LADY OF STONE

What Reviewers Say About Barbara Ann Wright's Work

The Pyradisté Adventures

"…a healthy dose of a very creative, yet believable, world into which the reader will step to find enjoyment and heart-thumping action. It's a fiendishly delightful tale."—*Lambda Literary*

"Barbara Ann Wright is a master when it comes to crafting a solid and entertaining fantasy novel. …The world of lesbian literature has a small handful of high-quality fantasy authors, and Barbara Ann Wright is well on her way to joining the likes of Jane Fletcher, Cate Culpepper, and Andi Marquette. …Lovers of the fantasy and futuristic genre will likely adore this novel, and adventurous romance fans should find plenty to sink their teeth into."—*Rainbow Reader*

"*The Pyramid Waltz* has had me smiling for three days. …I also haven't actually read…a world that is entirely unfazed by homosexuality or female power before. I think I love it. I'm just delighted this book exists. …If you enjoyed The Pyramid Waltz, For Want of a Fiend is the perfect next step…you'd be embarking on a joyous, funny, sweet and madcap ride around very dark things lovingly told, with characters who will stay with you for months after."—*The Lesbrary*

"This book will keep you turning the page to find out the answers. …Fans of the fantasy genre will really enjoy this installment of the story. We can't wait for the next book."—*Curve*

"There is only one other time in my life I have uncontrollably shouted out in cheer while reading a book. [*A Kingdom Lost*] made the second. ...Over the course of these three books all the characters have blossomed and developed so eloquently. ...I simply just thought this whole novel was brilliant."—*Lesbian Review*

"Chock full of familiar elements that avid fantasy readers will adore...[*The Pyramid Waltz*] adds in a compelling and slowly evolving romance. ...Set against a backdrop of political intrigue with the possibility of monsters and mystery at every turn, the two women slowly learn each other, sharing secrets and longing, until a fragile love blossoms between them..."—*USA Today Happily Ever After*

Not Your Average Love Spell

"Barbara Ann Wright mixes so much into her story–romance, comedy, drama, action, adventure–that it threatens more than once to collapse under the clash of themes, but those clashes and contrasts only serve to make it stronger and more engaging."—*Beauty in Ruins*

"...a solid little fantasy tale with a lot of really cool elements. ...Wright plays to all the tropes...in a way that keeps the story fresh while preserving the surprises. ...As for the romance, that was surprisingly sweet and amusing, with four women at the heart of the story who are entirely likable...the spark of attraction and the emotional connections are undeniable."—*Fem Led Fantasy*

"...a great story filled with magic, wondrous creatures and adventure but what I really enjoyed about the book was the way that the characters grew. ...It is a great thing to read in these trying times and I took hope from it. The story pulls with enough magic to feel like a fully fleshed out fantasy world while keeping our heroes relatable and engaging. ...I give it a full hearted thumbs up and you should definitely check it out."—*Paper Phoenix Ink*

"I thought this was a fun and entertaining adventure read…the fantasy aspects are very approachable. …The way the whole plot unfolded just felt different and I loved that. What also really impressed me was the amount of action this book had. It was one thing after another after another all keeping me completely glued to the book…I could not stop reading."—*Lez Review Books*

The Tattered Lands

"Wright's postapocalyptic romance is a fast-paced journey through devastation. …Plenty of action, surprises, and magic will keep readers turning the pages."—*Publishers Weekly*

House of Fate

"…fast, fun…entertaining. …*House of Fate* delivers on adventure." —*Tor.com*

Coils

"…Greek myths, gods and monsters and a trip to the Underworld. Sign me up…This one springs straight into action…a good start, great Greek myth action and a late blooming romance that flowers in the end…"—*Dear Author*

"A unique take on the Greek gods and the afterlife make this a memorable book. The story is fun with just the right amount of camp. Medusa is a hot, if unexpected, love interest. …A truly unexpected ending has us hoping for more stories from this world."—*RT Book Reviews*

"The gods and monsters of ancient Greek mythology are living, breathing entities, something Cressida didn't expect and is amazed as well as terrified to discover. …Cressida soon realizes being in the underworld is no different than being among the living. The heart still feels and love can bloom, even in the world of Myth. ...The characters are well developed and their wit will elicit more than a few chuckles. A joy to read."—*Lunar Rainbow Reviewz*

Paladins of the Storm Lord

"This was a truly enjoyable read. ...I would definitely pick up the next book. ...The mad dash at the end kept me riveted. I would definitely recommend this book for anyone who has a love of sci-fi. ...An intricate...novel one that can be appreciated at many levels, adventurous sci fi or one that is politically motivated with a very astute look at present day human behavior. ...There are many levels to this extraordinary and well written book...overall a fascinating and intriguing book."—*Inked Rainbow Reads*

"I loved this. ...The world that the Paladins inhabited was fascinating...didn't want to put this down until I knew what happened. I'll be looking for more of Barbara Ann Wright's books."—*Lesbian Romance Reviews*

"*Paladins of the Storm Lord* by Barbara Ann Wright was like an orchestra with all of its pieces creating a symphony. I really truly loved it. I love the intricacy and wide variety of character types...I just loved practically every character! ...Of course my fellow adventure lovers should read Paladins of the Storm Lord!"—*Lesbian Review*

Thrall: Beyond Gold and Glory

"Once more Barbara has outdone herself in her penmanship. I cannot sing enough praises. A little *Vikings*, a dash of *The Witcher*, peppered with *The Game of Thrones*, and a pinch of *Lord of The Rings*. Mesmerizing. ...I was ecstatic to read this book. It did not disappoint. Barbara pours life into her characters with sarcasm, wit and surreal imagery, they leap from the page and stand before you in all their glory. I am left satisfied and starving for more, the clashing of swords, whistling of arrows still ringing in my ears."—*Lunar Rainbow Reviews*

"In their adventures, the women must wrestle with issues of freedom, loyalty, and justice. The characters were likable, the issues complex, and the battles were exciting. I really enjoyed this book and I highly recommend it."—*All Our Worlds: Diverse Fantastic Fiction*

"This was the first Barbara Ann Wright novel I've read, and I doubt it will be the last. Her dialogue was concise and natural, and she built a fantastical world that I easily imagined from one scene to the next. Lovers of Vikings, monsters and magic won't be disappointed by this one."—*Curve*

By the Author

The Pyradisté Adventures
The Pyramid Waltz

For Want of a Fiend

A Kingdom Lost

The Fiend Queen

Lady of Stone

Thrall: Beyond Gold and Glory

The Godfall Novels
Paladins of the Storm Lord

Widows of the Sun-Moon

Children of the Healer

Inheritors of Chaos

Coils

House of Fate

The Tattered Lands

Not Your Average Love Spell

LADY OF STONE

by

Barbara Ann Wright

2020

LADY OF STONE

ISBN 13: 978-1-63555-607-0

This Trade Paperback Original Is Published By
Bold Strokes Books, Inc.
P.O. Box 249
Valley Falls, NY 12185

First Edition: September 2020

CREDITS
EDITOR: CINDY CRESAP
PRODUCTION DESIGN: SUSAN RAMUNDO
COVER DESIGN BY TAMMY SEIDICK

Acknowledgments

As always, thanks to the whole team at BSB. Especially Cindy, who let me fudge this deadline so many times.

Thanks to the Beavers and Writer's Ink: Angela, Deb, Erin, Matt, Natsu, Sarah, and Trakena. You are superheroes.

Thanks to all my readers. I had fun revisiting this universe. Let's go here again.

I love you, Mom. I love my cat, too, but not as much.

Dedication

To Matt and Nicole, always willing to help
and asking nothing in return.

Author's Note

This book takes place approximately two hundred years before the events in *The Pyramid Waltz*.

CHAPTER ONE

The air smelled of jasmine and honeysuckle, an aroma Sylph would have enjoyed if she hadn't been terrified someone would uncover her magic.

The enormous royal gardens contained a pond, a small forest, and a hedge maze as well as colorful blooms. A cadre of glittering nobles, all of them nearly as perfumed as the flowers, strolled at will, secure in the knowledge that two walls encircled them, a large one around the palace and its grounds, and a smaller, decorative wall so the royal Umbriels and their guests never had to see the plain wall that protected them.

Just like the cursed walls, everything seemed like an illusion, especially the calm nobles, those happy to be at court and among their own social circle, secure in the knowledge that all was well.

Sylph had never felt so apart from them, even though her father was a duke.

He stood surrounded by lesser nobles clamoring for his attention, and Sylph would have been equally courted—if only as a stepping-stone to her father—but every time someone approached, she moved a little farther into the trees and blossoms, her heart thumping at the idea that one of them might have a stray pyramid about their person. With her mind, she would reach for it without thinking, without even knowing how she did it, and the magic would be on her again.

No one would be in a rush to speak to her if they witnessed that.

Her father had only dragged her to court in Marienne to find a good marriage. It wasn't enough that she would be the duchess after he passed. In his mind, she *had* to increase their holdings before she inherited the title. He'd always hungered for land as most craved food and water. But she wasn't ready to chain herself to someone for a few acres.

Not that he cared.

If he found out about the magic, would that make him care? Easing behind a large tree with leaves dangling nearly to the ground, she sighed. She'd have to bend to her father's will someday, magic or not.

Clutching her fists, she nearly let loose a curse she'd heard one of the grooms use while she'd hidden in the stables. She couldn't even lament her tyrannical father in her own head without her thoughts going back to the spirits-cursed magic, to the fact that she might be a pyradisté.

She remembered the first time it had happened, nearly three months ago. She'd moved one stone without touching it, which made it a fluke, easy to dismiss. Then she'd felt a wall *pulling* at her another afternoon, wanting her to use the power lurking within her to touch it, move it, yank it from the ground as if it was no more than a blanket. She'd learned to stay away from the pyramids guarding the gates of her estate before they plucked at her emotions and her will as easily as a minstrel plucked at a lute.

In the garden now, she breathed deeply, trying to dispel the bile that rose at the memories. It was all a mistake. She did not have power, one way or another. Nothing ever had to happen again. She was not drawn to stone, had no urge to move it. And the mere presence of a pyramid did not pull at her like a haunting refrain.

I will it so.

But that wasn't how magic worked. Once a pyradisté, always a pyradisté.

A smattering of voices reached her, and she eased farther under the sweeping leaves, glad she'd picked a green outfit. Even the gossamer sleeves with their sprinkle of diamonds would help her blend with the dewy garden.

A group of courtiers strolled along the path beyond the tree. They were a privileged handful who were allowed to mix with nobility. They knew enough to be seen without getting in the way. Even without the leaves obscuring their faces, Sylph doubted she would have known them. The little she saw of their clothing gave away their station even before their conversation did.

Nobles only gossiped behind closed doors.

"Did you hear the prince will be putting in an appearance?" one courtier asked.

All of them sighed, presumably over the prince's beauty. He had turned quite a few heads. And quite a few mattresses, Sylph had heard.

Behind closed doors, of course.

"No sign of the queen?" one of the courtiers asked.

"She's too enamored of her new lover," another said, and the tittering began anew.

Sylph rolled her eyes, wishing they'd go away. Their gossip wasn't even interesting. She knew all about Lady Lucia, Queen Earnhilt's current paramour. Sylph had memorized her features and every fact about her that one could dig up. Her father had insisted she do so for every noble. One never knew what might be useful. And she had no doubt they all knew about her.

But they didn't know everything.

"The prince is enough of a thrill on his own," the first courtier said. "Adding in the queen would be too much loveliness and put the garden to shame."

They all clucked in agreement, clearly besotted with the Umbriels. Sylph supposed she'd become too accustomed to the royals too long to understand the adoration. The queen was beautiful as well as boisterous and not afraid to pick up a sword when the situation warranted. Not Sylph's cup of tea. Nor was the prince with his lazy drawl, half-lidded leers at most of the court, and glib wit. He'd always been friendly and courteous, but she'd never been interested in knowing him better.

Her father approved. In marriage, he wanted her to have the greater title and the upper hand. As a future duchess, there were few above her.

"Look," one of the courtiers said with a gasp. "It's the prince. At the end of the hedge."

They oohed and ahhed before one asked, "Who is that dour creature in black beside him?"

"The queen's pyradisté," another answered.

They paused as if searching their memories for either the identity of the person in question or perhaps for a definition of a word so outside their sphere.

"Peasant," one said dismissively, and that was that.

Sylph cringed and eased away, her cheeks burning. Her father would say the same. No noble possessed such an ugly, common little thing like magic.

Except her.

All thoughts of swearing and raging gone, she fought the urge to sag to the ground as she wandered farther into the scented trees.

Thana hated everything about this tea party, but she wasn't supposed to show it. Prince Gunnar had instructed her to smile and make cheerful conversation. She had promised to try not to scowl.

By the looks she was getting, she was failing at that.

"Why do I have to come?" she'd grumbled at Gunnar in his apartment before the stupid party. "I'm the monarch's pyradisté, the only one she has. Shouldn't I be with her?"

"Mother is busy." He sighed and shook his golden head, blue eyes twinkling as he added the final touches to his outfit. Even in the shadows made by flickering candlelight, he managed to gleam. "She's always *busy*."

Thana couldn't begrudge him the sigh and a touch of embarrassment. His mother's taste for beautiful women was legendary, and though she never shirked her royal duties, her private appearances when a new lover was on the scene were practically nonexistent. Even among her family.

"I should be here in the palace in case she needs me," Thana mumbled.

Gunnar gave her a look but said nothing. She knew what that meant. What would the queen need her pyradisté for when she was safely ensconced in the royal apartments behind hallways full of protective pyramids?

But Thana added another reason the queen wouldn't need her: She wasn't a very good pyradisté.

Gunnar would never say that, though.

He put a hand on her shoulder. "I need you. What if some over-amorous noble or courtier leaps upon me in the seclusion of the garden?"

"You can fight them better than I can."

"What if they use magic?"

"A noble would never stoop so low." She used a mocking tone of indignation. "There are no noble pyradistés, and they wouldn't stoop to use a pyramid that some lowly peasant made for them."

His affectional pat turned into a clap. "C'mon, Than. I need at least one member of the Order at my elbow, even if no one knows it but us."

Right. She couldn't forget that being the monarch's pyradisté also meant being in the Order of Vestra, the covert organization that protected the Umbriels and helped keep the secret that they all bore a Fiend. It was a necessary but unpleasant evil that had to remain secret at all costs.

Thana could help repress the Fiends if needed—she had enough skill for that—but could she subdue criminals or stop traitors? Hurl destructive pyramids of her own making and swing from the rafters into danger?

Give her a book and a cozy blanket any day.

She thanked the ten spirits that all the Umbriels wore a Fiend suppression necklace under their clothing. Unless they became overly angry, it would keep their Fiends safely out of the way. Legend said that a strong enough emotion could break the necklace and let the Fiendish Aspect out, but she'd never seen that for herself.

Since Gunnar had given her a pitiable look after his argument, she went to the spirits-cursed party. She'd taken an oath, too flattered when the queen had asked her to be the royal pyradisté for anything else. It hadn't occurred to her until later that they'd only asked her because she was Gunnar's friend. She *did* know everything there was to know about pyramid magic. She'd even studied with Allusian pyramid users, all the way to the east outside of Farraday's borders.

But powerful and energetic she was not.

She supposed she needn't be either to stand around in a black cassock under the hot sun at a garden party surrounded by sneering nobles.

Lucky for her.

She trailed Gunnar for a little bit, but he was in his element, surrounded by attractive, fawning minions dressed in the latest fashion of short-waisted jackets and tight trousers that ended at the knee, showing off silk stockings and crossed garters. Some bore bustles of tiered ruffles that splayed behind them as they walked, rather like a bird's plumage. Thana wondered how often they had to practice to keep the large feathers in their sleek hats from knocking into one another. Maybe they'd get tangled up and go down in a heap.

She'd have to practice not laughing her head off.

She let them get ahead of her and tried to enjoy the garden. Gunnar didn't really need any protecting. He was just trying to get her out into nature and sunlight and around people, three things she detested but that he felt necessary for a person's well-being. But without something to read, the garden was just another sort of frippery. She turned down a lonely path, and a flash ahead caught her eye. She paused, frowning before stepping forward, thinking of pyramid crystal, but it was only some ornamentation on a noble's sleeve.

The noblewoman stood along the path ahead near the decorative inner wall, staring at nothing. As well-dressed as the rest of them, she was clad in varying shades of green, and the cut of her clothing showed off her trim waist and the swell of ample breasts. Her bustle curled across her back, the hanging fabric nearly shrouding her hips, giving them an enticing fullness.

Thana cursed herself for admiring a noble, even one so... well-appointed.

This one wore no hat, and the sun caught her pale curls, a shade blonder than the prince's, nearly white. She turned, and Thana's mouth went dry at the sight of her tanned skin, round cheeks, and wide, mint-green eyes. Her full lips turned down in a frown or a pout, and she sighed as if infinitely sad.

Thana shook her head. The last thing she needed was to develop an obsession with some stuck-up, albeit beautiful, melancholic noble. She began to turn away when the noblewoman stiffened as if given a vision of her own grave. Thana looked for the source of her alarm but saw nothing.

When the noblewoman began to shake, Thana stepped forward to ask if she was all right, but the woman fell to her knees, and the ground let out an alarming rumble. Thana grabbed hold of a tree, her mind whirling, but before she could guess what was happening, the wall behind the noblewoman bucked like a runaway horse, the stones shifting and melting together before lurching toward the noblewoman like a wave, threatening to bury her.

Thana ran, heart pounding. She hit the noblewoman and heaved, carrying both of them out of the way before the stone crashed down. Thana rolled away from a spray of dirt and reached into her pocket for one of her pyramids. It was only half the size of her fist, but it blazed with enough light for ten of its kind. The five sides shifted like the wall had done, distorting the smooth crystal. Thana dropped it with a hiss, mystified about what was happening. She pulled another, a mild explosive pyramid that might weaken the foundation of the wall which was currently lifting again as if for another strike.

Desperate, she chucked the pyramid, trying to ignore her panic. The tinkle of breaking crystal disappeared in a roaring explosion. Thana gasped as the force of it hit her in the chest, knocking her down before shock had a chance to do so. Stone flew apart in hunks, showering everything in sharp little strikes.

Thana winced, wiping the dust from her eyes. Since when could she make a blast like that? She'd never crafted such a powerful pyramid in her life. She couldn't help a jot of pride.

The noblewoman moaned, and through a haze of dust, the wall began to rise again, smaller bits rolling back to join the whole. Thana's pride disappeared in worry. Now what? She patted her pockets, but she'd only brought two pyramids.

Her first had come through the explosion intact; it was still writhing in the grass. Thana pushed to her feet and lurched toward it, not knowing what else to do but eliminate whatever strangeness she could find. With a prayer to the spirits that this one wouldn't explode, she smashed the pyramid under her boot.

After a horrid grinding sound, the wall collapsed. Thana took a moment to breathe, a thousand questions hurtling through her mind.

She listened for more commotion but heard nothing. Gunnar would be all right. He could defend himself against a mundane attack better than she could, and the only magic seemed to be centered on this woman.

The noblewoman coughed and blinked, head lifting, her pretty features contorted in pain and fear. "Please," she said, her voice hoarse. "They can't know it was me. Please."

Thana hesitated, but voices echoed from the garden in all directions. They'd be coming to find the source of the blast.

"You don't know what they'll do to me," the noblewoman said.

Whatever else had happened, her fear was real, and Thana knew what it was like to have one's power be misunderstood. She rushed to the noblewoman and hauled her upright. Rumors circulated about areas of Farraday where pyradistés were still shamed or worse. She didn't have time to ask. She hauled the noblewoman into a clump of bushes and lowered her to the ground.

"Regain your strength, then sneak away."

"Thank you." Her grip tightened on Thana's sleeve. "Thank you."

Thana fought embarrassment, but her cheeks still burned. Gunnar would have known what to say to make the noblewoman swoon, but Thana could only mumble, "Welcome," before she returned to the shattered wall.

Sylph sat in the clump of bushes and tried to breathe. The fact that she didn't know what had happened should have unnerved her, but she'd become used to being unaware of what was going on from an early age. Her father had simply ordered her about, ensuring he got what he wanted and only preparing her for the future he'd planned.

So she wasn't really worried about why she'd been standing in the garden feeling miserable one moment and the next, the world had gone mad. She just knew what she'd felt when all the chaos had erupted: every single emotion. They'd boiled inside her. Anger, joy, regret, and so many more had rushed through her veins too quickly to sort one from another. She'd shaken from the force, nearly crying out when they'd wrenched free before she could burst. All she could think was *stop, stop, stop!* She'd have done anything to make the rushing cease.

The feeling of being hit, falling, rolling, had done nothing to soften the spirits-cursed feelings. She'd barely felt the sensations outside her body. Even the boom, the rush of air, the tiny impacts of stone against her skin had seemed as if they happened to someone else.

At last, the feeling had vanished like warmth on a cold day, and she'd seen a woman who was dark as a raven in a black cassock, with black hair and eyes nearly dark enough to swallow starlight.

Her savior.

No, no one could save her because now her father would find out. They'd all find out. This was magic no one would fail to notice.

She'd pleaded for that not to happen, and the raven had aided her again, hiding her in the bushes, but how would that help? Her father would want to know who was responsible for the upset, the source of the magic, and who but Sylph—

The cassock. A pyradisté. The queen's pyradisté.

Sylph breathed a little easier even as the first gawkers burst on the scene. It was chaos as everyone spoke at once, and the raven tried to make herself heard until the loud, icy voice of Sylph's father cut through it all.

"Be quiet," he said. He never raised his voice, but somehow, it always carried. The crowd went silent. They hadn't even done that for the prince.

"All is well," the raven shouted into the pause. She didn't balk when Sylph's father turned a glare on her that was worthy of a Fiend from a child's story. "Just a minor accident with a pyramid that—"

"Minor accident? You blew a hole in the deuced wall." Sylph's father's face inched from tan to scarlet, making his pale hair stand out like the heart of a flame. "If you can't control yourself—"

The raven bristled back at him with enviable heat, increasing her allure tenfold. But the prince stepped forward before the yelling could continue.

"Let's leave the magic to those expert in it," he said. Before anyone could argue that an exploding wall didn't instill confidence of expertise, the prince held up a hand and continued. "Explanations will be forthcoming after all examinations have been carried out. Right, Thana?"

The raven blinked at him before color darkened her cheeks, too. "Yes, right. Just what I was about to say."

As the prince shepherded everyone but the raven away, Sylph creeped from the opposite side of the bushes. She dusted herself off as she walked, her fear beating inside her like a bird's wings. After a few deep breaths, she circled a clump of trees and joined the rear of the gaggle of nobles. The courtiers parted like the sea to let her pass, and she hoped she looked as curious and bewildered as the rest of them instead of terrified.

Her father's sharp blue gaze cut at her. He dropped back to walk at her side, and the gap between the nobles and the courtiers widened, the entire party separating into natural circles.

"Where have you been?" he asked in a low voice, his anger a growling bass accompaniment.

Sylph couldn't yet speak past her fear. She waved vaguely over her shoulder.

He nodded as if that explained everything. He wouldn't question that she'd naturally come toward the chaos. He wouldn't have noticed her in all the commotion, but then, he rarely did under normal circumstances.

"Spirits-cursed pyradistés," he said. "Why doesn't the queen get rid of the lot? The only need for them is to combat other pyradistés, but if there weren't any left..."

Sylph felt his stare as he trailed away. She schooled her face to neutral and met his gaze.

"There's a leaf in your hair." He sounded confused as he removed it. "How did you get dirty?"

"One of the courtiers jostled me into a tree," she lied smoothly.

He frowned hard, appalled. "Spirits curse their hide. Which one? I'll—"

"It's all right, Father," she said with a bored wave. "I gave them a sound telling off. I don't even remember which one it was. They're nearly peasants anyway."

He chuckled. "Well done. And the deuced royal pyradisté *is* a peasant, never mind her manufactured status."

"And therefore, beneath our notice."

He seemed mollified at this and chuckled again.

Sylph repressed a sigh of relief. She didn't share her father's disdain of the less fortunate, but it was the quickest way to calm his ire or direct it elsewhere. While he was fixated on pyradistés who practiced magic openly, he'd never suspect that she was one.

Or that the queen's pyradisté was anything but beneath his notice.

CHAPTER TWO

Gunnar kept up his bored facade until the last of the visitors filed away, and then he turned anxious eyes on Thana. "What happened?"

"I'm not sure. One of the nobles had some kind of…reaction. Maybe to my pyramids. I don't know." She grabbed the end of the ponytail gathered at her nape but released it before she could thread the hair nervously through her fingers. Exploding walls were no reason to bring back childhood coping mechanisms.

"A noble pyradisté?" he asked with a cringe. "They won't like that."

"No, everyone knows magic is for the peasant class. It's only you noble shepherds who keep us herds in check."

He gave her a long, dry look. "We're not having this argument now. Which noble?"

Thana saw the large eyes again, the look of terror and despair. "Would you mind if I keep that to myself for now?"

"Why?"

"Well, I don't know her name. And she clearly didn't want anyone else to know what she can do." She couldn't meet his gaze, not knowing how to explain.

He put his fists on his hips. "If anyone knows how to keep a secret, it's me."

"I know, I know. I just…" She sighed. He'd probably never been told, *You're not one of us*, but it had never applied so much. "Just let me talk to her first, please?"

He mumbled something about not seeing the need for secrecy, but he waved as if relenting. "I do expect to be told eventually," he said, sounding pouty.

She chuckled. "And I expect to tell you, but I wouldn't tell your secrets without permission, either."

That shut him up.

"I need to investigate," she said, waving at the pile of stone. "Then I'll have some answers for you."

The prospect of knowledge to come seemed to mollify him. He nodded, but she noticed his hand going toward his throat where the pyramid necklace was hidden under his shirt, the magic that kept him and the other Umbriels from transforming into Fiends whenever they became enraged.

Spirits, she'd only ever seen the transformation once, when Queen Earnhilt, Gunnar, and the crown prince and his wife—both currently at home in the Western March—were safely chained beneath the palace for the Waltz, the ritual that pacified Yanchasa the Mighty, the great Fiend slumbering under Marienne. If they didn't perform the ritual periodically, Yanchasa would awaken and destroy the city, the country, and probably the world. So the Umbriels carried an Aspect of the Fiend, a little part of its nature, and a pyradisté used that Aspect during the Waltz to pacify Yanchasa. It was a burden they had to bear, a secret that could never be revealed, and the reason the Umbriels had to remain in power.

And the reason she had to keep her position even when she wanted to walk away. If her friend could carry around something so vicious inside him, the least she could do was watch his back. Not that Gunnar would ever need her for that, not when he could remove his necklace and unleash his Fiend if he was ever in real danger.

"Hey," he said.

She realized she'd been staring at where his necklace was and met his concerned gaze before looking away. "I'm sorry."

"It's all right." He cleared his throat, sounding as embarrassed as if she'd been ogling him. "It's a nervous habit I need to break."

Thana glanced around, but they were quite alone now. "Have you ever been tempted to take it off? When an enemy has backed you into a corner?"

He snorted and patted his hip where his sword rested. This one seemed a decorative piece, the grip and hilt slathered in gold and jewels, but the blade hidden in the sheath was as sharp as any other, a metaphor for Gunnar himself. "My skills have sufficed so far."

True. And what he couldn't do, his old pyradisté had managed. Thana flinched at the thought that she'd have to go on a mission one day and be the Order's magical arsenal. She sighed, letting her shoulders slump.

"You'll do fine," Gunnar said, resting another damned sympathetic hand on her shoulder.

"Stop pretending you can read my mind."

"Stop being so easy to read."

She snorted and waved toward the trees. "Catch up with your sycophants before they come looking for you. I've got an investigation to conduct."

He left without another word. She started shifting through the rubble, thanking the spirits that this wasn't the only barrier keeping riffraff out of the garden. A larger wall stood in the distance, one that encircled the entirety of the massive gardens. It was unadorned and harder to scale than this smaller wall, and it kept most people out. But the shorter one was the more dangerous.

It contained trap pyramids.

Like those that guarded the royal apartments, these pyramids were part mind magic and part destructive magic. They read intent and would explode if anyone approached them with murder on their mind. Thana frowned as she moved hunks of stone aside, searching for a telltale sparkle. Maybe the trap pyramids were why her own attack had done such massive damage. If she'd hit one with her explosive pyramid…

There, a rain of sparkling dust. So she had hit a trap pyramid with her own, igniting it. She tried not to let a well of disappointment overflow. It had been nice to be powerful for a moment. Then her frown deepened as she warned herself not to get mired in sentiment. She had to use her brain, and it was telling her that trap pyramids didn't go off just because they were shattered. They required evil intent to work. And a pyramid never shifted its function.

Or did it? She thought of the way the first pyramid she'd pulled from her pocket had seemed to writhe in her grasp, the crystal warping as it flared with light. And the noblewoman hadn't had a pyramid of her own. Then how had she controlled the stone? Thana had never constructed such a pyramid, had only read rumors of such. She was certain that no one in Farraday had created one for the noblewoman to use.

Had the noble figured out a way to…retune a pyramid to another purpose?

Impossible.

And yet a shattered wall lay at Thana's feet. Its trap pyramid could have been crushed. That wouldn't have set it off. She supposed it could have been smashed when the stone wall warped, or maybe it had been warped by someone—like the noblewoman—until it collapsed under the strain.

Then she'd used Thana's pyramid to control the stone?

Impossibilities on top of impossibilities.

Thana grinned as her excitement built. A pyramid puzzle, just the sort of thing she enjoyed. She'd have to dive into her books. Maybe she could consult a colleague or two, keeping her questions hypothetical, of course.

And no matter what, she'd have to speak to the noblewoman again.

Her belly warmed disturbingly at the thought. The warmth was due to attraction, she knew, but she could not, absolutely would not, allow herself to have any sort of feelings—no matter how transitory—for one of the spirits-cursed nobility.

As she stalked from the trees into the open paths through flowers and bushes, she made a mental list. First, find the noblewoman's identity from the castle servants. Second, order the destroyed section of the wall rebuilt and try her best to replace the destroyed trap pyramid. Third, research. Then she'd find time to speak with the noblewoman.

Thana sighed as that warm fluttering passed through her again. Fourth through sixth on the list would be chickening out about seeing the noblewoman and doing more research while berating herself. Finally, maybe, very probably, Thana would give in and go see her.

She gritted her teeth. She would not let some stuck-up beauty intimidate her.

Thana thanked the spirits that the garden party had broken up. She made sure Gunnar was heading back to the palace before scanning the stragglers, but the noble she sought was not among them.

After a few quick descriptions to the servants, she had the name she needed: Lady Sylph Montague, daughter of Duke Felix Montague of Baelyn. One day, she'd be Duchess Sylph, but according to the servants, she was quiet, icily courteous, and completely under the thumb of her father. Thana couldn't quite feel sorry for her. Sylph would still be a duchess someday. Then she could quietly and courteously dance icily on her father's grave, no longer under anyone's authority except the Umbriels, and even they wouldn't piss off anyone with as much sway as the ruler of a duchy.

Thana forced herself to calm. No use in getting angry before she'd even spoken to the woman. But angry was so much cleaner than…impassioned. No, no, better to not be anything. Calm, that was the way.

And clean wouldn't hurt. She hurried to her own apartment within the royal section, wanting to change clothes and comb the dust out of her hair. Because being clean would help with the calm. No other reason.

Sylph submitted numbly to the ministrations of her maid. Sometimes, she envied the woman her plain uniform and the fact that all she had to do with her hair was sweep it up under a simple cap. She never had to do all this primping.

It was all Sylph could do to control her pounding heart through the bathing and changing and redoing of her hair. She kept up a litany in her head of pleasant nonsense, trying to ward off panic or tears or hopelessness. Her father was safely tucked in his own room, out of sight and hearing. She wanted to believe her maid's sympathetic face, the invitation to confide, but she couldn't risk that.

Not when people could be other than they seemed.

She'd been seven when she'd learned about such deception, playing by herself on her family's massive estate. When some of the town's children had sneaked under the wall, she'd been thrilled. She'd seen them playing often enough through the windows of her carriage as it rolled through town. She'd glimpsed them at a distance as she rode the edges of the estate with her father, but she'd never spoken to any of them.

They'd *played* with her that day. They'd *spoken* to her as if she was *normal*. And it had been nice. She hadn't felt anything like it since her mother had died two years before. She'd felt a pang of grief then for her lack of a mother, but the visiting children had drowned that out.

Then her maid had found them. A different one than her current lady-in-waiting, but she'd had the same kindly expression as she'd shooed the interloping children away, gently chiding as she'd led Sylph inside. Sylph had asked the maid not to tell, and she'd winked. A friend. A confidante.

Or so it had seemed.

Then the maid had told all to Sylph's father. The children had been caned for trespassing while Sylph had been forced to watch. And he'd forbidden her to cry, but she hadn't been able to help a few tears, so she'd gone to bed hungry that night. The guilt had been worse than any pang. When she'd refused to let her maid come near her again, her father had fired the woman on the spot.

He could always find more spies.

So Sylph sat quietly as her maid now made her presentable should anyone come calling, but when further prodded to unburden herself, Sylph replied, "You may go."

After a curtsey, the maid left. Once the door clicked softly behind her, Sylph sighed and breathed deeply, straining her tight coat. The strength went out of her, and she drooped on the settee, leaning sideways until she fell over, unable to stop herself.

She let herself see it all again: the wall, the pyradisté, the explosion. She could remember having a gush of feelings but not what they were. She did not want to cry, not about the magic or about the memory of the children or her father or her maid or anything. She wished to be out of tears, a dried-up husk.

No, there they went. She sobbed into her pillow, keeping the back of her head up as much as she could so she didn't ruin the fall of ringlets her maid had produced. Even if this one was also a spy,

Sylph would help her keep her job, keep her fed. It was too much to expect that someone would resist her powerful father. And if he saw a head of flattened hair, he might fire this one, and she'd done nothing to deserve that.

Yet.

When a soft knock came at the door, Sylph thought she might have summoned the maid with her thoughts. She sat up quickly. "Just a moment." Wiping her face, she went to the mirror and took a few deep breaths, but that wouldn't help the redness around her eyes. She grabbed a bottle of perfume and spread some on her cheeks, wincing at the strong scent so close to her nose, but she needed an excuse for tears. She wiped at it as she called, "Come in."

"My lady, there's—" The maid stopped when their eyes met in the mirror. "You've been…crying?"

Sylph forced herself to giggle. "Went to spray myself with perfume and got myself in the face, I'm afraid."

"I'm so sorry, my lady. I should have been here to help." She rushed forward, taking another cloth and dipping it into a basin of water before dabbing at Sylph's cheeks.

Sylph fought the urge to sigh. Soon, the whole castle would no doubt think she was too stupid to put on perfume without help.

"No doubt a defective bottle," the maid said. "I'll replace it immediately." She scooped it up and nodded toward the door. "There's a visitor for you. The queen's pyradisté. Shall I tell her you're not available?"

Sylph's mind whirled. The raven. Come to visit her? To make sure she was all right? To ask about the magic? A pleasant thought and a terrifying one. She tried to speak and couldn't. After licking her lips, she tried again. "I…tell her…" She wanted to send her away, but the desire to speak to anyone who might be worried about *her* and not her station or what she could do for them was too strong.

And if today had proven anything, it was that the magic wasn't going to go away.

"I'll see her." Sylph stood, trying to ignore her shaking legs as she moved from her bedroom to the sitting room.

The raven nearly leaped from one of the uncomfortable sitting room chairs. Her cheeks had gone red, making her pale skin seem almost dusky. Her neatly combed ponytail shone like a fall of ink over one slender shoulder, even against the black of her cassock with its purple piping.

She made several noises as if trying to form the right word before she bowed slightly. "My, um, lady."

Sylph smiled, used to people being awkward around her, but there was something charming about seeing someone completely at sea. She waited until the maid moved around them and out the door before she said, "My savior."

The blush darkened. "Um, yes. My name is Thana. I'm the queen's pyradisté."

Sylph had heard the name in the garden, but she'd forgotten it in all the rush. "Sylph." She took a breath to continue with her surname and title and all the rest, but something made her stop. She didn't want to be a lady or the daughter of a duke or an heir or anything else in this moment.

"Please," Sylph said, gesturing to the chair before taking another. "I could ring for some refreshment."

"Are you all right?" Thana asked, nearly interrupting, then ducking her head as if realizing her faux pas. "I mean, I know you didn't want anyone to know, but if you're hurt…"

The raven asked questions as if answers were easy, as if secrets didn't exist.

"I'm not hurt," Sylph said. "You?"

"No." She licked her lips, thinner than Sylph's but so much more expressive as she chewed on the lower one. "Look, we have to talk about what happened."

Sylph fought the urge to order her out. She'd never uttered a word about the magic, and every part of her wanted to deny it now. Instead, she forced herself to nod and could nearly hear her tendons creaking.

"No one knows?" Thana asked.

Another bit of force, this time to shake her head.

"So you've had no training?" Thana looked at nothing as she asked, the question seemingly directed inward. She took a deep breath before meeting Sylph's eyes again. "This is what it looked like to me. You retuned one of my pyramids to another purpose, shaping stone.

Then you used it to move the wall. This means you're not only very powerful, you're impossible. It shouldn't have been able to happen."

"Can you make it go away?" All the other words bounced off her. This was the answer she had to have.

Thana stiffened. "I tell you you're very powerful, that you're an impossible puzzle, and all you want is to make it go away?"

"I cannot be a pyradisté."

Now those expressive lips turned up in a sneer. "Why? Is magic too lowbrow for a noble?"

"Yes." She regretted the word, but it was fact.

Thana laughed humorlessly and looked away. "No, I can't make it *go away*. I would love to have your strength, but unfortunately, I can't take it. You're going to have to learn how to control it."

"No. You can make it stop. You...have to." She willed it to be so, willed her savior to be happy for her, to lose that look of disgust and be worried for her again.

"I've studied pyramid magic for a long time, read everything written about it, but you think you know more than me?" Thana drew herself up, and Sylph thought she might stand, might bolt, but she sank back again and crossed her arms. "Being highborn doesn't give you knowledge as well as power."

Sylph wanted to crumble, but the derision on Thana's face wouldn't let her. This was not her friend, couldn't be if she didn't understand. "Then..."

"I can teach you how to control it so you don't use it."

"You'll teach me?" Her hope rose again, a little. If Thana wasn't going to insist she go to the Pyradisté Academy, then there was a chance her secret could remain silent.

When Thana looked up, her face softened as if she'd seen a bit of Sylph's need. "Yes. And no one has to know."

Sylph could have kissed her or wept or any of a thousand emotional reactions, but she kept still, not knowing if there could be trust.

Yet.

CHAPTER THREE

If Thana could have kicked herself in the ass while walking back to her apartment, she would have. She'd known nobles were arrogant and dismissive of anything or anyone they considered beneath them, but she'd never met one who wanted to just...throw power away.

Or who managed to look heartbreakingly beautiful while doing it.

And that was where the ass-kicking came in. Lady Sylph Montague had no right to look the way she did while spitting on everything Thana had worked her whole life for. She was extremely powerful without even trying, and she just wanted it *gone*.

Thana sighed as she reached her study and dropped into her chair. Deep down, she'd always assumed that the nobility scorned pyradistés because they were jealous, or they didn't know all the things magic could do, so they turned their noses up at it. But Sylph did know, at least a little, and still sneered.

No, that wasn't quite fair. She'd been terrified.

Another sigh, then Thana stood and paced, glaring at the books and at her worktable scattered with unworked crystal, tools, bags of sand, and rags. She'd tried so hard to be good at the thing she knew so much about, but true mastery always seemed just out of reach. Now along came a novice who could retune a pyramid without even thinking and summon enough power to turn a wall into a wave.

And she didn't want it.

Thana could have slapped her perfect cheek, then watched the sway of her full hips as she walked away.

"Ugh," she said aloud. "Stop."

Gunnar would tell her to take a lover, someone to have some fun with who didn't want anything serious. Then she could have a place to focus her sexual frustration. And all that would be left for Lady Sylph was scathing derision.

But who had the time?

Thana nodded, deciding that work was the best distraction. She gathered a few books, then retreated to the desk. She needed to figure out just what Sylph's abilities might be, then she could train her more easily. And the more Sylph wanted to dampen her power, too scared to embrace it, the more Thana could hate her and kill any fantasies about grabbing her waist and pulling her close and kissing her lips, her neck, her—

"I said stop," she whispered harshly, fully knowing that censuring her libido out loud placed her firmly on the road to lunacy.

She bent over a book, staring at the page and resisting the urge to blink. Maybe that would make her concentrate. She was so focused on getting focused that when the door to her study flew open, she yelped and leaped from her chair, nearly turning it over.

Gunnar stumbled to a halt in the doorway, his blue eyes wide, as if her shock had scared the wits out of him. "What?" he cried.

"What?" she yelled back. She shook her head to try to calm her racing pulse. "Don't what me." She pointed to the door which had flown open so hard, it bounced off the wall. "What's going on?"

"Come on," he said, gesturing her forward, his face the picture of confusion and concern. "It's Mother."

The queen. Thana moved with him, her pulse picking up again, and her throat tightening as if her heart had decided to lodge there. "She's not hurt, is she?" She swallowed and tried to bully her shaky legs into keeping pace with him as they moved out of Thana's apartment and into the hall. "I'm not a healer."

"I know you're not a spirits-cursed healer," he said. "I wouldn't come get you if it wasn't about magic."

He wanted her to do magic. The *queen* wanted her to do magic. She'd told Gunnar she wasn't as good at it as her predecessor, but he'd always said stupid things like, "You'll do fine when the time comes." As if the situation would somehow improve her ability. Fear, the great motivator.

Then she thought of the wall, the explosion, her certainty that the force of her strike couldn't have come from one of the trap pyramids. She'd been scared and desperate then. What if the situation *did* help?

Someone should have written that down by now if it was true.

"What's happened?" She tried to force herself to sound calm, but she feared the words sounded half-strangled, squeezed around the lump in her throat.

"She was with her new…paramour."

He couldn't say lover, not where his mother was concerned. "Lady Lucia, yes."

"And some pyramid in the sitting room went, as she called it, ass up."

Thana was surprised into a snort. Queen Earnhilt always did have a colorful vernacular. "Which means?"

"It exploded."

"Spirits above. Did you send for a healer?"

"The court physick is with her, but when I left, she was already waving him off. She says it's only a scratch, and Lucia wasn't hurt at all."

The suspicious part of Thana muttered something about that being awfully convenient, but while Lady Lucia might be after money or power or just the prestige of being lover to the queen, she'd never struck Thana as a murderer.

Even if Earnhilt's son didn't know what to call her.

As long as the queen didn't call her consort, everything would be well. No one wanted to see the queen betrothed to someone who *was* just after money, power, or prestige. Not unless she had the full approval of the nobles' council.

Thana rolled her eyes. The council wouldn't care what the monarch's betrothed was after as long as they could control her.

The door to the queen's apartment swung open much as Thana's door had earlier. Before they reached it, a tall thin man in a red belted jerkin was pushed courteously yet inarguably into the hall by a well-muscled arm.

"Yes, I have it, old man. Cold poultice for the swelling, ointment for the cut." Queen Earnhilt stepped out behind the man. Her disheveled hair stood out around her head like a golden cloud, and one sleeve of her purple robe was tattered and burned, dangling around the arm she was shoving with. "Take your bag of tricks and be off with you. Have no fear for me."

"But…Majesty…" The court physick's bag dragged after him like a willful dog. "I can tend—"

"I can tend myself. Don't you worry." She turned toward Thana and Gunnar, revealing a bruised right eye that had swelled shut. The other, cornflower blue just lighter than her son's, seemed to light up. "See, here's the prince and my pyradisté come to help. Run along now."

"But…but they're not—"

Earnhilt released him, hustled Gunnar through the door, then reached for Thana. Her hand curled nearly all the way around Thana's bicep, and the force of the grip almost lifted her off her feet. What a beast she must be in battle. Thana was glad they'd always be on the same side.

Earnhilt shut the door in the physick's face and crooked her finger for Thana and Gunnar to follow. She strode past them, going from her public sitting room into her private one, and Thana stopped to stare.

One of the couches had been blown over. It had a blackened spot in the middle and burned wool spilling out. Several tables lay overturned, and from the way the floor sparkled in the firelight, a great amount of glassware had been broken.

Earnhilt marched into the thick of it, and Thana noticed hunting boots under the robe, but by the way the fabric hugged her athletic body, she didn't have anything else on. At just over six feet tall—Gunnar's height—she'd be formidable in nothing at all.

She pointed to a blank spot on the floor, the epicenter of whatever had happened. "Spirits-cursed pyramid went ass up right here," she said loudly. She had no other volume. "Happened when Lucia and I were having a snuggle by the fire and *whoosh*."

Gunnar sighed. "She's going to need more than ass up and *whoosh*, Ma."

"But that's what it did, my boy." She looked at Thana as if for confirmation.

"Um, it exploded?" she tried.

Earnhilt nodded, gesturing at her sleeve, at the room. "Lucky we hadn't really gotten started, or it might have caught more than my sleeve and my eye." She barked a laugh.

"Your eye is…"

"Still there under the swelling." She gave a bit of broken glass a nudge with one foot. "Hit by a chunk of wood. If we'd have been on the couch, we might have both snuffed it. Lucia was lucky. I was on top."

"Ma, please," Gunnar said with a groan.

Thana waved at them both to be quiet. "Where did this pyramid come from?"

"Been here forever." She dusted off a chair and sat. "One of the last-ditch trap thingies. Here in case someone gets past the hall pyramids."

"A trap?" Thana eased closer, looking for something that was no longer there. She conjured the memory of this room as it had been with a long, low table in the center, a pyramid embedded in the wood. An intruder might not see it until it was too late, even one crafty enough to avoid the pyramids in the hall. "That's not possible."

Earnhilt clumped her boots onto the remains of a footstool and gestured around as if presenting all the evidence they needed.

"I told her about the incident in the garden," Gunnar said. "There was a trap there, too, wasn't there?"

Thana could only nod, going through all her research in her head.

"Are more of the cursed things going to be popping off?" Earnhilt asked. "A fat lot of people will be killed, all of us included."

"It…trap pyramids don't just…" Thana looked to Gunnar. Trap pyramids read intent. These would only detect murderous thoughts against the Umbriels. "Where is Lucia?"

He nodded as if they'd had the same thought.

"She's fine. In the bedroom." She looked back and forth between them before she stood. "Now, hang on. I know you in the Order of Vestra have to suspect everyone, but—"

"Ma—"

"She was in the room, Gunnar! If she was going to kill me, she wouldn't risk her own life, too. She knows what the traps can do."

"Exactly," he said.

Thana nodded. "And when people believe in a cause strongly enough…"

Earnhilt barked a laugh. "What cause? Lucia's never believed in a cause in her life except maybe to wring out as much pleasure as possible." When Gunnar didn't look away, she glowered and lowered her voice a fraction. "Spirits above, my boy, she doesn't have the brains for murder."

Thana didn't comment, but she recalled hearing gossip to back that up.

She squatted and picked through the shards, looking for the gleam of crystal among the glass. The incident in the garden kept coming to mind. A trap had exploded then, too, when there didn't seem a reason for it. But Lady Sylph the rogue pyradisté had been there. Neither Earnhilt nor Lucia had the gift.

Oh, what that would do for the status of pyradistés if an Umbriel was one.

"Was Lady Lucia your only…visitor today?" Thana asked.

Earnhilt offered a lopsided leer. "If memory serves. Why? Angling for a spot?"

"Mother," Gunnar said, reproof in his voice. When they'd been in their late teens, he'd often complained to Thana about his mother flirting with his friends.

Thana's cheeks burned, but she ignored the question and looked to Gunnar. "You?"

He shook his head. "I've been alone."

The door to the bedroom creaked open. Thana stood as a pair of doe-eyes framed by a curtain of honey hair peeked out.

"Is it all right?" Lady Lucia's voice was high and chirpy. She smiled widely and actually giggled. Thana tried to see it as an act and failed.

"Come out, love," Earnhilt said. "Watch your little toes. There's glass everywhere."

Lucia slipped into the room but stayed by the door. One of Earnhilt's robes swamped her, hanging over her hands and feet and making her seem much younger than her thirty-some years.

"Did either of you have any other pyramids in the room, Majesty?" Thana asked, going formal in front of Lady Lucia in spite of the fact that half the people in the room were wearing robes.

"Just Hilty's necklace," Lucia said with a titter, turning her chin into her shoulder.

Earnhilt winked, and Thana wondered what exactly "Hilty" had said about the necklace that held her Fiend inside. Probably that it was another trap, though it wasn't.

Spirits help them if those pyramids malfunctioned.

Thana glimpsed a shard out of the corner of her eye that still bore a bit of filigree, the corner of a pyramid. She pulled it out of the rubble and straightened. The edges of the break were as jagged as she expected. It had exploded, then, but what had set it off?

Or who? Could it have been retuned like the one in the garden? Again, by whom?

She glanced at Earnhilt and Lucia and wondered how in the spirits' names she was going to propose testing them for latent power. "I...need to run an experiment," she said. "To make sure neither of you has been...affected by this."

Lucia blinked, and Thana imagined she could hear the wind whistling between Lucia's ears.

"Affected how?" Earnhilt said.

"Hypnotized. Be right back." She hurried out before they could ask questions, grabbed the first mind pyramid she could find in her office, and strode back. She paused at the door to the queen's apartment. If she used this pyramid, and it retuned as the others had and exploded...

She cringed. But she had to know if one of the people now present was like Sylph, and the only way to tell for sure was to try to hypnotize them. Pyradistés were never affected by mind magic.

She'd test Lucia first.

It took Gunnar pleading and distracting Earnhilt to let Thana follow Lucia into the bedroom alone. Anger rather than jealousy colored Earnhilt's argument. She hated to be forbidden anything, especially information. Gunnar often complained that she stuck her nose into the Order of Vestra's business far too often.

Finally, she relented after Gunnar assured her that a true test had to be administered one at a time. His look said he trusted Thana even if he wasn't quite sure what she was up to. She only hoped she could live up to his expectations.

In the bedroom, Lucia kept up her vapid stare as she sat in a chair at the vanity. Thana held the mind pyramid up in front of her and fell into it, focusing on the facets in the crystal, letting it send her mind out to envelop Lucia's.

This came easier to her than any other sort of magic. Her confidence in her own mental powers had always been absolute, and Lucia's mind fell under the sway of hers with the ease of a fish slipping through water.

Not a pyradisté, then.

And while she was here…

Thana glanced over her shoulder, but the door was still shut. She absolutely should not be reading the mind of a noble without their express permission. If anyone ever found out she'd done it, the entire nobles' council would be calling for her head. But if she hurried…

She pressed the pyramid to Lucia's head and let the memories unfurl in her own mind. Deftly, she walked back through their discussion to when Lucia and the queen were alone. She sped too far, blushed at the image of Earnhilt's sweaty, passion-filled face, and leaped ahead to the moment the pyramid exploded.

Lucia had been hurrying toward ecstasy, and then the sound of the explosion had ripped everything else away. Her ears had rung. She'd barely heard Hilty's bellow of pain but had felt the weight of her body. It happened quickly. There hadn't been room for fright, just the sensation of being swept up in Hilty's arms and carried from the room, the feel of Hilty's robe against her bare side had made her feel vulnerable, never so aware of her own nudity, and she'd struggled into another robe even before inquiring about Hilty's bloody face and arm.

Thana pulled out of her memories and then out of her mind, hoping very little time had passed. She couldn't afford to be caught.

Lucia slumped as people often did after having their minds read. Thana shifted her in the chair so she wouldn't fall out, then left the room.

"Well?" Earnhilt bellowed from where she waited just outside the door. She stuck a finger in Thana's face. "You were checking to see if she's a pyradisté, weren't you?" She tapped the side of her head. "I've got a brain, you know."

"Sorry, Majesty. I didn't want…" Thana looked to the bedroom door.

"Didn't want her to scream the place down thinking you were insulting her with commoner's blood?" She snorted. "If I had any spirits-cursed power, you can bet I'd tell you."

Thana nodded, and her mouth went dry. She still had to suggest it. She raised the pyramid. "If I may?"

Earnhilt's face went still, dangerous.

Thana spoke as quickly as she could. "Just a quick moment, and it's done. You won't even lose consciousness…probably, since your mind is stronger than hers." Yes, that would cover Lucia's sleeping state nicely. "She'll nap for a little while. But as for you, Gunnar will be here the whole time. Majesty, please, you might not even know—"

"Oh, just do it if it'll shut you up." She crossed her arms and planted her feet as if Thana was going to try to push her over.

Thana lifted her pyramid, fell into it easily, saw that it could easily swamp the queen's mind, and fell out of the power. "You're not."

"Told you," Earnhilt muttered. She glanced at Gunnar, who nodded as if telling her that Thana had done nothing else to her. Even the queen didn't fully trust her pyradistés.

Thana didn't know whether to laugh, yell, or weep. None would be welcome. "I need to know if any other pyramids have malfunctioned."

Gunnar smiled. "I'll make some discreet inquiries. Any ass ups will be reported."

With a snort, Earnhilt turned toward the bedroom. "I want a report tomorrow."

"And the traps in the hall, Majesty?" Thana asked, envisioning them going off.

"Better disable some of 'em. I can keep an eye on myself." Then she was through the door, and Thana didn't want to linger and listen to what might happen.

"We're lucky there aren't many," Gunnar said as he followed her out.

Thana nodded. "I'm only going to do those closest to the rooms and leave those at the entrance to the royal quarters." Installing trap pyramids in the walls had been a project of her predecessor's that had never been completed. Thana tried not to feel too happy that she would have to dismantle part of it now instead of finishing it. Making pyramids inert was easier than creating them. She had a little while longer before her ineptness was known. And she planned to figure out what was happening before then. Maybe sheer knowledge would save her this time.

And it would save Sylph as well.

CHAPTER FOUR

Trying to calm her pounding heart, Sylph stared at the note, reading, "Had minor emergency for a few days. First appointment tomorrow. T."

Sylph was grateful it didn't mention pyramids or teaching. Even though Thana clearly disapproved of Sylph wanting to subdue her power, she still kept it secret. That boded well. She knew how to keep things to herself without being told. But Sylph didn't let her hopes rise too high. She'd thought her former maid would keep her secrets, too.

When her current maid had delivered the note, she'd waited as Sylph took it, probably expecting discussion or response. Sylph had waved her away before she broke the wax. She'd known it was from Thana. Suitors sent gifts with their notes. Would-be friends used signet rings to seal their wax. Only Sylph's raven would write such as simple note on plain paper with a thumbmark as a seal.

Now, with shaky hands, she burned the letter. She had no doubt her father would hear of the delivery. She already knew what she would say, a courtier had tried to get her attention with a simple missive, and she'd burned it, the best such an attempt rated. It didn't deserve to sit with the other notes and gifts awaiting her father's perusal.

And now that she knew her plans with Thana were moving forward, the room seemed much too small. She usually enjoyed hiding from court, but she couldn't stand the thought of waiting for an entire day, both dreading and anticipating her first session with Thana.

After a last check of her hair and clothing, she took to the halls of the palace, losing herself in admiring the works of art, tapestries, and sculpture. Courtiers thronged the halls as they always did, but Sylph did her best to stay away from the gossiping gaggles and turned at even the hint of voices. She'd been to the palace at Marienne enough times to know it by heart.

One quick escape took her into an alcove, and she paused to wait for some courtiers to pass, but they stopped as they met another group. Ah well. She'd just have to study the tapestry hanging in the alcove's center. It depicted some battle she couldn't place. If history lessons didn't involve her ancestors, she never learned them. Still, she could admire the artistry and wonder about the weavers, how long they'd labored, the pride they must have felt when their task was finished.

What did that feel like?

"The pyradisté?" one of the courtiers cried.

The others shushed him, but Sylph turned an ear toward the conversation and sidled closer to the alcove's edge. Her anxiety peaked at the thought of them gossiping about her. But how would they know? Were they talking about Thana, the one pyradisté they were certain to have heard of?

For some reason, that angered her.

"He killed the entire family," another voice said. "He claimed he lost control, but who knows with these peasants?"

Not her or Thana, then. Sylph sighed, and her heart slowed. She didn't recognize either of the voices, but she didn't memorize anything about the courtiers. With the nobility, she'd been forced to learn everything.

"I don't know why we tolerate them," someone said with a sniff.

Sylph suppressed a snort. As if courtiers had any say in policy. Maybe if one could get a noble to listen to them. But if a pyradisté had committed murder, that would get the nobles' attention. It certainly caught hers.

"Speaking of…there's the queen's pyradisté," one of them said, an excited note in her voice.

"Perhaps we should confront her about these murders."

"If we guided her in solving them, we'd be heroes!"

"We should at least demand she do her deuced job."

The first courtier laughed in an obnoxious way. "Why should we do anything but shun her?"

Sylph's anger bloomed again, and she stepped out among them, her best haughty expression in place. Thana was coming down the hall, so Sylph cleared her throat to get the courtiers' attention before they could put any plan into action.

The group of five whirled as if she'd shouted, faces startled, one with his mouth open as if to tell her off for scaring him, but another grabbed his arm, eyes wide in recognition.

"Lady Sylph." One of the women bowed low, and the rest followed suit as if tied together.

She kept her chin tilted up, her eyes half-lidded as she gave each a brief look. When she glanced down the hall, Thana had stopped, staring. "Pyradisté Thana," Sylph said politely. She lifted a hand as if signaling that the way was clear. "After you."

With a squeak, the courtiers hastened to get out of Thana's way, nearly pressing themselves into the walls.

Thana's mouth twitched, but she bowed to Sylph, ignoring the courtiers. "Thank you, my lady." She hurried past.

Sylph resisted the urge to walk with her, but they couldn't be seen as friends. She gave the courtiers another bland look, but as two opened their mouths, she strode past, hoping her frosty aura kept them from following. They stayed where they were, and as some of them cursed the one who'd nearly censured her, she fought the urge to smile.

No, no. She couldn't smile. It wasn't a happy occasion. Quicksand was what it was, as dangerous as any fen that bordered her father's land. Who knew what gossip would come of that encounter, how much would spread to her father, and then there'd be questions, and...

Sylph clenched a fist behind her back. Her father could do nothing to Thana. Even if Sylph marched into his study and declared them friends or lovers or betrothed, he couldn't touch Thana because she was the prince's friend and the queen's pyradisté, and those were two untouchables, even with his considerable reach.

She glided down another hall, found a vacant spot, and leaned against the wall, forcing herself to breathe. It was too dangerous to be out here at all. Too many eyes, too many secrets, and what would she do if the terrible magic reared in her again? Her father would... he would...

Disown her. Incredible, heartbreaking freedom opened up before her like a pit. A chance to get out from her father's reins but also the likelihood of starving to death with no money, no friends, and nowhere to go. Maybe Thana the raven would let her sleep on the floor in her apartment.

Sylph snorted. As intriguing as that was, it also wasn't likely.

No, she would continue her plan: learn to control her power, wait, inherit one day, be free.

She turned toward her apartment, strolling, aloof look in place, but she lingered whenever she heard gossip. Pyradistés had always been sneered at, but there was fear in some voices now. The tale of the murderer had spread, and so had others about rogue pyradistés running amok. Some were worried, but Sylph couldn't afford that luxury. Whether the rumor was true or not didn't matter. If the courtiers inside the palace felt secure enough to mock the queen's pyradisté, what would the pyradistés outside suffer at the hands of their class?

Thana couldn't stop censuring herself for mocking Sylph in her head. She'd been a bully, as bad a snob as those who looked down on her. She'd looked down on Sylph for wanting her power gone.

Well, she'd never be far enough above a noble to look down on one. Maybe sideways. Or up and to the side or—

She shook her head. It didn't matter. What did was that the faces of those courtiers had been as easy to read as a child's chapter book. They'd wanted trouble, and she'd been going to give it to them, but Sylph had stepped among their ranks like a queen carved from solid ice and made them give way.

And she hadn't had to bark an order. She'd just given Thana the courtesy she was due as a human being, not to mention someone who lived near the royals and worked with them, too.

As Thana stalked down the hall, she came around from gratitude to recrimination again. She couldn't fall for one kind gesture. Sylph wouldn't have done anything if Thana hadn't saved her earlier. By the spirits, she had to put Sylph and all these tangled emotions from her mind. She had exploding pyramids to deal with.

And she'd guessed why the courtiers felt they could confront her. She'd heard the rumors about pyradistés going mad. She'd paid a visit to the Pyradisté Academy, trying to find out more about the exploding pyramids, and while she'd been there, she'd heard a few stories. Headmaster Cyrus had told her that the man accused of killing his employer—and not the family, as rumor had it—had then been killed by household guards. Another pyradisté was supposedly imprisoned for another crime, but the stories disputed the location. She'd sent some contacts to check, wanting to get hold of the pyradisté as soon as she could and find out what had actually happened before they met the queen's justice.

In the meantime, she'd added her voice to the headmaster's and warned students to stay close to the academy and its walls. Pyradistés who'd been terminated from their positions had returned there, too, and they could quickly become overcrowded. A few had loudly declared that the people of Marienne should be taught a lesson in who possessed the power, but Thana had done her best to quell such feelings. The last thing they needed was fighting in the streets or a return to some of the darker days in Farraday's history when wielding pyramids was punishable by execution.

Thana needed to meet with Gunnar and the rest of the Order of Vestra. Luckily, Gunnar was already thinking ahead. She received a message from him that afternoon, just as she was going to send her own, a summons to meet on a secluded balcony accessible only by a secret set of stairs. Hanna's Retreat, Gunnar called it, after his grandmother, who'd built it as somewhere to get away from court life now and again.

There were a few more secret passages in the palace walls. Thana hoped they'd crisscross the whole palace someday, maybe when all the new construction was done. Then she wouldn't have so far to go and wouldn't have to wander the hallways until the entrance to a secret passage was clear of passersby.

She paused in the alcove where this passage was hidden and studied the tapestry that concealed it. Some old sailing ship or another. She didn't care and had to repress the desire to tap her foot as a servant wandered past. At least she wasn't politically active enough for any courtier to try to follow her.

That led her back to thoughts of Sylph and the deft way she'd gotten the courtiers out of the way. Thana smiled again, even in the face of the same dark thoughts that warned her to not get too attached and to mind her heart. Even if her thoughts wandered no further than admiration, Sylph could break her in two. It was just what nobles did, use people until there was nothing left.

Finally, the hall emptied, and Thana lifted the tapestry and stepped behind it. The wall slid soundlessly open, and Thana stepped through, letting the tapestry fall back and leaving her in the dim light filtering from the top of the stairs.

At the top, Gunnar waited on a balcony overlooking the fields surrounding Marienne. A hint of chill remained in the air, but the fields and forest beyond popped with every hue of green. The river sparkled in the distance, curling out of sight as it flowed away from the docks and down to the sea.

Thana leaned on the low wall beside Gunnar. His face was relaxed, with none of the languid airs he usually donned. Thana always saw through those to the coiled anticipation underneath, but here, out of the eye of courtly magpies, he could actually loosen up.

The chill of the bricks bled through Thana's cassock, numbing her arms, but she stayed still, mimicking Gunnar's thoughtful pose. "The others coming?" she asked.

He shook his head. "They're out collecting rumors. Have you heard any?"

"About the pyradistés? Or is there another crisis?"

He snorted. "When has there ever been just one? But yes, the pyradistés."

"I've heard about one in prison and another killed after committing murder. Those are the only confirmations I was able to get from the academy. All else is conjecture."

He shook his head, and his face tightened. "Not all. There was an explosion at the treasury."

Thana's stomach rolled over. "A pyramid?"

"It exploded while a pyradisté was carrying it."

Thana's head drooped onto her arms, and she imagined the cold penetrating through to her skull. "Spirits above. Was anyone else hurt?"

"Luckily no. And the treasury kept it quiet, not wanting anyone to think their money was in danger. They sent a note to my mother."

She rolled her eyes. "Well, thank the spirits the money's all right."

He glared. "Anything that keeps people from panicking is a good thing."

She wanted to retort, but arguing didn't seem important at the moment. "Where did you send the others?"

"Dina is collecting gossip from the chapterhouses."

Thana nodded. Even though Dina was a monk who worshiped the spirits of love and beauty, she'd be more welcome in the other chapterhouses, too, simply because she *was* a monk.

"I've told Ivar and Illis to go where they deem necessary in order to sort pyramid rumor from fact."

Another nod. The twin brothers were good at gathering info with one being very personable and talkative, and the other being quiet and contemplative. People warmed to the first and forgot the second was there. "Anything yet?"

"It's too soon. I wanted to talk to you in person, far away from anyone who might listen in." He sighed. "And away from any pyramids that might explode."

"Glad I'm not carrying any," she said with a smile she didn't feel. "At least your anti-Fiend necklace shouldn't go off with a bang." She put a hand on his shoulder and wanted to tell him it would be all right, but he'd always been the optimist. He usually only needed her to tell him when they were doomed. "My research hasn't uncovered anything except that what's happening shouldn't be happening." At his smirk, she added, "I know, big help. I'm going to work with the noble who was present at the first explosion tomorrow. With luck, I'll find a clue about this whole mess."

"And then you'll tell me who this mysterious noble is?"

She swallowed, still hesitant to give up that secret. She imagined what might happen if the courtiers and the other nobles discovered a secret pyradisté in their midst right when pyradistés seemed like the enemy. "Soon," she said, drawing the word out.

His mouth twisted with skepticism. "If she's a danger…"

"You'll know it." She waited a moment, staring at the river. "Because she'll explode."

He sputtered a laugh, and it was good to see him relax a little. "Please let me know before that…unless you've exploded, too."

"Deal." They went back to staring at the vista, and a wandering doubt passed through her head. What if Gunnar sent the Order away for more than just sniffing out rumors? What if he didn't want them to meet with Thana because she was a pyradisté just like those who'd become murderers or bombs? "You haven't…" She couldn't finish.

He turned and waited, never one to let a thought go unfinished. "Haven't what?" He lifted his eyebrows.

She tried to ask, but she couldn't accuse him of not trusting her. The very thought was almost too painful. "Never mind."

Now he laid a comforting hand on hers. "You'll figure it out. I have complete faith."

"Thanks," she mumbled. She prayed to the spirits of knowledge that he was right. "I'm sure the noble will give me a lead, then I can follow it up in my own books or at the academy." All information he knew or could at least figure out, but she was reluctant to leave him yet. Even if he didn't doubt her now, he might soon, but she didn't know how to ask for comfort.

She sighed. When had her thoughts become so jumbled?

"Something you want to ask?" He leaned against the wall, an elbow propped on the ledge and one ankle crossed over the other, the picture of relaxed, the master of putting people at ease. "Something about this mysterious noble, perhaps?"

She blinked, wondering how he could have known, but as his smile grew, she knew her reaction had just told him something. "You're guessing."

"And by the look of you, I was right. So tell. Is the noble terrifying, or have they caught your eye?"

Her cheeks burned as she turned away. "I should get back to—"

"Nope. Stay and tell. That's a royal command."

She hoped her look conveyed where he could stuff his royalty and his commands.

He barked a laugh. "If this noble is terrifying, I can yank a few of their fearsome teeth. If you find them intriguing, ask the master of romance." He opened his arms as if welcoming her in.

"Master of the one tumble and then a quick good-bye."

"Hey! Some were interesting enough for two or three."

She snorted a laugh. "No thanks." And there went the spirits-cursed burning in her cheeks again.

His eyes widened. "Are you in love?"

"Shut up," she mumbled as she tried to turn for the stairs again.

He raced around her and drew himself up to his full height of six feet, blocking her path. "Are you? You have to tell me, Than. I'd tell you."

"I wouldn't want to know." When he dodged to stay in her path, quick and lithe, she sighed. "I don't know this person well enough to be in love."

"But you can't get them out of your mind."

"The garden explosion was the day before yesterday. Of course, they've been on my mind." Sometimes naked, but she didn't mention that part. Her cheeks had probably told the secret for her by now.

He leaned back, the wonder on his face softening to consideration, the grin becoming a smirk again. She put her hands on her hips and waited, but he only turned to the side, gesturing that the way to the stairs was clear.

Thana stepped that way, trying not to stomp or sulk or blush any harder.

"When you tell me their name," he said behind her, "I want the whole story."

She strode on, glad the darkness hid her face.

CHAPTER FIVE

Sylph awoke feeling bold, something she hadn't experienced in a long time. She lay in bed and felt unworthy of the feeling even as she reveled in it. She hadn't done anything the day before except make a bunch of courtiers make way for the queen's pyradisté. She hadn't ordered them to go jump in the river or chop their own heads off, nothing that would make them fear her more than any other noble. And Thana had probably forgotten the incident even as it occurred. No doubt she viewed herself as above her station because of the royal company she kept.

That thought wrinkled Sylph's good feelings, and she sat up, staring at all her clothes and cosmetics and frippery. She took no joy in them today and focused on Thana. She didn't want Thana to forget her actions with the courtiers—a desire she did her best to squelch—because it had brought them closer…a little. She also frowned a bit at the thought of Thana being of such low station.

But that was truth and required no feelings from her whatsoever.

With a sigh, she nearly threw a pillow across the room. Even her own mind was starting to sound like her father.

She rose and dressed herself, not waiting for her maid. She pulled her hair back in a simple tail and donned one of the ridiculous hats so in fashion. It would cover her lack of artistry nicely. When she emerged into the sitting room, her maid made a little squeal from where she was laying out some breakfast things.

"My lady, I didn't know you were up!"

"You may go." Sylph gave her an icy stare until she fled. Her stomach was churning, and the thought of the impending pyramid practice left her thoughts scattered. She did not have the energy to field inquiries or school her face from the maid's searching glances. She sipped her tea and tried to make herself be calm. She'd endured many lessons in her lifetime. What was one more?

One more that could ruin her if anyone found out?

She set the cup down with a clatter that would have shocked her etiquette tutor and forced herself to breathe. She couldn't think of the pyramids without being nervous, so she thought of the only other thing this morning included: Thana.

Yes, Thana couldn't be her friend or anything, but that was only in reality. In her mind, Sylph could have anything, be anyone, befriend whom she liked, and love whomever she wished. She'd had many occasions to be grateful that her father couldn't read her mind while he lectured her, couldn't hear the many names she called him when he scorned or belittled.

She imagined that she and Thana *were* friends. She would be excited they were going to spend the morning together. They could talk about anything, not only the difficulties and triumphs in their lives but what they might do if let out into the world. They could go away together and have adventures. They could laugh. They could kiss. They could—

Sylph gasped as another thought occurred, a buried bit of trivia that fought through her imaginary nonsense. Because they had the power to read minds through pyramids, pyradistés never had to worry about someone reading their thoughts. The power shielded them somehow.

Having her mind read had never been a great worry, even with all her rebellious thoughts. Her father loathed pyradistés, but when she'd found out they had the power to read minds, she'd been fearful. Now, she had a certainty in her favor, an indisputable fact all her own. No one would ever know her thoughts.

The boldness returned.

She ate lightly. She would need sustenance for the tasks ahead, but she didn't want to be sick if her nerves assailed her again. When she finished, she waited in the hall, not wanting her maid or her father to catch Thana visiting. She would no doubt be coming from the royal quarters, so there was only one hall she could take, and Sylph waited at that junction, her nerves jumping so that she wasn't able to pretend to be admiring the art. She no doubt appeared to be waiting for someone and kept her death stare at the ready should anyone accost her.

When Thana turned the corner into the hall, Sylph blinked. With her dark hair and clothing, she looked like a shadow come to life, truly a raven who'd fluttered down the hall and become a woman. Such long, forceful strides. The sides of her cassock rustled like wings. Was it even within her power to stroll? Sylph imagined her hustling a lover down the street instead of meandering arm in arm. Maybe she always hastened to be behind closed doors, just like Sylph. Maybe she would be as energetic in lovemaking as she was in walking.

The thought would give Sylph's father apoplexy.

But he would never know it.

As Thana came closer, her dark eyes shone like obsidian. Sylph smiled, and Thana's stride faltered as if someone had pulled her back. She blinked a few times before her stern expression softened, and she returned the smile. It rounded her pale cheeks and gave her a winsome air.

"I...you're..." Thana cleared her throat, ducked her head, and when she met Sylph's eyes again, she closed to within a few steps, and the smile dropped. But a sparkle remained. "Thank you for meeting me."

"Of course. Thank you for taking the time." When Thana continued to stare, Sylph's confidence slipped. She searched her memory for any etiquette lessons on pyradistés but found her education lacking. Was there some sort of ceremony or initiation she was supposed to know about? The horror of being unprepared for any gathering rose within her.

Thana blinked again, and her cheeks reddened as she looked away. "Sorry, I was...um, I was thinking about..." She waved vaguely. "I have a place picked out for...what we're about, but I was just...briefly reconsidering." She breathed a nervous-sounding laugh and offered a smile of pure mortification. "This way."

Sylph fell in beside her as Thana started back down the hall. It took everything in Sylph not to laugh at the realization that they were both nervous. Perhaps Thana was also overjoyed that no one could read her mind.

She led the way to a door between the section of the palace where the courtiers were housed and where the servants' quarters began, a place Sylph had never visited. Inside was a room slightly bigger than her sitting room and bedroom combined. Musical instruments and chairs had been shifted into a corner and partly covered with white sheets. A large window let in plenty of sunlight, though it looked upon an expanse of stone, the part of the palace now under construction.

"A music room?" Sylph asked.

"Yes, soon to be incorporated into a bigger ballroom after the new construction." She gestured beyond the window. "But for now, it's got lots of light, and no one comes in here. Unless they knock the wall down while we're standing here."

Sylph smiled to show she appreciated the little joke. With Thana's words, though, she couldn't help thinking of the moving wall that had almost killed her. She shook the thought off. "How shall we proceed?"

Thana removed a black satchel that had hung crossways around her body and rested against her back. Sylph didn't even notice it until she took it off. "Well, even though you're only interested in suppression, you need to know about the various pyramids and how to use them. This will help you control your power."

When she started removing pyramids and setting them on a cloth-covered table, Sylph's heart began to pound. She'd pictured meditation or something of that sort, but this almost seemed like… weapon-craft. Still, she didn't want to argue and had to take it for granted that Thana knew more about being a pyradisté than she did.

Even if she dearly didn't want to be one.

Even after learning her mind couldn't be read?

She shook the thought away.

Thana pointed at the table. "Pyramids come in three basic categories: destruction, mind magic, and utility." She touched one pyramid that had steep angles and a sharp point. "This is a flash bomb. Like most destructive pyramids, these are made by pyradistés but can be used by anyone. They only have to be broken. Flash bombs create a loud bang and a flash bright enough to incapacitate those standing close to it when it breaks. There are other destruction pyramids: fire, disintegration, death, and explosive."

Sylph fought a grimace. All of them sounded awful.

"I've made them all, but I don't keep them on my person while in the palace. Disintegration is particularly nasty. It completely eradicates everything within its blast radius, taking the form of a black sphere, which, thankfully, is only the size of a single person." She tilted her head back and forth. "Roughly." By her lecturing tone, one would have thought she was talking about something as benign as the weather.

She glanced up, and something of Sylph's distaste must have shown. "They can be helpful," Thana said with a defensive look.

"Something called a death pyramid can be helpful? Or a sphere that disintegrates everything in a space that is *roughly* the size of a person?"

"I didn't invent them or name them."

Sylph held up a hand. "I don't mean any offense. Please continue."

Thana took a deep breath, but her finger seemed to stab toward the pyramids when she pointed again. "Destructive pyramids are hard to make." She shook her head as if that thought caused her pain. "For many people." Maybe she wasn't very good at crafting them.

Sylph gave her an encouraging smile. Not being able to make something with "death" in its name was a point in her favor as far as Sylph was concerned.

Thana returned the look briefly. "Some pyramids are a mix of types. Those that guard the royal quarters and the one you encountered in the garden are trap pyramids, a mix of destruction and mind magic, sensing murderous intent and then exploding."

Sylph pulled back, her mind reeling. "I never had any murderous intent."

"No, no," Thana said, holding up her hands as if pacifying a shying horse. "I didn't think you did. No, something definitely went wrong there."

Sylph forced herself to breathe. "I'm sorry. I'm just..." She didn't know what to say, couldn't begin to describe her feelings. She also wasn't used to apologizing to anyone below her station. But

Thana had already rescued her, seen her weeping and disheveled. She was owed a few apologies.

"It's okay." Thana touched another pyramid, her movements slow. "Um, this is a mind pyramid. It can hypnotize people, letting pyradistés sort through their memories. More complicated mind pyramids can control people."

"But none can read…us, right?" Sylph asked, gesturing between them. The thought of them being an "us" in any way made the heat rise in her face.

"No, mind magic doesn't work on pyradistés," Thana said. "For utility, I've brought a light pyramid, which is used, um, in the dark." She gave another nervous laugh. "If the name didn't clue you in. There are also utility pyramids that detect other pyramids being used, including trap pyramids, and cancellation pyramids, which render other pyramids inert. All of them can only be used by pyradistés." She held the light pyramid out. "Let's start with this one."

Sylph tried to keep from staring as if the thing was a rat, but Thana's flat look said she failed. And she couldn't apologize for that. This was a part of life she should have never had to deal with. That wasn't her fault.

Thana pressed her lips together and then released them with a little pop. "I know you don't want to do this, but you have to learn *what* you're trying to control in order to master it. And I need to see what you can do with a pyramid, so I can figure out what happened in the garden."

Sylph had to force her hand not to tremble as she took the pyramid, telling herself the smooth sides were glass, not crystal. It was an ornament. It meant nothing.

"Stare into it, see the way it's made, the way the five sides connect at the points. Look through it to the other side, at the way the light's distorted."

It drew the eye. She gave it that. Looking through it took the light and transformed it into an explosion of color, every hue she'd ever seen, many she hadn't even known existed. Strange how something half the size of her fist could seem to contain the whole world.

"Call forth the light," Thana whispered.

Simple enough. She was already inside the pyramid. All she had to do was step out and bring the light with her.

The pyramid blazed, a fountain of colors shining forth. Sylph cried out and tossed it into the air. Thana caught it and fumbled, coming to rest on one knee as she lost her balance and hugged the pyramid to her chest.

"What in the spirits' names?" Thana said, gasping as if she'd run a mile and staring at Sylph with wide eyes.

"Did I...was that wrong?" Sylph's heart was trying to beat forth from her chest, mostly from the pyramid but also from the fear in Thana's eyes.

"How did you do that?" She looked to the pyramid as if it might hold the answers. "So bright, all those different colors."

"They were all in there."

Thana didn't look at her. "All in where?"

Sylph took a deep breath. Nothing had exploded. All was well. "In the pyramid. Every color, every hue. Was that not what I was supposed to see?"

With a long sigh, Thana stood and put the pyramid back on the table. She leaned on it as if she needed it to stay standing. "I've read about people like you."

Fear creeped up Sylph's throat again. "People like—"

"Those so powerful, they can bring forth every bit of a pyramid's potential." She straightened, and the fear on her face morphed into hard lines and simmering anger. "You're the most powerful pyradisté I've ever met, my lady."

Fear tipped toward terror, clawing at Sylph's brain. She cast around for a chair but only saw those spirits-cursed sheets. She could sit on the floor—how long had it been since she'd sat on a floor— that was where she'd be when her father discovered this, beneath everyone's boots. How could she hide something that had built in her like some wasting disease until it came boiling out whenever she was near a pyramid?

"Are you crying?" Thana's voice sounded strained, as if she barely held in a scream. "You just found out that you're extremely powerful, and you're—"

"Ruined," Sylph managed to say. She would not weep, not when she had a choice. She'd wept in the garden, and that had been enough for the rest of her life.

"I don't believe this. Don't believe you."

"You don't understand."

"Oh, *of course*, I don't. I had to struggle with my ability, had to prove myself time and again, have to constantly contend with the fact that I might not be capable of doing my job as it needs doing. So, no, I can't understand unlimited power thrown at my feet along with being rich and titled and beautiful." She paced as if no longer talking to anyone but herself, waving her arms about and letting all her emotions loose upon her face. "No one should have that much spirits-cursed good luck in their life!"

She didn't understand, and Sylph didn't want to make her, not while she railed against her lot in life and bemoaned her fate. Meanwhile, Sylph was a hair's breadth from losing the title and money and security and being left with a power she didn't want. She drew on every one of her father's tactics and drew herself up. "The difference is, you're a peasant and I'm not, and these are a peasant's powers." She shrugged and made herself march to the table. "Perhaps if you spent less time bemoaning your fate and more time practicing, you could make something more of your life."

She could feel Thana's stare, could almost sense the anger. But if Sylph wanted to survive, to be a duchess one day, she had to keep moving forward. She had to be brave. She picked up the light pyramid when she wanted nothing more to do with the thing. "Now what?"

Thana's face nearly glowed red, and her shoulders worked up and down as if barely containing her fury.

Sylph lifted an eyebrow, telling herself it was all right. No one could read her thoughts, could see how badly she wanted to apologize, see how much she wanted to explain and ask for understanding. But that wasn't the path to a duchy. It led only to ruin. "Teach me how to suppress the power to control this pyramid, and perhaps some of my ability will transfer to you."

Thana took a few more breaths before slowly moving forward, each strike of her boots a thump against the floor. "It doesn't work that way, my lady." Her voice was low and as rough as if she'd been eating gravel. "And your greater powers aren't a gift of your title or your noble birth." Her head tilted slowly. "If these are peasant powers, what does that say about your lineage?"

Anger brought Sylph's teeth together. "Watch your mouth."

"Or you'll what? You might be able to flog your own *peasants*, but I'm a servant of the queen, at her service"—she leaned forward—"and under her protection." She plucked the pyramid from Sylph's grasp and stepped around her, placing it back on the table with an audible thump.

Sylph turned slowly. No one had ever just…disobeyed her before. Even her maid's betrayal didn't feel like this. There was anger, most definitely, and a vague sense of confusion about what to do next, but she also had a sudden desire to grab Thana's heaving shoulders and kiss her to see where all these passionate feelings might go.

She was quite certain her father would not regard defiance in the same fashion.

Nor would he be diplomatic, but Sylph had to try that if bullying wouldn't work. She cleared her throat. "Very well. I need you to teach me."

Thana barked a laugh.

"And though I may not be able to have you flogged," Sylph said loudly, "I can make your life in the palace as difficult as I made it easy yesterday."

With another deep breath, Thana leaned back against the table, her expression going calculating. Sylph had made the courtiers give way, but she could also make them block Thana's every move, make the nobles go from ignoring her to spurning her. And if that wasn't enough, if Sylph's father got involved, the queen might have to replace Thana as her pyradisté.

By the brief look of fear, then resignation, Thana didn't need to be reminded of all that.

"I will try to be a better student," Sylph said, hoping that greased the wheels.

Thana licked her lips and looked to her pyramids. "Well, I fear giving you anything stronger to practice with. Why don't you tell me when you discovered your powers, what you felt with the light pyramid, and what you can remember from the garden, and I'll think of a way for you to suppress it."

Sylph nodded. That sounded reasonable, especially since she really didn't want to touch a pyramid again.

❖

Thana tried to set aside her irritation and listen as Sylph described a moment three months ago when she'd reached for a stone with her power. It sounded the same as what had happened in the garden, only not as powerful. To Thana's frustration, Sylph didn't remember much from the garden, only a feeling of lightheadedness and a desire to pull at something inside her that she didn't recognize. It sounded like the rush a pyradisté felt when they fell into a pyramid.

Except Thana had never heard of someone being compelled to do so. At least pondering the problem gave her something to think about besides the desire to either punch Sylph or kiss her.

When their disagreement had started, the desire to punch had definitely been stronger. Heat rose in her cheeks again as she thought of all the garbage she'd spouted about her own struggles. Why in all the spirits' names had she said all that? Not only was it none of Sylph's business, but it could be construed as petty jealousy, and she was not jealous. Not much. Not to any degree that mattered.

And the last thing she needed was for Sylph to know that.

When they'd faced off at the end, Sylph's eyes had gone frosty, but her chest had heaved, revealing her emotions as much as her face had hidden them. Her gaze had wandered to Thana's lips and lingered, her eyes tightening as if she had to restrain herself.

Oh spirits, Thana had wanted her then. Desired her as much as she didn't *want* to desire her. And Sylph's eyes had said she wasn't alone.

"Do I need to say it again?" Sylph asked, breaking Thana's reverie and bringing even more heat into her face. She was going to set off the fire pyramid in a moment.

"No, sorry, I was just thinking." And getting nowhere with either the pyramid thoughts or the lustful ones. She clenched a fist and told herself to focus.

"No need for apology," Sylph said. "I'll do whatever I can to avoid having a repeat of the garden incident."

The garden incident. How could one person be so pretentious? "Thank you," Thana said, hoping some of her scorn remained hidden.

Sylph brushed a strand of pale hair off her shoulder. "Not at all."

Thana turned away and rolled her eyes, wishing they could go back to sniping if the alternative was this stilted, careful chatter. She shook her head and regarded her pyramids, feeling completely unqualified for her role once again. "I don't understand what happened in that garden. To be frank, I don't know what happened to you three months ago, either." She turned back around. "If you hadn't felt compelled to use your power, it would likely have gone undiscovered."

Sylph drew in a sharp breath. She opened her mouth but seemed to think better about saying something. Thana felt grateful she didn't have to remind Sylph that, yes, people were either born with pyradisté powers or they weren't. But peasants were tested.

How many other pyradisté nobles might be out there, undiscovered? Thana had the urge to tear from the palace and start testing all the nobles to see how many had dirty little bloodlines.

"Well," Sylph said, bringing Thana's attention back. "So this compulsion is unique?" She clasped her hands behind her back, stretching her lightweight coat tight across her breasts.

Thana forced herself not to stare. "As is your stone power."

Sylph shrugged. "If it's unique, then you need not feel badly about not understanding it. No one can understand a thing which is unprecedented." Before Thana could embarrass herself further by repeating her feelings of inadequacy, Sylph shook her head and took a step closer. "And I'm certain you would never have been named monarch's pyradisté if your competency was ever in question." Her eyes seemed kinder if still with a bit of frost.

And she was closer. If Thana took a step, she'd be close enough to kiss.

Enough! "You felt compelled," Thana said. "The answer must lie there. Do you feel compelled to use any of these pyramids now?"

Sylph looked around Thana and shook her head. "I'd rather not touch them, to be honest." Her eyes widened slightly, and Thana knew that anger must still be present on her face. "No offense intended, of course."

Breathe, Thana told herself. Nothing would be served by yelling again. "Something about that moment, then." She thought back to the garden but recalled nothing out of the ordinary.

Except her own abilities had seemed enhanced, too. She let her thoughts drift, thinking aloud as she always did with a difficult problem. "You felt compelled. I felt stronger. For someone like you, incredibly powerful under normal circumstances, some…special condition might force you to use a pyramid. Where the same condition made my pyramids more powerful." But the reason still eluded her. "Is that what happened to the other pyradistés? The murder? The explosions?"

"Murder? I heard some gossip, but—"

Thana waved for her to hush. "But did the pyramids explode without warning? Or were their creators compelled to set them off? But that wouldn't explain the queen's—" She cut herself off. That one was a secret.

"The queen's what?" Sylph asked, a bit of emotion in her voice, as if she'd thaw for a piece of juicy gossip.

Thana shook her head. "Did you see anyone out of place in the garden?" Sylph recited everyone she'd seen so quickly, Thana stared. "Did you memorize the guest list?"

"No, I have a good memory for faces, and I know what every noble looks like." She said it without crowing, a mere recitation of fact. Just like the tone she used when speaking about peasant magic.

Unable to avoid twisting that knife just a little, Thana asked, "What about the servants?"

Sylph's mouth tightened, the closest she'd come to an actual frown. "I remember their faces but not their names. Is that enough to escape your derision?"

"Maybe," Thana muttered, embarrassed again. "Were all the servants dressed in the palace livery?"

"Those I saw, yes." Her lips quirked now, a hint of a smile. "Did you not notice them at all?"

Someone had tried to serve her a drink, but the face was a blank spot in her mind. "I…"

Sylph took another step, close enough to touch. "You ignore the servants? Too far above them?"

"I ignore everyone, high and low, so there." How in the spirits' names did this woman bring her blood to boil so quickly?

That tiny smile was still in place, the most open Thana had seen her since she'd been terrified in the garden.

"Until I know what happened there," Thana said after a deep breath, "I can't help you contain your power. You might feel compelled again, and I don't know any pyramids that could keep someone from using their power." Maybe a modified version of the pyramid that kept the Umbriels from presenting their Fiendish Aspect, but she couldn't mention that.

She'd become the keeper of many secrets lately, and it weighed on her.

Sylph sagged as if Thana had destroyed her dreams. Thana couldn't resist touching her forearm lightly, a safe distance from the familiarity of a shoulder pat and the intimacy of holding hands. When Sylph glanced at her hand, Thana went to release her, but Sylph put her fingers over Thana's, a recognition that touched Thana as much as it frightened her. She dropped her arm and tried to think of what else to say.

"They'll shun me," Sylph said softly, looking at the floor. "If they find out about the...pyramids, the nobles will no longer see me as one of their own."

Thana fought the urge to grumble. So she wouldn't be invited to parties any longer? Thana would have been celebrating.

"My father will disown me."

"What?" Thana's mind reeled. "Really?"

Sylph nodded, and the little smile turned sad when their eyes met again. "You were honest with me, so I thought I might try it with you. Not that I'm usually a liar. Most times, I say nothing."

A habit Thana knew she should practice herself, but she couldn't do it now. "The duke wouldn't disown you. He can't, not if he..." She'd been about to say, "loves you," but Sylph seemed so sad and certain. And resigned. No matter what her father's feelings were, she clearly believed he'd throw her out with nothing.

Well, that was worse than not being invited to parties. Thana drew herself up, tired of the emotional gamut she'd run this day but determined to help. Strange that a barely emotive noble could put her through so much. "Can you feel the pyramids sitting here? If you're able to sense them without the aid of a detection pyramid, like some pyradistés can, you can at least turn and go in the other direction."

Sylph's smile was a little wider, grateful, and she glanced at the table. "Should we…stand away or something?"

Not a bad thought, considering the power she'd managed to pull from the light pyramid. "Let's start on the other side of the room. Then we can determine just how close you have to be in order to sense them."

They moved as far away as they could, nearly on top of some sheet-covered furniture. Sylph stared at the pyramid table with a worried look.

"Relax," Thana said. "Remember the way the light pyramid felt."

Sylph's intense face relaxed. As she breathed out a contented sigh, a burst of flame engulfed the table with a loud crack. Thana fell back amidst billowing smoke and a blast of heat, panic overtaking her as fire devoured the furniture and climbed the wall to lick at the ceiling.

CHAPTER SIX

S ylph came out of her pyramid stupor slowly.

The wall was on fire.

She blinked, but the flames remained, roaring and spewing heat and smoke. She remembered the pyramids on the table shining like diamonds before she'd focused on one that held flickering flame at its heart, contained destruction waiting for freedom.

She'd set it loose.

"Get down!" Thana jerked on her arm, hauling her around and sideways.

Sylph fell to one knee. Jarring pain vibrated up her leg. She gasped, and smoke burned down her throat, searing her chest into a coughing fit.

"Stay near the floor, the cleaner air," Thana said, her own voice ragged. "Where's the door?"

The door, yes. They needed to get out. The room seemed a maze around the dark smoke and crackling flame. Was the door on one end of the left wall or in the middle? Her eyes stung and bathed her cheeks in tears. She crawled left, tugging Thana with her.

"Wait," Thana gasped, choking.

No, they needed to stop talking and start trying to get out.

Thana sagged, coughing. "It's...not..."

"Come on." A tinkling sound filled her ears. A bell? No, a harsher, crunching sound, nearly covered by the fire, but it had to be coming from the hall. They were close.

"Wait!" Thana's cry was rough, and she caught Sylph's arm in a grip like stone.

Stone. Yes. If she could make a new hole in the wall…

A memory came floating back as if billowed by the flames. The pyramid in the garden *had* pulled her in, but it hadn't felt right. She'd felt herself reach but not with her arms. Her mind had gone tumbling into the pyramid, embraced by its power. She'd wanted her pain to end, so she'd changed the pyramid, and the wall had come for her.

And there were more pyramids in this room. She reached again as she crawled.

Tendrils of smoke parted, revealing a swath of stone before her and the glitter of glass. Covered in cracks, screeching and tinkling, it was the crunching bell she'd heard before.

She'd pulled herself and Thana deeper into the room, all the way to the window.

Despair tried to choke her along with the smoke, but she ground her teeth and reached again. There. She had a pyramid in the grasp of her mind.

She demanded it change itself into a now familiar mold.

One that could move stone.

The wall shuddered, and the grind of stone overpowered the sound of the fire. The glass shattered, a glittering fountain cascading away from the warped wall. The smoke *whooshed* outside, and the fire roared in a gout over their heads, but the path to the door became clear.

Thana tugged her around and into a crouch. Sylph let herself be led, forcing herself to release the pyramid as they reached the exit. The opening door let smoke into the hall until Thana threw it closed behind them. Sylph sagged to her knees again, coughing, fighting the urge to retch.

"Come on," Thana said hoarsely. "We need to get help and get you out of here."

Fear fought through Sylph's exhaustion and amazement. She stumbled after as Thana yelled, "Fire!" They slipped past the flow of people heading for the disaster.

In an empty corridor, they slowed. "What…" Sylph bent double, coughing. Her head pounded, and her eyes wouldn't stop watering.

"How…" She couldn't speak more than a single word without hacking again. Spirits curse her, she'd done this, created this nightmare.

No, it was contained. No one was hurt.

Yet.

"They'll put out the fire, don't worry," Thana whispered.

Sylph tried to breathe without coughing. Her hands and clothes were covered in soot. Tear tracks cut through the dark patches on Thana's pale face. Sylph took her hand. "All right?"

Thana nodded. "You?"

"Sorry, so sorry." She closed her eyes and fought her panic. She was not only a pyradisté; she was a menace. Being disowned was too good for her.

"It's all right. You ended up saving us."

Sylph opened her eyes to a look of such compassion, she almost sobbed. She wanted to be held but didn't know how to ask.

"Let's clean up," Thana said. "And you plead complete ignorance of the fire. Until I can figure something out, stay away from pyramids, especially the royal halls."

Sylph nodded, though her current fear was for more than herself. She didn't want to hurt anyone, least of all an Umbriel. She would claim illness and stay in her rooms for a few days. Her hoarse voice could serve as proof of a head cold.

"This way." Thana peeked down halls as she went, gesturing for Sylph to follow. She led them farther from the fire and paused at an open door near the courtiers' rooms, a dangerous place to linger if they wanted to avoid gossip.

After a glance into the room, Thana tugged Sylph inside and over to a washbasin. "Here." She grabbed a cloth and dipped it into the water before scrubbing at Sylph's face.

Sylph nearly sputtered, both at the roughest bath she'd ever experienced and at the used water. There had never been so many firsts in one day. She focused on Thana's frown of concentration and blocked out everything else. She was almost sorry when Thana finally stepped back and nodded, her dark eyes sparkling with a job well done. "There."

Sylph reached for the cloth, more than willing to reciprocate and caress Thana's face, but Thana shook her head and pointed to the basin. "Hands."

"What about you?" Sylph asked as she washed, wincing at the pain in her chest, her throat.

"Everyone expects me to look weird and half-exploded." She only wiped her hands clean and dragged her wet palms down her face, making Sylph want to offer a handkerchief, but she hurried out before Sylph could speak.

Thana pointed the way toward the nobles' apartments. "Remember, stay put."

"Thank you," Sylph managed to blurt before Thana could hurry away. The brief, embarrassed smile she received made her want to move for an embrace again, but she hurried toward her apartments as stealthily as she could.

Her maid was thankfully absent when she arrived, and she undressed and washed more thoroughly before hiding her sooty clothes in a wad under the bed, brushing out her hair, and donning a dressing gown.

She'd just settled in the sitting room with a pounding heart and a novel she was far too distracted to read when her father came in.

He stopped at the sight of her and frowned. "Are you ill?"

"A touch," she said, glad her voice still sounded raspy.

His brows lifted. "Did you send for the physick?"

"Oh no. It's nothing serious."

When he nodded and sat, she wondered if he'd asked out of concern for his heir or his own health. No matter which, he would never do a thing like bathe her face, no matter the reason. "Did you hear of the fire?"

Her heart thundered now, but she made herself shake her head and hoped her expression conveyed wonder and not terror.

It must have done both because he lifted a hand. "There's nothing to fear. It was doused quickly."

"Good gracious. Was anyone hurt?"

"No one of consequence."

Her hands ached, and when she glanced down, she saw her knuckles white around the book. In her father's mind, Thana was a person of no consequence. "Was anyone hurt...at all?"

His look was pure amazement, but she couldn't help asking. He sighed, and surprise changed to pity. "You shouldn't think such things, Sylph. Being kind to the peasantry will make you well-loved but soft. When they take advantage of you, you won't have the respect and fear to shield you."

Fear and respect weren't the same thing. And respect could be won many ways. The words pounded in her brain, but she couldn't speak them. It had taken all her courage to ask if anyone at all was hurt, and she hadn't even gotten an answer.

When a knock sounded, he called, "Enter."

His stoic valet slipped inside. "Court rumor paints a pyradisté as a reason for the fire, Your Grace."

"Of course," Sylph's father said with a snort. His look was pure prejudice, even though Sylph knew the rumor was true. "Who else could it have been?

"Which one?" It wasn't until they looked at her that she realized she'd spoken aloud. She bit her lip. She only knew one pyradisté, the only one who counted.

"Does it matter?" her father asked.

The valet cleared his throat, but his eyes remained half-lidded, as if he was a moment from falling asleep. "They say it's the queen's pyradisté, my lady."

Ringing filled Sylph's ears, drowning her father's scathing response. Her legs twitched as if desperate to run. She had to stand, causing her father to glance at her again as she paced behind the couch, clutching her book. She only hoped he'd put any odd behavior down to illness.

"Oh, Sylph, calm down," he said with a condescending edge. "We're safe here. The queen should have her servant on a tighter leash." He sniffed. "Even if she didn't cause the fire, she should be put to use snuffing this other pyradisté nonsense before we're all burned in our beds."

So much for keeping calm. She almost chucked her book at him. The very idea suggested that the boldness of the morning hadn't completely abandoned her.

Her father stood. "Stay here, daughter. Get well. I'll see what I can do to straighten this nonsense out." He smiled, a wan attempt at affection after Thana's open expressions. "If you need anything, I'm sure your maid will be along shortly. Come along, Hornby." His valet gave Sylph a more sympathetic look and followed in her father's footsteps.

Sylph sagged into a chair, fighting the panic beating inside her. Her father was looking for someone to blame. He could easily turn all the nobles against even the monarch's pyradisté, just as Sylph had threatened to do earlier.

She would have to apologize for that, too.

And she knew how.

Thana had to be warned.

Thana lined up arguments in her head as she strode toward the queen's apartment. She had to report the fire, had to report that it was a noble who'd started it, but she would stress that Sylph was untrained and not at fault.

She nodded as she passed the guards who were always stationed just outside the royal quarters, telling herself she had to remain strong in the face of Queen Earnhilt's temper. Sylph and her father could be removed to the countryside so Sylph couldn't do any more damage to the palace. But what would they tell her father? What if he refused to go or just threw his daughter out?

Thana gnawed her lip. Earnhilt could take care of Sylph, pay for her lodging, her training. Thana would stress that Sylph's stone-moving power could prove quite useful if she learned to control it. With her strength, she might be able to erect buildings by herself. Surely Earnhilt would see the value in that.

When Thana answered the call to enter the queen's chambers, she found Earnhilt pulling her boots on. "Have you heard of this fire in the palace?" Earnhilt said.

Thana shut her teeth on that very report. "Yes, Majesty, I was just—"

"Rumor has another spirits-cursed pyradisté behind it. No offense." She didn't look up as she buckled her sword belt around her trim waist.

"Um, none taken." Though there was a little and not just for her sake.

"Gunnar is in the city checking on some other tales of pyradistés gone mad. I suppose we'll add this one to his pile. With me." She strode out the door, and Thana had to hurry to catch up.

"It *was* a pyradisté," Thana said quickly. "I was there." Earnhilt gave her a calculating glance. She held up her hands and added, "It wasn't me. She's untrained, and I was trying to help her. She's a noble, and—"

Earnhilt stopped and ran a hand down her face. "Oh, spirits curse me, a fucking noble?"

"Yes, she—"

"As if we didn't have enough problems." She marched on, only pausing again when she reached the smoke-ravaged hallway near where the fire started. Thana stayed on her heels, all arguments shattered under the battering ram that was the queen's personality.

Earnhilt sighed loudly as she looked around the corner and saw the room itself, the stone and wood blackened by soot. "Dangerous, is she?"

"Very," Thana said without thinking. "Powerful, that is. Her power could be very useful if—"

"No help for it, then, if she's going to keep setting the castle alight and setting off pyramids in the royal quarters."

"I don't think that was her," Thana said, but Earnhilt didn't appear to be listening. Thana wondered how much trouble she'd get into if she shook the queen's muscular arm. Not from the guard. Earnhilt could rip Thana to shreds. "If we can convince her father—"

Earnhilt groaned. "Her parents are still alive? When the spirits curse us, they don't do it by halves, do they?" She glared at Thana. "No noble father is going to stand by while we execute his daughter. The whole lot of them would revolt." She stepped forward as she spoke.

Thana's heart dropped as ice spread through her veins. She winced, trying to meet Earnhilt's eyes but still not sure if any of her words got through. "Execute? But it's not her fault."

"Civil war," Earnhilt said, rubbing her chin. "We'd be back where we were when I first took the throne. We can't have that, not with Yanchasa." She took hold of Thana's cassock. "You are not going to argue with me on this. Farraday needs an Umbriel on the throne."

"I know." Thana went up on tiptoe to avoid being dragged off her feet. Her collar tightened around her neck, and she thought again of how terrifying it would be to have Earnhilt as an enemy. It was bad enough being her ally. "But things don't have to go that way. The lady can be taught."

Earnhilt dropped her and stared back at the smoky hall. "We'll have to kill her without his knowledge. I like a fair fight, but there comes a time…" She looked at Thana again, eyes wide as if seeing her for the first time. "You'll have to set it up. You and Gunnar and the Order of Vestra."

Thana's stomach dropped. The talk of execution hadn't quite penetrated her mind. The queen had only been musing, surely. But this, an order? "I…Your Majesty…"

"Who is this noble daughter?"

Thana coughed, both from the smoke hanging in the air and from the dread choking her. Earnhilt's blue gaze held her like daggers of ice. She thought of the Fiendish Aspect that all Umbriels contained and wondered if part of it could come leaking out at times like these, paralyzing people.

"Mother!"

Earnhilt turned, taking her power with her and letting Thana breathe. Gunnar came running down the hall, one hand on the hilt of his sword. "Is it an attack?"

"A fire." Earnhilt waved toward the destruction. "Out now. What news from town?"

"More incidents, pyradistés run amok. More witnesses this time."

"Multiple pyradistés, not just one?" Earnhilt's gaze flicked to Thana again.

As Gunnar confirmed that, Thana sighed in gratitude. Sylph couldn't set off pyramids across the city, though Earnhilt might add those disasters as fuel for Sylph's pyre.

"We might have to lock them all up," Earnhilt said, rubbing her chin. "At least until we find out what's going on."

The offhand way she spoke of mass imprisonment chilled Thana again, the ache spreading to her core. She covered her face, hoping to seem as if she was as alarmed by the news of rogue pyradistés as everyone else, but anger burned in her now, thawing her muscles. Her fellow pyradistés did not deserve to be shut in cages like animals or killed in secret halls and alleys.

It didn't matter how fearsome Earnhilt was. Thana couldn't stand for this.

When someone down the hall hailed the queen, Thana trailed behind her and Gunnar. He'd been Thana's friend since they were children, had seemed to care about their difference in status far less than other people. He'd treated her like an equal.

More or less.

She tugged on his sleeve, keeping him back. "The queen wants to lock people up before they've committed a crime?"

He frowned hard. "After an explosion in the royal quarters and a fire in the palace? Not to mention the other crimes throughout Marienne and Farraday? We have to stop this somehow."

"How many of these crimes are confirmed?"

"You were here for the fire and the explosion. And what about your noble in the garden?"

Thana gritted her teeth, forcing herself not to yell. "Your mother wants to execute *my* noble in the garden without even speaking to her first."

He looked away, but he didn't argue. She'd never felt a greater rift between them, never felt so far below his boots.

"You're not going to say anything?"

"I...give me time, Thana."

Time for Earnhilt to kill Sylph? She couldn't allow it, nor could she stand by while people were imprisoned. She refused to work with someone who'd take that action, no matter that the someone was her best friend's mother.

And the queen.

Thana didn't want to be the Umbriels' enemy, but greater than that, she didn't want to see all pyradistés in cages.

And she couldn't let Sylph die.

"We'll figure it out, Thana," Gunnar said. He squeezed her shoulder, but at the moment, it seemed less like reassurance and more like a threat. "We need to speak with the rest of the Order and get on top of this before anyone else gets hurt." He turned back to Earnhilt.

Anyone besides the pyradistés. Or Sylph. No, she was a pyradisté now, whether she liked it or not, but more than that, she was someone who needed help and didn't currently have the means to help herself. She was beset on all sides.

All but Thana's.

Thana stepped back slowly, and while everyone's eyes were turned on the queen and the smoke became a shroud between them, Thana turned and strode back down the hall, heading for Sylph's apartment.

CHAPTER SEVEN

When Sylph spotted Thana down the hall, relief washed over her. She hadn't really expected her father to oust Thana right away, but the sight of her walking free made Sylph's heart go from a gallop to a trot.

Until she came close enough to see the anger on Thana's face.

Something else must have happened. Thana was still disheveled, but her frown and the pinched look between her brows spoke of undertakings beyond her earlier agitation.

"What's happened?" Sylph asked quietly.

"You were supposed to wait for me in your apartment."

After everything, she was angry about *that*? "Forgive me for trying to come to your rescue."

"My..." Thana blinked and glanced around as if unsure of her surroundings on top of everything else. "Listen, I've been to see the queen."

"And I've seen my father. I have news."

"So do I!"

Sylph crossed her arms and said, "You must take care," just as Thana put her hands on her hips and said, "You need to leave."

They both took a step back and asked, "What?"

Sylph held up a hand, too confused for amusement. "My father blames you for the fire. If not for the actual starting of it, then for not controlling your fellow pyradistés. He's going to the queen to get you removed." Her mind repeated Thana's words, then, and she shook her head. "Why do I need to leave?"

Thana's brow darkened, and she opened and shut her mouth several times before closing her eyes and muttering, "Typical." After a deep breath, she met Sylph's gaze again. "The queen will no doubt be looking for him, too. She knows a noblewoman was behind the fire, and once they figure out it's you...well, you need to be gone first. Either with your father or alone."

Alone, such a huge word. Sylph's mind raced, fear and confusion spiraling inside her. "Why would I leave, even if she knows?" She swallowed hard. She needn't go anywhere a moment before her father ordered it. If the queen commanded Sylph to leave court, her father might keep her close out of spite, pyradisté powers or no. The nobles and the monarch had been at peace for years, but the civil war hadn't been so long ago that the nobles had forgotten it was an option. "If the queen commanded us to leave, it would be a huge insult, one my father would fight against."

Thana rolled her eyes. "That's exactly the point." She cast a glance around, then pulled Sylph to the side of the hall, her hands as warm as if she still stood in the fire. "The queen won't fight you, but she might...well, if she thinks it would help the kingdom, she might..." She nodded vaguely at Sylph.

"Might?" The queen couldn't simply strip Sylph or her father of their titles. They would have to commit a crime against the crown for that. Being a noble pyradisté was practically unheard of, but it wasn't illegal. Then what could the queen do? By Thana's worried face, it was serious. "You can't mean she'd...harm me?" she asked breathlessly, hardly daring to believe it. "My father would raise an army."

"I got the sense that it would appear to be an accident, one you wouldn't walk away from."

Sylph's stomach dropped to her shoes. She'd heard tales of Queen Earnhilt leading her troops in battle, of taking more than a few heads, but to cut someone down in cold blood? Unthinkable.

Or was it? Could she really say her father wouldn't do the same if it got him what he wanted? "He...I..." She didn't know what to say. "He won't just leave without an explanation."

"Then you'll have to go alone," Thana said.

There was that word again. Sylph barked a laugh, a bray of fear, before covering her mouth. "I couldn't possibly. The very idea is ludicrous."

Thana rolled her eyes. "Oh yes. One cannot possibly go without one's maid and chef and…horse trainer."

Anger spread hotly through Sylph's chest. "I shouldn't have expected a member of the peasantry to understand." They were words out of her father's mouth, but she couldn't say anything else to the snide look on Thana's face.

After another deep breath, Thana held up her hands. "All right. I shot at you. You returned fire. Now we're even, and nothing more will be solved by standing here sniping at each other. Your life is in danger."

"My father will protect me. He may not love me, but he will not allow the queen to take anything from him." Her anger washed away upon a wave of hurt. She'd never said some of those words before.

Thana's eyes went wide, and her burning touch engulfed Sylph's hand once more. "I'm sorry, really, but I don't think you want the nobles and the monarch to start fighting again any more than I do. If you aren't…done away with, it'll be something else." She couldn't seem to bring herself to say killed or murdered. "The queen is already talking about imprisoning all the pyradistés."

Touched, Sylph squeezed her hand. "Then you should flee, too. It seems neither of us has a very secure future." And she was becoming numb. Perhaps a person could only be so afraid before other emotions had nowhere to go. When Thana didn't respond, Sylph started back toward her apartment. "I'll leave my father a note, I suppose, to slow down the search. I'll tell him I'm too afraid of rogue pyradistés to stay in Marienne, and I'm going home."

Thana frowned as she kept pace. "Will he believe that?"

She shrugged. Fear still raged inside her, but it felt good to be moving, to be doing something other than hiding in her apartment and waiting for her father to either disown her or use her as a rallying point for rebellion.

Or waiting for the queen to kill her.

She tried to tell herself that a little jaunt in the country was all she needed. And the queen might find out her identity, but perhaps her father wouldn't. Then by the time she returned, she'd know how to repress her powers, and the current troubles would have blown over.

If only she could make herself believe that, all would be well.

❖

Thana tried to fight her impatience as Sylph packed. Every instinct shouted that Sylph needed to be removed from danger as fast as possible, but she wouldn't be dissuaded from taking everything in her apartment or writing her father a letter that probably wouldn't help.

Sylph went behind a changing screen and came out in a dusky pink riding dress with a tight-fitting bodice and a slit up the front that revealed tight trousers when she moved. The color complemented her tanned skin and blond hair so well, Thana had to look away to keep her jaw from dropping.

When Sylph swung a hooded cloak over her shoulders, Thana moved toward the door, thinking they were ready to leave, but Sylph merely gathered a few more things from her vanity table.

Thana ground her teeth. Maybe she could coax Queen Earnhilt in this direction. That might instill a bit of urgency.

"Instead of crossing your arms and tapping your foot, you could help," Sylph said as she packed some jewelry.

"Don't you have a trustworthy maid for this?"

Sylph didn't reply, so Thana sighed and stuffed some clothing in a bag, not bothering to fold it. Maybe wearing wrinkled shirts and the like would persuade Sylph to travel lighter.

Thana supposed she should be glad that she was busy saving someone. She didn't seem to be able to help all the innocent pyradistés who were as much victims of this rogue magic as everyone else. Locking them up likely wouldn't help anyone, but Thana doubted the queen would listen.

Gunnar might not listen, either, and that burned her still. He might not even argue when it was her turn to be imprisoned.

A soft sound came from the doorway. Thana glanced up, wadded garment in hand, to find a young woman in a plain dress with a shocked look upon her face.

"My lady," she said, gaze flicking between Thana and Sylph. "What's going on?" Red bloomed in her cheeks before she stepped into the room, crossing to where Sylph stood. "I beg your pardon, my lady. I meant, is there something I can assist you with?"

At last, a maid. Thana tossed the garment in with the others and stood back, happy someone else was here to pack. After a few quick words, the maid would probably be ready to go, too, and Sylph wouldn't have to worry about traveling alone.

But Sylph's eyes were wide, her complexion a few degrees paler, and she'd frozen, jewelry case in hand. She and the maid stared at one another for a moment.

"My friend is helping me sort through some clothing...for charity," Sylph said, her voice rough and wooden.

The maid stiffened, hands clenching as if she might strike, though her expression seemed fearful. "Can I assist—"

"No, thank you."

Thana frowned and moved to the door, looking out but seeing no one. What were they both so afraid of?

"Shall I..." The maid glanced at the bags. "Shall I inform the duke?"

Sylph frowned hard. "No." The word practically had ice dripping off it.

The maid took a step back. "I shall," she whispered.

"No!"

With a gasp, the maid dashed for the door, pulling up short before she hit Thana.

"Stop her," Sylph said.

Something about the panic in her voice made Thana obey. She stuck her arms out to the sides and lamented her lack of a mind pyramid. Then she could have hypnotized her instead of moving from side to side to block her.

All at once, the maid gasped in pain and collapsed. Sylph stood behind her, holding a candlestick as if ready to strike again.

"What in the spirits' names?" Thana said as she fell to her knees beside the maid. She let out a breath in relief as the woman's chest continued to rise and fall.

"She's a spy for my father." Sylph lifted a bag and her jewelry case and nodded toward the bags on the bed. "Bring those, too."

Thana grabbed two more bags and stumbled after her. She tried not to think of the downed maid, of why a father might set spies upon his daughter; it must be something else from the secret lives of nobles. When the queen planned secret killings, anything was possible. "What will your father think of your note now that it comes with an unconscious maid?"

"I don't know," Sylph said over her shoulder. "He'll figure out that someone helped me. If he finds out about my...power...he'll know that it's you."

Thana glanced at her as she took the lead, wondering if that was some kind of threat, but Sylph hadn't lost her pale, panicked look. "I'll just...have to lie low," Thana said. If she could have given herself a skeptical look, she would have. There was no more hiding now. Gunnar might try to help her, but the queen might sooner be rid of her. After all, once she'd considered killing one person for the sake of the peace, what was one more?

At the stables, Sylph's breathing had quickened nearly to the point of panting. Thana ordered a groom to saddle one horse. Sylph looked at her with such a stricken look, it broke her heart.

"Please," Sylph whispered. "Please come with me."

Thana had never heard such a heartfelt plea. "I..." She couldn't just leave her life behind no matter how shitty it currently seemed. She tried to say that aloud, but her voice wouldn't work. She told herself to think of how often Sylph had pissed her off, but the haughty noble who'd made her crazy seemed miles from this frightened creature.

Thana hadn't turned her back on Sylph yet. Why start now?

She sighed long and loud. She would have liked to pack a bag of her own but supposed Sylph had enough clothing for both of them. She ordered another horse.

Sylph's eyes still swam with tears, but her hopeful look spoke of gratitude rather than sorrow. Thana had the strongest urge to kiss her, but she pushed it down just as she'd pushed down all her feelings of passion.

"Follow me," Thana said when the bags were secured to the saddles, and they were finally ready to set out.

Sylph nodded without argument, managing only a soft, "Where are we going?"

"Not far." She didn't want to say it aloud even though no one rode near. It seemed prudent not to mention pyradistés unless she had to, especially as she was headed toward the most powerful one she knew, the head of the Pyradisté Academy.

Thana might be able to get away without clothing, but if she was going to defend them both, she'd need pyramids.

❖

All her life, Sylph had felt as if the wind was simply blowing her along. Each day had been incredibly ordered. No decision had been hers. It led to a different kind of numbness than the one that came from too much feeling. Most of the time, she'd felt nothing at all.

Now she seemed mired in decisions. She'd left her life, her father. She'd hit her maid over the head, for spirits' sake. She was completely adrift. No schedule, no spies.

No father.

How in all the spirits' names could she exist without her father?

"Are you all right?" Thana asked.

"I've never been…" Sylph didn't even know how to say it. That terrible word, alone. But she wasn't alone. She had Thana, the one person who'd ever cared about her enough to risk life and liberty. And Sylph didn't know what to say, was afraid to speak in case more of her father's words came out, and she cut this delicate cord between them.

"It's all right," Thana said, and there was that compassion in her eyes again. It simply appeared as if summoned. How could she just… care?

Sylph stared at her saddle. How could she feel so drawn to Thana and still so afraid? It couldn't last, couldn't be real. Thana wanted to keep the palace safe from Sylph's power. True enough, but in her heart, Sylph knew that wasn't the only reason Thana was helping her.

Thana didn't want her to get hurt.

Should she apologize again? For not having the right words?

"Where are we going?" she said instead, grasping for any other topic. "Shouldn't we be…hiding or something?"

"The Pyradisté Academy," Thana said softly. "I need pyramids and information. As for hiding, we have a little time. I have no doubt that people will begin looking for us shortly, but Marienne is a huge city, and they won't know where to start even after they discover we left together."

Sylph supposed that made sense. And her father certainly wouldn't expect her to go to the Pyradisté Academy. An entire building full of pyradistés? The mad peasants currently running wild? Her father would equate it with a den of thieves and murderers. Sylph shut her eyes to banish such thoughts. She might be out of her father's reach at the moment, but how long would it take to banish him from her mind?

And what would she be when she did?

"It's not much," Thana said. A quick glance revealed that her defensive look was back. "Just a regular building. Before all the troubles, before the civil war, they had a grand old building, but that got taken over by a bank. I've always envisioned a grander structure one day, like a giant pyramid people can see across the city, something to rival the palace itself."

"The troubles before the civil war," Sylph said quietly. Thana had mentioned the war before, when the nobles had clashed with the monarch, the very war Queen Earnhilt had put a stop to in her younger days. "Some nobles refer to the civil war as the Troubles." Not her father. He rarely spoke of it at all. The nobility tended toward forgetting their past mistakes when they could.

Thana stared, and Sylph realized her court mask had no doubt been absent for some time. Did she even need it anymore? She shook her head. Of course she did. When things went back to normal, she'd need everything she'd ever learned.

Sylph tried to keep up a blank look as Thana pointed out various structures around the city. She barely listened, looking at the people instead. She'd only ever ridden among the peasantry on her own estate, when the residents lined the road as she and her father rode through town. Whenever they came to Marienne, they rode down the main street to the palace, but a wall of guards had always ridden between her and the people.

Now, hardly anybody paid her or Thana any mind. They went about their business, walking, talking, calling out to one another. Their faces and bodies were so alive. She read happiness and anger and sadness from a distance, as if they didn't care if their fellows knew what they were feeling.

"Wonderous," she whispered. Her father would have sneered, but these people must have so many words for what they were thinking, how they were feeling. They would've had the right words for Thana, but Sylph didn't even know if such words existed within her.

"Hello, Thana, dear. How are you?" someone called from across the street. A short young woman with an enormous basket was hurrying in the opposite direction.

"All right, Miss Chambers. You?" Thana said.

"Can't complain. Take care." And then she was gone. No bows, no courtly maneuvering. Just hello and then gone. Sylph felt like laughing but feared looking like a lunatic.

Others greeted Thana, too. Some seemed a bit wary of her, no doubt a sign of the recent pyradisté troubles. Thana frowned at that, and the pinched look between her brows said she was hurt.

Sylph couldn't stand to see it and grabbed for the first words that came to her. "Any anti-pyradisté sentiment is no doubt due to our proximity to this academy of yours. Most people seem quite friendly, and there is comfort to be had in that." Spirits, she sounded like a formal letter. She tried a smile, hoping her feelings came through. "That is the norm, correct?"

Thana gave her a crooked smile. "Are you asking if people usually like me?" She shrugged. "I don't have many close friends." She looked away. "Still, people out here are a lot nicer than the nobles in the palace."

"Yes." Sylph didn't even have it in her to be arch. Thana spoke the truth. "Were people friendlier toward the pyradistés when they had their grand building?"

Now Thana frowned at her. "During the rebellion? I don't think any non-pyradistés felt very charitable toward them."

Sylph thought through her lessons but couldn't recall a rebellion concerning the pyradistés.

"You have no idea what I'm talking about, do you?" Thana asked. When Sylph stared, Thana sighed hugely. "During the reign of Queen Earnhilt's grandfather, a group of pyradistés banned together to try to take the kingdom."

Sylph knew her surprise had to be showing, but they were out in the world now, and she doubted anyone cared. Still, she reined it in a little. "They what?"

"Yeah," Thana said slowly. "I'm not surprised you don't know. The nobility has probably written it off as embarrassing."

"I had the same thought."

Now Thana gave her a slightly condescending smile. "When Farraday was formed, the king's sister and her pyradisté husband defeated a Fiend using pyramid magic. These rebel pyradistés I mentioned took that as the reason why pyradistés should rule the kingdom. When they were defeated, the monarch declared magic illegal. Pyradistés were either locked up, executed, or banished."

Sylph frowned, both at the thought of rebellion and that a past monarch's sister had married a peasant. Her father would have said those were dark days indeed. Sylph tried not to mirror his feelings, but it felt like trying to pull something out of herself. "How were they defeated?"

"We're only as powerful as the number of pyramids we have. The monarch cut off the routes to where the crystal is mined, and when the pyradistés ran out, that was it."

Sylph nodded. Had the king let the pyradistés run amok amongst the populace until they ran out of pyramids, knowing they couldn't get more? Or had he fought them tooth and nail beforehand, losing troops, losing nobles, perhaps? If a great many had died, they would have declared that period in history a great embarrassment indeed.

"We lost a lot of knowledge," Thana said, her gaze far away. "And it wasn't until years later that pyradistés were allowed to practice again. It's gotten to the point where we aren't completely under suspicion." She frowned hard. "Or it had until now."

Sylph put a hand on her arm, surprising herself, but she had to do something, some show of support. When Thana smiled at her, she thought she might not need so many words after all.

CHAPTER EIGHT

Thana was happy that Sylph seemed thoughtful about the history of pyradistés. Or maybe her look of intensity was due to the fact that she was out of the palace with only Thana for company. Or it could have been the fire or the threat of death.

Or any of a thousand things.

At least she hadn't responded with scoffs and angry denials. If she had, Thana might have abandoned her to continue this journey alone. And even that outcome would have been better than the mistrust she'd seen in the eyes of the people who lived and worked near a place she'd spent years getting to know.

Oh, there had been smiles. And Miss Chambers, who Thana had exchanged many flirtations with, had called a cheery hello. But others who should have known better scowled at her or hurried past. The same was probably happening to pyradistés all over the city. The closer they came to the academy, the lonelier the streets became.

So many emotions swirled through her, it was hard to process them all. To her horror, she wanted to weep with all the sadness and frustration and anger. Maybe she could do so while throwing things. But she took a deep breath, not wanting to fall apart in the open and give the passersby any more reason to think pyradistés unstable.

And she cringed at the thought of Sylph trying to comfort her. They'd both be so embarrassed and out of their element, they might combust.

The Pyradisté Academy looked incredibly nondescript from the outside. It could have been any old brick apartment building, its windows unadorned, its door simple with no markers or banners proclaiming what was inside. Thana had thought it a sad building at first, but now she was happy to see it remained depressingly normal. If everyone in Marienne decided to hunt down pyradistés, many wouldn't even know where to find them.

Unless the people who'd seemed scared of her in the street decided to shout her whereabouts across the city.

And now she was back to angry again. Wonderful.

Thana dismounted to hitch her horse near the side of the building. She tied the reins and turned to Sylph, who held her own reins and stared at the hitching rail as if waiting for it to come to life and offer assistance. Thana resisted the urge to roll her eyes or laugh, even as her anger wanted her to lash out and relieve some tension.

Maybe she was finally learning diplomacy.

"Like this," she said, moving aside so Sylph could see her loose, then retie the reins. "See?"

Sylph blinked and held the reins forward as if urging Thana to do it for her. Thana's frustration must have registered because Sylph frowned slightly, and a bit of color came to her cheeks. "I don't want to...tie it incorrectly." She ducked her head, then raised her chin in the air unnecessarily high, her face a darker shade.

"Spirits give me strength," Thana muttered. "Here, watch." She waited until Sylph stood beside her. "Copy me." Sylph finally tied the reins under her direction. Thana didn't want to be a teacher, but she would not be a servant. She hoped Sylph was dreading the day when Thana finally decided to be neither and went her own way.

"I do know quite a lot about horses, you know," Sylph said, not making eye contact. "I've just never had to use a..." She nodded toward the rail.

Oh yes, she probably knew all about breeding and hunting or racing or whatnot. But how to tie a strip of leather to a piece of wood was beyond her. Thana prayed to the spirits for patience. She led the way around the front again and through the simple doors which were well-oiled into boringness, so they matched the rest of the building. Inside, she stopped and breathed deep.

A huge pyramid rested in an open area just past the foyer, separating the staircase from the rooms and halls leading in different directions. It was an ancient artifact, a masterwork of facets that caught the light from the windows in the foyer and sent it shining in all directions, lighting the room as if it sat outside at midday.

Sylph gasped, and Thana smiled proudly before she frowned. She rounded so quickly, Sylph took a slight step back. "Please do not reach for that pyramid with your power. In fact, don't reach for any pyramid. Don't even think of them."

Sylph shook her head hurriedly. "I won't. I promise."

Thana nodded, grateful they were both terrified by the prospect of Sylph retuning a pyramid that was taller than they were. With her odd ability to move stone, she could probably make all the buildings in Marienne dance.

"This way." Thana led the way up the staircase. She couldn't wander around looking for unattended pyramids to take, so Headmaster Cyrus would have to help. And he'd want to know why Thana was leaving Marienne. She could warn him that Queen Earnhilt was considering imprisoning pyradistés. More of them could flee. That sounded like the right thing to do, but Thana had pledged her loyalty to the crown above all else—she was part of an order designed specifically to protect the Umbriels, after all—and to inform others of their plans would be treason.

If she'd stayed, Gunnar and Earnhilt might even have been able to convince her that their plan was the right one. No, not when she thought of the offhand way Earnhilt had spoken of killing Sylph, who hadn't asked for her power. There was right and wrong, and treason didn't matter.

Then why did her stomach churn so?

"The headmaster's office is this way," she said softly as they came to the second landing and turned down a hallway.

"I see." It was a noncommittal, barely listening sort of answer, but it was far better than if she had pushed ahead and shouted demands. Thana's heart was beating so quickly that if Sylph had put a foot wrong, Thana might have yelled the place down.

The little card pinned to the headmaster's door brought Thana's heart into her throat. She knew what it would say before she reached it, but she hurried forward anyway to stare at the note stating that Cyrus was currently in class and would return in an hour.

But was the hour up or just starting or somewhere in the middle? There was no water clock in the hall, and no one stood nearby to ask. Thana tried the door and found it open, but of course it would be. It only led into Cyrus's sitting room with its handful of chairs and low table. When Thana tried the door to the actual office, she found it locked.

Her limbs felt heavy as she rested her forehead against the door. She could feel time getting away from her. Sylph's father would find the maid and be looking for Sylph. Gunnar and Earnhilt would notice Thana's absence. They'd look through the palace first. Sooner or later, they'd compare notes. They would shout at one another and begin to ask questions, and it might take time, but they would track Thana here. She and Sylph had made no effort to hide.

"Are you all right?" Sylph asked softly.

Thana turned. Sylph had shut the door to the hall but rested a hand on the knob as if she didn't know whether to flee or try to hold the door against intruders. At the moment, Thana didn't know which to do, either. "The headmaster is teaching."

A ghost of a smile flitted across Sylph's face. "Hence the card."

Thana chuckled. "I don't want…we can't wait."

"I know."

Thana's mind raced even as her stomach sank. What in the spirits' names was she even doing? She should have stayed in the palace, let Sylph make her own decisions. The queen had been in a position of power much longer than Thana. She knew what she was doing, knew the best course to take in any situation. She could prevent civil war and keep the peace just as the monster inside her—inside all Umbriels—kept the great Fiend under the palace in its prison.

Sylph was staring, and Thana thought she saw a slight tremble in those full lips. Her imagination, perhaps, or maybe it was fear. It wasn't just Sylph's inheritance at stake. Thana pictured her lips bloodless, her sparkling eyes lifeless, and her murder blamed on some other poor soul so the duke would have a target for his anger. Then that poor soul would be killed by the duke, but Thana couldn't imagine that one, couldn't see past Sylph's life being snuffed out.

It was enough to make her ache.

She turned and regarded the office door again. She needed pyramids in order to defend them both. "I don't suppose you know how to pick a lock?"

"That would be lucky, but no."

Thana nodded. "Right." Her mind hit on a solution, and before she could rethink it, she dragged a chair closer to the door.

Surprisingly, Sylph moved to help. "What are you going to do?"

"Break my foot, most likely." She positioned the heavy chair close enough that she could lean on its back and raise her leg high enough to kick the door right next to the lock. She took a deep breath, glad of the chair. She imagined falling flat on her back if she tried this any other way, and she and Sylph didn't need another reason to be embarrassed around each other.

Thana kicked as hard as she could. The contact made an impressive noise but didn't give, and pain vibrated up Thana's leg. She groaned and limped for a few steps, trying to hurry the pain away, never mind the keen disappointment.

"Are you all right?" Sylph asked, face creased in concern.

"Mm-hmm," Thana said, clenching her teeth. "Nothing broken."

"Let me try." She mimicked Thana's position and kicked. The door flew open with a splintery crack. She beamed so widely it was hard to hate her. "All in the heel, I think."

No, Thana could still hate her a little. She hurried into the office, fighting not to limp. Someone might have heard that, narrowing their window of time even more. Luckily, Headmaster Cyrus kept quite a few pyramids in his office. He liked to trot them out to show new students, and his hobby was research. He would have loved the chance to teach Sylph, but there was no time to explain.

Thana borrowed a satchel from the coatrack and put the pyramids carefully inside, separating them by type into the pockets, never so glad that everyone who taught at the academy practiced meticulous labeling and categorizing of pyramids as rigorously as they taught it.

When she'd filled the satchel, Thana said, "Let's go," and led the way into the sitting room before remembering the other task she'd been considering: Warning Cyrus about the queen's plans. She turned back just as Sylph pulled the office door as shut as it would now go.

The outer door to the hall flew open.

Thana whirled, heart flying into her mouth so fast, she couldn't help making a strangled sound. A man in a black cassock with the white piping of a teacher stared at her curiously before smiling, revealing a row of white teeth amid a dark beard.

He pointed past her. "Is he back yet?"

Thana couldn't think of who he meant, couldn't even recall who she was at that moment. Sylph stepped past, a slight smile in place. "We were just knocking, but the headmaster hasn't returned, it seems."

"Oh." He sagged a bit, then shrugged, dark eyes twinkling. "He'll hear soon. With all the commotion, every student will no doubt be poking their head out." He smiled wider, someone with news and desperate to be the first to share it with the higher-ups.

"Huh?" Thana managed, her body slowly returning to normal now that she knew they weren't caught, though he'd spot the damaged door if he looked closely. She cleared her throat. If this teacher had something to share, maybe he'd settle for telling them, and they could slip away. "C…commotion?"

He brightened even more. "Come see!" He turned and led the way into the hall.

Sylph muttered, "He's too trusting," and followed. Thana stumbled on her heels, wanting to argue that this wasn't the palace, that they were all friends here, but in the current climate, maybe Sylph was right.

"It's a new shipment of the crystal, just a small one," the teacher said as he led the way. He winked and laid a finger against his nose. "But mum's still the word and all that."

Who exactly where they keeping mum from? But Thana couldn't ask that. Still, her curiosity won out over her awkwardness. "Shipment from, um, the same place as before?"

"Yes, the mountains to the northeast. A safer source than Allusia, as they say. I hope they have enough for everyone to try one now."

Thana frowned and fought down a million questions. A new source of crystal? Why hadn't she heard about this? The headmaster wasn't supposed to be scouting sources of crystal on his own. He should have at least told the monarch's spirits-cursed pyradisté.

People were starting to filter into the halls and staircase, but the teacher pushed through. "They say they'll have a bigger shipment soon, once they get the route sorted out."

Thana's face was starting to ache from frowning. She hadn't heard of any of this, and if Earnhilt or Gunnar had, they would have mentioned it. What in the spirits' names was going on? This teacher obviously hadn't taken a good look at her, or he would have noticed the purple piping on her cassock, the sign of her position. Even if he had, no doubt he'd assume she knew all this. Maybe he was just happy someone was listening to him.

But Headmaster Cyrus had deliberately left her in the dark. That was the only conclusion she could reach. This teacher wasn't the only one who'd been too trusting.

The sounds of banging and swearing filtered through the large room downstairs. Thana paused by the huge pyramid and looked down the wide hall that led toward the back doors. She craned her neck to see over the crowd. Cyrus would no doubt appear soon, and Thana could ask all her questions, time be cursed.

But Sylph grabbed her arm. She'd gone pale, her lips mashed together until they were as bloodless as in Thana's vision of her corpse. "Something's wrong."

Thana's heart rate picked up again. "What is it?"

Sylph groaned, and light blazed from the huge pyramid behind them. A kaleidoscope of color shone through the halls, and people cried out in surprise and wonder. Sylph's power. Her grip tightened. "Thana, I don't know if I can hold on," she said, eyes unblinking. Sweat broke out on her forehead as if someone had splashed her.

Thana's fear had her moving almost before she realized it. She yanked Sylph toward the doors. "Move!" she shouted to the throng. She shoved people aside and nearly dragged Sylph toward the door. Plaster rained from the ceiling as the building began to shake. A few people fell on the staircase. More began to scream. Thana shook Sylph's arm. "No! Do not retune that pyramid, Sylph. Fight it." She clenched a fist, tempted to strike her, but that might make her lose control completely. "You have to fight."

"Trying."

But there had to be so many pyramids here and now this new crystal. The bricks near the door shuddered, twisting slightly. Thana charged through the door. "Focus on me. You can do it. Just breathe." She met Sylph's eyes until their breathing matched. "That's it. You can do it. If it's too much, focus on the big light pyramid. Just make it shine. That's all. Nothing else. Just light."

"Just light," Sylph whispered. A few other people ran out around them, crying out to each other or just calling in fear as the rumble in the ground slowed. "It's just light."

Thana tried to reach for the light pyramid, too, but didn't know how when she couldn't touch it. When her mind fell into the facets of a pyramid that now stood behind a closed door, she nearly stumbled in surprise. She'd used this one before, of course, every pyradisté had, and it surrounded her now so she could barely see where to put her feet. "Feel my mind in with yours?"

"Yes," Sylph whispered, and there she was, her presence in the pyramid like another shining light, but one that sought to stretch forth, no doubt to touch all the pyramids and reshape them, to bring in the raw power of the new crystal, to make the city fall. "It hurts."

"I'm sure." Trying to touch so many pyramids and raw crystal, it had to feel like she was being torn apart. "Stay with me. Follow me." In the street, she guided Sylph toward the horses as she sent her power through the myriad facets of the light pyramid.

Sylph's bright light followed her mind just as their bodies stayed together in the street. Thana had used pyramids with others before but not as if she was playing some odd game of tag. The ground ceased to rumble, but Thana kept her concentration. "Stay with me."

"I am. I'm scared." Her voice was high, almost childlike.

Thana squeezed her arm. "It's all right. I have you." But they couldn't stay like this. They had to get away from the academy, and Thana didn't know how long she could keep her focus. Sylph's reach was undoubtedly greater than hers. Would she continue to hold on to the pyramid after they left?

When they reached the horses, Thana dug in her borrowed satchel, fumbling over the pyramids as her mind tried to be in two places at once. Her control on the large pyramid slipped, but just as Sylph gasped, Thana pulled a light pyramid and fell into it. "Here, Sylph, follow me here."

Her gaze snapped to the small pyramid in Thana's hand, and Thana felt her focus shift as if it was a tangible thing. By the spirits, she was strong. Thana's jealousy was nearly swamped in awe and fear and pity. Her pyramid blazed, shifting through radiant colors as if it was all the world's jewels combined. It was beautiful, but more than that, Thana could now function. She helped Sylph mount her horse, then climbed on her own. She kept up a soothing litany of nonsense even as her mind wanted to panic and run. With both horses under her control, it was slow going until they were a few streets away, and Thana didn't feel Sylph's power reaching for something else to control.

"It's okay." Thana had hidden the light pyramid in her cassock, but she glimpsed the light peeping out everywhere, as if she'd swallowed a star. "You can let go. Come with me. Come out." She let her mind slip slowly from the pyramid, and Sylph followed like a moth, but this one running from the flame.

They released it at the same time, and Sylph sagged in the saddle, sighing, her eyes slipping closed. When she opened them, tears filled her lashes and spilled down her face.

"It's all right," Thana said, amazed she could still feel anything after all the turns her emotions had taken, but she managed relief. "Everything's fine now."

Sylph breathed a laugh that had no humor. She wiped at her cheeks hurriedly. "Thank you."

"Of course." Thana looked away, awkward.

Sylph took back her reins, and her touch lingered on Thana's hand. "No, please. You have to hear me…to know that I mean it. You stopped me from hurting anyone, and you didn't hurt me to do it. Thank you."

When Thana looked at her again, she had a grateful smile, and Thana wanted to be embarrassed, wanted to say that it was all right or that it was nothing really or that anyone would have done the same, but none of those responses seemed to fit. If they'd been standing, she would have embraced Sylph, and that surprised her nearly as much as Sylph's entreaty. "I do hear you. And you're welcome. Truly." She led the way again. Maybe her pride would keep the fear and anger at bay for a while.

❖

They rode from the city and entered the forest surrounding Marienne, and the trees offered a cool stillness that seemed perfect for calming runaway emotions. Sylph pressed a hand to her fluttering stomach. All the myriad feelings she'd experienced since she'd met Thana paled when compared to now. She was grateful and tried to focus on that, but underneath was a mélange of terror and confusion that made her ache for the safety of home. After all that had happened, she craved a life laid out for her in neat little rows. Her excitement at the prospect of freedom had been nothing but a moment of foolishness. Her freedom meant danger for others. It was only dumb luck that she hadn't yet killed anyone.

Maybe the queen was right. Maybe the pyradistés should be confined until this magical mess could be cleared. Maybe it was better if some were dead.

"Pyradistés are as dangerous as everyone says." She didn't know she'd meant to say it aloud until it happened, but when Thana turned thunderous eyes upon her, she couldn't take it back. She even added, "The queen was right."

"How can you even think such a thing?" Thana said, her voice low and gravelly, as if emotion choked her.

Tremors started in Sylph's core, passing all through her. She felt tears gathering again, but she dug her nails into one hand and pointed at Marienne with the other. "How many people could I have killed, including both of us? And this new crystal the teacher spoke of? I saw your face. You didn't know what he was talking about. Do you even understand what any new crystal can do, how it works? Do they? Or are they just playing with danger?" She stiffened in the face of Thana's anger and pulled her horse to a stop. "You're the monarch's pyradisté. They should have consulted you, consulted the queen, before doing anything."

Thana sneered and groaned, rolling her eyes so hard, they seemed to turn her head with them. "Did you know that pyradistés are the only group in Farraday without autonomy? The nobles and chapterhouses and merchant guilds don't have to consult the crown for every decision."

"They can't kill people so easily."

"A blade can kill as easily as a pyramid."

Thana's cheeks grew red, and she was breathing hard, her eyes shining with outrage and conviction. And also fear. Sylph forced herself to calm and bring her court mask to bear, not yet willing to leave everything from her old life behind. "People rarely lose control of a blade and kill without meaning to."

Thana leaned back and sneered. "The only one out of control is you."

Hurt replaced anger, the emotions clashing against one another so harshly, Sylph wondered that she couldn't hear them. Only a flex of will kept her court mask from slipping.

Thana looked away, her frown easing as if she realized that what she'd said wasn't fair or true, but she didn't take back the words.

"There are…" Sylph cleared her throat and started again. "From the rumors, I'm not the only one."

Thana wouldn't meet her eyes. "At least the others had their own pyramids. They didn't go lashing out for any old pyramid lying around."

The hurt spread as if she'd come too near a fire. She remembered the heat of the blaze in the castle, the quaking in the academy. Yes, no one had been as great a menace as her. "You should have let the queen kill me." The words reminded her of petulance, but she only felt truth in them.

"Don't be stupid." Those words weren't said with malice or recrimination. They were soft, apologetic, Thana's feelings as free as air. "I wouldn't be helping you if I thought any of this was your fault. Just like with every rumor, you weren't in control." She sighed. "And I was wrong. You aren't the only one lashing out, or pyramids wouldn't be randomly exploding."

"Quite," Sylph said, taking a little comfort in that. And in the fact that Thana didn't seem angry anymore. She hadn't truly apologized, but maybe that was where she faltered as Sylph faltered with…every emotion.

"And it doesn't happen to you all the time," Thana said almost cheerfully. "I'm sitting here with a satchel of pyramids, and nothing's on fire." After a wince, she smiled, seemingly committed to a facade of happiness.

"Yes." Sylph tried to smile for her sake, but she didn't want to be happy or calm. She wanted to run off in any direction, to ride until the emotions blew away from her.

Leading the way deeper into the woods, Thana said, "Tell me about what happened in the academy, what you felt."

Sylph wanted to say, terrified, but that wasn't what Thana was asking. She made herself think about the incident as if she were an outsider, a mere spectator, untouched by the experience. "As when I first discovered this power and in the garden, I felt pulled, compelled to reach for the magic wherever it lay."

"Hmm. Might have been proximity to this new crystal. But why would that have been near your home or in the garden? I suppose someone could have been carrying the crystal near your home up north, but there's no road near the garden."

"Perhaps then, whoever was carrying the crystal didn't want anyone to see them and sought out a clandestine avenue."

Thana grinned over her shoulder. "If you're thinking out loud with me, does that mean you've given up the notion of turning yourself in? Is that because it's a mystery that needs solving?"

A mystery? Sylph supposed it was. And though they held no particular allure for her, solving this one might mean fewer incidents and lessen the chance of deaths. "I'll help." After the destruction she'd caused, it seemed the least she could do.

And then, perhaps she could leave all pyramid magic behind.

"But are you sure you want my help?" she called when Thana turned back. "I'm a liability."

"No, you're my crystal detector, if the crystal is indeed the problem. And if you're worried about hurting people, you need to learn control, and I can continue to teach you." She turned in profile, and her cheek was pink. "And you don't deserve to be hurt either."

Sylph smiled, her chest warming for a different reason. Strange how different feelings caused similar reactions in her insides, but she could tell the difference. And Thana seemed to be making up for her harsh words, very touching. Sylph was still frightened, but being afraid with someone felt so much better than being afraid and alone. She'd gone through a fear of the dark and all its terrors as a child, and that by herself, after her father instructed her maids not to "coddle" her. Yes, having someone was better.

Again, she tried to say thank you, but Thana deserved more. As they reached a clearer track, she nudged her horse abreast with

Thana's. "I appreciate you." No, that was just another thank you. "It's very good of you." That didn't sound right, either.

Thana chuckled. "Don't mention it."

Sylph fought the urge to frown, recalling her lack of words earlier and how she'd wanted Thana to truly hear those that went unspoken. "I fear you're not listening."

She expected anger again, but Thana smiled softly. "It's all right. I know what you mean, and I know why you seem to be having trouble saying it. You've been at court a long time, and it must be hard to speak to a peasant."

Before Sylph could argue, Thana winked. Sylph smiled back, recognizing teasing even if what she'd said was also the truth. But those weren't the only reasons Sylph couldn't speak. What she felt for Thana was...unprecedented. She recalled how mystified she'd been when her father first told her that she'd eventually marry well. She'd understood falling in love. She'd read about romance and had spied on some servants kissing in the hall. But nothing had seemed to recommend love beyond the simple slaking of lust. And even *then*, she'd had no one. She hadn't even had friends. How was she supposed to find a spouse?

Every flirtation she'd experienced at court had felt false, a mere grab for power and influence. But Thana didn't care about such things. And unlike those at court, she kept secrets for others and helped without asking for anything, and her emotions fluttered all about her for anyone to see. She cared.

She was a friend.

And they'd shared little moments of something more. Thana's occasional heated stares said she felt attracted to Sylph. And in every mood of Thana's, there was something to desire in her.

It grew easier to think of such things the longer she spent in Thana's company. Now she just had to find a way to say them.

CHAPTER NINE

Thana didn't know whether to be pleased or frustrated with Sylph, a state of half-emotion she hadn't become accustomed to. Sylph was undeniably beautiful, and when they argued, Thana wanted to leap on her and lose herself in combustible passion. But then Sylph would turn vulnerable and open, and Thana wanted to cradle and protect her, kiss her gently and tell her everything would be all right.

It was all so stupid.

And impossible. There would be no kissing or leaping or losing herself. Sylph would be offended beyond belief if she tried anything romantic, would probably be offended at the very thought. Sylph might admit her vulnerability, had pleaded some ignorance, but she would never seek comfort from a peasant. She'd hit her maid over the head with no hesitation, and ladies were said to be very attached to their maids.

At least in the stories.

But that maid had also been a spy, so the stories were probably all wrong.

Either way, if Sylph hit her maid so easily, she'd never be kissed by some peasant she hardly knew. Worse still, she might do something extra offensive like tip Thana for the service. What else could Thana expect from someone who couldn't even express her thanks?

Her head hung a little at that thought, but she couldn't argue with it.

She focused on the path ahead, wondering if her theory about Sylph reacting to the crystal was correct. The teacher had mentioned a second shipment. Perhaps if she and Sylph investigated a path near the palace gardens, they'd run into this larger shipment and test her theory. And if they were out in the middle of nowhere when Sylph lost control, the danger to bystanders would be less, even if Sylph brought the outer wall to the garden down.

One worry taken care of, at least. Another was the middle of nowhere part. Where would they stay? Thana knew nothing about sleeping rough, and Sylph probably knew less than that. She might not even know the word camping, no doubt called it peasant sleeping or something. Or maybe she thought only animals slept outdoors.

Thana pulled her horse to a stop and glanced around. The light was dimmer in the forest than in the city, but it had to be getting late. Everything that had happened, from the fire to the incident at the academy, had seemed to go by in a flash, but it had taken all day. They'd be sleeping rough sooner than they thought.

"We need to pick somewhere to bed down for the night." She looked at the dense trees lining the path, wondering how to tell a good place from a bad one.

As expected, Sylph looked at her blankly before staring at the forest. But then she glanced away as if thinking and pointed ahead. "If we are where I think, Countess Carisse Van Umberholme's estate isn't far."

Thana shook her head. "Where? Who?"

Sylph's smile was only slightly condescending, a vast improvement. She drew a circle in the air. "Marienne and its lands to the west are held by the Umbriels," she said. "All the way to the Lavine River, and then stretching slightly north, so that they own the harbor there." She swept her hand to the left and up, then right. "But the lands abutting theirs are owned by the Umberholme family, distant cousins to the Umbriels, who hold this area." She made another wave. "All the way to the Lake of Umber north and then down to the village of Longside. Indeed, if their population gets any bigger or they acquire more land, they'll be a duchy." When Thana continued to look, wondering at this vast wealth of knowledge she knew nothing about, Sylph's smile faltered. "Countess Carisse inherited her title after the death of her husband four years ago, and she merely holds it now until her daughter is of age."

"Sorry," Thana said, shaking her head. "I didn't mean to stare. I just had...no idea that you knew...well done." She felt the heat in her cheeks and wondered when in the spirits' names she'd stop blushing around this woman. "Good." She cleared her throat. "Do you think she'll welcome us?"

Sylph's smile was wider this time.

"Right," Thana said before she could speak. "Because you're the daughter of a duke, and she's just a countess, so she'll be happy to have you."

"Indeed. And though I'm certain my father is on our track, he will probably assume we will go north toward my home rather than stay with a countess who owns a lonely estate in the forest." She took the lead now, blessed with knowledge of geography even if her camping know-how was probably minimal. "And the countess should be home. She does not often come to court because she doesn't want to fend off any suitors hungry to take control of the estate before her daughter can claim it."

Thana frowned, both at the politics and at someone trying to steal from a child. "But even if she married, that person wouldn't have real power, right? Because they're not blood, and they weren't married to the original count?"

Sylph grinned over her shoulder. "That wouldn't stop them from trying. Especially some particularly nasty individual who planned to take the countess's life and have the child be under their influence alone." She tilted her head. "Or if it were a man, and he could persuade the countess to have another child with him, he might later do away with both the countess and her daughter."

Thana knew her mouth was open but couldn't close it. "Queen Earnhilt would never let anyone get away with that."

"It would look like an accident, Thana," Sylph said drily. "The queen would have to prove otherwise."

"That's...sick." Thana shuddered. "How can you talk about murder so calmly? Of anyone, but especially a child? What is wrong with nobles?" She couldn't stop the words but didn't want to start another argument.

Even if every noble deserved to be condemned.

But Sylph laughed loudly, a startling sound. "I've often wondered that. And most of them deserve your censure. In case you were wondering, I've never considered murdering anyone."

"Good to know." She paused before smiling at Sylph's back. "But if you had, you wouldn't tell me, would you?"

Sylph winked over her shoulder, making butterflies tumble in Thana's stomach.

The path wended through the trees so far, Thana feared they'd be caught outside when the sun fell, but thankfully, the path ended at the lawn of the manor before sunset. To her surprise, Sylph paused and dismounted, digging a mirror and comb out of her pack and going to work on her appearance.

Thana scoffed but took the opportunity to dismount and stretch. When she was done and Sylph still wasn't finished, she sighed.

"I can hear you," Sylph said. "And I know what you're thinking, but appearance is a helpful tool when dealing with nobility." She didn't take her eyes off the mirror. "I don't know Countess Carisse personally, but as my father always says, if one needs a favor from another noble, it is best to go with an outstretched hand rather than a bended knee."

Thana frowned and tried to work that one out. "Isn't that the same?"

Sylph gave her another of those condescending smiles that made Thana want to throw dirt at her. "One cannot look too desperate when asking for a favor. The price for said favor will be considerably higher."

"So if you look good when you meet her and not like you've been riding for your life through a forest, she won't think you really need her help that much."

"Exactly."

"Even though we're asking for a place to stay, and there's nothing else around for miles."

Sylph shrugged. "We will not look as if we have no other options."

"Right," Thana said with a snort. "Because looking better will make lodgings magically appear."

Sylph ignored her. Thana waited for her to finish primping. She couldn't really argue about how a person should ask for a favor, even from a friend, because she hadn't done it often. And she didn't have many friends. The most she'd ever needed from Gunnar was reassurance, and he always seemed to know she needed it before she did. She hung her head at the thought of him and hoped they weren't always going to be on separate sides of this conflict.

"Now," Sylph said as she put her mirror away. "The countess will know we need lodgings. What we are hoping to conceal is that we have fled from the palace. If Countess Carisse suspects we are on the run, she might send word to my father in order to curry favor. Or she might hide us, then use this information for future blackmail."

Thana's belly went cold. "What is wrong with nobles?" she said again.

Sylph put a finger to her lips. "Not so loud. Now, come here."

She still hadn't put away the comb. Thana eyed it warily. "Why?"

"As I've been saying this entire time, our ruse will not work if one of us looks as though she's been in flight." She walked around Thana, looking her up and down and making her skin crawl.

Thana fought the urge to hug her elbows. "I'm fine."

Without a word, Sylph took her mirror back out and held it up. Thana's hair was disheveled, and she still had some lingering soot from that morning, marred in some places where sweat had run through. She fought a blush and failed. "Okay, I need a wash."

"And a change. I'm sorry, Thana, but you'll have to hide the fact that you're a pyradisté."

With a sigh, Thana realized she was right. She began to unbutton her cassock, revealing her sleeveless black top and trousers. "Isn't she going to wonder why I'm out without any sort of coat? And why are you sorry?"

"That you have to hide what you are," Sylph said distractedly. "And these won't do." She gestured at Thana's clothes, but before Thana could yell that these were all she had and that she didn't want to impress any snooty countess, Sylph began to dig in her packs. She pulled forth a pair of dark trousers and a green shirt with a bit of poof in the long sleeves. She thrust them at Thana, who grabbed them before they could fall. Then Sylph added a waterskin and a soft cloth to the pile.

Thana waited with the armload until Sylph looked at her. "Do you need assistance?" Sylph asked.

Thana knew she was blushing again, so she turned away, imagining Sylph helping her dress. Maybe they'd pause in the middle and make eye contact. Then before they even realized what was happening, their lips would be together, and they'd tumble to the forest floor…

Shaking her head to stop the flood of images, Thana marched behind a tree. She hurriedly washed her face and neck, then donned the clothes. The trousers were too long, so she stuffed them in her boots, and the poofy shirt nearly reached her knees, so she tucked it far into the trousers. Everything bagged a bit, even after she fastened her belt.

She was certain she looked as stupid as she felt, though the silk shirt seemed to caress her skin, and the trousers were so soft they felt like a blanket.

Stupid nobles.

She tied the shirt's cuff strings around her wrists and stepped out from behind the tree, her old clothes under one arm. "She's still going to wonder about the coat. And I can't wear one of yours because…" She was about to say that the coat would be too large because Sylph's breasts were bigger, but any mention of Sylph's anatomy had more blush-inducing visions dancing in her head. She stuffed her old clothes in one of the saddlebags, and when she turned, Sylph began assaulting her with ribbons, tying them around the sleeves here and there so that the shirt bloused between them. She then tied one around Thana's middle, tucking the shirt around it until it clung to Thana's breasts.

Spirits above, her cheeks were going to melt.

She sputtered and tried to ignore the many touches, not even arguing when Sylph combed her hair back and plonked a hat on her head.

When Sylph stood back to survey her work, Thana fought the urge to shuffle her feet as she frowned. When Sylph's gaze reached her face, she snorted a little laugh, then flashed a dazzling smile. "Like this," she said through her teeth, gesturing at her own mouth.

Thana kept frowning. "I won't smile about the fact that I'm headed into a viper's nest wearing silly clothes and ribbons. And it's still not a coat."

"You're my fashion-forward companion."

Thana's eyebrows shot up. "Not your servant?"

Sylph *tsked*. "A companion is a son or daughter of noble birth whose family has fallen on hard times. They rent out their... friendship, for lack of a better word, so their family will have some income." She went around Thana again, tucking and fluffing. "The families are usually tied by some past marriage."

It sounded stupid enough to make Thana want to tear the hat from her head, but when Sylph held up a mirror, Thana had to admit that the green hat looked all right on her. "Why don't they just borrow money from these relatives?"

Sylph blinked at her.

Thana sighed from her toes. "That must just be for peasants, right. Okay, who am I?"

"Miss Justine Theroue, a poor cousin from a tiny holding north of mine. As the daughter of a lady, you have no title of your own, and you are not the heir to the handful of farms your family owns."

"Great, nobility and farming, two things I know very little about."

"Just smile," Sylph said, again demonstrating, and there was a bit of real twinkle behind the fake show of teeth. "And let me do all the talking." She gave Thana a stern look as they remounted. "And no grumbling."

Thana bit back a groan and tried to smile, but she knew it either looked fake or insane. Maybe the countess would think her family was poor because they were all mad. That would have to do.

They walked into a clearing, and the manor house sat in the middle, but it didn't have the cleaner lines of the newer buildings in Marienne. It looked like a pile of stone blocks, more of a fortress than a house. She counted three stories, but the far side was in crumbling disrepair. A few wooden additions stuck out from the other side, and a turret in the front had crenellations for archers, though none stood there now.

The sound of voices came from the rear of the manor. Thana craned her neck as someone came around the side, starting when he saw them before he jogged away and returned with another man, both in leather and homespun. They tugged on their caps almost absently before reaching for the reins of the horses and holding the stirrups so Sylph and Thana could dismount.

Thana opened her mouth to say thanks, but Sylph swept by them without a word. Right. Nobles only had manners for the *right* sort of people. She suppressed an eye roll and came to a halt behind Sylph as the large wooden door of the manor swung open. A pale woman with iron-gray hair peered out at them, hands folded in front of her dark shirt and trousers. The belt around her waist had a ring of large keys dangling from it: a housekeeper.

"Lady Sylph Montague and Miss Justine Theroue to see Countess Carisse Van Umberholme," Sylph said, her tone bored and her gaze wandering as if the housekeeper was no more than a piece of paper to write messages on.

The housekeeper nodded as if that was indeed her only function. "This way, my lady." She didn't lose her stern, suspicious look as they trooped past. Thana tried to look imperious but guessed she was somewhere between awkward and apologetic. A cold stone hallway greeted them with a bare stairway to the right and an open room to the left. They followed the housekeeper into a heavily carpeted room with tapestries hiding the walls. A cold fireplace dominated one wall, and the chandelier did little to dispel the dimness. The entire place could have used more windows.

The housekeeper beckoned to a wooden bench and chair that sat before a low table. She then swept from the room without a word.

Sylph took the chair. Thana took the bench, wincing at the creak of ancient wood. At least it was clean. She peered at the hall, but after the housekeeper ascended the stairs, she saw nothing and heard only silence.

"She doesn't seem to like company," Thana whispered. "I wonder if it's because of what you said about the countess fearing attack."

Sylph frowned slightly. "Why would the servants care about that?"

"Some servants actually like their bosses, you know. It's even possible that they're friends." She thought of herself and Gunnar and winced. But he'd never treated her like a servant.

Sylph frowned at nothing as if working out a complicated arithmetic problem.

"What?" Thana asked. "Never been close with the help?" She wanted to take the words back as she thought of Sylph hitting her maid. She hadn't meant to sound so snide.

But Sylph just shook her head. "No, Father wouldn't allow it."

Maybe the countess hadn't had such strict, bigoted parents. Or maybe, if she was close to her servants, it was because she didn't have anyone else.

A rustle of fabric preceded the countess's arrival. Thana stood as she always did when someone entered a room. Sylph stayed seated, but she didn't command Thana to do the same. No doubt Thana had complied with some status rule without knowing.

Like her house, the countess seemed to date from some years ago. Her dress was nothing like the tight trousers, frilled shirts, and coats or vests popular in Marienne. Made from blue silk, it had a high collar, and laces ran down the side from her left shoulder to her waist, the cord and eyelets in startling silver. Maybe she wanted to match her house.

Or maybe she was saving her money for the fight she knew might be ahead.

Her graying blond hair was pulled behind her head, but stray ringlets lay over both shoulders. She seemed very pale in the dim room, but her dark eyes snapped like fire as she glanced between them. Thana bowed, happy she'd received protocol lessons from Gunnar even when she didn't want them.

"Lady Sylph, Miss Justine," the countess said. "Welcome to my home." Icicles could have formed in the wake of her words. Her face didn't twitch. She didn't sit, which meant Thana couldn't either, and her eyes practically screamed at them to state their purpose.

"Thank you, Countess," Sylph said. "My companion and I were out riding, and I'm afraid time escaped us. Now that night has fallen, we have come to beg accommodation." She smiled, and it had some charm, Sylph putting on the lady-in-distress mask like a professional actor.

"Of course," Countess Carisse said, and she seemed a little relieved, though Thana didn't know what she was expecting. A challenge to her or her daughter? A marriage proposal? Maybe she thought they'd at least pretend to be suitors, but when they didn't propose, she decided to relax.

"This way." She led them up the stairs.

Thana wondered why she was leading them herself. Maybe she knew Sylph was the daughter of a duke simply because of her name. Maybe it was mere status that made the countess nervous.

Thana had never met Sylph's father, but the fear he put in everyone didn't make her anxious to do so.

"With the disrepair of the east wing," Countess Carisse said, "I'm afraid we have only one guest room available."

Thana's stomach sank. One room. With Sylph. Who Thana had been fantasizing about since they'd met. She didn't know whether to be overjoyed or horrified. They'd also been arguing since they'd met.

When Sylph said, "Of course," in that smooth manner, Thana ground her teeth. Sylph would probably command her to sleep on the floor. Spirits, Sylph might have demanded that Countess Carisse give up her own room, but that would probably cause a diplomatic incident.

When the countess let them into a room with a huge wooden bed and a near-acre of mattress, Thana let out a breath. In that monstrosity, they'd be hard-pressed to *find* each other, let alone make love. People in the old days must have lived in them. Or maybe they'd hardly ever changed the sheets and just slept in another corner if one got dirty.

"Dinner will be soon," Countess Carisse said as she left and shut the door.

Thana breathed out and stretched. She'd been holding herself so stiffly that her back was starting to ache. "I'll have to remember the prince's lessons on table manners," she said, and her stomach growled in approval.

Sylph smiled faintly. "Just copy me, and you'll be fine." She glanced at the bed, and her cheeks colored as if she'd just realized they had to sleep together. Thana waited for her order to take a blanket and find a spot on the carpet. She'd tell Sylph to take her blanket and shove it. Then they'd fight, and then…

"Left or right?" Sylph asked.

Thana blinked. "Pardon?"

"Side of the bed. Which do you prefer?" She had wide, innocent eyes, but she wasn't demanding anything. If Thana had been reading her right, that meant she was nervous.

It felt good to not be the only one.

"Oh, um, I've never had a side." She wished her own blush would take a rest. "I've only ever slept in single beds." She stopped before admitting that she'd shared a single bed a time or two, at least for an hour or so, but just the thought made the spirits-cursed blood rush to her face again. She turned away.

"Oh," Sylph said softly. "Try the right?"

Thana barked a laugh. "Sounds like you're offering wine." And everything sounded as if it had a second meaning at the moment. She wanted to bite her cheek to stop talking.

Sylph sat on the left side of the bed. The mattress sagged, lifting her feet off the floor. She gave a delighted little laugh that made Thana want to hold her even more.

And if the mattress sagged that much, they'd both wind up in the middle, thrown together by fate...and an old mattress. Then neither of them could be held responsible if they—

A gong sounded from below, a deep hollow reverberation that made Sylph roll out of bed. "Dinner," she said, all false brightness that said she might have been thinking about that mattress, too.

Chapter Ten

S ylph tried to control the tension in her body as she descended the stairs. The presence of Thana behind her should have given her some comfort, but then she thought of them sharing a bed, and the anxiety stayed put.

In the palace, the thought of Thana pressed close had made her excited, eager even, despite the differences in their station. Perhaps she hadn't been upset by it because she'd known that they could never be together. Here, on the run, adrift from their roles, forced into proximity...the possibility seemed right in front of her.

Thrilling, terrifying, all exhilarating feelings she couldn't recall from her former life.

But she couldn't dwell on them at the moment. She had to shove her feelings down and put her court face on, and it felt as uncomfortable as cramming herself into a small box. The countess was clearly wary of her and her intentions, and she had to exude an aura of relaxed condescension, or Countess Carisse might become suspicious enough to ask questions, maybe even tell someone she'd seen them.

Her father would make a powerful ally for a countess who feared other nobles. And Countess Carisse might not realize until later that being under his arm was as dangerous as being in front of it.

Sylph schooled her face before entering the dining room, clearing her throat so Thana would also remember to stay calm. The room was as old-fashioned as the rest of the house. Larger than the chilly sitting room, this one reached high into where the second story would be. Exposed wooden beams ran across the space, displaying tattered banners that didn't brighten the stone walls so much as fade into them, making a palette of drabness.

A long wooden trestle table dominated the room, but it stood empty, leaving a smaller wooden table at the head of the room, the lord or lady's table. The countess sat at one end with a bearded man on her right, facing the room. If they'd been having dinner when this manor was new, the countess and her honored guests would all be behind the table, facing the room, and the long trestle table would be occupied by the countess's vassals and men-at-arms.

But the time for nobles keeping their own armies was over, though the Troubles had proved that such troops could be raised quickly if needed.

The countess wore a calm expression, but Sylph could see her true feelings around the edges: the slight pucker between her eyebrows, the pinched corners of her mouth. Maybe she feared Sylph had some mercenaries waiting in the forest, a grab for power on her father's bloody command. A foolish thought. Her father would never risk her that way, though not for sentimental reasons.

Countess Carisse and her companion rose, the countess gesturing to the other end of the table where two place settings mirrored hers. As she came closer, Sylph's insides stirred. She felt something from the man, some sense of danger. He peered suspiciously at both her and Thana and leaned toward the countess as if ready to shield her.

A suitor? If he was noble, Sylph would know him. A servant? Surely not. The only reason Thana was allowed to sit with them was because Sylph had lied about her heritage. Well, Sylph took comfort from Thana's presence. Maybe this man provided similar relief for the countess.

She and Thana weren't as unique as she'd thought.

"This is Timmony," the countess said, offering no other explanation. He inclined his head.

Sylph glanced in his direction before pretending to dismiss him. Thana smiled awkwardly, then looked to Sylph. She fought the urge to narrow her eyes as the danger-sense continued, only looking down when the servants served the soup.

The silence was broken only by the sound of spoons against bowls and the occasional slurp from Thana. Sylph might have been amused by the noise, but the warning inside her continued. There had to be a reason she was so ill at ease, and when a memory came to her, she nearly dropped her spoon.

During her brief training session with Thana, she'd felt something similar to this from the table of pyramids. A sort of tingly awareness, but not of any person.

Timmony had a fire pyramid.

Sylph kept eating, hoping the motion didn't look too wooden. She had to find a way to tell Thana without alarming anyone. Perhaps Timmony was a pyradisté. That might explain his presence. He was here as a protector.

Thana didn't seem particularly afraid. She had no court face. If she'd sensed the pyramid, she would have given a sign. When their gazes met, Thana's was only curious.

After the soup, the servants brought a haunch of venison and bowls of greens. When everyone had a portion, Timmony cleared his throat loudly.

Everyone froze as abruptly as if he'd produced his fire pyramid and held it aloft.

"Tell me, Lady Sylph," he said, the words brittle through a polite facade. "During your stay in Marienne, have you heard any rumors about rogue pyradistés?"

The question was so artless, she might have laughed, but Countess Carisse fixed her with a keen look. Thana sputtered on her wine, and Sylph nearly kicked her under the table. "I am surprised news of such events has spread all the way out here," Sylph said, hoping to convey that the countess's estate was so remote as to be beneath Sylph's notice and therefore safe from her.

"Everyone knows," Countess Carisse said. "Some pyradistés are dangerous."

"Are either of you one of them?" Timmony asked, bringing the table to silence again.

Thana froze with a forkful of greens at her mouth and stared at Sylph, an obviously guilty expression on her face. Sylph dabbed her lips with a napkin. If Countess Carisse thought either of them a pyradisté, then their nobility was in question. But surely everyone had heard of Lady Sylph Montague.

Sylph looked Countess Carisse in the eye. "I have heard that some pyradistés are dangerous, but I know none who are. Why would I?" She glanced at Timmony. "I know some nobles employ them, and I wonder what other roles they might fill if they, for instance, eat at their employer's table."

She hoped to make the countess uncomfortable enough to change the subject, but Countess Carisse said, "Indeed. If one were to live or dine or travel so accompanied, it would no doubt be for protection from the very threat Timmony just brought up and not because they are looking to cause trouble themselves."

Sylph put her hands on the table, trying to keep from reaching for that pyramid and making it burst to life, but the more her heart pounded, the stronger the desire to ignite it rose inside her.

"I would expect someone wanting only to defend themselves would not travel with too many offensive pyramids," Timmony said. The countess briefly turned a glare on him.

Sylph cocked her head. He couldn't have gone through Thana's satchel, so he had to have sensed her pyramids, probably with one of the utility pyramids Thana had mentioned before.

"Okay." Thana put her fork down. "Enough dancing around. First of all, protecting yourself from an attack requires a weapon as well as a shield, but dinner requires neither. So that leads me to my second point." She put her hands on the table, palms up. "I'm unarmed."

Both Timmony and Countess Carisse took deep breaths and seemed to relax slightly. Sylph was relieved that the subject might now be dropped and annoyed that Thana had spoken so bluntly. Since she hadn't said pyradisté, she probably thought she'd been talking in code, but she gave entirely too much information away for Sylph's liking.

"What happened that's got you two so nervous?" Thana asked as she took a big mouthful of food.

Sylph wanted to kick her so badly this time that her leg twitched.

Thana looked to Countess Carisse with a wry smile. "Sorry, Countess, but where I'm from, um, north of my cousin here"—she nodded awkwardly at Sylph—"we talk out our worries, especially when we encounter a stranger traveling through who might be bothered by them. If there's a rampaging bear nearby, we don't keep mum just because bears are…gauche this season or something."

The countess stared. Sylph fought the urge to do the same. Timmony's lips were mashed together, but his eyes were merry, as if he was trying not to laugh.

"How long have you been at court, Miss Theroue?" the countess asked, a smile creeping out.

Thana's cheeks colored slightly. "A few, um, weeks," she muttered. "My first trip."

"Ah." Countess Carisse nodded and gave Sylph a sympathetic look, but she surely couldn't believe Thana was both a noble and a pyradisté, even if she was at the bottom of the hierarchy. Maybe she'd decided to let the noble deception go and just pitied Sylph a chatty traveling companion. Sylph displayed her best put-upon look.

Thana rubbed her temples. She'd started the evening being amused by all the doublespeak and nonconfrontation, but in the end, she had to say something. Timmony had clearly detected her pyramids at some point, but he couldn't know about Sylph. Thana supposed her lesser noble persona might be crushed, but Timmony and Carisse seemed more relaxed.

"We have heard some rumors about rogue pyradistés," Carisse said, "from some travelers our groom spoke to. Murder. Explosions. Is it true?"

Thana fought the urge to bite her lip. She waited for Sylph to answer. She wasn't any good at lying, and Sylph seemed a natural. That was a bit worrying for other reasons, but she didn't let herself think of them at the moment.

"We've heard the rumors, too," Sylph said. "But it's hard to know what's true."

"Did you ride out today because you feared staying in Marienne?" Timmony asked.

Carisse gave him a tiny frown, but Sylph shrugged as elegantly as she did everything else. "I don't need to worry about such things."

Thana frowned. Was that an acknowledgement of Thana's ability? If so, why didn't she just say so, for spirits' sake? But that was just Thana's nervous aggravation talking.

And the ribbons around her sleeves were cutting off her circulation.

Revealing that she was a pyradisté would probably lead to her real name and position. A noble like Sylph could waste time riding around, but why would she have the monarch's pyradisté with her? Especially when there was a pyradisté crisis going on. And it seemed as if they hadn't had any magical troubles out here. Because the new crystal hadn't come near here? Or was there something else at work? Nothing strange had happened at the academy when the crystal was there, apart from Sylph's trouble. Maybe the other problems were more than accidents.

As a servant handed around bowls of custard, Carisse and Timmony added another piece to her puzzle: a story they'd heard from a servant who'd been traveling back to Marienne after visiting family in the country. She'd told the servants that a pyradisté in the local lord's holding had set the house on fire, but afterward, the pyradisté couldn't be found. The household had assumed he'd perished in the fire, but what if he'd been conducting experiments with the new crystal? Or even just using it? Maybe it only reacted badly to some people, like Sylph. Thana sighed. She didn't have enough information, but she added this new town to her mental map.

She also wondered where Carisse's daughter was. Maybe the child never ate with strangers, or maybe she always ate with her nanny while Carisse ate alone or with Timmony, who seemed to care about her more than a paid servant might. By the warm atmosphere, Thana could imagine Carisse, Timmony, and the child together. Maybe if she married him, she wouldn't have to worry about other nobles trying to steal her land.

Or maybe she feared he'd become a target of those same nobles.

Or she didn't want to marry a peasant.

Thana fought the urge to sigh. She'd spent too much time in Sylph's world, like another planet, especially where family was concerned. She'd grown up in a lively foster home manned by a variety of monks. They believed in hands-on learning and frequently took the children into the city for outings. When Thana had met Gunnar on one such trip, she'd thought him just another child and had treated him as such, including him in games, teasing him, and protecting him from the jibes of others. When she'd found out he was a prince, she hadn't cared. He was already her friend, and he'd needed one.

Like Sylph. She was lonelier than Gunnar had ever been.

When dinner ended, and Thana trailed Sylph upstairs, she rethought their status. They wouldn't be friends much longer. Once they lay in that monstrous bed together, Thana wouldn't be able to think of them as friends anymore.

"Since you were caught out at night," Carisse called after them, "is there anything you need?"

For Sylph, no, but Thana hadn't had the chance to pack and said, "Anything you can spare would be appreciated."

Sylph didn't respond, not speaking even once they were behind closed doors. Thana shifted from foot to foot as Sylph kept her back turned and dug through her pack. The rustling sound seemed loud in the cavernous room. Thana thought of a hundred words but discarded all of them. Maybe they'd end up going to bed in silence and stare at the ceiling all night. Then they'd just be awkward friends.

When someone knocked on the door, Thana jumped, barely holding in a screech. A maid brought in two long nightshirts, soap, a comb, and a basin of hot water. Sylph still didn't turn, not even when Thana splashed in the basin, washing her face.

Maybe Sylph didn't want her but couldn't think of a way to say it, so she was going to paw through her luggage all night. Thana's stomach soured. Had she imagined every glance, every lip bite, every ounce of heat?

She turned, thinking to take her own advice and speak, but the words died at the sight of Sylph's bare back. Her golden curls brushed across her tanned shoulders. Lean muscles flowed under her skin, drawing Thana's eye to a smattering of freckles in the small of her back. Thana's mouth went dry, and she couldn't think of anything but what it would be like to run her hands over that skin, to trace those freckles with her lips.

Sylph glanced over her shoulder as if she'd felt Thana's gaze or heard some small noise of appreciation. She turned, clutching a shirt that barely shielded her naked breasts. Thana waited for a smirk or some other expression that would piss her off, but Sylph only took a step, the shirt dipping a bit lower.

Thana mirrored her step. When Sylph took another, Thana reached for her, determined to embrace her before that shirt could hit the floor.

They touched, and a boom sounded from outside, drowning out Thana's pounding heart.

❖

Sylph almost kept reaching for Thana, thinking the fire between them had ignited in a thunderous boom, but Thana broke eye contact and moved toward the door.

Sylph's breath left in a rush, and she slipped her shirt over her head as goose bumps broke out along her arms. The desire in her belly had probably kept them away until now.

"What was that?" Thana asked, her ear to the door.

Sylph wanted to say, "Who cares. Come back to me." She had never had a romantic partner and wasn't quite sure what lovemaking entailed, but she wanted so badly to find out. When their eyes had met, when Sylph had realized her state of undress and how it had spawned such desire in Thana's eyes, she hadn't thought once about the difference in their stations.

Curious.

And wonderful.

Worthier of exploration than any feeling she'd ever known.

Someone yelled in the corridor. Thana opened the heavy door, and muffled voices became clearer.

"Is there someone out there, or did the east wing collapse?"

"The grooms are looking."

"I'm going with them."

"Timmony, get back here!" That sounded like the countess.

A draft of air rushed through the old house, making the doors shudder.

"I'll find out what's going on," Thana said.

"Wait," Sylph called.

Thana turned. Her gaze filled Sylph with desire again, but Thana was out the door before she could say or do anything.

Sylph *tsked* and had to bottle her feelings as she hurriedly donned a vest over her shirt so she wouldn't appear in public less than half-dressed. She thanked the spirits she hadn't removed the trousers that went with her riding dress. She tightened the laces as she left the room, her heart pounding with fear for Thana's safety instead of in anticipation of her embrace.

After her irritation at being interrupted faded, she wondered if the boom could be because of her presence instead of a collapse or some enemy of the countess. No matter what, Thana would want to help. Sylph's father would call helping strangers and asking nothing in return the height of foolishness.

But he'd been wrong about so many things.

Thana needed someone to watch her back. Sylph dashed into the room again and grabbed the pyramid satchel.

Downstairs, someone screamed.

Sylph's heart flew into her throat, and she hesitated as she left the room again, trying to swallow her fear. She took a few careful steps down the narrow staircase even though every instinct told her to run and hide. Thana needed her. She had to be brave. Amid the fear, she felt something else. She thought it might be the awakening of her courage, but no, it was the pyramid pull, the undeniable drive to reach out and connect to a power she barely understood.

"No," she whispered, her feet sliding until she sat on the cold steps. "Stop." She clenched her fists but couldn't stop the call. Somewhere outside, a pyramid sang to her.

And the spirits only knew what it might do.

She fumbled with the satchel, seeking to distract herself as Thana had before. Her fingers skimmed over the crystal inside, and she grabbed on to a familiar pyramid.

Light suffused the dim stairway. The whole bag was alight, blazing with color, and the pull from outside lessened. Breathing hard, Sylph struggled to her feet, one hand on the wall and one in the bag. She stumbled down, hearing raised voices and another boom.

"Thana," she called, all she could get out past the tightness in her chest. Her mind kept trying to reach further. "Thana!"

A figure appeared at the bottom of the stairs, and Sylph nearly cried out in relief until she focused on the countess's face.

"What did you do?" Countess Carisse cried. Before Sylph could withdraw, the countess reached for the satchel, the source of Sylph's hard-won control.

CHAPTER ELEVEN

Thana stepped outside and peered into the darkness. She heard someone calling from the forest nearby where the light of a torch bobbed through the shadows. Off to her right, near where the ruined part of the house stood, another torch pushed away the gloom.

A pop came from the trees, a reverberating sound that caused a tinny echo in her ears. An explosive pyramid? There was one of Carisse's questions answered. That sound they'd heard hadn't been the ruined wing collapsing. Someone was attacking them.

From the woods? But that torch she'd glimpsed in the trees seemed to have gone out.

Thana felt at her side where her pyramid satchel should have been if she'd remembered to grab it. Swearing, she turned for the door, but a figure blocked her way, and as she stepped toward it, it screamed and slammed the door in her face.

"Shit," Thana whispered. She raised a hand to bang on the door but feared drawing too much attention. She slapped her palm against the wood, hoping the sound carried inside. "Let me in, spirits curse you," she said in a loud whisper. "I'm a guest, not the enemy."

No one answered, and she cursed herself again for forgetting the damn bag. She'd never get better at using pyramids if she was always forgetting them.

She turned back to the darkness. The moon spotted the yard with shadows, but she didn't see anyone. She backed up against the manor wall, hoping to stay out of sight. Down the yard, the other torch she'd seen creeped toward the forest. Thana clamped her teeth on a warning cry as the torch slipped inside the trees. A scream followed, a horrid sound that cut off too quickly to be natural.

The light vanished, the silence deafening. The singing of insects slowly creeped back, filling the air with all the noise of an orchestra. Thana edged to her left, keeping her back to the wall. If she remembered correctly, the stables were in that direction. She could get under cover.

Her brain tried to remind her that a simple roof over her head wouldn't be enough to stop an exploding pyramid, but the terror inside her drowned out that voice, insisting that she needed to hide or share the same fate as the torchbearers.

Another boom sounded against the far side of the manor. Thana clapped a hand over her mouth, holding in a scream. As the boom faded, she heard the scrape and slide of falling rock. She glanced that way, her feet frozen. A cloud of dust flitted through the moonlit yard like a ghostly horde. Why attack the part of the manor already in ruins?

Because they knew they couldn't get through the stout doors? Did they think the walls would be easier? Well, the exterior ones, no, but at a place where the structure was already weak?

The questions gave her rational mind a foothold, and her heart calmed a little, giving her control of her senses. As she peered around again, listening for footsteps or voices, she caught a glint of light within the trees and heard a soft sound, either the susurrus of leaves or people whispering. She hurried to where the shadow of the manor's corner jutted across the lawn like a pointing finger, then followed it into the trees.

The same trees where the torches had disappeared, and people had screamed.

Not smart.

She clenched a fist and told herself to get a grip on her fear. She couldn't stay stuck to the side of the manor or hide in the stables if someone was throwing pyramids around. She was a spirits-cursed pyradisté in service to the crown. Stopping enemy magic users was her purpose.

Straining to listen, she edged forward. A glimpse of light came again, not the flicker of fire but steady pyramid light, and by the way it came and went, she guessed someone was covering it, probably hiding it in their hand.

"It's not working."

Thana froze again, then crouched. This voice sounded angry. Another murmured a response.

"I don't care," the first voice said. "And we shouldn't have used one of the new pyramids on some random person who happened to wander out of the fucking manor."

"We didn't know it was some random person, and keep your voice down," the second voice said, a tone just this side of calm.

"Shut up and keep throwing," a third voice added near Thana's side.

She squeezed her lips together to keep from crying out. She hadn't realized she'd gotten so close to someone.

"The rest of 'em will have to come out eventually," the third voice added, and the other two didn't seem inclined to argue.

Light bloomed shortly, uncovered then covered again three times in a row, the burst ruining Thana's night vision but letting her see a clump of undergrowth in front of her face.

Another boom came from the manor house, then silence for a few moments before the angry voice said, "Let's just set fire to it."

"It won't burn easily," the second voice said.

"Stay calm," the third voice said, a slow, threatening tone. "We don't want to kill everyone inside, just the traitor."

Thana fought to keep quiet. Who? The countess? Sylph? What had either of them done to be branded a traitor? Sylph could be a traitor to her class, maybe, but Thana couldn't picture a bunch of nobles or courtiers skulking through the woods to teach the daughter of a duke some lesson about not making friends outside her social station.

Thana's stomach shrank. Oh, spirits, it was *her*. She'd told Sylph of the queen's plan and had run off with her. Now Queen Earnhilt had come to flush her out. Thana scowled, her anger driving away her fear even as she continued to think. Earnhilt wouldn't use pyradistés. She'd march up to the door and demand Thana answer for her crimes. And this couldn't be Sylph's father, either. He'd never use pyradistés. Then who?

And what could she do to stop them? Even if someone considered Countess Carisse or someone in her household a traitor, bombing their house until they surrendered didn't seem exactly law-abiding.

She had to distract them. Or at least make them think there were more enemies in the forest than they thought. Maybe if she spooked them, they'd leave.

After a long, silent breath, she eased back, waiting for them to make a rustling sound before she moved. When she'd taken a few steps away, she felt for something small enough to throw. She found a stick and launched it into the trees, listening to the attackers try to discern the source of the noise and praying for the spirits of wisdom and intelligence to abandon them.

Sylph clutched the satchel tighter as the countess demanded to know what she was doing. "Don't take it," Sylph cried. "I'll lose control." Already, it was slipping. The pulsing need to reach for nearby pyramids lessened somewhat, but she could still feel them out there, waiting. And she didn't know if she'd set them off or retune them. She might kill everyone outside the manor house and inside, too, and just the thought made her hold on to the light pyramid all the harder.

"What do you want? Are those your friends outside?" Countess Carisse gave the bag another yank.

"No!"

"Liar. You won't take my child's inheritance."

The satchel slipped from Sylph's shoulder. She grabbed the strap, but her senses were already stretching, called by some pyramid outside. She tried to see, to keep her eyes and mind on the satchel, but the light pyramid didn't call to her like the others did. She couldn't lose herself in it without Thana guiding her.

Unless she changed it.

She liberated the light pyramid as the countess tore the satchel from her. She clutched it to her chest and looked for the stone through it, twisting it until she could feel the walls of the manor rising like sentinels around her. Part of the wall was broken, lying in ruins outside, and as she kept her mind on it, another crack tore through it, chunks of masonry raining down as if they'd been smacked with a giant hand.

She could fix that.

Everything else began to fade: the staircase, the countess, the sound of a child crying, and voices raised in alarm. She grabbed the stone with her power and yanked the broken pieces upright, pulling large slabs up to be one again with the whole. She let herself flow with the power instead of fighting as before, and it didn't hurt, didn't howl through her like it had in the garden. She had something to focus on here, something to fix.

Sylph lost herself in the feeling, the rightness of fitting seam to seam and mending cracks and holes. These walls had stood far longer than they'd been in disrepair. If she concentrated, she could feel the history in the rock, the miles it had traveled, the quarry it had come from, the millennia it had lain dormant. And before that, a whisper of an echo spoke of countless ages spent under the sea.

The land had once been a sea. She'd never dreamed such things could change.

She'd nearly finished when the staircase and the countess came back in a rush. Sylph had forgotten they'd ever existed. Countess Carisse's face seemed panicked, desperate. She clutched the remains of a vase in her hands, ceramic bits cascading from her fingers.

Sylph's own body came back slower, the haziness around the edges of her vision, the pain in her head, the slight scent of blood. She couldn't think what had happened, could barely think at all, and she couldn't control her body as it fell backward, and the haziness overtook her eyes, dropping her into blackness.

"Shut up and listen," one of the voices in front of Thana said with a growl. She could almost feel them listening.

When another started to protest, she threw another bit of forest flotsam.

They shuffled, sounding as if they were headed in the direction of where it landed. Maybe if they wandered far enough, they'd just leave. And without these three signaling, the bombardment of the manor house had stopped.

Now she only had to decide what to do next. Find whoever was using the explosives? What if they were pyradistés, but they weren't in their right minds? A concerted attack didn't sound like any of the other incidents. Those had sounded spur-of-the-moment, acts that came from being overwhelmed. Journeying to a manor house in the middle of nowhere to hunt a so-called traitor seemed the height of deliberateness.

A screech sounded from the manor. Thana leaped from her hiding place. In the moonlit-dappled forest, a pair of wide eyes stared back at her. Light blinded her for a moment before she realized it was someone holding a pyramid.

The signaler.

Another shrieking noise came from the manor, followed by the grinding sound of stone and the rumble of shifting rock. Thana jumped, her heart in her mouth. The pyramid-holder let out a gasp of alarm, and the light tilted. Thana caught a glimpse of dark hair, a beard surrounding an open mouth.

He was going to call out.

Thana leaped without thinking, wanting to stop any warning cry. Her breath left her as they crashed together. The pyramid bounced into the undergrowth as Thana's target fell, taking her with him and cutting off a brief cry in a whoosh of breath.

Thana tried to disentangle herself and get up, but her hands and feet kept sinking into flesh as her captive squirmed. He gasped or coughed, the wind knocked out of him, but that wouldn't last forever.

As if goaded by her thoughts, he flailed, and Thana clamped her teeth on a cry as an arm connected with her cheek, sending pain rattling through her skull and making stars streak past her right eye.

Panicking, she lost her balance. Her captive bucked. She threw herself forward, one hand landing in the dirt and the other smacking him again. A small cry answered her, so she pressed down and felt for a weapon with her free hand. She groaned as another blow caught her in the stomach. Aches radiated through her midsection, but she pushed the feeling aside as her fingers closed over the roughness of bark.

"Get—"

His words cut off as Thana brought a broken branch over her head and sent it down without looking, without thinking, only hoping she wouldn't have to do it again.

He went still. Shuddering through a few deep breaths, Thana fell to the side. The rumbling from the manor had stopped, but the rattle of cascading stones filled the silence. She had to move before someone came looking. She felt for the light pyramid in the undergrowth. When she felt the smoothness of crystal, she snatched it up, holding it close.

She cradled her aching stomach as she moved back to the captive and riffled his clothing. Another pyramid. She grinned and stuffed it in her pocket. After she'd found another, she stood, having no room for more. She wondered if she had enough time to discern what the pyramids did before—

Light blinded her again, this time coming from between her and the manor house. She gasped and fell into her pyramid, fighting through fear to sense its fiery nature. She cocked her arm to throw, but Timmony's voice stopped her.

"Lady Justine?" he whispered.

Sylph's first thought was that she was walking. Funny, she'd never walked with her eyes shut before. Was she sleepwalking? The air passed over her back, and her arms swung beneath her. Sleepwalking was much more...horizontal than she'd expected.

A funny thought, but she couldn't laugh, couldn't do much of anything. She tried to stop, but her legs met resistance, as if someone was holding them. Another aspect of sleepwalking she didn't expect.

"She's waking up," someone said, the words more than a little breathless.

"Quickly." This voice was near her feet. The other at her head. She was being...carried. Why? "We have to get her outside."

"We don't know that she was attacking us, Your Grace."

"Then why did it stop when I hit her? Stop talking and move."

The words fell into place as memory, but Sylph still couldn't do anything about them, could hardly move at all. She'd have to fight harder if she wanted to escape this dream…memory…whatever. She couldn't open her eyes, and all she could hear was the huffing breath of the two people carrying her and the shuffle of their footsteps over carpet and stone. Her head began to pound, made worse by the musty scent of the old manor house. If they were taking her into the fresh air, that could only be a good thing.

Or not. Because…

Pyramids.

Now that she'd thought about them, she could feel them. She tried to call out a warning but could only cough, prompting her bearers to go faster, the one near her head making little whimpers of alarm. Sylph tried to focus on the feel of the normal pyramids, the relatively safe ones, but there was also a siren-like call like the one at the garden party and in the academy, and it made panic flutter through her chest.

She tried to breathe deeply to keep it from consuming her and forcing her to lash out in an effort to stop this ghastly pull, but it felt too much like trying to relax when something sought to pull her off a precipice. Not panicking felt too much like succumbing to doom.

No, Thana would argue that staying calm would help her avoid the abyss, too. Thrashing would only speed her fall. She pictured Thana's dark eyes, her lips saying, "Breathe, breathe." She demonstrated deep breaths along with the words, smiling proudly when Sylph copied her.

Ah, the pride of another. She never knew how much she'd needed it until Thana.

A rush of cool air rewarded her. "Do your dirty work out here or begone with you," the countess said.

Sylph thumped lightly against the dirt. The pull of the pyramid became stronger. She clamped her teeth and balled her fists, trying to picture the struggle as a physical one. Finally, her eyes opened.

The countess stood above her. "Timmony," she called. "I've gotten her out. Come back."

"Countess?" two voices called from a distance, one male, Timmony, but the other was like a sweet balm to Sylph's frazzled nerves.

"Thana?" Sylph wanted to reach for her even more than she wanted that pyramid, but she couldn't risk moving. The pyramid called for her like a long-lost love. "Thana, help."

"Go back in," Timmony cried as Thana called, "Watch out for—"

Sylph lost the rest of their words as a pyramid took flight. It wasn't the siren, but she reached for it anyway. In her mind, its invisible presence was as bright as a shooting star.

At a brush of her mind, it detonated, and the sky overhead cracked, the sound washing over Sylph in a rush of air. Countess Carisse cried out, several other voices with her, but hers faded behind the boom of a closing door.

Sylph struggled to rise as the relief from touching the pyramid faded. The siren was still out there, and she had to get away from it before she hurt someone. "Thana?"

"Let me go, curse you, she needs me."

Sylph nearly wept at the words. Thana was coming. Thana would save her. Again came all those feelings she didn't have names for. With her mind occupied, her heart ran free, wanting Thana, needing her like a garden needed the sun.

Then she was there, merely a shadow in the night, but Sylph knew her.

"Are you all right?" Thana asked, her touch fluttering around Sylph's face, her hair. She tried to kiss those quick fingers but couldn't manage it. "Sylph? Did they hurt you?"

"Pyramids. They…" Thana had some on her, too, but their pull was nothing compared to what was coming closer. Oh spirits, what if she killed them both?

"Easy, Sylph, breathe. Here."

Smooth pyramid crystal pressed against her palm, but it felt like dead stone as the siren tried to claim her mind.

"It's light, Sylph. Remember? Light it. Hold on, please."

"It's coming," Sylph whispered, and she felt the destruction at the siren's core. She wouldn't be able to retune it. It would swallow her before that, forcing her to ignite its fiery heart and take them both, take them all, the manor and all the world.

Soft lips landed on hers, a fierce pressure, desperate hunger. She could see no more than shadow, but as with the pyramid, she could feel Thana beyond the kiss, feel the heat of her body, of her breath, the way she cradled Sylph's face with tenderness but also need. A distraction, yes, but also a release. The way Thana's mouth moved said she'd imagined this kiss many times.

Sylph had imagined something like it, too, ever since she'd known what kissing was, and this was nothing like she'd expected while being so much better.

The siren faded to a pinprick of distant light as the pyramid in her hand blazed. The siren was just a tool, carried by someone who had more tools at their disposal, all of which could be weapons.

But she was not helpless.

She threaded a hand through Thana's hair as she warped the pyramid in her hand, retuning it as she'd done in the manor and calling through it to the stone. The ground rumbled, and she brought part of the manor wall arching around them, shielding them from all the world.

CHAPTER TWELVE

Thana had been wild with the idea that Sylph needed a distraction, that the light pyramid wasn't enough, but she'd been drawn to kiss her for more reasons than that.

Sylph seemed to need it.

For comfort, yes, but also to know that someone saw her struggle, cared about her and wanted to help. As much as Thana had been jealous of Sylph's power, she'd also been sympathetic about the way Sylph felt forced to use it. Thana had been forced into enough situations in her life to resent them on another's behalf.

And of course, Thana had really, *really* wanted to kiss her, too.

When Sylph had kissed her back, Thana had melted, forgetting the danger, the questions. The earth seemed to shift around them, and when she finally drew back from Sylph's soft lips, she was surprised to find it really had moved, creating a little dome over them, with a hint of light coming from one side where the stone sloped downward.

Sylph's stone power. Of course. Thana's cheeks heated at the thought that she'd ever assumed differently, even for a moment. Then she also realized the barrier wouldn't stop an explosive pyramid for long.

She scooted nearer the hole and called, "Come out and give up, or we'll blow up the rest of your pyramids. You've already seen it once."

A beat of silence passed, then another. Sylph groaned, and Thana knew that no matter how much stone she manipulated or how many kisses she received, she'd eventually be compelled to touch the enemy pyramids again, maybe to vaporize everyone.

"Come out or retreat," Thana yelled. "I know you're still out there." She licked her lips, trying to think of something to make them respond, that would let her know where they were. Even Timmony had gone silent.

"One of you talked about a traitor," she called. "If you're talking about me, why didn't the queen come herself?"

"The queen can't protect you any longer."

Thana peered into the darkness of the forest, trying to determine where the voice was coming from, but sound echoed strangely in the dark. She frowned, trying to think of what the words could mean. So it was her they were looking for? But if this pyradisté thought the queen had been protecting her before, whom was she a traitor to exactly?

"Just...get out of here," she yelled. "Or give up. She'll blow you to the spirits if you don't." Something brushed her leg. Sylph was trying to sit up. Would moving make the desire to reach for the pyramids better or worse? Thana clasped her hand, fear rising but not for herself, for what it would do to Sylph if she had to hurt someone.

A cry came from the forest, then a shout, the words lost in pain or anger.

Sylph's grip tightened on Thana's. "It's coming closer."

"Fuck," Thana muttered. Any closer and an explosive pyramid might hurt the people inside the manor, too, but by the way Sylph's breathing grew sharper, that was inevitable.

Thana bit her lip, torn. Sylph seemed to fear hurting people more than anything, but what choice did they have when it was between the two of them, the innocents in the manor, and some idiot determined to attack? With her heart in her throat, she leaned toward Sylph's ear. "Do it."

Sylph sucked in a great breath, then slumped as if all the air had left her.

An explosion rocked the night outside, and light gleamed through the hole in a blinding flash. Thana cried out and curled over Sylph as the ground shook, and tiny flecks of stone trickled from the dome.

But nothing crashed atop them, and Thana opened one eye, blind in the dark. When a soft orange glow came from the opening, she launched herself forward. The forest was alight, the heat from the flames billowing toward the manor and filling the air with smoke and a high-pitched whistle as the fire pulled in the surrounding air.

"Sylph, there's a fire. Can you use your power to smother it?"

Sylph nodded weakly, and the dome around them fell away, the blocks collapsing outward. The earth of the forest lapped into the trees, smothering the fire and looking for all the world as if the land was eating itself.

Thana shook the thought away, stopped marveling at the sheer power, and rubbed Sylph's shoulders for a lack of anything else to do. "Are you all right?"

"Yes." She rubbed her neck as she sat up, her pyramid clutched in one hand. Light from the fire dappled across her as the flames died. Her face was tight and pained. She cradled her head and winced. Thana helped steady her. "It's not so bad with that…siren pyramid gone."

"You just felt one?" Thana frowned, but Sylph didn't elaborate. This siren she was talking about might have been unique simply because Sylph hadn't encountered its type before, but after her reaction at the academy, Thana bet it was made with the new crystal.

She looked at the dying fire. Rows of broken trees stabbed the sky like spears. Every pyramid the faceless attacker had been carrying must have gone off when Sylph touched her siren. When the fire dribbled out, darkness returned, though the smoke diffused the moonlight, brightening the yard as it put the forest in a haze.

Thana marveled at the woman in her arms. For her, accomplishing the impossible took far less focus than simply *not* using her power. "You did wonderfully."

Sylph moved, her eyes glinting. "I killed someone."

"You didn't have a choice."

Sylph shifted away, and guilt stabbed at Thana's heart. She hoped that wouldn't be a scar between them.

Something moved at the forest's edge. "If you're finished doing…whatever the hell that was, would you mind helping me?" Timmony called, his voice sharp with fear and anger.

Thana stood and took a few steps toward him, not feeling particularly charitable. After all, he'd tried to prevent her from going to Sylph's aid. He'd whispered something about keeping under cover to avoid attack, but she hadn't cared about his reasons.

He and another person dragged someone else into the yard... which was now significantly larger than it had been with the flattened trees. "What in the spirits' names happened?" He dumped his burden and gestured wildly, as if trying to take flight. "You asked about the queen, and that man said she couldn't protect you. From what? Who were they? What happened with that fire, the soil? What...are you?"

Thana didn't know where or how to begin. She nodded at the lump and Timmony's helper. "Who are they?"

"This is Jamie, one of the grooms," he said slowly, as if she was an idiot. "*You* tell *me* who in the spirits' names this is?" His finger stabbed toward the lump before he threw his arms in the air. "You know what, it doesn't matter. This clearly has nothing to do with the manor or Carisse, so you need to leave."

The way he pointed imperiously toward the forest almost made her laugh, and his use of the countess's name confirmed that she was more to him than just an employer. "I don't know who these people are or what they wanted, but they're clearly..." She pointed at the destruction, at the lump in the grass. "Dealt with. We can't go anywhere right now. It's the middle of the night, and we're both exhausted and..." She'd been about to say hurt, but she made herself stop, not wanting him to know how close Sylph seemed to falling over. "Tired," she finished lamely. "And I'd like to search your captive and try to find out what happened. Did you find anyone else?"

She bent over the lump, trying to see his features, but she didn't know if she'd recognize the person she'd hit before. If the others weren't dead, surely that last fiery explosion had driven them off.

"We found one more, dead," Jamie said. "And I saw two others blown up. And Owen, the other groom. They only wounded me, but they got him."

"There, you see?" Timmony asked. "You've done enough damage. Go."

Thana took several deep breaths. "We *can't* go in the middle of the night." She put a hand to her pocket, to the fire pyramid she'd... liberated from an enemy who was probably dead. She didn't want to use it, not on someone who was simply frightened. And she couldn't threaten him with Sylph. Thana had wanted to prove that Sylph was more than a living weapon. That was why she'd sneaked her out of the palace in the first place.

And then she'd used her as one.

Thana made a fist and held her temper in check. "Look, I can't explain right now. I barely understand what's going on myself, but we're...no threat to you." They would probably continue to attract threats, but she made herself keep that thought inside. "Please, have pity. We'll be gone in the morning."

She could see his shoulders moving as he breathed, and she prayed to the spirits of wisdom that he would back off. Finally, he shook his head and said, "You can sleep in the stable. Jamie, you come in the house with us." He pointed at Thana again. "Don't try to follow us."

She nodded, though anger burned in her to tell him that she and Sylph could come in any time they wished, right through the wall, but she told herself not to be cocky.

Guilt should keep her from that.

As Timmony hurried past her and knocked on the door, speaking softly to someone on the other side, Thana put her hands on her hips and looked toward the stable. It didn't seem secure, but if the night had proved anything, it was that they weren't safe anywhere.

And if the attackers came back, she and Sylph could ride away while the manor was attacked again.

The thought satisfied her and made her guilty at the same time. She wouldn't run if they needed her help again...though she wouldn't be happy about it. Maybe a little smug that she and Sylph could do what Timmony couldn't.

She shook her head. If a jumble of feelings told her anything, it was that she was too tired to think clearly.

After a deep breath to settle herself, she helped Sylph into the stable. They didn't speak, though Sylph leaned on Thana's shoulder, so she couldn't be that upset. In the stable, a lit candle sat on a small box behind a partition, illuminating one of the groom's beds: a blanket on top of a pallet of clean straw. Thana lowered Sylph onto it and moved a jug of water and a cup closer. Sylph only leaned against the wall and closed her eyes.

Thana bit her lip but didn't speak. She took the candle as she left the room. The horses were whickering and shifting in their stalls, eyes rolling, no doubt scared stiff by the noise and the smell of smoke, but they weren't kicking the place down, so Thana supposed they were all right.

She headed outside and set the candle near the captive's head. She didn't know if this was the one she'd felled, but it didn't matter. This one was dead, his head caved in. Maybe Timmony had thought he still lived, or maybe he'd dragged him out in order to search for clues. Whichever, Thana went through his pockets, trying not to think of him as a dead body, trying not to dwell on the fact that she'd never killed anyone before that day, and now she had several deaths on her conscience, and staying near Sylph might mean more.

This body had several more pyramids hidden in its clothes, so it wasn't the person she'd hit. The explosion or smoke had done that one in, or he was still lying unconscious in the forest. She didn't want to look for him, not really, didn't want to know, but she took the candle anyway and headed into the smoke. If he was alive, she could help, maybe get some answers, maybe assuage her conscience. If anyone else lingered, she'd make a handy target, but she deserved a little pain for all of this.

But did she deserve to die?

After a sigh, she hurried but stayed low. She didn't remember where exactly he'd been. How could she possibly find—

Through a gap in the foliage, she saw a foot, the boot still smoking.

"Oh, spirits." Retching, she turned and voided the countess's nice dinner into the bushes. As if summoned, the scent of charred meat wafted past her nostrils. She threw up again, gagging. Meat, yes, it was only meat. Nothing else. Not a person, just an accident with a campfire.

She was almost tired enough to believe that.

In the clearing again, she sank to the grass and leaned her head against her knees, breathing, thinking. If she was a traitor, but not to the queen, what was happening? Did other pyradistés consider her a traitor for working with the Umbriels, the people who told the academy what they could and couldn't do?

She clenched a fist. She'd always considered herself part of the solution. The more people who saw the Umbriels embracing magic, the fewer thought magic was something to be feared or outlawed. Pyradistés couldn't be the traitorous usurpers of yesteryear if the queen took them to her bosom.

Well…kind of.

After all, Queen Earnhilt had been the one to casually suggest killing Sylph and locking away every other pyradisté "for their own protection." Thana grimaced. Instead of staying and advocating for them, she'd taken Sylph and ran.

And the other pyradistés didn't know that Sylph was in danger. If Earnhilt had begun her mass incarceration, the academy might think Thana was either in on the plan or had run to save herself without warning anyone.

After she'd *robbed* the head of the academy, no less.

She groaned, wondering what other shambles she'd left in her wake.

But, a little voice reminded her, the head of the academy hadn't told her about this new crystal, so he'd stopped trusting her long before she'd complicated everything. And then when she'd pilfered his pyramids, he'd made up his mind to have her followed, captured, maybe even killed.

He probably thought she was out here recruiting nobles for the queen's anti-pyradisté cause or was arresting the pyradistés spread throughout the countryside, like Timmony.

Or it was simpler than that. The head had found out she'd heard about the new crystal, feared she would tell the queen, and set these pyradistés on her trail. Maybe he'd told them she was a traitor to get them to go, or they'd come to that conclusion themselves.

Thana sighed and rubbed her temples. What a mess. One she wasn't going to figure out tonight.

With a tired groan, she stood and went back into the stable. Sylph still sat against the wall, and her eyes opened as Thana entered. In the faint light, her light green eyes seemed almost colorless. A tiny smile seemed to ghost across her lips, but that could have been the way the candlelight flickered across her face. She lay down on the pallet, shifting so there was room for two.

Thana blew out the candle and lay beside her, putting her captured pyramids close to hand. Memories of the kiss danced across her thoughts as they lay shoulder to shoulder. She began to drift, smiling wryly at the idea that they were sharing a bed after all, but it was nothing like she'd imagined.

❖

Sylph's eyes drifted open, and confusion reigned.

The ceiling above her was bare wood, and she smelled straw and horses. The air felt heavy, each muted gust carrying the scent of smoke and char.

And someone was lying beside her.

Of all the times she'd slept outdoors with her father's retinue, no one had ever slept beside her in her enormous tent. But then, she'd never slept on a bed of straw, either.

If one had to sleep on chaff, she supposed it was nice to have company.

As she recognized Thana, her recent memories rushed back. It had been a night of firsts, including a first kiss that still made the forbidden stir inside her, made her imagine what would have happened if the manor hadn't been attacked.

If she hadn't killed someone.

Another first.

Also initiated by Thana.

Sylph slipped out from underneath the thin blanket. Thana's eyes stayed shut, her black lashes standing out starkly against her pale cheeks. She looked so peaceful as her chest rose and fell rhythmically. Her lips were a very pale pink, and Sylph thought again about what it had been like to kiss her. For a moment, she wanted to repeat the experience, but the death seemed to stand between them.

When Sylph stepped from the small room into the stable proper, soft light greeted her, and the horses whickered. She set about feeding them, a task she'd often undertaken at home. She wondered where the pasture was, if the grooms just let them mill about the yard under watch or if they grazed nearby. The manor no doubt had fields, probably a village, but she didn't know where it would be, so she left all of them in their stalls.

Even with all her musing and with all the busy work for her hands, the deaths kept a steady drumbeat in her mind. It had felt so good to let go. And that seemed different than self-defense, different from a desire to protect Thana or the countess and her family. It felt like…murder.

Thana's idea.

With a snarl, Sylph turned from the horses and stomped outside. The air was still smoky, and no one in the manor stirred, though she noticed that her things had been piled just outside the door. That was for the best.

What would Countess Carisse do with the blasted and burned trees? Pull them down? Even if she replanted, she wouldn't erase last night for many years to come. And new plant life couldn't replace human ones.

She told herself she was being maudlin, not fair to herself or Thana. She would have lost control eventually. She could still recall the feel of that siren pyramid; it had felt like trying not to touch a thing that already lived inside her. If its wielder had come any closer, she would have slipped anyway, would have killed Thana and herself and maybe destroyed the manor and those within. Even with her guilt, she couldn't believe that outcome would have been better than this.

Would Thana feel guilty, too? Or would her conscience be clear when this destruction could lie at Sylph's feet? Thana had shown many kindnesses, but doubt still lingered. Sylph didn't know people, had always had a hard time reading them ever since her maid had betrayed her when she was little. Was everyone capable of that kind of turnaround? Even Thana had a hidden self, keeping passion behind anger.

Oh, that kiss.

Sylph turned her face up, trying to find cleaner air, and breathed deeply. That kiss seemed almost worth the guilt that followed.

A soft sound made her turn. Thana stood in the stable doorway, blinking wearily. When their eyes met, Thana smiled, but Sylph saw an edge there, some twist that spoke of an emotion she couldn't read.

Anger? Embarrassment? Disgust? Doubt? Nothing positive could cause a smile to slip.

Sylph turned away, anger burning her chest. She had not asked to be so far out of her depth, nor for any of this. Thana began speaking, planning, clearing her throat a lot and talking as if nothing had happened, but her voice had a strained quality that set Sylph's nerves on end. Thana chattered as she rummaged through the luggage. She nattered as she put things in the stable, and she moaned about the countess's hospitality until Sylph wanted to put her hands over her ears. It all sounded so false. How in the spirit's names were they supposed to keep going like this?

"I mean, they haven't even left anything to eat," Thana said before looking in another bag. "Oh, here's some bread. I guess they did leave something, but how are we supposed to get the horses ready?"

"Why don't you stop talking and figure it out?" Sylph snapped. It felt as if her father spoke through her, and the surprise on Thana's face shamed her, but her father got things done. No matter what, he kept moving forward, even if on the wrong course, and that was what Sylph needed right now. She needed to get out of this place of death, and she needed Thana to come with her.

So...

Sylph grabbed a bridle from the wall and stopped in front of her horse. "Pay attention."

The words or the tone seemed to spark something in Thana, and she obeyed. Sylph took her brusquely through the process, then had her repeat it on the other mount, correcting her quietly but firmly when she erred.

"Get the bags," Sylph said when they finished with the saddles.

Thana's mouth dropped open. "Why don't you get them?"

Sylph mimicked one of her father's epic sighs. "If you require help, all you need do is ask."

"I...you..." Face flushed, she marched to the luggage and picked some up, stomping past Sylph to load the saddlebags.

"That's the way," Sylph said, guessing the condescension in her voice would only make Thana move faster. "Softly now," she said as she packed. "You don't want to pull the saddle out of place or cause the horse to stumble onto your foot."

"I hope it steps on yours," Thana said in what she probably thought was a mumble.

"What was that?"

Thana's ears went red. "Nothing."

Sylph nodded, and when they set out, she took the lead, all her other emotions buried under the satisfaction that everyone and everything was in its place.

Thana ground her teeth. Sylph had been leading them for an hour, and she'd been mercifully quiet after her behavior that morning. Thana was torn between wanting to tell her off and wanting to plead that they go back to the closeness of the night before.

But they'd been in danger, even during the kiss, even before that, in the bedroom. No doubt that had been the source of their feelings. Peril and forced proximity had spawned something they'd mistaken for actual passion.

She rolled her eyes, much as she would have done if Gunnar had used those words to excuse away his feelings. She still wanted to kiss Sylph as much as she wanted to shake her. Her hesitance sprang from the idea that Sylph was back to denying that she felt anything. The thought of being the only one who wanted a relationship was too humiliating to live with.

So she would be silent.

And seethe.

At least being angry distracted her from the guilt of telling Sylph to use her power to kill someone. Maybe that same guilt motivated Sylph's lady-of-the-manor routine. She hadn't wanted to hurt anyone, and Thana had made her. Sort of. And when it came down to facts, Sylph was a lady, would one day be a duchess, and she owned much more than a manor. Thana had no place in that life.

After another clench of her jaw, Thana made herself focus. She was lucky Sylph was as good at geography as she was at recognizing nobles because Thana had no idea where they were. Thana had told her that they should go north of Marienne, to the road Sylph had taken when traveling from her home to the city. It was the closest road to the outer wall of the palace, where the massive gardens lay and where she'd experienced the pull of these new pyramids. Thana didn't quite know what she expected to find there, but it was a place to start. From there, they could visit the other sites of pyradisté attacks or mishaps. Maybe they could piece together a likely location for the source of this new crystal, and then...

Thana bit her lip. She didn't know what then. Deduce how it was different from regular crystal? Academically, she was curious, but did it matter? Perhaps she could convince those mining it to stop. If she couldn't, she supposed she'd have to ride back and tell the queen.

Which would make her a traitor in the eyes of most pyradistés. The Umbriels controlled magic by controlling the flow of crystal from the mines north of Allusia. Headmaster Cyrus clearly hoped this new crystal could put some of the power back in his hands.

Maybe he'd even start the civil war back up again.

Thana leaned her head back, stretching her neck. She missed the moments in this adventure when her biggest problem was whether to kiss Sylph or not.

It was nearing midday when they finally reached the road that led from Marienne to Farraday's northern territory. Sylph remained chilly and silent. Thana went back and forth between wanting to soothe her and wanting to throw something at her. From the road, she could just see the large wall surrounding the palace grounds and thanked the spirits that they would now be forced to speak.

"Can you feel the pyramids in the wall from here?" she asked, hearing the archness in her tone but unable to do anything about it.

Sylph narrowed her eyes and shook her head. She dismounted and took a few steps toward the wall, letting the reins of her horse slip through her fingers.

Muttering, Thana dismounted, too, and grabbed the reins of both animals. She wanted to snap that she wasn't m'lady's groom but hesitated. If Sylph wanted to piss her off, she wasn't going to give her the pleasure.

Except she couldn't hide her irritation. She never could. "Nothing?"

"No." Sylph sighed. "I might not even be able to feel a special pyramid at this distance." She turned, frowning. "And this is only the outer wall. If someone had been bringing the new crystal down this road, I wouldn't have felt it from inside the inner wall, in the garden proper." She shook her head and stared into the middle distance. "Unless they were carrying it in the wall's shadow, but why would they do that when they wanted to hide from the Umbriels?"

"Even if they wanted to avoid the road," Thana said, "they wouldn't travel closer to the palace."

Sylph strode back, hand out for her reins. Thana practically threw them at her. She only turned her chin up farther. Fantastic. If it rained, she might drown.

When Sylph remounted, Thana opened her mouth to ask where she was going, but Sylph heeled her horse toward the wall, and Thana had to hurry to catch up. Sylph pulled up so quickly, Thana nearly ran into her, horse shying.

"What are you—"

Sylph lifted a hand for silence and dismounted again.

Gritting her teeth, Thana followed. "Listen—" When Sylph kneeled in the dirt, Thana stuttered and finished with, "What in the spirits' names are you doing?"

"No one's been through here recently," Sylph said, studying the ground. She stood and brushed off her hands. "And I can feel the pyramids from this distance."

"How would you know if anyone had been through here?" Thana asked, not bothering to hide her ire.

"Hunting is a noble's pastime," Sylph said loftily. "I'm a fairly proficient tracker."

"And here I thought hunting was mostly about having enough to eat."

"Only for peasants."

Thana felt her cheeks catch fire. "I thought we were past this nonsense, yet here we are again. What in the spirits' names is wrong with you?"

Sylph was the picture of pretty confusion, eyes wide. "What do you mean?"

"You know exactly what I mean. This nobles and peasants shit. You don't talk to me all day except to say nonsense like that?"

Her confusion remained, but Thana couldn't believe it was genuine. "What is it that we're supposed to be past?" Sylph asked. "There are nobles, and there are peasants, and we are part of those respective classes. Why does that make you so angry?"

Thana clenched her teeth and stepped forward, determined to be heard. "If we're so far apart and will always remain so, why did you kiss me back last night?"

Sylph swallowed, and her gaze flicked to Thana's lips. "I... wasn't thinking at the time."

"How about now?" Thana took her face in hand and kissed her again, swallowing her gasp.

CHAPTER THIRTEEN

As before, when Sylph's lips met Thana's, her mind became quiet. Only this time, it wasn't to avert some great catastrophe. Class and status and worries fled. Anger and fear and frustration mutated into hunger, and she put her arms around Thana and drew her closer.

Thana's hands went from her face to tangle in her hair. A thousand options flashed through Sylph's mind as Thana's soft body molded to hers, but her hands seemed to wander without her permission. She caressed Thana's back, her hips, giving her buttocks a firm squeeze.

Thana moaned, and when her touch skimmed over the curve of Sylph's breast, her legs threatened to buckle. She tried to stay standing, but Thana half collapsed with her, both kneeling before lying down, and Sylph clung to every sensation rocketing through her body.

Thana's lips delighted her neck, her ears. When Sylph found the gap between Thana's shirt and trousers, she seized the opportunity to explore the bare skin until Thana panted in her ear and began a journey of her own, finding the most wonderful places to linger.

Thana mumbled something, a question.

"Yes," Sylph said. Whatever it was, she wanted it. Thana's ear came near her mouth, and she traced it with her tongue.

"Ah," Thana said with a gasp. "Wait, wait."

The last thing Sylph wanted to do was stop, but she pulled back, forcing her hands to still as Thana pulled her shirt down between them. "What?"

Thana swallowed and breathed hard. Her eyes seemed like pools of ink, and her hair spread over the grass like a raven's wing.

"My raven," Sylph asked, "what's wrong?"

Thana looked at her curiously, amusedly, before she sat up, taking Sylph with her. "Someone's coming." She squinted into the distance toward some moving shapes.

Right, other people existed. Sylph stood and straightened her clothing. Whoever it was couldn't find her rolling around in the grass like a—

Like a peasant. With a peasant. Shame flooded her. She tried to argue against those thoughts, but they were as much a part of her as any other. She gritted her teeth and helped Thana up. There, she told herself, as if helping Thana to her feet would dismiss all she knew about the circumstances that separated them.

"Come on," Thana said, plucking her sleeve. She grinned as she led them back to the horses. "I know you're still reeling from those kisses, but we should get under cover."

"Yes," Sylph said, returning her smile, happy to let her think that was the reason for her hesitation, not wanting to ruin the moment by speaking the truth again, even if it had been truth that made Thana kiss her in the first place.

Part of Thana wanted to ask herself what in the spirits' names she was playing at. She'd been pissed that Sylph said they were noble and peasant, but that didn't mean it was wrong. All the kisses in the world would not erase it.

And none of it mattered right now, she told her busy brain. She wouldn't have stopped what had been shaping up to be an epic session of lovemaking just to philosophize. Someone was coming this way, and there was a chance that it was someone they didn't want to meet.

Sylph's dazed demeanor made Thana preen a little. It was good to know that a long stint of celibacy hadn't robbed her of her skill. Though from what she'd gleaned, Sylph didn't have much experience for comparison.

She told her mind to shut up again.

The trees on the opposite side of the road had been cut far back, a deterrent for brigands and footpads. Thana was certain that the other travelers saw their dash for cover, but there was nothing for it.

It was slower-going under the trees, but they continued north while watching the road. When the other travelers didn't pass, Thana looked back. If they'd entered the forest in pursuit, they weren't yet close enough to see.

"What do we do?" Sylph asked.

"I don't know." Her plan had been to follow the tales of rogue pyradistés until she found the source of the crystal, but it was clear they couldn't do so in a day. And how could they rest when every other sign of life had them fleeing?

"They must have turned a different way or stopped," Sylph said.

"Maybe." Thana pulled to a stop, giving in to aggravation. "I don't know what to do," she muttered. She wanted to ask if they could just go back to kissing but didn't have the confidence.

Sylph gave her a sympathetic look that became a blush, and Thana wondered if they were of the same mind, kissing-wise. She grinned.

"All we can do is keep going," Sylph said.

True. If the travelers had pursued them into the forest, they would be slowed by the trees, too, and could be outpaced.

"Can you feel any pyramids?" Thana asked. She brought the detector out but sensed nothing. Then again, she'd never been a skilled hand with it. Her inadequacy struck again.

"No," Sylph said faintly. Then, "Wait."

It was good to know that even her skill had limits. Thana handed the detector over. "This should help."

Sylph stared at it for a moment before she turned away. "No, thank you." Her cheeks were crimson, but by her arch tone, Thana knew it wasn't from passion.

"I know you're worried about setting them off—"

"About being *forced* to do so."

Thana took a deep breath, now guilty as well as irritated. "I didn't intend to make you feel forced. They were trying to..." She didn't know exactly what they'd intended. Kill or capture, she was sure of that. Or had *she* been the only one at risk? With the comment about the queen, the enemy pyradistés might have only been after Thana. At the time, it hadn't seemed that way. She'd felt like they'd been willing to hurt everyone to get at her.

Before she could even begin to explain or apologize, Sylph gave another haughty sniff, her chin inching up, and Thana's stomach dropped. *Lady* Sylph was about to put in another appearance.

"I don't need the detection pyramid because I shall never need it. It's enough to know I can feel pyramids from a distance. I simply need more practice ignoring them."

Thana's first instinct was to yell, an urge she'd been repressing for hours. Her second was to return to the aggravated, ashamed state she'd been stewing in all day. But they'd connected, both emotionally and physically, and a new emotion rose in her now, a stubborn anger that refused to be hidden.

"After all that's happened," she said, forcing herself not to yell, "do you really believe you can ignore your gift? There is another fight going on around us, some conflict between pyradistés and the Umbriels, and we can't avoid it forever." She lifted her arms, then dropped them and shook her head. "Well, I'm the only one who's truly caught. If you leave me now, you might be spared until the queen remembers you. Or if Headmaster Cyrus gets hold of you, spirits know what he'll force you to do." A wave of sadness washed over her, and she turned away, not willing to show how vulnerable this irritating woman made her. "And since you haven't left me yet, I thought you'd realized all of that." Cursed tears pricked her eyes, and she blinked them back. Had she been this soppy before their kissing session?

Sylph didn't respond, and the seconds drifted by, marked only by the sound of hooves through the foliage. Thana couldn't look at her, not knowing which expression she might see. She didn't know what would be worse, that she'd affected Lady Sylph or that she hadn't.

As Thana nudged her horse forward, the chance to speak passed along with her. Sylph couldn't help feeling grateful for that even as she berated herself for not saying what she was feeling.

As if she could. What would Thana say if Sylph admitted that being together filled her insides with embers? That being with Thana was like discovering a new world, one she'd been certain existed only in myth? When Thana had suggested that Sylph leave her, it had felt like a blow. How could she abandon this marvelous new world just as she clapped eyes on it?

And why had she said what she had, why draw a wall around herself again? Deep inside, she knew she could not be rid of her "gift" and return to her old life. But stubbornly, she wanted to find a way to ignore it, and she and Thana could be...

Mistress and servant?

Employer and pyradisté?

Noble and shabby little secret?

Sylph would never let her raven be seen that way.

And she should say so. But she was still her father's daughter and would always be. When they weren't writhing on top of each other, there would always be...considerations.

Still, she couldn't just quit this field without a word. Thana deserved more. She took a breath, paused, then took another as the words deserted her. She would not say, "thank you," again, curse it.

"Thana..." When she felt the flutter of a pyramid on the edge of her mind, she rejoiced even as she named herself a coward.

Thana turned in her saddle, her hopefulness prompting heartache.

"Someone behind us is carrying a pyramid," Sylph said. "I just felt it. If you like...I'll use the detector. I can't tell which kind it is yet."

"No need," Thana said softly, her expression saying she recognized the gesture, at least, but she probably wasn't ready to forgive. "If it's not pulling at you, it's not one of the new ones we're really worried about." She gripped her pyramid, and her eyes took on a vacant cast. "There are a few that...ow!" She rocked in her saddle as if struck, and her pyramid went dark.

Sylph reached to take her reins as she put a hand to her head and winced. "What is it?"

"Spirits-cursed bastards canceled my pyramid," she said with a growl. "Hurts like a dozen wasp stings." She flinched. "I probably made it easy for them somehow." She blushed, the pretty effect ruined by the shame in her eyes.

A peculiar feeling raced through Sylph's veins, similar to what she'd felt for the courtiers who'd sought to snub Thana, but this was so much more. No one made her raven feel less than she was.

She turned her focus behind again, watching that way as if she could see through the trees. Canceled, was it? She pictured a pyramid with a blanket pulled over the top, but that garnered her nothing. "What does it feel like?"

"A cancelation pyramid? I don't have one. Why?"

"I'll use theirs against them."

"From a distance?" She laughed. "You can't possibly..." After clearing her throat, she spoke again, awe in her voice. "Let's see if you can. It shows all surrounding pyramids as bright lights, and you have the power to snuff them like candles. It feels...dark, consuming."

It was enough. Sylph searched through the pyramids with nothing but her mind. Fire, detection, light, all these she ignored until she sensed one that seemed like a blank spot among the others, an absence of pyramids cast in pyramid shape. She sensed it reaching toward her and Thana like the tentacles of some beast, but as she touched them, they crumpled like paper. Following them was as easy as breathing, and there she was, inside the pyramid that cast them.

One by one, she snuffed the surrounding pyramids as easily as if she threw them to the ground. Then she turned this pyramid killer in on itself, shutting it off like a closing door as she withdrew.

Someone howled among the trees, someone closer than expected.

Thana held her darkened pyramid, her eyes wide. "Did you... you did, didn't you? You're like...like pyramid magic brought to life." She leaned forward as if to stress her words. "No matter what happens, Sylph, you can't repress a gift like yours. It would be like destroying art, silencing music, taking every actor who ever walked a stage and—"

Sylph held up a hand, not knowing whether to be flattered or terrified by such a speech. "We should be going, should we not? They sound close and are no doubt angry."

Indeed, the pounding of hoofbeats thundered behind them. Thana turned her horse, and Sylph put heels to her mount, and they created their own echoes in the trees.

Fleeing for their lives had one point in its favor: Thana didn't have time to think about her spirits-cursed feelings.

She gripped the reins until her hands felt numb. With every shuddering step, she felt as if she might be jolted from the saddle. Sylph pulled up beside her as if having no trouble keeping her seat, but as she'd said, nobles often hunted, so she was probably as accomplished at riding as she was at many things that didn't matter.

Until someone chased them through the woods.

Sylph glanced back, her hair streaming like a cape. Her eyes went wide, and she looked to Thana as if for help. Thana thought that if she glanced back, she'd lose her grip for sure, or her horse would run into a tree.

As if she was steering now.

She risked a look and spied a halo of golden hair with a tinge of red that framed a strong, handsome face. Only one person looked that good while riding breakneck through a forest.

Gunnar.

Thana slowed her horse before realizing he might not have come as a friend. But even with all that had happened, she had to give him the benefit of the doubt.

"Thana?" He pulled up his own steed, and the Order of Vestra followed suit, including a face Thana hadn't seen before, one that glowered at her. The stranger had a blond ponytail lying over one shoulder, wore a satchel around her skinny frame—a pyradisté, then—and she seemed far from happy.

"What are you doing here?" Gunnar and Thana asked at the same time. Both scowled before saying, "No, what are *you* doing here?"

On Gunnar's left, Dina laughed. As muscled as someone from a strength chapterhouse, she wore the white of a love and beauty monk. With a grin on her exquisite face, she said, "Sounds like you two never parted." When Gunnar glared at her, Thana resisted the urge to do the same, not wanting to invite further comparison.

"Did you come out here after me?" Thana asked. "I won't help you or your mother lock pyradistés up or kill them."

"You didn't give me a chance to convince her to do otherwise."

"Have you done so now?" He blinked before opening his mouth. She wasn't interested in hearing excuses. "Why did you cancel my pyramid?" she asked.

"You canceled all of mine," the pyradisté said with a snarl. "How in the world did you do that?"

Gunnar held up a hand. "It's gotten worse in Marienne, Than. More accidents and some attacks that don't seem like accidents at all. We've been chasing a pack of rogue pyradistés and thought you might be them."

"Before we realized it was you," Dina said. "Because we wouldn't attack you." The mercenary twins, Ivar and Illis, nodded with her.

Thana felt tears prick her eyes. She hadn't let herself think of what the consequences of her actions might be as far as her comrades were concerned. They didn't want to hurt her, and she almost couldn't breathe for relief and gratitude.

Gunnar seemed as if he might have more angry words, but after a glance at Sylph, he sighed and dismounted. "Let's set up camp. Seems we have a lot to talk about."

Thana looked at Sylph, who had her placid noble mask firmly in place. Thana wondered how much Gunnar would share with her and how Sylph would react. Perhaps knowing her prince consorted with peasants and regularly fought by their side would loosen her up a little.

There was one way to find out. She and Sylph dismounted, but Gunnar nodded toward the trees, then headed that way as the Order began setting camp.

Thana gave Sylph a small signal to stay put before following Gunnar. He stopped near an elm, and she said, "We haven't seen any pyradistés today, but a group attacked us last night, claiming that the queen couldn't protect me anymore."

His mouth closed, and he frowned hard. "I…wasn't expecting to hear that."

"I just wanted you to know that whoever is making the purposeful attacks you mentioned seems to be after me, too." She sighed. "Unless we have two enemies."

His smile was lopsided. "Ever the optimist. I never thought of you as my enemy, Than. I hope you know that."

She felt those cursed tears again. "Not even when I abandoned you to help someone I'd just met?"

"Oh, for spirits' sake." He pulled her into a rough hug. "Yes, I was angry. I understood, but I was mad, just like you were. But now we're both here. Let's work together. And I promise not to kill your lady if you promise not to overthrow my mother."

She laughed into his shoulder. "Deal."

"So have you kissed her, yet?"

"Spirits above," she said as he pulled away. "Is your mind ever truly out of your trousers?"

"We're talking about your trousers, not mine, and that blush tells me there are stories to be told."

She rolled her eyes. "Can we talk about the kingdom's problems first?"

"I can wait," he said, glancing at where Sylph stood. "Can you?"

She didn't answer, knowing he could help with her Sylph problems but unwilling to bring them up when the kingdom might be at stake. "Later."

"I will hold you to that, and I won't even try to seduce her, on my honor."

She wanted to laugh in his face and tell him to try his luck, but even the thought was too much, and when he grinned, she knew she was being baited. "Shut up, Gun."

Sylph didn't know where to look, let alone what to do. Prince Gunnar had arrived and didn't seem to be acting like his normal, carefree self. He hadn't attempted to flirt with her at all. Instead, he'd taken Thana aside to have a quiet conversation while his servants set up camp.

Except they didn't act like servants. Retainers, perhaps, or bodyguards. But none bowed to her. They simply gave her curious looks. Perhaps they didn't recognize her.

Preposterous.

They were all armed, even the beauty monk, and all seemed as disinclined to speak to her as she was to them. At least that was a positive.

But one of the dark-haired men stepped toward her, and she resisted the urge to back away. Like the other man, he wore a leather coat sewn with metal disks and had a general appearance of unkemptness. The two looked nearly identical, clearly brothers, except this one's cheeks bore pockmarks under his startling green eyes.

"Are you thirsty, Miss…" He raised his eyebrows.

Miss? She nearly sputtered.

His smile turned a little hesitant. "My name is Ivar. That's my brother Illis." The other nodded from where he was putting up a tent. "And our compatriot Dina." The monk gave a little wave. "And our new friend, Calla." He pointed to the pyradisté, who snorted, still glaring at Thana and Prince Gunnar. No doubt she thought Thana had disabled her pyramids. For once, Sylph had a strong desire to admit that it had been her. It seemed only fair that she finally be the one to instill fear in someone else.

But she didn't need magic to do that. She'd been born into power. She began to admit her title but hesitated, all at sea when it came to who was allowed to know what amongst the prince's peasant companions.

"Sylph," she said. Someone had once mentioned that the name had grown in popularity since her birth. Naming a child after the nobility supposedly brought luck.

Ivar's smile widened, and he held out a water skin. "Good to meet you, Miss Sylph."

She took a small sip. "And you, Ivar. Tell me, how do you come to ride with the prince?"

"Companions of old," he said.

He wasn't a noble, and she didn't know any courtiers who wore armor. Some of the queen's cronies did, those who'd fought beside her during the Troubles, but he seemed too young for that. Perhaps all these people knew the Umbriels through Thana and her position as royal pyradisté. But why would the prince bother with them?

And why hadn't they asked why she was riding with Thana?

Because they already knew. They were agents of the queen who wished her dead, and she'd been a fool.

Sylph struggled to keep her face neutral as her heart thundered. Ivar hadn't needed to ask her name, but it had put her off-guard enough to drink the water. She handed the skin back woodenly.

His eyes seemed to glitter as he took it, and a tinny sound filled her ears. Any moment, the forest would spin as darkness descended, and she hadn't even had a chance to tell Thana that—

Ivar took a long pull from the skin, and sound returned to normal, the only upsetting thing being that he hadn't wiped the spout first.

"Sylph?" Thana asked as she rejoined them. "Are you all right?"

"Perfectly," she managed.

"Good. Come on. Let's all sit down together. We've got some information to share."

Sylph wanted to ask, "With people who want to kill me?" But she wasn't dead yet. And she wasn't poisoned. She took a deep breath. There was still time for answers.

What a quandary life had become.

Frightening. Invigorating.

She'd never equated the two before.

CHAPTER FOURTEEN

Prince Gunnar stared at Sylph from across the campfire, but he might as well have been someone she'd never met. His face seemed open and yet more closed than she'd ever seen. His real self—if that was indeed what this was—seemed serious and secretive, his eyes probing and unnerving, a quality she'd never associated with the greatest gadabout in the land.

"You may have heard of the Order of Vestra?" he asked.

"It's a child's tale," she said. "The secret protectors of the crown, bogeymen for traitors." She shrugged. "Or children who won't eat their greens, though why such creatures are named after an ancient Farradain noble, I've never been able to guess." She thought it might be another way of maintaining noble control, but she wasn't about to say so in this crowd.

"We're very real," he said.

"We?" She looked to his comrades as pieces fell into place. Who would want to push the image of control more than the highest nobles in the land?

"It's not bandied about," he said with a trace of his usual drawl. "Secret order and all that. I'm glad it's been relegated to a threat for misbehaving kiddies. Maybe one day, it will pass out of public remembrance altogether."

"And you act as agents for the crown? Why not leave that to the royal guards?" Anxiety fluttered in her chest at her own daring. In the past, she would have remained quiet in front of the prince, put on a show of meekness, but the fact that he had a secret identity made her want to throw off her old life, too. She could show that she was clever, that she pondered the world at times.

That she was so much more than what her father had made her.

And if she couldn't express her feelings to Thana, she could at least impress her. Thana was watching her proudly already. Something in her soared.

"Too conspicuous," he said. "The people we chase are normally in the shadows, and they rarely expect the prince to be after them."

She nodded. That explained why he recruited help outside the nobility, like Thana who—as monarch's pyradisté—was already privy to many royal secrets. None of which Sylph had heard until now. Anxiety gripped her. Steady, she reminded herself. She had to keep her wits. "And you have decided I am trustworthy because Thana has found me worthy of aid?"

"No, my lady. It's because you are a noble pyradisté and have as much to lose as any of us."

Her chest froze. So he knew. And yet he sat so casually, as if she wasn't an abomination. None of his cronies batted an eye. They all knew. The queen must have guessed after she and Thana had fled. How far had the knowledge reached? Her peers? Her father?

"Breathe," Thana said softly. Her touch on Sylph's arm was like a cool cloth to a fevered brow. "Watch me, Sylph. One, two, three."

They breathed together for a few moments, and Sylph forced her facial muscles to relax, relax, relax, and admit nothing.

Prince Gunnar sighed. "It really got you in a tizzy, didn't it? I almost don't want to tell you the rest." After scrubbing one hand through his hair, he said, "You know of the pyradisté rebellion in the past?"

She managed a nod. "Thana told me. The pyradistés tried to take control of the kingdom."

"Well, what's not commonly known, not even by Thana, is that those pyradistés were led by the king's cousin."

Everything inside her balked. "There are no noble pyradistés." She felt a fool the moment she said it, living proof that she was.

"There were many," he said. "After the uprising, the noble families killed or banished their pyradistés. Even now, in the oldest families, if they discover one in their midst, they quietly get rid of them."

Thana shot to her feet. "You can't be serious. Queen Earnhilt allows this?"

He flinched. "Well...she doesn't exactly investigate when it happens."

"Spirits above!" Thana paced, hands atop her head, face flushed. "It's murder."

"She can't control the nobles," Ivar said.

"Most of the stubborn mules wouldn't listen if she tried," Illis added.

"Begging your pardon, Lady," Dina said with a beatific smile.

"Not necessary," Sylph muttered out of habit. She could barely think through her own elation and fear. She wasn't alone, wasn't an abomination?

Except she'd been right to be afraid. If her father knew of such a grisly tradition, would he follow it? But most of her family's wealth and lands were newer, acquired long after the pyradisté rebellion. Perhaps they'd changed too much to remember such casual murder.

"We don't do it, Thana," Prince Gunnar said. "The Umbriels don't kill their pyradisté relations no matter how close to the throne they are."

"Where are these relations, then?" she asked with disbelief thick in her voice.

"And why target me if you don't kill your own?" Sylph asked, anger taking over. "Did the queen seek my death simply because I am not a member of her family?"

"You've already met one relation." Prince Gunnar motioned to Calla, who flipped her straight blond hair over her shoulder.

"Distant cousin," she said with a smile that was more a baring of teeth. "Trotted out when needed."

"And," Prince Gunnar said loudly over Thana's exclamation of disbelief. "My mother overreacted to you, my lady, because you lit the palace on fire, and she thought you part of the greater pyradisté problem."

Ah yes. That.

❖

Thana couldn't believe her ears. It didn't matter that the events Gunnar spoke of were over a hundred years in the past. She couldn't believe no one remembered.

But the victors had written the history, and they didn't want anyone to remember, and what the nobility did was so far outside of the normal person's sphere anyway…

"I can't," she said. "It's so hard to think of, let alone believe." But if he was telling the truth, the proof sat just across the fire. "Why me, Gun? If you already had a pyradisté you trusted, why am I the monarch's choice?"

He looked pained. "Because I wanted it to be you, Than."

Calla snorted and rolled her eyes. "They need to keep my lineage secret, remember?" And that clearly didn't sit well with her, but something in Gunnar's eyes said he wouldn't have had her anyway.

Thana's cheeks grew hot under the weight of his trust, his affection. "Thanks," she muttered. Before he could smile too widely, she added, "But how could you keep this huge secret from me? All the times I had to listen to garbage from the courtiers and nobles." She pointed to Sylph. "And all the fear she had to suffer."

"None of that would have changed if you'd known, except you would have been tempted to mock the courtiers with the information."

She ground her teeth. That was true. And the fact that she had to keep quiet would have eaten a hole through her stomach. But she couldn't shed her anger so easily. "Keeping the whole thing secret was a stupid solution."

"I agree." He smiled softly. "But the nobles and monarchy thought the lack of a possible noble leader would keep the pyradistés from revolting again."

"As if we'd need one," she said with a snort.

He gave her a flat look. "Whether they were right about that or whether it was lack of access to crystal that stopped the rebellion, the situation has changed."

"Because of the new crystal," she said, arching an eyebrow.

He sat back, hands pressed together. "And because the pyradistés of Marienne have another noble to guide them."

Thana's heart thundered. Sylph had gone white, her eyes huge. They said, "What?" and "Who?" at the same time.

He looked between them. "I'm hoping you can tell me."

"It isn't Sylph," Thana said, her ire rising again at the thought of Sylph being accused.

Gunnar looked at her as if she was an idiot. "I know that."

And there was that embarrassing flush again. "Sorry." But Sylph gave her an affectionate look that made the embarrassment worth it. Sylph had to be off-guard indeed for her mask to have slipped that much.

"Tell us about this crystal," Gunnar said.

Thana told the little she knew, happy to unburden herself. She related what had happened at the academy, that all the pyradistés seemed to know about and be excited by the crystal. She left out Sylph's desire to bring the building down and spoke about the attack at the manor. She downplayed Sylph's struggles there, too, and said that the attackers' pyramids had gone off and that she and Sylph had decided to trace the rumored pyradisté attacks in an effort to find the source of the new crystal.

"We think the early attacks and explosions could have been caused by pyradistés like Sylph, who are more sensitive to the crystal and had accidents when it came near them," Thana said.

Sylph had been sitting stiffly but quietly, and now she shook her head. "I'm not sensitive, Prince Gunnar," she said as she stared into flames that made strands of gold dance through her hair. "I'm inexorably pulled to it, captivated, imprisoned. It's terrifying and yet so beautiful to touch. I could tear the world apart with it, and that would feel...right." She finally looked up with tears in her eyes and an expression of horror that became a snarl. "The person who attacked us at the manor? I set off his pyramid made from this new crystal, and it blew up the others, and at the moment I did so, I'd never felt so free. No remorse, no thoughts for anyone's safety, not even my own. I was just so happy to merge with it and so relieved to stop resisting." Her voice had climbed until she was nearly shouting.

Thana couldn't move, caught by the raw emotion in Sylph's voice. Not even when they were kissing had she seemed so open.

"If there are others like me," she said quietly, "I pity them. And I hate those who would use this crystal after knowing what it does to us."

Gunnar stared for a few moments. "I am truly sorry, Lady Sylph, for what you've endured. Will you help us end this?"

"Yes," she said, almost hissing. "If the secret of noble pyradistés comes to light." She stood and marched into the darkness.

Thana held up a finger to Gunnar, indicating that he should give her a moment. She followed Sylph, who stood not far into the trees, her pale hair like a ghost among the black trunks. "Are you all right?" Thana asked. She snorted. "No, of course you're not."

"Why of course?" Sylph asked as she turned. "Do outpourings of emotion normally leave a person feeling as if they've run for miles? Because I've never had one before tonight."

"An...outpouring?" Thana asked, wondering if she'd heard right.

"Yes. My father would have frowned on it, and there was no one to talk to anyway." The firelight glinted in her teary eyes, and her tone seemed somewhere between heartbroken and disbelieving. "I feel as if I can barely breathe, Thana. The world is not what I thought it was."

Thana took her hands. "Isn't that a good thing? You can have everything you want. You can be a noble and a pyradisté. You can have friends. Love." Her breath caught. They weren't in love, but they could certainly fall.

"I wanted to ignore my power, if you'll recall."

"And now you don't have to."

Sylph made an inelegant snort. "Because the secret will be revealed? You think it that easy?"

Thana let go of her hands but resisted the urge to cross her arms. "Why not?"

"And if I don't wish to be a pyradisté?" Her voice was cold, pure noble.

Thana's mind raced even as anger overcame her pity. "Even though you know that nobles can be pyradistés, that it was possible all along, you'd still choose not to embrace it?" Her own spirit seemed to be straining from her chest, begging Sylph to let go just a little, to consider the possibilities now that her world was not what she thought.

"You sat beside me at that fire but didn't hear a word I said."

"I..." Thana shook her head. Perhaps they'd only ever misunderstood each other. "After we take care of this new crystal, after we...convince these rogues not to rebel, you want all to come to light, and you can be free." The convincing part sounded lame, but she would avoid bloodshed if she could.

"Free?" Sylph still sounded colder than a winter's morn. "And you've decided what that means for me?"

"It won't be easy, I know, but—"

"I will still be under the control of my father, and you would have these pyradistés order me about as well?"

"These pyradistés?" Thana asked, no longer fighting to keep her tone civil. "After the rebels are stopped, who are these pyradistés? Or do you mean me?"

"You'd have me be lost in a world that should not concern me, with continuing terrors that I want no part of."

"It doesn't have to be like that," Thana said through her teeth, but no amount of anger seemed to penetrate the chill.

"We will never understand each other," Sylph said, and she had the decency to sound a little sad. "Perhaps that is for the best."

"Don't do that. Don't turn all *noble* on me again."

Sylph drew herself up, and Thana knew what was coming, but there was no way to avoid it. "I know of no other way to be."

Thana thought about kissing her again, but she was tired. And at least Sylph hadn't called her a peasant again. "And you clearly don't care to learn." She turned back to the fire, not waiting to see if Sylph followed or stayed in the dark.

❖

In a way, Thana was right. Sylph could now have everything she wanted. If there were other noble pyradistés, her father couldn't disown her, and the queen had no reason to execute her.

Apart from the little fire incident.

But when this secret of noble pyradistés came out, she could find another teacher who'd give her what she wanted: a way to suppress her power. Then the queen wouldn't have to worry about her, and her father could pretend she was normal.

And Thana could go back to her life, too, and...

That thought hurt like angry bees swarming inside her chest. A new future might be possible, but it wasn't the one she wanted. Better if her power proved she wasn't a noble after all, just some cuckoo left in a duke's nest. She could learn how to be a peasant with her raven's help.

If she hadn't driven her away for good.

Sylph rubbed her aching shoulders. She still had her power and a queen who feared it, two problems that must be solved no matter what future she wanted. With a whispered curse, she kicked a tree. It remained unimpressed, and now her foot throbbed in time with her heart.

Just perfect.

She told herself to quit acting so childish, to stop thinking herself into corners. Taking her frustration out on Thana solved nothing. It didn't matter if she barely comprehended Thana's insane ideas. She should enjoy their time together and throw herself into solving the problems right in front of them. Right now, she had the opportunity to prove herself to the crown. Thana would have to help her suppress her power in front of Prince Gunnar. Then she could cease worrying about one possible future, the one that included her execution.

Sylph sighed. So far, she'd proven herself completely incapable of not worrying about that.

Unless she was in Thana's arms.

Which wasn't likely to happen again if the sorrow in Thana's voice was any indication.

Sylph rubbed her temples. She'd been such a fool, but she couldn't think of a way to apologize. She wondered if Thana wished for a magical way to simply end Sylph's nobility. She would never wish for the opposite and become noble herself. She clearly loathed everything about Sylph's class. When she bothered to care about such things at all.

How in the world had she learned how to do that?

Simply not caring was probably how she'd become friends with a prince. Sylph tried to feel the same, to be disinterested in her station and that of others. She imagined fraternizing with…people, as the prince did. They would call her by name alone. None of them would have titles, and she would learn about their lives, their families. And no one would care about anything except the safety and happiness of the group. It would feel partly like her bond with Thana and be friendship made outside of danger and secrets.

Her father would have no control over it.

The thoughts were pleasing even as they made her queasy. It seemed a step away from anarchy.

But at least it was some kind of step.

She walked stiffly back to the fire, tired of her busy head. The others quieted as she approached. Thana didn't look at her, and the prince's gaze held a hint of censure. She balked. He was one of the few above her, people who could name her guilty.

Without title, how would she know who could command her heart like that?

An easy question. Thana could do it just by being Thana. Friendship could do it, and romance had an even greater power.

"Everything all right?" Prince Gunnar asked.

"Yes," Sylph said, trying to let some emotion into her words, but it was difficult when it wasn't rage. She wanted to say she was sorry, anything to get Thana to look at her, but there were too many eyes. She had to put her mask back on, or she'd fall to pieces.

And while wearing it, a different solution presented itself, one for the present and the future. As much as it hurt, driving Thana away would solve many problems. After all, Sylph would be a duchess one day, and she wouldn't be as free to have friends or lovers as a prince was.

Or a peasant.

And if a wound could heal, so could a heart. "Tell me of your suspects for this pyradisté noble."

His nod was slow, his look still a bit accusatory, but he began.

Thana barely listened as Sylph and Gunnar discussed Lord Whosits and Countess Whatsits and the Earl of Who-Gives-a-Shit. The very last thing she wanted to talk about was more stuck-up nobles, many of whom had dismissed her as trash twice over, once for her birth and again for her magic. And some of the bastards had known all along that a noble could have magic, too.

She cursed all of them with never-ending boils.

At the moment, she wanted to include Sylph in there, too. Gunnar and Queen Earnhilt barely escaped. All of them were too much trouble, too set in their ways. Too shortsighted and stupid and beautiful with soft lips and great skin.

Spirits above.

Thana's dumb feelings wouldn't just die, even after Sylph had made it clear that she would not bend, even a little. In the midst of danger or lovemaking, she could change her tune, but once her head cleared, she sang the same song. She would never truly embrace her so-called peasant magic or the peasant who wielded it.

Clearly, it would take a lot of work before Thana could finally say good riddance. Work she did not need to be focusing on in the moment. "How did this mysterious pyradisté noble keep themselves secret for so long?" she asked, interrupting.

Gunnar blinked before he shrugged. "No idea. We're operating on intelligence that Calla gathered."

Calla glared, which seemed the only expression she was capable of. "I heard that Headmaster Cyrus is working with a noble who's ready to lead a rebellion now that we...they...have access to a new source of crystal."

Well, that slip of the tongue wasn't worrying at all. "And you believe this, why?"

Her scowl built until she looked as if she'd eaten an entire lemon. "Because my source had no reason to lie, and he told other pyradistés the same at the time."

"But it could simply be a rumor?" Sylph said with a hollow quality to her voice. "A story made up to give the rebels someone to believe in?"

Thana snorted. Most of the pyradistés she knew would rather not have a noble in charge. "Gun, a word?" She stepped away from the fire without waiting.

"If everyone gets a private convo in the forest, when's our turn?" Dina called, and the brothers laughed, though it didn't seem to have much humor in it.

"Who is this Calla person?" Thana asked when they were out of earshot. "How come I've never even heard of her?"

"I told you. She's a cousin."

One who had led the Order out here on no one's word but her own. Thana's insides went cold as the weight of that came home. She'd been too wrapped up in her conflict with Sylph to keep her guard up.

Which made more sense: that Calla was an Umbriel cousin who was also a pyradisté, and Thana had never met her; or that Calla was a rogue pyradisté who had captured the Order and used a mind pyramid to control them?

And now that same group of pyradistés was attempting to take Thana and Sylph without a fuss because a mind pyramid wouldn't work on them.

"What are you thinking?" Gunnar asked. "That Calla's a traitor?" Skepticism dripped from his voice. He wouldn't know he was being controlled. The trick with mind pyramids was to only change little things, nothing fundamental. The addition of a cousin who could be trusted wouldn't take much. And he would have been told to defend Calla, too, if Thana knocked her teeth in.

She cursed the fact that she had no mind pyramid to check whether it was true. At least it was a problem she could do something about, even if she didn't know what. Whatever she did, she couldn't tell Gunnar and couldn't let Calla know and give her time to act.

"You know me," she said, hoping she sounded natural. "Suspicious of everyone."

He rolled his eyes, and she tried to think fast. Calla now knew all about Sylph, but Sylph had destroyed her pyramids, so she couldn't attack them. No wonder she was so grouchy. And no simple mind pyramid would be able to convince Gunnar and the Order to kill Thana. That much tampering would show.

"Fine," Gunnar said. "Feel free to keep an eye on her. Is that all you hauled me away for, or are you taking me up on my romantic advice?"

Spirits above, he sounded just like himself. Was he really under hypnosis? She couldn't just sit around waiting to find out. "Yes," she said, buying time but not listening as he began speaking of seduction. Maybe she and Sylph could find a way to immobilize the Order before Calla's comrades arrived or whatever her plan was.

"Got it?" Gunnar asked.

"Yep."

"Okay, now you also have to remember…"

She needed to get Sylph alone again. Wait until everyone went to sleep? That might be too late.

"It all depends on how long you want the, um, session to last."
By his lascivious wink, he wasn't talking about a session of the
nobles' council.

"Right," she said, telling herself to remind him later that she
didn't need actual sex instructions.

"But that was just my experience," he said. "You might want to
be more flexible."

Spirits, she did not want to know what kind of flexibility he
meant. "I've got it."

"Okay," he said with a chuckle, holding up his hands. He pointed
toward the fire before leaning in. "Are you going to try it on tonight
after the lights are out?"

She was about to snap that they were in the middle of a crisis, but
his suggestion was one way to be alone. "Yep, right now."

He leaned back, eyes wide. "Now? Than, we haven't finished
discussing—"

"Nope, sorry, right now. Loins afire and all that." She nearly
raced back, snatching up a candle Illis was using to dig around in his
tent.

"Hey," he said, but she paid him no mind.

"Sorry, everyone," she said. "Time to be alone. Romance and
such." She laughed, knowing she sounded awkward, her hatred of
lying mixing with her sense of impending doom. Maybe they'd think
it was passion.

Sylph gaped as Thana grabbed her arm and forced her into a
stumble toward another tent. "What—"

"Just play along," Thana whispered. "Good night, all! Good
sleeping, and if not…good…other things, too." Her laugh sounded as
merry as two pots grating together, but she hoped it would be enough.

CHAPTER FIFTEEN

Inside the tent, Sylph snatched her arm back. "I beg your pardon!" Her ire was up, even though part of her was curious about what was happening. "I will not be commanded into your bed like some kind of..." Words failed her, but the look of shock and fear on Thana's face stilled her anyway. "What's going on?"

"I think the word you were looking for is prostitute, but I wouldn't try to push one of them around if I were you." She was babbling, the words running into one another. "My friend Marcus has tossed many a client out on their ear." She was sweating and shaking, far from a paramour.

"What's going on?" Sylph repeated, narrowing her eyes.

Thana took a deep breath. "I think the prince and the Order might be under the control of a mind pyramid." She spoke quickly of convenient cousins and false memories, all of it in a quiet rush that Sylph barely followed.

"And what can we do about this?" Sylph asked.

Thana stared at her hopelessly before a nervous laugh escaped her. "I was hoping you'd have an idea. Can you make one of my pyramids into a mind pyramid?"

"I wouldn't know where to start." She tried to think of a way, but all her experience had been with destructive or utility pyramids. And though a description had helped her find a cancelation pyramid, creating one seemed quite a different matter.

"Me neither," Thana said. "I never even heard of it before you, and you've only created your stone pyramids." She nodded. "Maybe that's the key. You can use the ground to restrain them until we can get a mind pyramid."

Sylph frowned. She didn't want to doubt an area where Thana had more expertise, but she had to ask, "Are you certain about this course of action? This is the prince."

"I know."

"An Umbriel."

"I know!" She took another breath and bit her lip as if that would keep her voice down. "It's Calla. I can't believe her, and this situation is too important to be working with someone I don't know and can't trust. If Gunnar is not under pyramid control…I have to hope he'll understand."

Sylph's heart went out to her, and she was beyond touched that Thana trusted her, especially after their last conversation. She hoped all her faith shone in her eyes. When Thana smiled gratefully, Sylph knew it was so. Then she looked away, expression pained as if she was remembering their earlier words. Before she could ask, Thana brought out the stone pyramid.

Fear bloomed in Sylph's belly, but she took the pyramid anyway. "What would you have me do?"

"I don't know. Bury them up to their waists?"

Sylph frowned. "That leaves them awfully vulnerable."

"And you'd have to keep a close watch, or they might dig themselves out." She hit her forehead with the heel of her hand. "Why am I so bad at planning? Or being a pyradisté? Or everything except stupid pyramid trivia?"

"You are not—"

"We can run," Thana said resignedly. "It's sort of worked so far. Even if some mystery attacker comes, maybe you can cancel all their pyramids so we don't get blown to pieces. But if they have a mind pyramid, there might not be time to spare it, even with your skill."

"And yours," Sylph said, daring to clasp her arm. "You are not useless." The desire to prove it rose within her. "I'm tired of running. We can do better than burial, and your prince will only have to forgive a minor inconvenience if we're wrong." A feeling of calm washed over her, and she wondered if there was a way to bottle this feeling for when she needed it again.

Undoubtedly not.

She moved toward the tent flap, but Thana caught her arm. "How can you want to repress your gift one moment, then use it so readily when asked?" She ducked her head as if fearful of the answer.

"Because it's for you." The words came out so easily, another gift of calm.

Thana's face lit up, then quickly dimmed again. Perhaps she realized that Sylph's insistence on learning to deny the magic would keep them apart once the danger had passed. A sad thought, but...

Then Thana's hangdog look evaporated for the most part, and she clasped Sylph's hand. "Thank you for believing me." So much hope and admiration shone in those eyes.

Beautiful eyes. Sylph nodded. If nothing else, she would use magic to ensure that Thana lived.

They peeked outside. The others were gathered around the fire, whispering. Calla frowned hard, a sign of thwarted plans or an escalation of her normal expression? There was nothing for it but to trust in Thana.

Sylph closed her eyes and focused on her pyramid. She dropped into it as quickly as if she'd leaped down a well. The feeling of earth surrounded her, stable and eternal. What was forest had once been many different climes, the ground constantly churning, though the living were too quick to notice. What was soil had been sand, and the rock beneath remembered journeys from snowcapped mountains and towering spires of ice.

They stirred at her call. Thana made a little cry as the ground began to tremble. More cries came from outside, prompting Sylph to hurry even as the earth had no such concept. The rumble became a crash, a shuddering roar, then the scream of long dormant stone rising past its fellows. She dared another look.

The Order was on their feet, crying out as spears of stone rose around them. Calla's wide eyes met Sylph's, and she pointed, mouth open to accuse. But now that the stone was free, Sylph taught it how to be as water, and it flowed around the Order, snuffing their campfire and entombing them.

Well, not quite. She commanded windows to open on the structure, apertures too small to climb through. When she eased everything into stillness, she couldn't help a smile.

In the light of the candle, Thana seemed in awe, and part of Sylph considered it might be worth embracing the forbidden if she could see that look all the time.

"Curse it, Thana," the prince yelled. "What are you playing at?" His pale face shone at one of the windows.

"I…" Thana licked her lips but crawled out of the tent, Sylph following. "I think you may have been manipulated by a pyramid, Gun."

"You have gone mad."

"By Calla," Thana said, her chin lifting as if confidence was rushing back. "This cousin I've never heard of."

"Clearly, we don't tell each other everything," he said, the words clipped. "Nothing you told me of Lady Sylph included her masonry skills. Now let me out."

"She cannot," Sylph said. "They are my *masonry skills*, after all. The stone is under my power." She bowed. "I must beg your forgiveness, Highness, for I will not set you free until Thana is certain your mind is clear."

He slid his lip through his teeth, no doubt holding in a wealth of expletives. "And do you possess a mind pyramid?"

Thana glanced at Sylph and swallowed. "No."

"Then how, in your spirits-cursed brain, do you propose to *clear* us?"

Luckily, his angry tone seemed to make Thana more determined, a reaction to an angry royal that Sylph had never witnessed. "If I'm right, I'll steal one when Calla's cohorts catch up to us."

"Curse you, I don't have any cohorts," Calla yelled from another window. "And if you haven't heard of me before, trust me, you'll remember me after I get my hands around your neck."

Sylph's gaze shifted back to the prince. He didn't censure his so-called cousin for threatening his friend, but that could be for many reasons, the most obvious being that he wanted to strangle Thana, too.

"Highness," she said, ignoring Calla. "We are acting in the only way that makes sense to us at the moment. If you have not been hypnotized, I am certain you will understand in time."

Several cries of protest came from behind him. He closed his eyes, then opened them and said in a calmer voice, "And what do you intend to do when these supposed cohorts arrive?"

"Best if you don't know," Thana said quickly. She pulled Sylph some distance away. "What should we do now?"

Sylph blinked and nodded at the prison. "This concludes what I had planned."

Thana ran her free hand through her hair. Sylph took the candle so she could pace and gesticulate as she liked. "Well, I have some pyramids, and you have your stone power. If anyone tries to cancel our pyramids, you can turn it against them. And Calla is unarmed."

"Quite." Sylph was still proud of that.

"And it's not cold, so the Order won't be that uncomfortable. And they'll live."

"Yes." She suspected Thana's questions were rhetorical but thought she should contribute something.

"Traps," Thana said, snapping her fingers. "You hunt. You can make traps."

Sylph frowned, casting her mind back to the hunt but finding nothing useful. "I believe riding down prey and shooting it is a separate skill from laying a trap."

"Makes sense," Thana said with a sigh. "And it's just our luck. Illis is the person I'd ask, but I don't think he'll be in the mood to help." She lifted her arms, dropped them, and blew out her cheeks.

Too adorable. Sylph bent slightly and kissed her, lingering for just a moment before she stepped back.

Thana smiled. "What was that for?"

"Inspiration."

She tilted her head as if confused, still grinning before her eyes widened. "I may not know how to lay a complex trap, but I know how to dig a pit." She tapped the stone pyramid. "If you don't mind, of course."

Sylph found she didn't mind, not even a little, not in this moment. "For you? I never mind."

Sylph's abilities were awe-inspiring, worship-worthy, and a thing of beauty to behold.

And Thana was so jealous, it felt as if she were eating her own liver.

Before, she'd been too swept up in the moment to ponder how unfair it was, but now, as she waited among a sea of wide pits and a prison of stone, she could really sink her teeth into some old-fashioned envy.

As Sylph had dug the pits, Thana had labored with her hands, covering their work with piles of branches. Sylph had covered other holes with a brittle crust of earth that wouldn't hold any weight. And now came the waiting, the pondering, and the spirits-cursed jealousy, the kind that could easily bake into resentment and kill a relationship.

As if they had one.

Now that the crisis had been temporarily suspended, Sylph had gone back to silence, though it didn't seem as tense as before. Thana didn't know what to do. Their every interaction seemed a lot harder than a relationship should be.

She wandered to the prison. Gunnar leaned against his window, the picture of idleness, but she recognized his coiled grace, the ability to react at a moment's notice when his enemies didn't expect it.

"I'm not your enemy, Gun," she said. "I'm trying to help."

"I know that's what you think. What you're actually doing is wasting time, and you're not even doing that in your beautiful lover's arms. I don't know if I can forgive that."

Partly a jest but partly not. It stung. "I don't know what to do about her. When I need her, when there's action to be taken, she's there. When it's over, she...freezes, and she says things that make me want to smack her."

"Are you seriously asking my advice after imprisoning me?"

She shook her head. What else was there to do? "I just don't know what to do."

"Unbelievable. You could let me go. There's idea number one."

"Nothing like this has happened to you before?"

The light from the newly made campfire flickered in his eyes as he looked at her without expression.

"I'm not letting you out, and I can hear snoring in there, so I'm guessing you don't have many people to talk to at the moment."

He sighed. "Why would you want the advice of someone who's been hypnotized? Advice I've already given you, by the way, and which you clearly did not attend to."

"I attended enough to know it was sex advice, which I do not need, *by the way*. And if you have been hypnotized, it would only work if they manipulated a little of your memory, enough to make you trust Calla and perhaps mistrust me when the time came."

He pointed at the ground, his eyebrows up. "And that's now, right? You didn't need Calla's help, then."

Thana's irritation rose, and it felt nice to be angry at someone besides Sylph. "I bet that if I asked you to punch her, you couldn't."

His jaw dropped. "No, I wouldn't, you ass, because why would I strike an innocent person on nothing more than your say-so?"

And he was right, but so was she. "You *couldn't* do it even if you wanted." Maybe she could prompt Calla to attack him, and then…

No, that was madness. She was getting too tired to think straight. "I'm sorry."

His smile was brittle. "Nothing says apology like freeing your chum from prison."

She chuckled and reconsidered for the hundredth time. Maybe she was wrong. It would take a master of mind magic to tinker with someone as she suspected. But it wasn't impossible, according to the lore, and the academy had many masters.

And Gunnar wouldn't speak with her, it seemed. She couldn't blame him. She went and sat by the newly made fire, trying not to drown in all the assumptions she'd made, hoping this didn't spell the end of their friendship. She'd never hoped that someone had been hypnotized before.

If Calla was the enemy, Thana hoped her reinforcements would come to her. If she was supposed to lead the Order to them, Thana might be waiting a long time, and she couldn't keep the Order locked up forever. She and Sylph would have to sleep eventually. There were so many ifs and too few people she could trust with pyramids thrown in the mix.

No wonder so many people disliked pyradistés. She wasn't feeling very charitable toward them at the moment.

Sylph settled beside her, and Thana hoped she wasn't going to compare nobles and peasants again. That would definitely lead to a fistfight.

"You're tired," Sylph said, and Thana wondered how she looked if her fatigue was that noticeable in dim light.

"I can't sleep."

"I wish I knew how to make a bold, romantic speech," Sylph said. "A way to invite you to spend this time in bed with me, not sleeping."

Thana gaped, unable to believe what she'd just heard. "Well, you…say exactly what you said, but you flower it up a little." Her cheeks burned, and to deny her own lust would have been a lie, but she raised a hand. "Please don't try. I wouldn't be able to concentrate, and I wouldn't want…" Her face grew even hotter.

Sylph smiled. "To give less than your best?"

Thana rubbed her forehead. "Is there any way to make this more embarrassing, so I can just die?"

"I know we can't…do anything," Sylph said. "Because of the danger."

Thana bit her lip. She didn't want to start another fight, but she couldn't remain quiet, either. At least she wasn't embarrassed about the point she had to make. "For more reasons than danger. I don't know what you want from me, Sylph. Am I your teacher? Your servant? Your partner in crime against the crown?" She gestured at the stone prison. "All of those? None? Until I have the answer, I don't think I can be your lover, too."

Sylph's eyes were steady, her posture as correct as always, and Thana braced herself for *Lady* Sylph or a frosty exit, but she said, "You want me to be someone I'm not."

Thana resisted the urge to shake her, to say she could change. But Thana hadn't exactly been willing to do the same. "Do you want a relationship with me or just a fling?" She put a hand on Sylph's arm before she could look away. "Don't look into the future. Tell me what your gut says."

That got a little smile. "My abdominal organs don't usually speak."

"Well, summon some indigestion, and tell me what it says."

"I have to think about the future."

"Not right now."

"Always."

"Why?"

"Because!" Sylph leaped to her feet, facade cracking. "Property, peasantry, money, crops, connections, the future of a noble is always around us. If we don't plan, people may starve, land can be lost, and laws can go unrevised. Each decision affects every other, don't you see?" The pain in her eyes cut Thana to the quick, and she had to admit, she'd never considered most of what Sylph said.

She stood slowly. "And despite all that, when I asked you what you wanted us to be, you felt something inside here." She tapped her own chest. "Some answer. You don't need fancy speeches to tell me what it was."

When Sylph breathed out, it was half sob, and Thana resisted the urge to embrace her. "The thought of being without you is like…a hole in my chest. That's what I felt. A void. I would survive, but all that you've brought out in me, feelings I have never considered, would fall into the void and never be seen again. I won't say I love you because I'm not sure what that is, but my…abdominal organs would miss you all of my days."

Her gaze was earnest, even if some of her words were ridiculous, and Thana had to kiss her gently before she could point out their differences again. "Then I'll make you a deal. You try harder to enjoy the time we have together now, and I'll think about the ways in which we might have a future." She raised a hand before Sylph could protest. "I'll keep in mind that you will be a duchess and not a pyradisté, and I will be a pyradisté and not a noble." She grabbed Sylph's chin. "But I will think of something we can both be happy with." And she wasn't sure at all that she could keep such a promise, but she couldn't leave it unsaid, not after demanding that Sylph bare her feelings.

Sylph had tears in her eyes, but she still smiled. "That will give us both something to do until the danger finds us again."

Taking her hand, Thana sat. "Thank the spirits for that." She couldn't resist leaning in, giving Sylph the choice of how they were to enjoy their time together, even if retiring to a tent wasn't an option.

Sylph brushed her lips softly before she opened her mouth, an invitation that Thana gladly accepted. When Sylph gasped, Thana put a hand on her back and pulled her closer, pausing only when Sylph made a sound of fear. She pulled back to see an expression of horror and had a moment to hope she wasn't the cause.

"They've come," Sylph whispered. "And they've brought a new pyramid." Her face creased in pain, but it had a touch of wonder as her gaze went far away. "I've never felt…it's like a hole in the world, a well of destruction."

Only one kind of pyramid fit that bill, one that obliterated everything caught in its sphere-like blast: a disintegration pyramid. And by Sylph's expression, they'd made it from the powerful new crystal. "Spirits help us all."

Sylph curled her hands into fists as Thana implored her to breathe. She sensed her stone pyramid being pressed into her hand, and she was able to channel some of her desire into it, to fall there instead of into the well of darkness coming ever closer.

Thana's voice was gone before it came back again. "Feel for a cancelation pyramid, Sylph. Get your focus off that new crystal and see what else they have."

She tried, but she feared abandoning her link with the stone, and she could not split her focus three ways, nor could she fully ignore the crystal that yanked at her attention as forcefully as a chain. "I'm trying," she said with a gasp.

Thana rubbed her back, kissed her cheek, murmured, "I'm with you," over and over.

Sylph focused on her presence. The earth began to tremble while she leaned her power there and pulled some of herself away from the well of darkness. She felt the presence of many crystalline lights. They shone so brightly in her mind that it was hard to believe they didn't also light the forest. Mostly destruction, none as powerful as the one she fought against. She sensed many she'd never encountered, thought they might be mind pyramids, and Thana needed one of those.

Pain rocketed through her temples, and her focus was wrenched from the earth. She cried out as pain arced across her palm, leaving her hand feeling empty. She opened her eyes, expecting to see her pyramid gone, but it was merely dark, its magic fled.

"They canceled it," Thana said breathlessly. "The *bastards*."

And without it, the pressure built again. They were bad people, coming to hurt her, Thana, maybe everyone. They deserved to have their disintegrator set off in their midst, ending their lives and gobbling their pyramids.

Perhaps taking this camp as well. Then it could all end.

"Don't kill them, Sylph, there has to be a way to resist it."

Now Thana felt merciful? Had there been a way before, at the manor house? The well of darkness was drawing her in with each breath, making her hate anyone who kept her from it.

Thana gave her another pyramid. "Here, try this light pyramid. Focus on it." She kissed Sylph again, but it would not be enough.

Sylph snarled and gripped her dead pyramid, casting the light one aside. No, she would not bow. Her father would choose death first, and she would follow his example, but she would also spite him, tired of obeying. She would do as Thana suggested and live in the now.

And now, she would fight.

With a new cry, a sound of battle, she flung her power into the trees, searching out the pyramid that had attacked her own. She ignored the others and called to the feeling she remembered, the pyramid that felt like the lack of one. She found it quickly and began to snuff those around it, barely able to focus on destruction pyramids alone.

Someone in the woods cried out in surprise, no stealthy killers these, and she wondered what their plan had been. They couldn't stop her in her quest to cancel all their destruction pyramids.

Then she came to the disintegrator.

It sucked her in, begging her to set it off rather than kill it, but there was more at stake than just lives. Thana needed a mind pyramid, so Sylph could not consider any future without it.

She would consider no future at all. There was only now.

The disintegrator resisted, no common crystal to be snuffed like a candle, no lesser power to be covered. It wanted her touch, craved her as she craved it, as inexorable as the tide or as her father's orders or the queen's whims.

She screamed. If it wanted her so badly, she'd take it. On her terms.

Her mind hammered at the dead thing in her hand, cursing it into remembering what it used to be. Her magic kept hold of the cancelation pyramid and vaguely felt the enemy pyradisté trying to use it along with her. She brushed him aside and pounced upon the special crystal, the dark well, but instead of trying to kill it, she commanded its power to be elsewhere, using the cancelation pyramid like a lever.

The power inside the disintegrator leaped from its home as if joyful to be free. All magic was really the same, she saw, raw power drawn into a pyramid that had been shaped for a specific purpose. She left the purpose of this one behind and drew the raw magic to her.

Her stone pyramid blazed back to life, all the power of the special crystal infusing it and leaving its former home naught but a shell.

"Sylph!"

She opened her eyes. People swarmed through the trees, some falling in pits, but others found their way through. Pyramids sailed through the air, but all their destructive powers had been wiped away, and they hit the ground to shatter harmlessly. Thana batted one out of the air, keeping it from crashing into Sylph.

"Enough," Sylph said and fell into her pyramid.

And felt all the world.

Or near enough. She sensed it was a great sphere, too large to contemplate, and she could lose herself in all the textures from sand to diamond, but she pulled back to the now, guided by Thana's cries. She opened the ground under every nearby pair of running feet, dropping them into pits of their own, and the noise of battle became cries of alarm as they all fell.

It felt so wonderful, she could see why most people embraced the training.

Thana's look of awe was something she would never tire of, even as it seemed rather wistful at the moment. "Yes." Thana squeezed her hand once, then pulled a pyramid from her pocket. "Now to find a mind pyramid." She pointed at Sylph's paragon of stone. "We'll talk about that later."

"All right. I'll guard your back in the here and now."

CHAPTER SIXTEEN

The entire forest was alive with complaints, voices raised in anger, condemnation, fear, and a host of other emotions. Thana didn't bother to try calming any of them. She just used her detector to find what she was looking for, a mind pyramid.

Its owner glared from the bottom of a pit. She didn't know how many pyradistés were gathered in the forest, but they would probably all be as reluctant to cooperate as this fellow seemed to be.

And Thana was too tired for persuasion. "Give me your pyramids, or my friend will fill in your grave."

Before he had time for words, the earth churned around him, pebbles raining down. His eyes went wide in the candlelight, and he flung a satchel up. Thana barely suppressed a cry as she caught it. She hadn't even had time to ready herself.

Among a slew of other pyramids, some canceled, she found what she needed in the satchel and marched back to the stone prison, gratified to feel Sylph with her.

Sylph, who now seemed as powerful as one of the ten spirits. But now wasn't the time for such thoughts.

"Thana," Gunnar called from his window. "What is going on? Is this what you were waiting for? I—"

She held the pyramid aloft, catching him easily and hypnotizing him. "Keep the others back, please, Sylph."

"As you wish."

The walls of the prison drew back like melting wax, giving Thana room to get to Gunnar while separating him from the others, who cried out in protest. Relieved that mind magic came easy for her, she pressed the pyramid to Gunnar's forehead. She searched his memories, frowning.

And found nothing out of the ordinary.

She frowned harder. Tampering wouldn't be easy to find, but it had to be there. She looked through his recent memories, events unfolding through his eyes. He'd gone hunting a pack of rogue pyradistés with the Order and his difficult cousin, someone he didn't see very often, whose company he didn't enjoy.

He'd missed Thana.

She bit her lip as he'd lamented that he must keep silent about Calla. She'd clearly resented the fact, too. Even if she hadn't wanted to use her power, she still had to be kept a secret in case her abilities became apparent in some other way. The desire to keep the common people from knowing that nobles could be pyradistés was that great. It was all for the good of the kingdom.

And even though Thana knew why the Umbriels had to stay in power, she hated them in that moment. She'd been wrong about Calla, but there seemed to be plenty of wrongness to go around.

She let go of Gunnar slowly, and he slumped. He'd come around soon enough.

Sylph touched her arm. "Well?"

"Nothing," she said. The weight of someone else's emotions left her a little sick. Well, the weight and the guilt. "He wasn't tampered with."

"Oh." The single word carried a lot behind it.

"Yeah." Thana wiped the back of her mouth. "He's not going to be happy."

Luckily, she hadn't been very deep in his memories, just enough to see that he'd known Calla a long time. Memory erasure worked in threads, so if someone wanted to *erase* Gunnar's memories of someone, they'd have to take every incident closely connected with that person. That would leave gaps that another pyradisté would notice right away. Making new memories required an overlay of older memories and took a more skilled touch. There were still seams, though, and the memories would all be recent. To replace someone's entire mind was unheard of.

Thana had seen no gaps, nothing amiss. There wasn't a pyradisté alive who could rework a memory seamlessly.

She checked the rest of the Order, just to make sure, leaving Calla alone in the prison, cursing Thana's name. Parts of the forest had gone quiet, but some of the captured pyradistés still yelled their heads off as the light of dawn began filtering through the trees.

Gunnar finally stirred from where he lay among the Order. Thana had tried to make them all as comfortable as she could. Her nerves were high, the bile bubbling in her stomach. When Gunnar blinked confusedly at her, she blurted, "I'm sorry, Gun. I had to make sure, and I'm so sorry. I wasn't completely wrong. Look!" She pointed into the forest.

He continued to stare. "I take it from that babbling that you found nothing?"

She knew his tired tone wouldn't last long. She had to turn this back around a bit, prove they were a little bit even. "Yes, I know you weren't lying about Calla the way you've been lying about other things, like the existence of noble pyradistés."

He sighed loudly as he sat up and stretched, rubbing his back. "Not hypnotized into lying, anyway." He looked into the forest, to where the cries of the enemy had grown hoarse. "Yet the attack you envisioned happened all the same. Where did they come from? How many are there?"

"I didn't want to count in the dark," Thana said as Sylph said, "Seventeen."

Thana glanced at her in surprise, but she only shrugged. To capture them all, she no doubt had to pinpoint them, but it was disturbing to think that the stone had told her where everyone was.

Gunnar stood, glanced at the Order before giving Thana a reproachful look, and stepped farther into the forest. "That's more than the five we were chasing. If this is them, they found reinforcements."

Thana hurried to catch up. "Don't go among them alone, for spirits' sake." Her own anger wasn't enough to overrule her sense of duty. She leaned close to his arm. "One of them might have another mind pyramid, and you are still susceptible."

He gave her a steady look. "I suppose it was a good thing I was locked up when they arrived. Is that what you're going to say next?"

So he wasn't ready to forgive her just yet. Even though she'd been a little right. Sort of. Tangentially correct. But he wasn't yelling. Maybe he felt a hint of shame for all the secrets and a soupçon of gratitude that this attack hadn't caught them all sleeping.

He peered into a pit until a string of curses came from the occupant, and then he leaned back. "What in the spirits' names are we going to do with them?" he muttered.

"Excuse me," Illis called from the campsite. The others were up, and he pointed at the prison. "Can we let Calla out, too?"

A look of amusement flashed across Gunnar's face before he raised an eyebrow at Thana. "Oops," he said flatly.

She glared and looked to Sylph, who lifted her hands. "I was awaiting instructions."

"Please let her out," Thana said, trying to sound calm.

Calla lunged out of the prison as it collapsed. Dina caught her by the waist and held on as she shouted and raged, arms whirling as if she wanted to swim through the air. "Let me go. I will kill her. I will kill—"

Dina put a hand over her mouth and said something in her ear.

"Making friends wherever you go," Gunnar mumbled as he strode back to camp. "Lady Sylph, if you wouldn't mind, will you keep an eye on our prisoners until we decide what can be done?"

"My pleasure, Highness." Her placid mask was back in place, and Thana envied her in that moment. She felt as if she was coming out of her skin with emotion.

Calla had quieted in Dina's arms, but her shoulders heaved with every breath, and her pale face had turned nearly purple. She glared at Thana, but if her eyes strayed toward Sylph, they took on a sheen of fear.

Thana couldn't blame her. Sylph's stone pyramid shone like a star to her senses and put her even further on edge. "I'm sorry, all right?" Thana said. "I couldn't take chances."

No one seemed happy with that answer. Ivar cocked his head in the captives' direction. "If they hadn't come, how long would you have kept us in there?"

"Until just now," she lied, gesturing around them. "Dawn. That was always the plan." She consoled herself with an excuse Gunnar often used: they didn't need to know any differently.

Illis scratched at his stubble and echoed Gunnar's earlier words. "What are we going to do with them all?"

Thana frowned. She didn't know now any more than she had known before, but she promised herself that she wasn't going to let them be put to the sword. As far as she was concerned, these pyradistés had good reasons for some of their actions, reasons the crown and the nobility had to answer for, and anyone who committed murder or other crimes needed to have their time before a magistrate.

Gunnar was staring, and she met him look for look. He had to know she wouldn't see a slaughter hidden away, nor would she be willing to ignore the existence of noble pyradistés. It wasn't one of the problems the Order could erase from history. There were too many lives at stake, too many pyradistés already cold in the ground. And she would protect all she could, nobles or not.

He sighed as if reading her thoughts. "Some of us will take them to Marienne and lock them up. The others will track where these came from and see if we can figure out what they were up to."

Thana let out a breath, happy he was still who she'd thought he was.

Sylph had never felt so capable in all her life. The pyramid in her hands felt ten times heavier than it was, fit to burst, never mind that the power wasn't in its original cursed pyramid. And she felt swollen with power, too, capable of anything now that the world itself was her companion.

Even her father wouldn't turn his nose up at that. He'd probably march on his neighbors and demand they sign over their land, or his daughter would turn it against them. More than that, he'd eye the throne, seeing the value of magic if it could deliver the world.

Literally.

She sighed as she leaned against a tree, watching and ready to act as the Order divested these pyradistés of their meager weaponry and bound them in a line so they could march back to Marienne. She was tempted to go with them. She'd be torn between finally securing her father's approval and encasing him in stone.

Better to stay put. Neither plan would endear her to the queen.

As for the prince, he kept up a chilly facade. He and Thana traded several barbs and recriminations, but she couldn't detect any real malice, though her ability to deduce emotions was somewhat stunted. By the way Thana smiled at Prince Gunnar when he wasn't looking and the similar expressions he made to her back, they remained friends. Sylph wondered how long it would be before they smiled at each other's faces.

Thana could hurl angry retorts in one moment and dole out kisses in another. Sylph had pushed her often enough to see it, feel it. But Thana never walked away. She cast many a glance Sylph's way, as good as saying they would continue to walk the same path, wherever that might lead. After all that she had said to Thana, all the nasty little thoughts…

She did not deserve such loyalty.

But she couldn't flee from it or betray it and not just because it felt as warm as a thick blanket on a cold day. A rejection of that loyalty would break Thana's heart, and Sylph had to protect her from everyone.

Including Sylph herself.

Calla shuffled up nearby. "What is that?" she asked, resentment roiling off her like heat off molten rock.

Sylph turned, her mask in place. She didn't know how to treat this woman, a noble with a peasant's power—like her, she admitted—an Umbriel secret.

"Don't insult me by saying, 'It's a pyramid,'" Calla said, sneering. "I've never felt one like it."

"I don't know how to explain." She tried to be patient, but she felt as tired as everyone else and was still unaccustomed to anyone's anger except her father's. Well, and Thana's. Even at the manor house, the countess had the good manners to knock her unconscious before insulting her.

Calla's nostrils flared. Perhaps she was trying to suppress her acid tongue. "What does it do?"

"Connects me to stone. I can command it." She wasn't ready to talk about the extent, frightened to speculate.

"How did you make it?"

"Again, I cannot explain. I haven't the vocabulary." Time for another subject. Perhaps the two of them were more alike than she thought. "Have you always known your status?"

Calla blinked, uttering a clipped, "What?"

"As a noble. Were you brought up as one?"

"Of course. What's that got to do with anything?"

"It must have been quite a blow." She recalled her own panic at facing discovery, but Calla had no doubt faced it immediately if the Umbriels were always looking for magic in their kin. How had she borne such a thing? "Even if you were excited by the power, you were stripped of your old life, your peers. It must have been unsettling."

Her cheeks went scarlet. "It's not like they moved me into a cave above the sea."

"It was still exile." Sylph tilted her head as Calla seemed perplexed. "I quite understand."

She sneered again as if to say that no one understood her, and they shouldn't dare try. "You've been going through this for how many days, and you think you know my life story? Oh, please. Even if we did feel the same, my family is letting the secret of noble pyradistés out because *you* demanded it. You'll sacrifice nothing."

Both somewhat true and mostly false. And Sylph had no interest in explaining. A small part of her had thought she and Calla could bond, but she no longer cared to push where she wasn't wanted, not in this moment, when she was supposed to be completely in the present. "I cannot answer your questions now. Perhaps I will one day, but our time seems at an end." She nodded at the captives as Calla went from scarlet to indigo. "You will accompany them to Marienne, I take it?"

"Why should I?" she asked between her teeth.

Sylph frowned, genuinely confused. "Because you will have deduced that Thana and I will most likely remain on the hunt, and you loathe us. And the prince, to a point." She lifted a hand as her father often did at the end of an argument. "And the escorts will have need of a pyradisté, and you have rearmed yourself."

Calla put her hands on her slender hips. "With a bunch of useless junk, no destructive pyramids left."

Sylph smiled as brightly as she could. "Even so, the loathing remains."

"Oh, fine. I guess I'll do it. At least you're somewhat intelligent." From her, it seemed like high praise. She marched away stiffly, as if on parade, and Sylph knew she'd continue all the way to Marienne just as the prince would remain behind.

The brothers joined Calla in escorting the prisoners, leaving Prince Gunnar, Sylph, Thana, and Dina the monk to follow the rogue pyradistés' trail and find out where they'd come from.

The rogues had made no attempt at disguising it. Sylph couldn't blame them. The hunting parties she was used to never attempted to cover their tracks, either.

Of course, she'd never hunted people before.

But Prince Gunnar had. He tracked with Sylph in the front, and neither had to dismount to see the path. The pyradistés might as well have hacked their way through the undergrowth.

"They seemed in quite the hurry," he said. "I wonder if that was the plan of the original five all along, to lead us out where their allies were waiting."

"But when you spotted and followed Thana and me, you disrupted their plans." She nodded. It made sense, though it couldn't be confirmed. The pyradistés hadn't seemed willing to talk before they'd left—aside from chains of expletives—and since they were pyradistés, their memories couldn't be read.

He shook his head. "How did it come this far? Were we blind to miss rebellion brewing in our own city?"

Like Thana, he seemed prone to thinking aloud and likely did not require an answer, but as before, she felt she should contribute. "Why should you have noticed, Highness?"

He blinked as if he'd forgotten she was there. Then he frowned, and though he was as handsome as ever, she wondered how many nobles and courtiers would still be smitten if they saw these genuine expressions. She'd heard that his lackadaisical personality was part of his charm, just like his mother's passion was part of hers.

Though they rarely appealed to the same people.

"You don't think I should have seen this coming?" he asked.

She shrugged. "The pyradistés did not tell Thana, your link to them, and even though you clearly work with"—she glanced back at Thana and Dina—"those outside your station, you do not seem to socialize there in public." She tilted her head. "Unless you sometimes mingle with the populace in disguise?"

He seemed intrigued but still shook his head. "I still should have…" He sighed. "I wish someone would have told me." He chuckled as if realizing how ridiculous that sounded.

But her mind was already working. "Use spies. The pyradistés know of Thana's connection to you, so someone else must serve as your eyes and ears in their camp. After this current rebellion has been dealt with, of course."

"A spy in the academy?" he said, frowning.

"And wherever else one might be needed." She thought of her maids and tutors. Her father would never hire someone who couldn't be bought, and his pockets were so deep, he never feared being outbid.

The prince's frown said he found the idea distasteful. She nearly laughed, tickled that his conscience extended so far. She liked him. Her father would have laughed himself sick, but it would have been all disdain.

"Or recruit a spy master," she said. "Someone whose loyalty you trust but who knows how to buy it in others."

A step removed from dirtying his hands seemed to please him, and he looked at her as if seeing someone different.

She nearly laughed again, prepared to tell him to look elsewhere for his tender of secrets, but perhaps the lessons her father had inadvertently taught her could be put to good use.

And even he would be impressed that she'd found another way to be useful to the crown.

But that was the future, and she didn't have to think of that just now.

"What do you suppose they're muttering about?" Thana asked as she and Dina followed Sylph and Gunnar through the forest.

"We could ride closer and eavesdrop," Dina said.

"I think they'd notice."

"Well, that leads to my next suggestion. We could ask."

Thana snorted. "For a monk of love and beauty, you're much too straightforward."

"Oh?" Her full lips quirked up. "Love problems?"

Thana scoffed, feeling a cursed blush betray her. "No. I...have a...beauty problem that..." She sighed. "Fine, yes. I do."

"Relax, I already heard what you said to Gunnar when we were locked up."

Thana had known that was possible, but she still bristled. "I thought the rest of you asleep."

"You and the lady seem to have reached an accord since then."

With another sigh that came from her toes, Thana nodded. If Gunnar wasn't going to help...but she already knew what Dina's ultimate advice would be.

"You know what you really need to clear the air?" Dina asked.

That hadn't taken long. "A long romp in a soft bed," they said together.

When Dina gave her a surprised look, Thana ground her teeth. "That's what you always say, Di. Those exact words."

"Doesn't make them wrong."

"You suggested it for Gun's problems with his tailor."

"Would have worked."

"And when Illis was fighting with his upstairs neighbor."

"That would have been a joy to witness." She chuckled when Thana sighed yet again. "We servants of Elias and Elody seek to understand the universe through love and beauty, and I seek my understanding through the awe-inspiring, gorgeous realm of the physical."

It made sense. Dina was beautiful enough to be one of Elody's statues. She probably got offers wherever she went. "But not everyone feels the same way."

"Everyone should try."

"I know you think so." And as frustrating as these conversations were, she'd missed them after being too long apart. If only the brothers had remained to take Thana's side while Gunnar stood with Dina.

If only...lots of things.

"All right, fine," Dina said. "You have to have an honest conversation with her."

"I just had one. That's why we're currently at peace. Or at least at a standstill. She's not good at admitting emotion. Or showing it." She frowned. "Or feeling it, based on what she's said."

"Uptight?"

"More like hidden. I don't think she's ever felt free. Or even safe." The emotion she'd exhibited most often was fear. Of other nobles, the Umbriels, even her own father. It pulled at Thana's heart.

"She might not know how to be honest, then."

"She's trying," Thana said, overcome with the need to defend her if no one else was going to.

"I believe you, but she still might not be very good at it, even in her own thoughts."

"She considers herself a realist. Keeps bringing up the differences in our stations and ruining the mood."

Dina *tsked*. "Realism with facts doesn't equal honesty with feeling. And why should such an obvious fact ruin anything for you?"

Thana rolled her eyes. "I know nothing ruins the mood for you." When Dina didn't take the bait, Thana watched the trees for a few moments and listened to the birds calling from the branches. "I don't like having her status thrown in my face."

"Or your own status repeated."

"Yes," she said as a groan.

Dina stretched her arms over her head until her impressive physique clicked all over. Then she met Thana's eyes. "You're a snob."

Thana blinked, certain she hadn't heard correctly. "Excuse me?"

"You have a negative attitude where nobles are concerned."

"Doesn't everyone?" But her cheeks were beginning to burn again.

"You don't like to be reminded that she's a noble because you hate most of them and wish she wasn't one."

"You don't know me that well," Thana said, knowing it was a lie before Dina gave her a flat look, but she still had to protest. "Well, you and I have never had a romp of any kind, so your understanding of me is imperfect." There, undeniable logic.

The smile Dina gave her said she was welcome anytime, and it forced Thana to look away before her face caught fire. "You like Gunnar, and he's a noble," Dina said after a laugh. "And the queen is the ultimate noble."

And not Thana's favorite person after recent information, but she stayed quiet.

"Why can't you like a duke's child, too?"

"Because."

Dina waited a heartbeat before she said, "Is that it? Oh well, I can't argue with that."

"Because," Thana said again, lengthening the word to eat up time while she searched for a reason besides the real one. Finally, she had to admit, "If we hadn't met through extraordinary circumstances, she would have been as mean or dismissive as the rest of them." It hurt to even think of, let alone imagine, but she couldn't help picturing Lady Sylph with her cold expression twisting into one of derision.

"You don't know that for certain," Dina said softly, sympathy so heavy in her voice that Thana teared up.

She clenched her fists, rejecting the sadness. She would not be so childish. "My experience with court life suggests otherwise."

"Nobles are mostly asses, so what? You know two very notable exceptions. There is no reason Sylph wouldn't have been one, too."

Thana had to admit to the remotest possibility. She nodded. After all, Sylph only brought out the frosty persona when she felt threatened. Since Thana never would have threatened her, either emotionally or physically, if they hadn't met the way they had, the odds were that Sylph would have simply ignored her.

As she had before they'd ever met. And since Thana couldn't recall her before that day in the garden, Thana had been ignoring her, too.

And only focusing on the asses.

A thought that made her laugh until Dina insisted she share, and they both chortled like miscreants until Gunnar gave them a warning look, and Sylph smiled over her shoulder, a beautiful look that Thana would have been a fool to ignore. And Sylph only showed it to those who mattered to her, those she liked, perhaps those she could someday love.

If they could see past her title.

"Fine," Thana said. "I'll think on that."

Dina nodded. "And if that doesn't work?" She grinned.

"Please don't say it."

But her mouth was already open. Thana began to repeat the line about romps and beds, but Dina said, "You'll have to have more honest conversations." When Thana sputtered in surprise, Dina snorted. "Really, Thana, that's what you always say."

CHAPTER SEVENTEEN

L uckily, the pyradisté camp wasn't far. A few tents stood in a small clearing, as well as flimsy lean-tos made of logs and blankets. The pyradistés had put their fire out before venturing forth, but everything else spoke of haste: utensils scattered about, clothing left in piles, a picketed horse that still wore a saddle, and a few books still open, waiting for the readers' return.

Sylph began tending the sad-looking mare while the others searched for clues. The horse shivered and nickered as she brushed it. The pyradistés must have advanced as soon as they'd scouted the prince's camp and hadn't wanted to risk riding in the dark. Too bad they hadn't been as concerned with the mare's well-being as they had been with their own.

And that also meant someone had spied on the prince's camp before the attack. And Sylph hadn't noticed because she hadn't been looking for pyramids, but maybe she should have been. She tried to shake the guilt from her shoulders. Thana hadn't noticed either.

But she didn't have Sylph's ability, which she was forever pointing out. Sylph couldn't help thinking that, since she had all this power, she was obliged to use it when needed.

She cast her senses out now, pausing in her brushing, hoping she wasn't too late to catch an ambush if that was what the future held. She sensed no pyramids lurking in the trees and breathed a sigh of relief.

Until…a spark of something caught her senses.

"Stop," she cried, whirling around, unsure of what the signal meant or where it came from, but everyone needed to halt until she found out.

Everyone froze, well-acquainted with the suddenness of magic, it seemed. Thana's eyes were wide as she bent over a blanket near the campfire. Dina paused while halfway inside a tent. Prince Gunnar held one foot aloft, freezing on the way to another tent, this one set apart from the others.

Barely there, the signal slipped around Sylph's senses, slippery as an eel or an elusive secret. "Thana, use your detector. I can't quite search it out." And quickly, as Prince Gunnar seemed a bit wobbly on one leg.

Thana dug in her satchel and brought her pyramid forth. No sooner had her eyes closed, then she pointed at the tent nearest the prince. "Gunnar, back up. They might have left quickly, but they took the time to set a trap."

He did so, stepping as carefully as if away from a sleeping bear.

"Don't go poking around it, Sylph," Thana said. "You might set it off. The rest of the camp is clear." Dina sighed in relief and joined them. Thana smiled sheepishly. "I should have checked. Sorry." Her cheeks went red. "Maybe you should have brought Calla."

The prince gave her a sympathetic look. "I doubt Calla would be able to figure out how to disarm that trap without a cancelation pyramid."

Thana had barely said, "There are a few theories," before Prince Gunnar gave her a gentle push in Sylph's direction and joined Dina in a different search.

Sylph smiled, hoping to convey complete confidence. "Tell me these theories."

Thana spoke about the transference of energies and mind locks and all sorts of things Sylph didn't understand in the least. But she nodded and tried to seem interested. The idea of learning more magic still made her uneasy in her abdominal organs, but she told herself that this was another instance in which she was obliged to use her power, when she could further prove her worthiness, and she could help Thana in the here and now.

It felt nice to accomplish all those things in one go and nice to prove that she was getting better at corralling and categorizing her thoughts. Even if no one appreciated that last one but her.

Thana fell silent and looked at her expectantly.

Oh, bother. "Which would be your recommendation?" Sylph tried.

"The lock, I think. We don't have the right pyramids for the others, not really. But we should be able to lock the trap and create a circumstance where only we can set it off."

"How?" And she had to admit to a spot of genuine intrigue.

Thana pulled another pyramid from her satchel. "Trap pyramids are a mix of destruction and mind magic. We need to fall into my detector together, so you can see the trap, then into this mind pyramid so we can configure the lock. You'd normally only do this for a pyramid you didn't want anyone else to access, using a memory no one else has, but we're going to make it so the trap only goes off if someone is actively recalling our memories when they get close, and since no one can do that…"

Sylph nodded slowly. "All we have to do is not think of those memories when we remove the trap."

A smile flashed quickly before Thana shifted and cleared her throat. "Or to be extra safe, we'll let Dina actually remove it."

Sylph felt her own flush. "Right. Of course." She expected Thana to make the entire situation worse by saying that Sylph would get the hang of it or by making reference to further training, but Thana only nodded, quieting some of Sylph's fears and lessening her desire to rebel against a pyradisté future.

Sylph used the detector, marveling at the way it cast the world in darker tones, all but the pyramids, which shone like gold in a land of shadow. Once she'd felt the trap, she had it pinpointed. When Thana directed her to do so, she fell into the mind pyramid.

Delight infused her at finding Thana there, her mind like a happy beehive buzzing with intelligence. Her light shone as brightly as any pyramid. And though they could not read each other's minds, Sylph caught a hint of her wonder and excitement.

"I haven't done this often," Thana said aloud, her voice carrying through the faceted semi-darkness around them. Sylph let her eyes slip closed. She didn't need them in this place.

"Carefully," Thana said. "Focus there." A gentle nudge guided Sylph's senses through the detection and mind pyramids and she saw the trap as a spiderweb, a complex puzzle that would have to be disassembled one strand at a time.

"No," Thana said firmly as Sylph reached to touch it. "Try to disable it like that, and we'll set it off, no doubt destroying whatever they're hiding. Fix a memory in your mind."

What to choose? It seemed so important. What if she picked something common, something Dina might have experienced?

"I can sense your fear," Thana said. The comfort of her warm hand curled around Sylph's fingers. "It doesn't matter what you choose since no one can access your memories, and no one will have experienced any event the same way as you."

"Will I lose the memory?" It could be something she'd always wanted to do without, like the sounds of her childhood friends being lashed for sneaking onto her land to play.

"No, you don't need to fear that."

Pity, though she couldn't go giving parts of herself away, she supposed. She thought of the first time she'd looked into Thana's face and had seen how a stranger could worry for her, how someone could extend a hand while wanting nothing in return.

"Got it?"

"Oh yes." She tightened her grip on Thana.

"Good. Hold on to it and follow me."

Sylph observed as Thana's power flowed through the mind pyramid and from there to glide along the web, weaving strands of gold over it, through it. She guided Sylph next, and as Sylph kept the memory at the forefront of her mind, she felt a little pull all over her body, a sensation she fought through like a serpent shedding its skin.

Afterward, the trap seemed more tapestry than web. The magic faded, and she opened her eyes to Thana's smiling face.

"Now only we can set it off, and only if we're recalling those memories when we approach."

Sylph couldn't resist kissing her. "I thought of you."

Another blush appeared. "I thought of you, too." And by her smile, it seemed to be a happy memory. Sylph was tempted to ask, but depending on the answer, she might crave another kiss. Or something more and Thana would either have to deny her or embarrass them both before their prince.

Thana licked her lips as if reading Sylph's mind or perhaps her expression. Before either of them could begin embarrassing the other, she called, "Dina, you can get the pyramid."

Prince Gunnar didn't bother to argue that he could do it. Even in his Order, everyone seemed to recognize that his life was too important to risk when there were others who were willing.

❖

"Well, this was certainly worth all the trouble," Dina said as she surveyed the items from the trapped tent. After Thana had implored her to take care with the trap pyramid, she'd chucked it far into the trees where it had shattered unceremoniously. She'd given Thana a look that asked if she was satisfied.

Thana had restrained herself to muttering, "Here's to being unappreciated in my time." What she and Sylph had done had been glorious, beyond noteworthy, though she was going to document the whole experience when she got...

Home?

Who knew when that would be, if ever? She tried to push it from her mind. It fell into the category of futures to be on the lookout for rather than futures to be pondered. She would write about it when she could, and that would have to suffice.

She turned her attention to the articles Dina had found in the tent. She'd gone through everything twice, even feeling along the tent's seams, but it held little more than shovels, picks, and other digging apparatus like lanterns and rope. There was also a map of the surrounding area with a few indiscernible markings. Thana only recognized the wall around the palace and the edge of Marienne.

Gunnar studied it now, biting his thumbnail. "Do you think they were trying to dig under the palace wall?" Dina asked as she looked over his shoulder.

He shook his head. Thana went back to looking at the equipment with Sylph, who seemed more mystified by it than the rest of them.

"This is all for digging, what, a hole?" Sylph asked.

Thana shrugged. "Maybe, though the picks could mean they had more substantial work to do, like mining or making a well or a tunnel."

Sylph tilted her head. "You could have just said, a very stubborn hole." She glanced at Thana from the side of her eye, a small smile in place.

"Yes, all right," Thana said with a grin. "A stubborn hole for a stubborn person."

"But look." Sylph kneeled and touched the tip of one shovel. "This dirt seems fresh." She touched the others. "Compared to what mars the other tools."

Thana opened her mouth to make a joke about a lady being an expert on different types of earth, but then she remembered Sylph's power. If anyone was an expert, it was the woman who could commune with the ground.

Sylph slipped a hand into the pocket where she kept her pyramid. "It's dark like the soil in this forest." Her eyes took on the unfocused look of someone using a pyramid. "I sense a void." She held her free hand over the ground where the tent had stood, and a small square of earth parted like water, bringing a piece of leather into the light.

"Spirits above," Thana said, watching in awe as Sylph took the leather and revealed a slim book wrapped within.

Sylph presented it to Gunnar without ceremony, as if she accomplished amazing feats every day. Which she did, but Gunnar clearly wasn't used to it if his dropped jaw was any indication. By the spirits, Thana wasn't used to it, either, and she'd seen that fantastic power again and again. She had to restrain herself from imploring Sylph to embrace this power, to promise she would never forsake it.

Her choice, Thana reminded herself. It was up to Sylph to embrace or ignore it. Even if it made Thana writhe in envy or want to shake Sylph until her teeth rattled.

Her. Choice.

"Nice," Dina said, nodding.

Thana turned slowly. "Is that all you have to say?"

She blinked. "And impressive?"

"Is that a question?" Her ire rose now that her frustration had a target other than Sylph's stubborn refusal to accept a gift from the ten spirits.

Sylph put a hand on her arm and smiled. "There's no need to be angry. I'm not offended. It was a compliment."

"See?" Dina asked, smiling wryly.

"I just…never mind," Thana said, beyond belief at the pair of them. "Gun, what's in the book?"

"I'm not sure."

She read over his shoulder. It looked like a journal written in a tidy hand, but the words were fragmented, as if the writer noted their thoughts as they'd had them and hadn't bothered to explain.

"Five spirits, doubled," one entry read. "The ten spirits? Relatives?" This was accompanied by a crude sketch of a person with something bulky surrounding them, like heaps of clothing, armor, or a blanket. "Check founding of the city," the notes underneath it said. An asterisk set off the next line. "Bring more lanterns to save pyrs. Knowledge monks?"

Thana pointed at those last lines. "I know it's obvious, but that probably refers to light pyramids being saved."

"And lanterns can be left behind for the supposed knowledge monks," he said. "Or the monks could be a thought the writer is saving for some future date." He flipped through a few pages. "This is homemade, doesn't feel old." He brought it to his face. "The leather cover smells new."

"Meaning these are likely notes the rogues are making now?"

"Hmm." He paused on another page and pointed. "Here's a reference to tunneling." His tracking finger paused on a symbol that meant nothing to Thana, but he brought out the map again, and she held it while he made comparisons. "There." He tapped a marking on the map that stood well inside the palace. "The tunnel entrance?"

She frowned. "I doubt it. Wouldn't someone have noticed a group of pyradistés tunneling through the pantry floor?" She squinted at the map. "It's too vague to see exactly where in the palace that is. Maybe it's the goal?" She scanned the map again before thinking of her own attempts to track the movements of the new crystal. Some of the locations on the map seemed the same as those where pyramid accidents had been reported. Then there were others she hadn't heard anything about.

"These could be the sites of more pyradisté incidents or something completely different," she said.

Like a tunnel opening.

She grinned at Gunnar to find him smiling at her, too.

"You two are cute when you're sleuthing," Dina said with a wink. "Care to elaborate for the rest of us?"

"We have a place to start," Gunnar said as Thana announced, "We should head here." But to undermine their portrait of closeness, they pointed to different places on the map.

"Perfect," Sylph said wryly.

Gunnar closed the book with a snap and gave Thana a lofty look. "I'll hear the reasons behind your choice." But he began striding toward the horses.

"When?" she asked as she hurried to catch up, cursing his longer legs.

"On the way to my choice."

She muttered a few phrases she definitely should not say in front of royalty, glad for once that he outpaced her by too great a distance to hear.

Not far from the pyradisté camp, they set up camp themselves, all of them exhausted from the night before and needing a longer night so some could sleep while others kept watch. Thana didn't even have time to anticipate another night with Sylph because she fell asleep as soon as she lay down.

There was nothing left of the farm but a hole in the ground.

Sylph and the others had ridden hard just after dawn, following the enemy map. They only found this place because Sylph had sensed the disturbance in the earth. She'd been connected to her stone pyramid for miles, looking for this tunnel entrance Prince Gunnar hoped to find.

Instead, they'd found torn soil strewn about, along with a scattering of green leaves that might have been vegetables. Clumps of torn thatch spread along the ground. Apart from the dark earth that blighted the lighter soil like some malevolent creature, Sylph might have guessed that a cart had overturned, and here remained the scraps that could not be salvaged.

But with her pyramid, she didn't have to guess.

If it had been a farm, what of those who'd lived here? Had they been a family? More than one? While the others gathered around the sunken patch of ground, she looked for tracks but saw only their own horses. No one else had come and gone.

Not aboveground, anyway.

"It's like the earth swallowed everything," Dina said. "It's sure not a tunnel entrance unless it was filled in."

"No one left that I can see," Sylph said as she wiped the dirt from her hands. She slipped a hand in her pocket, running her thumb along the edges of her pyramid as she fell into it and scanned the area closely. "There is a tunnel down there, but…there was a cave-in," she said softly. "The tunnel makers dug themselves out, then filled this area behind them as they left."

"But why bother filling it in?" Thana asked. "And what happened to the farmers?"

Prince Gunnar wiped his forehead. "They couldn't leave a hole, didn't want anyone to follow them."

"And the farmers?"

"Like I said, they didn't want anyone to know." He took a deep breath, his face grim. "If we hadn't found that book or didn't have Lady Sylph, we might have thought this some sort of sinkhole that had swallowed the farm and farmers, too." He nudged a bit of thatch with his foot. "The pyradistés probably blew the house apart to support their ruse."

"No," Thana said, her tone still striving to be light. "Okay, maybe the pyradistés destroyed the house, but…" She looked at Sylph, her mouth working. "The farmers ran away, right? I mean, who would have believed them if they'd said a group of pyradistés had come up through their house like giant moles? There was no reason to kill them."

Sylph fell into her pyramid, her senses cast into the earth. She found eight voids in the ground not far away, the right shape and size. Her heart fell for Thana. "I'm sorry. It's true."

Thana turned away as if sick, and Sylph heard her sob. The pyradistés might be her people, but the farmers were her people, too, in a way, being peasants. Or perhaps it was more than that. Perhaps Thana would weep if these were nobles or visitors from some distant shore. She'd always wondered if Thana had originally helped her out of a sense of duty, both because of their respective stations and because of Thana's being an agent of the crown, but now she knew differently. Thana had helped her because she was a person who'd needed helping.

Sylph had suspected it before, but to have it confirmed atop an unmarked grave sat heavily on her chest.

She put her hands on Thana's shoulders. "What can I do?" she asked softly. She didn't want to explain her thinking, didn't want to trot out words like peasant or status, not here where it ceased to matter. For those who'd lived here, with nothing but each other, perhaps it had never mattered. But Sylph still had her life, her many powers. There had to be something she could do.

"Help me catch them?" Thana asked.

Catch, not kill. She was still Thana. "Yes."

Thana took her hand and kissed it.

"Shall I create a way for us to climb down, or shall we move on?" Sylph asked.

Prince Gunnar stared at nothing for a few moments, but Sylph didn't know him well enough to guess at his thoughts. She'd never really known him, and she pitied him his mask. At least she didn't have to pretend to be jolly all the time at home.

"We go down there," he said. "At least for a little way. Maybe we'll get lucky." He nodded at Dina. "Picket the horses. We'll be back for them." He glanced at Sylph. "Do what you can to…make the entrance…efficient."

She nodded, certain he meant that she was not to disturb the nearby bodies. Sometimes, doublespeak came in very handy. Even Thana didn't implore the prince to say what he meant at the moment.

"Thank you," Thana said, wiping her tears on her sleeve.

Sylph couldn't help a cluck of her tongue, but she didn't have a clean handkerchief to offer.

Thana gave her a crooked smile. "I know what that was for. I'm going to lick my thumb and clean your cheek next."

Sylph fought the urge to flinch. "Please don't. And stand back now, away from the hole."

Thana nodded, but before she got far, Sylph kissed her quickly on her tear-stained cheek.

The ground was easy to part, the earth already disturbed. She sensed the force that had cracked the larger stones, an explosive pyramid that left some edges jagged and raw like open wounds. She went carefully by the sad voids in the sea of earth.

It amazed her, as it never would the unfeeling ground, that an element she'd grown so close to in so short a time was partly responsible for these deaths. She was surprised by her depth of feeling. If these crimes had been discovered by someone who'd believed a lie about a sinkhole, it wasn't as if they could put the ground on trial or injure it with slanderous whispers.

As much as she felt moved by the earth's history, what she'd come to think of as memory, the stone that all the world rested upon was not alive. She had to be the closest to it out of anyone, taking comfort from its power and security, but she could not fool herself into thinking that it cared.

Even so...she cared for it.

Thana looked awed again as Sylph created a stairway down into the darkness. She was glad someone else could feel emotional about her power. Maybe one day, her magic might be understood.

"What do you think we'll find down there?" Sylph asked. "Besides the culprits."

"Answers, I hope." Her face creased with concern. "For all we know, the source of the crystal might not be far away. Will you be all right?"

Impossible to know. Even the feel of unworked crystal at the academy had her flailing, desperate to latch on to any pyramid. "I have this," she said, looking at her stone pyramid. "It holds much the same power. I can only promise to try to keep my head."

"That's all anyone can promise," Thana said with a snort. She stared at her feet. "I want you to know how proud I am. Of you," she added, speaking quicker after the heartwarming words. "I know that sounds awkward coming from someone that you..." She cleared her throat. "Anyway, I wanted you to know. I mean, I don't want to sound like a parent or your aunt or anything."

Sylph grabbed her hand. "Thank you." When Thana smiled and went to pull away, Sylph tightened her grip. "No, you have to understand, to hear the words I'm not saying, like you did before." Shame burned in her. "No, wait, I want to try." She lined the words up in her head, everything she'd tried to express during every clumsy attempt. She didn't want to blather on about holes in her heart or other organs. She wanted it to be true and right.

And to her surprise, Thana didn't blush and turn away or make a joke to fill in the silence. She waited.

Sylph breathed deeply, feeling as if she'd just taken the stage. "You are…I am…" She fought a stab of frustration. "We're friends. Right now. And whether we are ever more or not, I will always cherish all the moments with you. And I look forward to my future moments because no matter what we will be to one another, every moment spent with you feels like a gift. If that's love, then that's what I feel. I don't know if it's the love of a friend or if my ever-present desire to kiss you means it's more, but it sits inside me like a light, and I never want to see it dim."

The words that had started as a trickle became a flood, washing away her mask as they came, so she had no idea what her face was doing, nor did she care.

Thana's eyes sparkled like black jewels, and she practically leaped into Sylph's arms, burying her head in Sylph's shoulder. "You said you weren't good at words, but you are," she said around her sobs. "You're good at everything, and it's not fair, and I'm sorry I thought of you badly at times, even when you deserved it, and I feel the same way, and if you die in this hole, I will be so angry with you."

The muffled rant tickled her, and she laughed through her tears, kissing Thana's head. She heard another small sob and glanced over to see Dina crying, though she had the decency to look away. Prince Gunnar stared at something in the distance, but he was blinking rapidly and had his arms crossed as if holding his emotions inside.

He cleared his throat after several moments of silence. "Come on, you two. No time like the present and all that."

Thana pulled away, sniffling, and Sylph had to look away before she wiped her face with her sleeve again. Love and such was well and good, but some things just weren't *done*.

CHAPTER EIGHTEEN

Gunnar caught Thana's shoulder as they lined up for the stairs Sylph had created in the rock. He leaned in to whisper, "That was beautiful, Than. I'm so happy for you."

She grinned, too pleased to even kick him for eavesdropping. Still, she had to get herself together. They had business to take care of. "Easy," she said. "We're not engaged or anything. Get your mind on the task ahead."

But then, by the spirits, she and Sylph would find some time to be alone. *That* was her plan for the future.

He winked as he pushed to the front with Dina. He carried his sword in hand, and Dina had hers as well as a shield she'd retrieved from her horse. They'd both covered their riding clothes with studded leather armor.

Thana stayed just behind them, carrying a light pyramid and fighting her nerves. She'd changed back into her cassock and had her stolen satchel slung around her. Sylph brought up the rear. She'd changed into a gray coat and dark trousers. She carried her stone pyramid and Thana's detection pyramid, which extended her already exceptional senses and would warn her of any traps.

Of course, if they encountered any new crystal, it would captivate her all the faster.

A chance they had to take.

Sylph had to sift through the dirt until she found the tunnel, a narrow passage braced by wooden beams. Gunnar looked down it and frowned. It led in the opposite direction of Marienne, and he'd clearly hoped to follow the pyradistés and catch them as they worked.

"If we hurry," Dina said, "perhaps we can find where this crystal is coming from before we ride back to report."

Gunnar frowned but nodded. "I suppose you're right."

Thana shivered. It was one thing to be brave in daylight, but anyone would balk at squeezing through that narrow, lightless passage. "We could collapse this part of the tunnel, but I guess that won't do any good if they're no longer using it."

"I was just thinking that," Sylph said.

Thana grinned. "Really?" She squeezed her arm. "Nice to know we're so in sync."

"Yes, you're very cute together," Gunnar said. "Let's get going before the ground gets jealous of you two and squashes us dead."

Dina barked a laugh as she took point. Thana glared as Gunnar followed, but she fell in behind him. They moved as quickly as possible, everyone but Thana having to stoop. Pebbles rained down whenever they had to squeeze, and she couldn't imagine hauling crystal through the airless gloom. No wonder they'd encountered so few pyramids. If the pyradistés succeeded in taking over, they could travel overland, and Marienne would be flooded with this stuff.

And pyradistés like Sylph would wreak havoc unless they were sent away. Or killed. She wondered which road the rogues would choose. Either decision would make them just like the people they rebelled against.

The tunnel seemed endless, dusty and draining, but before Thana could ask for Sylph to make them a bigger space to rest in, they broke into a natural cavern. By the groans and stretches of the others, they were as happy to see it as she was.

She held her pyramid high, illuminating jagged walls that stretched fifty feet end to end and ten feet high. Slender columns of rock connected the floor to the ceiling, and the slow drip of water came from one corner under a low-hanging ledge. A veil of humidity coated everything in a layer of dampness, and Thana wiped her face as the close air made her sweat.

"No one dug this," Dina said softly. "Do you think the pyradistés knew it was here and aimed for it?"

Gunnar peered down several natural tunnels that ran off the cavern before pointing to one. "This seems the most traveled. The pyradistés probably used these caves to go as far as they could and only tunneled when they had to."

Sylph moved to the center of the cavern and stood with her eyes closed, holding her two pyramids. She seemed serene, and though Thana smiled to see that, she wished she could share it.

"Are you all right?" Thana asked.

"Such age," she said. "Difficult to comprehend but strangely comforting."

Thana didn't quite understand, but falling into a pyramid often made one slightly tipsy. For all she knew, communing with stone while underground could make one full-blown drunk. "I'm glad none of us is claustrophobic." She tried to laugh as her skin crawled.

Sylph opened her eyes. "You need never fear the stone's collapse while I'm around." Affection shone from her gaze, as if being underground let her emotions fly free. Or maybe it was because she was hidden from all but a few eyes.

Thana squeezed her arm, glad no matter what the reason. "I'll keep that in mind." She cleared her throat, desperate to change the subject before she couldn't resist kissing her. She nodded toward Gunnar and Dina, who were looking down the other tunnels, one of which would require them to crawl on their bellies.

Spirits, it couldn't be that one.

"Do you think Gunnar is right," Thana said, "about the tunnel we need to follow?"

She expected Sylph to examine the tracks, but she closed her eyes again. "The memory of stone is tricky when it's not been disturbed."

"The memory of stone?"

Gunnar peered back at them, proving that he'd been listening in again. Thana might have to kick him soon. "How can stone remember?" he asked.

Sylph opened her mouth, closed it, and shrugged. "I don't know how to answer. You stand outside a gift I take for granted, and I know no way to describe it."

"A gift?" Thana echoed with a smile.

Sylph chuckled. "Grudgingly admitted."

"You can speak with the rock?" Dina asked, her face alight with the chance for new knowledge. "Do beautiful stones know of the pleasures they give?"

"I have received no indication of such," Sylph said with a smile. "But the idea that we converse is erroneous. It is..." She waved vaguely. "Intuition, I suppose."

"And what does your intuition tell us about the right tunnel to take?" Gunnar asked, his tone a little teasing. Thana glared, hoping he saw the future in her cocked foot if he added poking fun to eavesdropping.

He winked as Sylph shrugged again. "That tunnel seems as good as any," she said. After another moment with her eyes closed, she nodded. "There are more caverns in that direction, and something is moving through the stone, sending vibrations."

Gunnar nodded, all business again as he took the lead. Thana's heart thundered as they followed. They'd found someone at last. She supposed she should hope it was the pyradistés. The idea of "something" moving through the stone was unnerving, especially considering what slept under the palace in Marienne.

❖

Sylph kept her senses open, keeping a link with her stone pyramid while the detector let her power flit before them. Though surrounded by stone, she felt freer than she ever had. Thana had been right. She couldn't turn her back on this gift. That had likely never been an option, as much as she hadn't wanted to admit it.

And truly, there was no reason Thana *had* to know it now.

Sylph smiled, tempted to reach forward if only to touch Thana for a moment. But something caught her senses. "Stop."

Everyone halted, and she focused. No traps glittered in these walls, but a tantalizing pull came from ahead.

"New crystal," she said. When Thana turned with a look of panic, Sylph shook her head. "Unworked. I can...resist it." And it *was* easier. The stone at the academy had caught her attention, but she'd faced pyramids made from it since, and her stone pyramid granted her somewhere to focus.

Thana's presence didn't hurt, either.

Prince Gunnar peered back at them. "Thana, is everything all right?"

"It's okay," Thana said. "Do you sense any other pyramids?"

Sylph handed over the detector. She could resist the new crystal, but it still made her want to touch every pyramid within reach. There was no reason to tempt herself needlessly.

Thana rattled off a few pyramids, mostly light, a few explosive, but no traps, no detectors, and no cancelation pyramids. They clearly weren't expecting to have to defend themselves.

"But," Thana said. "If they were actively using any of those just now, there's a chance they felt my detection."

Prince Gunnar nodded with a grim look. Unless they wanted to bury everyone, the pyradistés might not have a way to defend themselves. The ones in the forest hadn't been armed apart from their pyramids. Arms and armor were expensive, after all.

And pyradistés were peasants.

For the most part.

Thana's people. And she wouldn't want to see them hurt.

Sylph shook her head. No, Thana was with her people right now. Anyone on the right side of the law who needed her help was one of her people. These rebels, who hated her, who didn't seem to care who got hurt, were no one to her.

Still, Sylph caught the tension in Thana's shoulders, the worried look on her face. "We capture, not kill, right?" Sylph asked.

Thana gave her a grateful look. Prince Gunnar tilted his head. "Of course." He got a similar look from Thana, and Sylph hoped his assertion had been sincere and not prompted by her. She'd hate to begin thinking poorly of him now.

They came on slowly and soon heard voices coming from ahead. As they turned a corner, the tunnel opened into another cavern. Prince Gunnar waved Sylph forward, and she squeezed past him to see light glinting from a number of pyramids scattered about the floor. One person kneeled near a crate, sifting through it, and she didn't need to cast her power out to sense what it was. She tore her eyes away in case she fixated on the crystal and looked to the others in the room. Two stood to the side, near another tunnel, their voices echoing in the small space, distorting their words into noise.

"Can you trap them all?" Prince Gunnar whispered.

"Easily." The only problem would be to stop using her power once she started. The crystal pulled so strongly, she imagined she could hear it, a persistent hum that could only be banished by using her power. She could almost see it as a shimmer in the air.

"Do it."

She sighed as she used her power at last, wrapping the three pyradistés in stone, leaving only enough room for them to breathe and leaving their heads clear. When the shouting began, she almost reconsidered leaving them room to speak.

She forced herself not to act, though the presence of the crystal argued vehemently, even when Thana and the others burst into the cavern, telling the pyradistés to be quiet or be robbed of consciousness. Whether the threat was genuine or not, they complied.

Still, her power said it wasn't enough. She could make a prison for them, a fortress for the prince, a mountain, a pit to the center of the earth. The itch to use the stone became an ache, and she stirred the rocks, listened to the cavern groan around her, singing of all she could do. In such a place, with such abilities, she need never fear anything again.

A touch on her arm made her jump. She'd nearly forgotten there was such a thing as flesh.

"Are you all right?" Thana's brows were furrowed, worry etched in every feature. "Maybe you should go back in the tunnel, away from temptation." She looked to the open crate, to its glittering contents. The man who'd been kneeling beside it glared. Sylph sent him away on a ripple of stone, and he cried out. When she brought him to a halt, he cursed them, not stopping until Dina stepped to his side and had a word in his ear.

Sylph didn't realize she'd taken a step toward the crate until Thana grabbed her arm. "Sylph, listen to me. Go back to the tunnel."

Sylph could move her away as easily as she'd moved the man, but everything in her rebelled at that idea. She clenched her teeth, glaring at the crate now. She would not let it harm Thana through her.

She turned, using all her will, and started for the tunnel, her legs like lead, and the crystal crying out behind her. She buried herself in her stone pyramid, letting her senses fill the other parts of this cavern, finding the crevices and corners, the paths cut long ago by ancient rivers, the long dead creatures entombed in the earth, little more than stone themselves.

The vibrations of the pyradisté she'd missed.

She turned, crying out, trapping the pyradisté in stone, but his pyramid was already falling and burst before she could form words.

A boom shook the cavern, stealing her hearing in a burst of pain that rattled through her skull. The stone betrayed her, throwing her to the ground before tearing itself apart as if it was paper and swallowing one of the pyradistés she'd trapped. Bits of ceiling fell like rain, and dust clouded her eyes, her nose, the stone she'd come to love seeking to cut short her life. She screamed, or perhaps not, too deafened to hear, panicked and not just for herself.

Thana.

The crystal still called to her, this time as if to name her an idiot and say, "It is *stone*, yours to command."

Yes. She drew the ground around her, stilling it before moving it up the walls to hold back the ceiling. It flowed around her like water, carrying her to the cavern's edge, and she fell deeper into the rhythm of it until she could sense the vibrations of all that stood apart from it, limbs slapping, breath coming fast, and the fragile beating of hearts. She grabbed them and carried them to her, all of them covered in dust that she could will away if she chose.

But why bother? She could do so many better things. Her mind followed the branches of this cave system. It went on for miles, meeting other caves, dipping far into the earth to lakes that would never know the breath of wind, down rivers that carved the rock with the patience of millennia.

Finally, her senses came to the mountains north of Farraday, a land filled with this new crystal. She sensed the hole where a glacier had slid away from its brethren, carrying some of the crystal close enough to be found by Farradains, but there was so much more of it about.

And some of it lived.

Beings made of pyramid stone? It couldn't be. Yet she sensed them as they scented the wind as if feeling her touch. It had been a long time since something had commanded them. They'd missed that. They were ready to destroy at an order for those with the right tools.

"Sylph?"

Someone called her name, or perhaps it was the wind sighing across the glacier.

"Sylph, please."

Thana's voice, rough with tears. Something was wrong. And a warm hand clasped hers. She was flesh and blood and needed no cold mountain creatures to wreak havoc for her.

She opened her eyes to find Thana kissing her forehead, her lips. Light shone weakly around her, and tears made tracks through the dust on her cheeks. "Come back," she said with a hiccupping sob.

Unacceptable. Whatever hurt Thana would be buried and stay that way.

Sylph collapsed the cavern beyond, filling it all the way to where the pyradistés had found their crystal, taking with it those still in the tunnels. There were only a few, a small sacrifice that didn't sicken her as much as it should.

She did not venture into the mountains again. The rest of the crystal was too high for any in Farraday to reach. And it already had its guardians.

She sat up from where she'd nearly encased herself in stone. Thana threw her arms around her, and Prince Gunnar and Dina peered at her. His face was bloody, and she held her left arm awkwardly, a line of blood trickling over her ear.

"Wow," Dina said. "The rock was like water, and...wow."

Prince Gunnar nodded but didn't speak. None of the captives had survived, it seemed. It made sense, as they couldn't scramble away from any newly opened pits or debris. Still, Sylph embraced Thana and said, "I'm sorry," both for those in the cavern and those she'd buried along the way. "I was able to collapse this path and bury the crystal they found. It's so deep now, no one will ever find it."

Thana looked at her in awe before kissing her. "Don't ever go that deep again."

"Without the crystal's presence, I don't know if I can." Her stone pyramid begged to differ, but she didn't want to test it, preferring to stay in the present with Thana.

They were a sorry lot as they limped away from the collapsed cavern. Thana kept her hand on Sylph's shoulder as they went, scared of losing her to the stone again, even if there was no chance of them losing each other in the dark.

Gunnar had spoken about going above to travel back to the horses, but they'd all gotten turned around in the dark, and he wasn't certain of the way. Thana thought about insisting. Anywhere was better than down here. She couldn't get the image of Sylph's body encased in stone out of her mind. Only her face had been left uncovered and one of her hands.

And she'd looked so happy.

When they came to the first cavern they'd rested in, they paused again, all of them breathing hard and sweating, creating mud from the dust. Gunnar gestured to a corner. Thana swallowed hard, fear rising. He was going to say that Sylph was too powerful, that even after everything she'd done for the crown, she was going to be exiled upon their return to Marienne. She followed him ready to argue.

"I can't lose her now, Gun," she whispered. "I feel more for her than I've ever felt for anyone."

He frowned. "Who said you have to give her up, you nitwit?"

She blinked. "Oh, I thought…what did you want, then?"

"Not to talk about your cursed love life. I've been thinking about all this tunneling, about the marks on that map that were under the palace." He lowered his voice even further. "What if the pyradistés don't want to break into the palace itself? What if their goal is underneath?"

It took her a moment to remember because she'd known him far longer than she'd known his secret. One of the primary reasons for establishing the Order of Vestra was to protect the fact that each Umbriel carried part of the great Fiend that slumbered under the palace. And they kept that Fiend asleep by using the massive pyramid that sat atop his prison.

Her belly went cold. She'd been forcing herself not to think of that while down here in the dark. One of her main duties as royal pyradisté was to conduct the magical ceremony that let the Umbriels commune with Yanchasa the Mighty. She'd never done it, but she'd seen it. It was conducted via a pyramid under the palace that was itself a capstone for a larger, buried pyramid, the actual prison. She'd felt its malevolent power.

"How would they know about it?" she asked.

He shrugged. "Maybe with all their tunneling, they came close enough to sense it if not use it."

"We'll have to go and..." She paused as his gaze flicked to Sylph. "Oh. She'll sense it, too."

"Probably inevitable at this point if she's going to help us. We'll have to think of a lie for it."

She winced about lying but breathed a little easier because he didn't suggest they leave Sylph out of their plans. Or send her away. "She already knows about the Order."

His eyes hardened. "I don't care. This isn't your secret to tell or hers to know. And her father or one of his cronies could use the knowledge of Yanchasa to rebel against the throne again."

Thana's temples burned, and she resisted the urge to argue that Sylph would never tell her father, but Gunnar couldn't take her word for it. Sylph had been right when she'd said that their station trapped them in many ways. "You're right."

His expression relaxed. "We can't afford to find their new tunnel and chase them. We need to ride to the palace and get ahead of them."

"If Sylph can collapse their tunnel—"

He shook his head. "That worked back there because there's little out this way except some isolated farms to the north." He winced, no doubt remembering the dead farmers, and Thana prayed to the spirits that no one else had suffered from Sylph's collapse. "Even if she can strengthen the ground after she collapses the tunnel, there are too many homes closer to Marienne, not to mention the city itself. And we can't have her filling in the capstone cavern."

She nodded. They still needed to use it from time to time to pacify the Fiend. "I hate the idea of lying to her."

His smile wasn't unsympathetic, but he didn't let her off the hook. "You'll think of something. Put it on me."

"Oh, okay," she said with a snort. "I'd tell you what that pyramid is, Sylph, but the prince would rather lie to you."

He clapped her on the shoulder, reminding her of how sore she was. "Perfect."

By the time they reached the staircase and got above ground again, night was falling. Thana rejoiced when Gunnar said they couldn't risk riding in the dark, even with a light pyramid. Any roads this far in the country were so little used, it would become too easy to get lost or risk a broken leg for one of the horses. They did venture away from the farm, into the beginning of a forest before setting up camp.

Sylph had filled in the staircase, though Thana had made sure to watch her, the image of her entombed in the stone rattling around in recent memory.

Thana helped picket the horses, and when she turned to the small camp with its merry fire, she couldn't help noticing that the two tents sat quite far apart. She stared, her mind kicking up too many thoughts to sort until Dina slipped an arm around her shoulders.

"Not trying to push or anything, but now's your chance," Dina said. "Quiet night following a brush with death, very good for the libido. We don't need to set a watch because no one knows we're out here. You and the lady can get cozy." She shrugged. "Or be so energetic that you get tangled in the blankets. Whichever you prefer."

Thana's heart thundered even as she tingled all over. "I..." She wanted to be with Sylph, alone in that tent, but Dina looked so smug, and she hated being set up. "The mud..."

"Lady Sylph," Dina called. "We found a small spring just past those trees there if you want to wash up." She grinned.

Sylph thanked her, and Thana glared.

"Your turn after her," Dina said. "Or catch her at the spring. I don't care."

"Will you be outside our tent praying to your patron spirits?" Thana asked.

"Sort of. By being in my tent giving the prince a rubdown after all our exertions." She winked. "And getting quite the rubdown in return, I might add. A moment of leisure after a brush with death isn't just good for your libido, you know." After a laugh, she sauntered over to her tent.

Sylph had already finished when Thana got to the spring. She worried slightly all through her own quick wash and on her journey back to the tent. She felt almost as she had at the manor house, but she and Sylph had come so far from the sniping pair they'd been.

At least the sniping had led to bursts of passion.

Though it was cowardly, she told herself she'd let Sylph lead the way. After using her pyramid so deeply, she might be tired, might want to cuddle or sleep on opposite sides of the tent or…

Sylph kissed her as soon as she ducked her head inside, pulling her the rest of the way in. Thana's fears flew out the tent flap and disappeared as Sylph's arms went around her. Thana half stumbled, half fell into a nest of blankets, and when she reached out, she found bare flesh.

She moaned and gasped for air as Sylph pulled back slightly.

"Is this all right?" Sylph asked breathlessly, her voice small, hesitant, so far from a duke's daughter that Thana pulled her in again without thinking.

"So right." She lost herself in Sylph, more than happy to be explored. For someone new to love in all its forms, Sylph seemed keen to learn. And it was better than Thana had imagined as each assured the other, mumbled loving words, and discovered how best to please each other.

"I feel like I almost lost you," Thana said as she breathed hard, the truth spilling out in the wake of ardor.

"Will never happen," Sylph mumbled into her shoulder. "I'm right here. I'll stay here." She pulled Thana close again as if she meant they could stay here forever.

Thana wished that were true as Sylph's touch roamed her body again as if seeking to coax more passion out of her. For a moment, she thought she had no more to give, but she returned the caresses and kisses and found an undiscovered store.

Tomorrow didn't matter, not now when they had each other.

CHAPTER NINETEEN

Sylph woke up smiling, the first time in her life that she remembered doing so. The night's events replayed in her mind as she looked at the dark hair poking out from under the blanket. She feared moving, scared to wake Thana and break this blissful peace. It was even better than being one with the stone, which had been as soothing as she imagined the womb to be.

She shifted slightly, seeking Thana's warmth under the covers, but the prince called from outside, and Thana's head shot out from under the blankets.

"Is it?" Thana asked sleepily, blinking at the tent.

Sylph smiled and tilted her head. "Is what?"

"What?" Thana glanced around, frowning, before her mind seemed to come back. "Hello." She yawned, then cursed as Prince Gunnar called again. "We're coming, all right? Give us a moment to wake up."

"You said, 'is it?'" Sylph said. "When you woke up."

Thana shook her head. "End of a dream, gone now." She smiled happily, her eyes half-lidded, and Sylph had to bring her in for a cuddle.

Reminding her that they were both incredibly naked.

When the prince called again several minutes later, Thana broke free with a huff, pulled on her shirt, and poked her head out of the tent. "We are coming," she said stiffly.

The prince mumbled something like, "That's what I'm afraid of," and Dina brayed a laugh. Heat suffused Sylph's cheeks, and she donned her clothing. When she emerged, Dina and Prince Gunnar gave her polite smiles, and she thanked the ten spirits that they didn't tease her. She wouldn't know quite how to respond. "Are we going to sneak inside the palace?" she asked, steering the conversation as Thana emerged, and they began to break camp.

"We'll not make a grand fanfare when entering the city," Prince Gunnar said. "As for the palace, is there some reason we shouldn't walk right in? The pyradistés in their tunnel won't know we're coming."

"My father…" She didn't want to outline their difficulties, not while still carrying the bliss of the evening before. "If he knows I have returned, he'll want to see me." And perhaps throttle her. No, that was too hot a reaction. Depending on what he'd heard, he'd order her to her room to be kept prisoner, or he'd icily shun her, as good as announcing that she'd been disowned.

At least until the news that nobles could be pyradistés was released. She clenched a fist. And it *would* be released.

Thana took her hand and squeezed, and Sylph relaxed her fist as the pressure in her chest eased. She was not alone anymore.

"Don't worry," Prince Gunnar said. "I'll assure him that you've been on important business for the crown, business that continues until further notice."

It might work. For a moment. "He'll demand answers."

He seemed amused, then nodded as if remembering who he was speaking about. He'd no doubt been to more than one council that had been taken over by Duke Felix Montague of Baelyn. "What if we promise that answers are coming?"

She had to chuckle. "His heir disappeared from the palace amidst a string of bizarre pyradisté incidents, which were no doubt the target of his ire. Now she returns in the company of the prince, the monarch's pyradisté, and a monk from a love chapterhouse. At best, he might conclude that Thana spirited me away so that you and I might be married by Dina, Highness."

Dina shook her head as she saddled the horses. "I'm not senior enough to do weddings. Or a fertility rite, before the young couple can ask." She grinned, even when Thana glared daggers at her.

Sylph chuckled. "Facts he will not inquire about before he implores the nobles' council to censure Your Highness and have the assumed marriage forsworn. And remember, that is the *best* scenario if you leave him without answers."

Prince Gunnar looked utterly offended. "What proud parent would object to their child marrying me? I'm not the crown prince, but I'm still royalty, for spirits' sake. Just how protective is your dear da?"

She sighed, glad of Thana's touch again.

"He's not protective," Thana said. "His feeling is all possession."

Sylph gave her a peck on the cheek, happy that someone could put it so succinctly. "Particularly possessive where land is concerned. He wants my eventual marriage to increase our holdings. If I were to marry an Umbriel—"

"We'd get your land, not the other way around," he said. "I see." He seemed relieved as he swept a hand through his hair, his ego no doubt assuaged. Then he grimaced as if just realizing that their discussion meant her father would be angry about his family's potential loss of holdings rather than his daughter's happiness.

Or her safety, for that matter. He wouldn't bother to inquire if she was all right before attempting to put her under guard again.

"Well, no matter what," the prince said, "I don't want him thinking you were abducted, that I blackmailed you into marriage or something."

Dina bristled. "No proper monk would conduct a marriage like that."

Prince Gunnar waved her affront away. "What would you suggest, Lady Sylph?"

That they all disappear into a world where she and Thana could be together, and everyone left them alone. That would be nice.

And it was the first time she hadn't immediately wished she could go back to the way things had been before she'd ever had magic. Was that because of Thana or the power?

Why couldn't it be both?

She made another fist and imagined the future, saw herself walking up to her father and admitting every deed, every feeling she'd had since this crisis started, throwing them in his face, rejecting every lesson, being free. It seemed like what Thana would do.

And it was…sadly, still moronic. At least for the moment.

"What we don't need is my father actively working against us. And the minute I show my face, that is what he'll do. No matter what he knows, history has proven that he'll want to control my actions, and any defiance will cause him to take steps."

Thana looked pained as they mounted their horses and began the journey back to Marienne. Prince Gunnar seemed thoughtful, but he said nothing, glancing at Thana as if awaiting her input.

"You could be free of your father," Thana said as Sylph knew she would. "Just tell him to—"

"It wouldn't matter," Sylph said before Thana could prove her ignorance about how noble life worked. "What we want to avoid is the aftermath." She tried to smile reassuringly, but her own words pained her now that she'd been shown a different way to live, and Thana's hangdog look hurt even more. "My father is powerful. In some ways, even more than the queen."

Thana's head swung toward Prince Gunnar as if hoping he would argue, but he flinched and nodded. "Duke Felix could sway the nobles' council if he convinces them there's a threat to their power."

"And he'd say whatever he needs to. There's only one way to get around someone who has no concept of fighting fairly."

Thana blanched, jaw dropping. "You can't mean to…" She swallowed. "I know he's an ass, but he's your father."

It took a moment to catch her meaning, but then Sylph had to laugh. "Thana, nobles haven't solved their problems with murder for ages." She thought for a moment. "Well, haven't solved most of their problems with it, anyway." The quiet deaths of noble pyradistés came to mind. "What I meant was, we tell him nothing. The prince rides in the front door, but we enter surreptitiously."

Thana blushed and stammered. She'd been thinking like a noble at last, but Sylph supposed she shouldn't compliment her on that.

❖

For once, Thana didn't have a problem with deception. Much as it pained her that Sylph had to hide from her own father, Thana was glad to keep her out of his clutches.

Perhaps that meant that after their night together, they understood each other more. Dina would be smirking at the thought. She'd already smirked quite a bit that morning, making Thana want to kick her as much as she'd wanted to injure Gunnar yesterday.

But all the smirking in the world was worth it. She had to keep stopping herself from grinning at Sylph like a lovestruck idiot.

She forced herself to think of the task ahead, bringing her back to Sylph's father. All the times she'd imagined having a family as a child, she'd never conceived of cruel or uncaring parents. The few accounts Thana had gleaned of them were, "Nice enough. Kept to themselves." It had been better than nothing.

Gunnar's father had died around the same time as Thana's parents, victims of the same illness. But records of her low-born parents were scarce, unlike those of the man who'd sired a child with the queen. By all accounts, he'd been a carefree, boisterous man, quite unlike the father of Earnhilt's first child, and he'd suited her down to the ground as a longtime friend and sometime lover. Thana had often imagined her parents being just as happy.

Now she had to deal with a father of quite a different stripe. A not at all nice fellow in everyone's business. Unless Sylph's plan worked, and they could avoid him.

But if she wanted to be part of Sylph's future, she couldn't avoid him forever.

"Isn't your father afraid that by treating you so badly, you'll undo everything he's worked for after he dies?" Thana asked as they rode for Marienne.

Sylph tilted her head. "I doubt he thinks of his actions as being bad. He sees them as lessons that I will no doubt come to appreciate. Everything else is inconceivable."

"What if you threatened him by saying he has to let you do as you please, or upon his death, you'll donate all your lands and money to charity."

Her laugh was high and sweet, as if they weren't speaking of a parent's lack of love. "I have plenty of cousins who would love the chance to inherit in my place."

Thana rubbed her roiling stomach. "Ugh. You should all team up and overthrow him. Then you can split the cash."

"You're awfully bloody-minded all of a sudden. Is rebellion the future you have planned?"

Thana shrugged, hoping to seem as if she was in on whatever joke had put a twinkle in Sylph's eye. In truth, she had no more ideas about the future than she'd had when they'd decided she should be the keeper of it.

❖

Even while riding at a good clip, they didn't reach Marienne until nightfall. Even with the cover of darkness, Thana fought to control her jangling nerves.

As planned, Gunnar and Dina went ahead. They'd meet up with the rest of the Order and bring them into the secret passages nearest the entrance Sylph and Thana would use. Everyone bid farewell hurriedly, and Gunnar started down the main thoroughfare while Thana led Sylph to the right of the gate, down a few of the darker streets, where they found a hostler and left the horses.

"We'll be less conspicuous on foot," Thana said. They'd already raided Sylph's clothing for darker outfits and had borrowed hooded jackets from Dina and Gunnar. It was a little too warm for them, but they hoped the breeze and the darkness would give them enough reason to avoid suspicion.

Still, Thana steered them around large groups of people and kept to the shadows. Sylph gawked as if it was another world. She craned her neck to peer at people milling around taverns or chapterhouses. She slowed as they passed various tradesmen closing for the night. Thana would have thought the whole of Marienne a fair in her eyes.

"Are you nervous to be back?" Thana asked, trying to puzzle out her behavior.

"Hmm?" Sylph asked, engrossed in watching someone call in their children for the night. "Is it always so…lively?"

"People's lives? Usually. Apart from the graveyards."

It was a tasteless joke, regretted instantly, but Sylph only said, "Yes," in a distracted way.

"It'll quiet down as it gets later."

Sylph finally looked her way and smiled sheepishly, like a student caught not paying attention. "Most of my days have been quiet, you see, and anytime we rode out among the peas...people, they were always quiet, too. Was that from fear?"

Thana pulled away from irritation, her first reaction to the cluelessness of a noble, but she remembered what Dina had said about snobbery, and Sylph's quick change from saying peasantry to people spoke of effort.

Thana took her hand and intertwined their fingers. "Maybe it was fear. Or maybe it was more like what you're feeling now, curiosity about what's different, each side treating the other as something glimpsed at the village fair, except the villagers aren't part of the body that can send you to prison...or the scaffold."

"Yes," Sylph said distractedly, but Thana could see by her frown that she was listening. And her grip on Thana's hand didn't waver. And though Thana had said the last part a little archly, it was just a fact of life for Sylph.

Thana told herself that it was a fact of life for everyone, that someone had to be in charge, and right now, she was part of a team working to keep the status quo. At least she could comfort herself with the fact that she'd joined that team out of friendship and that the Umbriels were good leaders.

Even if some of their nobles were complete asses.

Not her noble, but still.

"You can always talk to them more after you're a duchess," Thana said. "Your father must have people who act as go-betweens for him and farmers or shepherds or whatever." Most of country life was still a mystery. "You could talk to those same people more often and find out what they have to say." Though she imagined they'd be astounded into speechlessness.

"I could, couldn't I? You know, it never really occurred to me to undo my father's legacy." She seemed almost delighted by the idea, even though they'd spoken of it before. Thana was just glad it seemed to add spring to her step.

Soon enough, they reached a section of the palace wall that would have to be scaled in order for them to reach the secret entrance. Thana cast about for anyone watching, then said, "Up and over," and cupped her hands to give Sylph a boost.

"Thana," Sylph said quietly, her tone affectionate. Darkness concealed her expression.

"What?"

A grinding sound came from the wall, and a darker patch appeared in the center, a door created with Sylph's power.

Warmth suffused Thana's cheeks as she hurried through. "Fine. Just don't be so noisy." And after what had happened underground, Sylph's power still unnerved her as much as it awed her.

The sound was slight as the wall closed behind them. At the end of a short passage, Thana pressed her hand to a pyramid inset in the real wall that led into the palace, and the door swung open, admitting them into the secret passages. Safely inside, Thana lit a light pyramid and hoped she remembered the way to the caverns beneath the palace.

Sylph couldn't help feeling a sense of privilege as Thana led her through the dark. Here were halls even mightier than the ones she'd grown up in, a sight few outside of the Umbriels had ever seen, that her father would likely never know.

But Thana knew them. And the rest of the Order, strange denizens of somewhere in between noble and peasant. She thought of the areas of town they'd gone through, with as many layers of poverty and privilege as there were strata in the earth.

And Sylph belonged here now, thanks to power she'd been born with rather than her social status, though she hadn't discovered it until it threatened to strip that status away. But it was also a power that no one could take from her.

She touched her stone pyramid to remind herself of this fact, not immune to the irony of taking comfort where she'd once found only terror. The solidness of the palace embraced her like a friend, and she sensed the other pyramids that were part of it, mostly traps, which fled like ghosts through her senses.

But there was another. Made from crystal that felt closer to the new variety than any sort that came from the Allusian mines. It didn't flee but sat below the palace, pulsing like a heart, a malevolent energy that drew the mind like a flash of movement drew the eye.

She slowed, sensing another unknown magic. "What is that?" she whispered, unable to keep the awe from her voice. "That pyramid?"

The look on Thana's face said she knew, but she didn't want to say or perhaps dreaded admitting. "Uh. I was hoping you wouldn't feel that, at least not yet."

Sylph waited for an answer to her question before she asked a hundred others, but Thana seemed reluctant, a suspicious turn in such a normally eager teacher.

Finally, Thana sighed. "Gunnar wanted to be the one to explain." Her face said volumes Sylph was only beginning to learn how to read.

"He can't explain it better than a pyradisté," she said slowly. "So do you mean he wants to hide something, perhaps tell me the official explanation if one is ever required?" And though she was suspicious, and her father's lessons urged caution, she also couldn't help being relieved that Thana didn't want to lie to her. Quick on the heels of that came anger. Weren't they past the time for secrets? "Haven't I earned some trust?"

"It's…not my secret to tell."

Not good enough. Sylph stopped, a wealth of feelings bubbling away. She wanted to bring up everything they'd meant to each other, the time they'd spent in each other's arms, but she couldn't use something as beautiful as that for any reason. She took a deep breath. "If this pyramid affects what we're doing—"

"It doesn't. At least, I hope not. If the rogue pyradistés have discovered it, it could be what they're after in the palace. They'll be as curious as you are." She frowned hard. "But it's nothing they can use, nothing we can use. The less anyone touches that thing, the better."

Sylph fought her temper, banning her emotions as she'd done so many times. "If *you're* saying this, it must be true, with how often you've encouraged me toward magic."

Thana gave her a little smile. "Please tell me that means you'll forget about this." She offered her hand.

Sylph took it and squeezed. "Not a chance." She gestured for Thana to lead the way again.

Thana groaned as she complied. "Tell me I'm not going to be caught between you and Gunnar." She sighed heavily, and Sylph patted her shoulder.

"If the pyradistés are after that pyramid I feel below, then it is a part of our current predicament, and if they get their hands on it, I should know what it does in order to defend against it. Would the prince not agree?"

"I don't know. Ask him."

Sylph chuckled. She would help him either way, but she wasn't above letting him think she might walk away. If he thought her talent invaluable during their current trouble, she had more power than she'd thought.

And she was tired of being kept in the dark.

However, she wasn't willing to let Thana be confused for a moment regarding her loyalty. She turned her and kissed her soundly. "No matter what's said or done, I'm on your side, and I won't leave you in peril."

"Likewise," Thana said, giving her a kiss in return.

Sylph cocked her head. "Even against the prince?"

Thana groaned again, and Sylph had to chuckle. "There's no reason for you to be on opposite sides. Ever," Thana said. "He won't ask you to share all your secrets either." She hung her head. "And I'm sorry to have to keep this from you, but I can promise I will do as good a job keeping your secrets from him. Or haven't I proven *my* loyalty?"

Yes, when she'd first smuggled Sylph out of the palace against the queen's wishes. And such loyalty deserved future trust. "All right," Sylph said with a sigh of her own. It wasn't until Thana began walking again that she muttered, "I'm still going to ask."

Thana gave her an exasperated look over one shoulder, but she kept going.

They halted in a dark corridor similar to every other dark corridor. Thana frowned and looked in both directions, craning her neck as if she could see around the corner they'd just passed.

"They should be here," she said. "They came straight here. And this…is probably the right spot." She glanced around as if the hall had developed clues in the past few seconds.

Sylph rubbed her shoulders, feeling guilty for adding to her anxiety earlier. "There are many reasons for tardiness."

"I know." She leaned into Sylph's touch. "The queen probably wanted to talk. Ivar and Illis might have still been dealing with where to put all the captives. There might have been some court nonsense Gunnar had to take care of."

"He might have needed to speak with the nobles' council and calm my father if he isn't already out stirring up trouble."

"Won't he be out looking for you if he's doing anything?"

Sylph snorted and quoted him. "Never waste time doing anything someone lesser can do in your place. Focus on those tasks which only you can accomplish."

Thana turned slowly, a look of pity and horror on her face. "Looking for you isn't wasting time." She closed her eyes and breathed hard as if calming herself. "If necessary, I will always find you myself."

With a laugh, Sylph kissed her nose. "I will endeavor not to become lost. And I'll find you, too. Provided I'm not busy with something else, of course." She lifted an eyebrow to Thana's look of affront and then squeaked as Thana tickled her. They laughed for a few moments until Sylph noticed that Thana stood on tiptoe, leaning against her, and the passion of the night before came rushing back.

And there was nothing else to do except try to help Thana relax.

It was medicinal, really.

Sylph kissed her and found eagerness returned. Thana's hands ran along her body, and thought became lost to sensation. She had a brief moment of wonder that a dark, dusty hallway could be a place of possible ecstasy before Thana took her breath away.

Then, slowly, a siren call wormed into her thoughts, merging briefly with passion before pushing it aside.

New crystal, shaped into a power similar to that of the malevolent pyramid.

Sylph tried to lose herself in Thana while also summoning the words to warn her. But this pyramid promised delights equal to Thana's. No rage or destruction here, no mere power of cancelation. She could surrender to this without consequences, be carried away with a feeling she was tired of fighting.

"Sylph? What's wrong?"

Thana's fiery touches stilled, but sensation still carried through Sylph's mind, ecstasy from the inside out.

"Sylph? Is it…okay, don't panic. Here." Something cold and unbreakable slid into her hand, her pyramid, but how could it match this promise of flesh, a host of possibilities beyond unfeeling stone?

"Don't you feel it, Thana?"

"No, but I'm trying."

Sylph grabbed her hands, falling with her through the facets of a detection pyramid. It took them through the earth, past the beating heart she'd felt earlier, itself an echo of this power. There, the siren call, far below but moving closer.

"Fiend magic, spirits above," Thana said, her voice a harsh whisper in this place of revelation. She yanked the pyramid away, but Sylph barely needed it now. "Sylph, stop. Let it go. Focus on your stone, please. Come on." Desperation and tears flooded her voice. "Don't let it carry you away."

Fiend magic? Evil monsters from children's stories had their own magic? It was absurd. "Come with me, Thana. Feel this."

"No, break free from it. Now. It's evil, Sylph, please. It's the magic of the pyramid you sensed before, and I should have warned you. Break with it. I have no idea what will happen if you use it, and that should scare you because I know everything, remember?"

Sylph managed to open her eyes, drawn by that distress. She was lying in Thana's lap, her pale, anxious face hovering above. Tears ran down her cheeks as she pleaded. She wiped them on her sleeve. Sylph *tsked*.

Thana's face brightened. "Stay with me. Keep your eyes open." She brought Sylph's hand into view with the stone pyramid inside. "Stay here." She squeezed, and the sharp points dug into Sylph's palm, making her gasp.

"See?" her pyramid seemed to say. "Flesh is ephemeral. I am eternal." And through it, so was she. And it wasn't cold, she saw as she let it capture her senses. The world had been born in fire and carried that flame at its core, a force of such magnitude, it tore itself open on occasion and spread molten rock that birthed new land.

The siren still called, but it only reminded her that flesh had one point in its favor: Thana. And she was in pain.

Sylph struggled to sit up, forcing herself to breathe and letting Thana's words and touches ground her. "It's still there," she managed. "And coming closer." And the large pyramid, the heart that scared Thana so, was beginning to beat in time with the new pyramid as if coming alive.

A rumble began in the stones around them, and Sylph asked her pyramid for answers.

Far below, something stirred.

CHAPTER TWENTY

S pirits above," Thana cried. "What now?" The palace rumbled around them, but at least Sylph seemed to be out of the grip of the new crystal. Thana pulled her upright and kept her close until the rumbling died down. "Did you do that?" she whispered.

"No," Sylph said, the words mumbled in Thana's hair. "It's something under the palace."

Thana breathed in so sharply, her chest ached. There was only one *thing* buried under the palace: Yanchasa the Mighty.

"Shit." Thana's mind raced. Sylph had sensed a Fiend pyramid made with the new crystal, though the spirits only knew how the rogues had managed that. In their tunneling, they must have detected the capstone, the pyramid that kept Yanchasa prisoner.

But who knew what they planned to do with such a pyramid? She couldn't let them get to the capstone, and she couldn't wait for Gunnar. She couldn't let two Fiend pyramids be brought together, or the rogues could awaken Yanchasa.

"I have to go into the caverns below the palace," she said, heart thundering in her ears and her stomach roiling. She leaned Sylph against the wall. "Wait for Gunnar and tell him where I've gone."

Sylph pushed upright, far paler than usual. "I'm coming with you."

"You can't. The crystal—"

"I'll be fine so long as I have this." She held her stone pyramid aloft. "And you."

Thana's heart ached to say yes and for more than loving feelings. She absolutely did not want to go alone, but…"I'm the royal pyradisté. It's my duty. And the closer we come to that pyramid, the more it will pull at you." She grabbed Sylph's hands before she could argue. "And you might use it without meaning to." She kissed Sylph's hands and threw caution out the window. Now wasn't the time for secrets. "The capstone, the pyramid you first detected below, imprisons a Fiend. Of the monstrous variety. You've probably heard of them in stories, but they're real. Or this one is. The capstone is Fiend magic, a discipline known only to royal pyradistés. Or it's supposed to be. The rogues have made their own Fiend pyramid, and no matter what they think it does, I have to stop them using it near the capstone and waking a monster."

Sylph frowned hard, her eyes unfocused as if she'd fallen partway into a pyramid or was slightly drunk. It was absolutely the former, but Thana's mind was reeling, babbling away.

Thana backed up a few steps. "If Gunnar doesn't come, you have to find him. Please, Sylph. I…" But she couldn't say that her task might be impossible while alone. It couldn't be.

Sylph took a few steps after her, but she was slow. Thana lit another light pyramid and commanded it to stay on. She set it on the floor and turned, blocking out the sound of Sylph's few footsteps. She didn't know how long Sylph's control could last—another ticking clock to worry about—but it would weaken the closer Sylph came to the new crystal. Better to be alone in this even if that thought made Thana want to vomit.

And what in the spirits' names could she do by herself if the rogues had reached the capstone cavern? She wanted to try a lock, though she'd never done that alone. And she didn't know if she could fight a host of her peers, especially if they started canceling her pyramids.

She clenched a fist. She could yell, plead, warn them to stop. They couldn't know what they'd be doing by tapping into the capstone. Yanchasa's awakening would kill them all. It would most likely kill everyone in the palace, then in Marienne, once the great Fiend was loose. She'd tell them that, too. No matter how motivated they were to be autonomous or even in charge, they had to possess some self-preservation. And hopefully, some reason.

She hurried through the secret passageways, going lower until the bricks gave way to natural stone. When she arrived at the stout door to the capstone chamber, she pressed her hand to the lock, and the door opened with a groan of rusty hinges.

The cavern stood empty, the capstone protruding from the floor to at least half her height. It glowed softly, a homey counterpoint to its general malevolence. She stepped inside, searching the shadows and breathing easier when no one peered back at her.

Now for the lock. She didn't have the pyramid that let her communicate with the capstone. It was in her office. But she didn't think she'd need it. It was only used in conjunction with the four sets of manacles at the capstone's base, where the Umbriels stood when they shed their anti-Fiend necklaces that kept their Aspects inside during a ritual known as the Waltz.

And after all this was over, the Waltz might have to happen sooner than anyone thought.

But not right at this moment. She pulled out her mind pyramid and prayed to the spirits of knowledge that she'd be strong enough to lock the capstone alone and keep anyone else from using it.

Sylph wanted to protest as Thana left her behind, but it took most of her energy just to stand. And part of her knew Thana's argument made sense. The closer she came to that pyramid, the harder it would be to keep from using it, whatever it did.

Like awaken a great Fiend, some fairytale made life. The new siren-like pyramid she'd sensed hadn't felt as evil as Thana seemed to think it was, but it had been very seductive, and she sensed its ability to change those around it. Into what, she didn't know. It might change people into whatever she'd felt underground, a thing that seemed eerily similar to what she'd sensed in the mountains.

Fiends?

Impossible, surely.

But she'd never get any answers by lingering here.

Thana seemed to think she'd need more help than just the two of them, so Sylph would find it for her. She scooped up the light pyramid and looked back down the hall, wondering which way to go, but there was no time to figure it out. She could find her way easier inside the palace proper. Running into her father didn't seem as great a problem compared to saving Thana's life.

She fell into her stone pyramid, wrenching her senses away from the siren pull below. She focused on the bastion of stone around her, block upon block, and made herself ignore their history, fighting to feel the present and view the palace like a map until she found a nearby gap that signaled a hallway.

She'd have to work quickly or she might destabilize the floors above. With a groan of sliding rock, the wall opened before her, then reformed as she stepped past, fitting together from memory. She passed through the wall into a light-filled hallway.

A slight shudder rumbled through the building, nearly lost as someone screamed and fled from her. She ignored them and studied the hall, seeing no furnishings on the walls, no rugs to protect the slipper-clad feet of courtiers or nobles. Servants' halls. She needed to go higher.

She imagined the wall before her as a staircase, and it was so, reforming as she passed, but warning her again that pulling at the stone around her could damage the palace in other areas, and she was forced to keep her senses wide open, trying to move quickly but with care.

Hopefully, anyone who saw her would think her a dream.

She emerged into a large room with the rug bunched into a corner by her power. It was a place where the queen often held court, but it stood empty now. She hurried to the hall outside, got her bearings, and strode as fast as she could toward the stairs that would take her toward the royal quarters.

Courtiers thronged this area of the palace. As she threaded through them, she ignored any comments or questions. Word of her arrival was no doubt already on its way to her father's ears, another reason to hurry. She kept her focus tight on her pyramid, though the siren call had dimmed. Even so, she nearly sprinted up the next staircase.

And stopped. No guards stood at the entry to the royal quarters.

That wasn't right. She sent her senses out again and noted the trap pyramids nestled in the walls. They hadn't been canceled or set off, so the royal apartments might still be safe, but even if the queen and the prince weren't in their rooms, someone should be on guard.

She turned, frowning, searching, and spotted movement down the hall, turning the corner toward where the council chambers waited. It seemed a likely place to find out what was happening.

Even if her father might be there.

Sylph took a deep breath, spurred into motion when she heard footsteps on the stairs. She couldn't linger and be questioned by curious courtiers or palace guards, so she rushed for the council chambers. As she turned the corner, she saw guards on the room, but the door stood slightly ajar.

She drew herself up as the guards stepped in front of the doors, barring her way. "Lady Sylph Montague," she said archly. "Stand aside."

They didn't even look at her, didn't seem to be looking at anything, not even the pyramid in her hand.

They didn't even blink.

And she didn't have time to figure out why. She pulled a block of stone from either side of the door—making it sag slightly on its hinges—and used the stone to pin the guards to the walls. They didn't protest, certainly hypnotized.

She stepped closer and slowly pushed on the door. Her father's raised voice greeted her, and she paused. He rarely yelled, and she tried not to let it unnerve her as he berated a small group of men and women clustered in one corner.

"You've gone too far," he cried.

Sylph edged closer. Her father stood in front of a group of his peers on the far side of the table. At the head sat the queen and prince, both with vacant expressions similar to that of the guards. Sylph clenched her jaw to steel her nerves and took another step. Her father turned at the movement, gawking. She nearly laughed to see him so discomfited, so human. She recognized all those who stood with him, but the group in the corner were strangers to her.

All but one, she realized as she focused on a lone woman who stood to the side of the queen's chair. Lady Lucia, the queen's current lover.

❖

Thana stepped back from the capstone, not happy with the hasty lock, but it would have to do. At least the rumbling had stopped, so she supposed she'd accomplished something. She didn't want to detect the rogues' pyramids again, not wanting them to know they'd been discovered…if they didn't know already. The last thing she needed was for them to try to cancel her pyramids.

Or, spirits forbid, the capstone.

She needed more pyramids than those she carried. She'd have to raid her office. She could check on Sylph, too, escort her upstairs if she was still waiting on Gunnar or collect him if he'd made it.

She raced out of the cavern and up into the secret passages. When she rounded the corner to find Sylph gone, she wasn't even that surprised, though she'd been hoping for a better outcome.

"You did tell her to find the Order if they didn't show," she mumbled. Maybe she'd get lucky and run into all of them in the royal quarters.

She had to exit the passages and go up the main stairs, hoping again that one day, she could travel the entire palace within the walls. The halls were buzzing with the news that Lady Sylph, dressed all in black like a mummer, had appeared out of nowhere. As Thana wound her way through gossiping courtiers, the story grew from simple gossip about Sylph's purpose to more bizarre stories, with everything from a murderous gleam in Sylph's eye to the image of her screaming about wild Fiends.

It seemed no one had seen her pyramid. Or perhaps they hadn't cared to see a noble with peasant magic. And it wasn't snobby to think so. She was trying to give more nobles the benefit of the doubt, but these were courtiers, deserving of scorn, especially when the comment she heard most was some variation of, "Did you see her hair?" followed by mocking laughter. Thana was tempted to shout the truth about noble pyradistés and give them something real to talk about, proving that Gunnar had been right not to tell her.

She turned away from the stairs that led to the royal apartments, not wanting to bother with the guards or give any watching courtiers a reason to follow. Instead, she ducked into an empty alcove and slipped behind a painting, entering the secret passage that led to her office. Once there, she took a moment to breathe in the scent of leather and old books, catch her breath, and gather her courage. People needed her, and she wasn't going to let them down.

After stuffing her satchel with useful pyramids, she hesitated at the Fiend pyramid that linked with the capstone, then packed it, too, keeping it in the box so she didn't accidentally grab it and help the rogues destroy the city.

Now she'd have to risk the royal halls, but at least she'd be on the other side of the guards and away from prying eyes. She opened her office door and hurried toward the queen's apartment. Gunnar had to have explained things to her by now. He was probably with her at that—

The door to the queen's apartment stood open. It was never left that way. Earnhilt valued her privacy too much.

Thana slipped a hand into her satchel and readied a flash bomb. The rogues couldn't have gotten in here. She glanced at the traps in the walls that she hadn't disarmed earlier. They were still clear, gleaming with warning for those who approached with murderous intent.

She leaned around the door, surveying the room. Lady Lucia, the queen's lover, lay on one of the couches, her eyes closed. Thana envied her ability to nap during a crisis. But why leave the door open?

And why was she so still?

Thana took a step inside, pyramid at the ready. When someone grabbed her from the side, yanking her into the room, she managed to toss the pyramid, but someone else dove from behind the couch and caught it before it could shatter.

"Illis?" Thana said. Someone pulled on her shoulder, and she whipped her head around, flinching away from a fist poised to strike, but it paused, revealing Dina behind it.

"Thana," she said. "Thank the spirits."

"Sylph?" her father said, brows drawn in confusion. Then his jaw tightened as if seeing his daughter made him more in control. "Go to our apartment. I'll be there shortly."

Her recent practice at maintaining control made it easy to ignore him, even as much as her body wanted to automatically obey.

But she was finished with his tyranny. "No."

His jaw fell with such alacrity, it was a wonder it didn't drop from its sockets and fall to the floor.

Lady Lucia laughed. "So she does have a tongue in her head." Her eyes widened as she glanced at Sylph's pyramid. "I was hoping I wasn't the only pyradisté with noble blood. Come to join the cause?" She rested a hand on the queen's shoulder and lifted her own pyramid.

Sylph kept her face blank. Thana would have shouted defiance, but she had no idea where the battle lines stood, only that she should keep the Umbriels safe for Thana's sake and all her talk of Fiends.

And Lady Lucia clearly had the upper hand. The queen and prince sat like statues, hypnotized. Could the lady kill them with a thought?

"I've come to learn," Sylph said carefully. "I've heard much in the past few days."

Lady Lucia inclined her head. "Clearly, you've discovered that noble pyradistés aren't as impossible as once claimed. The crown feared us and so attempted to eradicate us, but we have now returned, and with our brethren"—she indicated those who stood with her—"we will create a new ruling class."

"That is not what we agreed," Sylph's father said. He slammed his hand against a chair, but his outrage seemed to stem more from Lady Lucia's words about the ruling class than from the revelation about noble pyradistés.

He knew, then.

Perhaps had always known.

All her worry, her anguish, and he'd already known about noble pyradistés but had never said a word? She felt a weight in her chest, a simmering pit of anger.

No, not now. She had to pay attention.

The six nobles behind her father were nodding and muttering to themselves about how they'd been duped, and pyradistés would never rule. Sylph wondered where the rest of the nobles were. Assembling another faction, or had they been silenced by this crumbling cabal?

"We were to secure the rule of Farraday in the hands of the council where it belongs." Her father gestured at the people in the corner, who moved closer to Lady Lucia and the Umbriels. "Not in the hands of the cursed peasantry."

Several of the "cursed peasantry" had pyramids, which they didn't hesitate to brandish as they muttered, but none of them attacked. They'd had practice biding their time.

Lady Lucia barked a laugh. "They have more nobility than you ever will, Montague. But don't worry, they'll have titles soon enough. All except yours, which will be Lady Sylph's." She gave a beatific smile and inclined her head. "Duchess."

A clever ploy. Would she hypnotize the nobles into signing away their lands before she killed them, or would she even bother? "What of those pyradistés who oppose this scheme?" Sylph asked. "Like the royal pyradisté?"

"Any traitors who choose them over us shall be dealt with," one of the pyradistés said, the gravel of hatred in his voice. "We'll soon have enough crystal to deal with all comers."

Not anymore, but she didn't mention that she'd buried it.

"Quite right, Headmaster," Lady Lucia said. "But if you've any favorites among them, Lady...I beg your pardon, Duchess Sylph, I'm sure we can leave you to persuade them."

Sylph's father turned a chair over like a child throwing a fit. He wasn't used to being ignored. "Sylph." He breathed hard, his disbelief so clear, she expected it to take shape. "I..." He glanced at the pyramid in her hand at last, and she expected disgust, even hatred, but Lady Lucia had clearly changed him, at least a little.

"Are you going to ask me to save you?" Sylph could hardly believe he wasn't commanding her to do so. It was almost enough to make her want to give Lady Lucia's idea a try.

"Must I ask?" He blinked, and she would have given her eyeteeth to know what he was thinking.

She sneered as she stepped farther into the room. She couldn't let time get away from her, not while other pyradistés were skulking in tunnels and sniffing around ancient pyramids. Still, she had to ask. "Are you expecting filial affection?"

Her father took a step back as if the idea of affection scared him more than anything. "Family loyalty is—"

She laughed. "The pyradistés I've met have been more like family than you ever have." Well, one had anyway.

Lady Lucia joined in her mirth, eyes sparkling. She wasn't at all the stupid creature rumor painted her to be. And the differences didn't stop there. The closer Sylph came, the more she spotted. She'd memorized the looks of every noble, and this one had a slightly different curve to the mouth than Lady Lucia and fewer dimples, and the eyes were a bit closer together than the simpering moron the queen doted on.

This wasn't Lady Lucia, but they could be sisters. Even twins.

Oh, it made sense now.

Two noble daughters, the powerless to inherit and go to court, the pyradisté to be hidden. Then opportunity had struck, and so had she. If that was true, this woman was brave, at least, a person who hadn't let fear paralyze her into ignoring her gift.

And Sylph's father had embraced her.

As petty as it was, Lady Lucia's sister would have to pay for that. Sylph gripped her pyramid and set the floor to moving.

CHAPTER TWENTY-ONE

Thana was torn between the desire to hug the members of the Order and punch them as they ceased trying to attack her and fired questions instead.

She slashed a hand through the air, silencing them. "Sylph and I were in the secret passages when she sensed someone bringing a new pyramid, Fiend magic, toward the capstone, and we have to stop whatever they're doing before they awaken Yanchasa." She took a deep breath and gestured to Lady Lucia's still body. "Now you explain."

"She came in while we were discussing Order business with the queen, so we hid until the queen could get rid of her," Dina said. "When a few minutes had passed and we heard nothing, we checked, and the queen, Gunnar, and Lady Lucia had left."

"We went down the hall," Ivar said, "and found the guards gone, and the lady stuffed into a room outside the royal section. We brought her here, thinking we could help her, but she died soon after. We don't know why."

"Died?" Thana peered around him at the body. "I thought she was sleeping." She swallowed a lump in her throat. She hadn't known the lady well, but her death was as much a tragedy as any other.

"I'm thinking poison," Illis said. "Something's been up with the nobles for days. People have been dropping out of sight and back in, but they act changed. We thought to take the queen's secret passage and find you, but you found us."

Thana held up a hand, something else catching her in the torrent of information. "The queen's secret passage?"

The brothers looked to one another. Dina seemed sheepish as she answered. "Yeah, they didn't know either before I told them. I only knew about it from the one time the queen and I—"

"I don't need those details," Thana said, her anger rising. "Are you telling me the queen has a secret passage leading to these rooms, and she never told me?"

"She only uses it for assignations."

"I got that part, thank you!" They waved and whispered to shush her, but she was livid. "What it is, however, is another way in and out, a path her enemies could exploit." When Dina looked skeptical, Thana nearly kicked her. "There are pyramids at work here, and even the most ardent paramour can be hypnotized. Show me."

Dina led her to the bedroom mirror, then toggled a switch, and the wall opened. Thana found what she'd expected inside. Trap pyramids dotted this passage, but every one had been canceled, no doubt slowly and carefully over time, letting someone with ill intent come close enough to this door to set off the trap pyramid in the queen's sitting room even before Thana had first left the palace.

Had any enemies used it since? Or had they feared more pyramids in the queen's apartment, a place they wouldn't have unfettered access to in order to carefully disarm the traps? She imagined them lingering here, awaiting their moment. And after the explosion, Earnhilt hadn't told Thana about this, still certain her secret was safe, that the traps of old would protect her, maybe even that Thana would insist the passage be sealed until the current pyradisté crisis ended.

But then the queen wouldn't be able to sneak her lovers past the guard or the nosy nobles and courtiers. Spirits knew her trysts were too important to give up for a little while.

Out in the open, she breathed deep. "Where does this go?"

They took it together, the Order already armed. They arrived in a rarely used guest room outside the royal apartments and near the council chamber. When the floor shuddered, Thana knew they were out of time for figuring things out. That had to be Yanchasa stirring again. She needed to find Gunnar and the queen and stop the pyradistés below. And she needed to find Sylph, though the order of those goals changed every moment.

When someone cried out in the hall, at least the question of where they should head first settled itself.

In the council chamber, several people screamed at once as the floor shifted. Sylph's father staggered and fell. With her stone magic, Sylph trapped the legs of several pyradistés, but others took cover behind the queen and prince. Sylph hesitated to bring the floor up around them, not wanting to encase the royals and the pyradistés together.

Or move enough bricks that everyone plummeted to the rooms below.

A pyramid sailed at her from across the room, and she dove for the floor, rolling under the table as a crack echoed through the room, and light exploded as if from a miniature sun. Sylph cried out with several others as pain speared across her forehead, and the vision in her right eye showed only a mass of bright blobs. One of the nobles collapsed while several pairs of legs ran in different directions.

Sylph scooted back and sent another ripple through the floor, wishing someone would use a cancelation pyramid so she could poach it, but no such luck. Someone screamed just before another horrible flash. Sylph slid out from underneath the table on the opposite side.

And met her father's eyes where he'd also dropped to the floor.

He stared as if he didn't know her. Well, he never really had. "If you don't want to hang for treason," she said, "I suggest you help me." Several of his cronies were trying to fight the pyradistés but were thwarted by mind pyramids or those awful flash bombs.

When another pyradisté pulled a pyramid, Sylph focused on it, hid her face in her sleeve, and set it off in his hand. The light faded quickly, and she risked a look. The pyradisté had fallen over backward but so had one of the nobles, and neither of them moved, stunned. A trapped pyradisté fumbled with a satchel, and Sylph commanded the floor to creep up her body, cementing the bag shut.

And making the walls groan again. It would be so much easier if the room was near the exterior of the palace, with a handy outer wall to manipulate. Sylph scrambled up behind the pyradisté she'd just secured. The woman screamed, slapping at the stone. Sylph ignored her and looked past, seeking a path to the Umbriels.

Lady Lucia's sister smashed a pyramid into a lord, and he collapsed with a scream. She scrambled for the queen just as someone hurtled through the door and leaped upon the table. Sylph recognized Dina as she careened into the lady, not even flinching when a pyramid smacked into her chest.

It shattered into harmless splinters, canceled.

Sylph nearly cried out when Thana stepped into the room, pyramid in hand. "Sylph, use this!"

"Yes." She took hold of the pyramid with her mind as Illis and Ivar scrambled into the room, headed for the pyradistés. Everything faded to the dull gray of pyramid sight, and Sylph moved the power of the cancelation pyramid like a blanket, covering every enemy pyramid and snuffing their power. For a moment, the pyradistés continued to throw the useless crystal at the Order and the nobles, but Dina and the brothers succeeded in carrying the Umbriels from the room.

Lady Lucia's sister was an unmoving heap, as were most of the pyradistés and some of the nobles. The standing pyradistés froze as if they didn't know what to do.

"Sylph!"

She turned, saw the man coming at her, saw the knife, but he was already collapsing before she brought her power to bear. Her father stood behind him with a wine bottle held like a club. His expression was as confused as ever, and she wanted so badly to believe he cared.

But she couldn't risk sentiment at the moment. "No one leaves," she said, edging around him toward the exit. "We'll wait for the queen to—"

Queen Earnhilt barreled back through the door, bellowing at full volume. Thana had obviously released her, and Sylph left her to cow everyone into obedience.

In the hall, Thana was speaking rapidly to the prince, something about mind pyramids. Sylph released the guards from their stone shackles, making everyone jump. "They need your help, too," she said, thankful that Thana was adept at mind magic.

Thana squeezed her arm. "Are you all right? Is Calla one of the traitors in there?"

"Yes, and no. Do you still doubt her?"

"I don't know." She scowled as she released the guards and sent them in to help the queen. "Why isn't she here if she stands with us?"

"I hope you're not talking about me," someone called from down the corridor. Calla led a contingent of palace guards, who saluted the prince. He led them into the council chamber to take possession of the captives.

Calla glared at Thana and Sylph. "What is it with you two and trust? I went for reinforcements quietly, unlike some. We don't want to cause a panic." She snorted. "Honestly, as if I'd betray my own family."

If she'd lived her entire life among the nobility, she might not be so quick to say that. She marched past without another word.

Thana grabbed Sylph's arm again. "I need your help protecting the capstone, but…with this new crystal nearby…"

"I'll just have to face it. With you, my raven, I know I can."

Thana beamed. "Well, me and this." She held her cancelation pyramid aloft. It would be enough. Anything else was unthinkable.

Thana left all the arresting and questioning to Calla and the queen. Yes, she had suspected Calla, but she wasn't ashamed of that. She was beginning to think she should be suspicious of everyone. Especially when the queen's lover had a sister who no one seemed to have known about or had forgotten.

Or she'd been hidden away like Calla, and excuses for her disappearance had been made until her existence had faded past memory.

Who knew how many more of them were waiting in the shadows?

Gunnar led the way to the nearest secret passage, the Order and Sylph in tow. He'd given the queen a brief explanation, and then they were off with barely a moment for Thana to tell Sylph how proud she was.

"Lady Sylph?" Gunnar asked as they walked. "Can you tell if the pyradistés have broken into the capstone cavern below?"

Thana guided her as she focused. "I sense them," Sylph said, her tone dreamy. "Crudely moving through the earth, chipping away. I dare not extend my senses close enough to find their exact location."

"But if they're still traveling, they haven't gotten there yet," Thana said, hopeful and worried at the same time. Her reasons for leaving Sylph behind the first time were still valid, but without her, they wouldn't be able to reach the rogues. "Are you sure about this?" she asked, knowing Sylph would get her meaning.

Sylph squeezed her hand. "If it starts to pull me in, we can use your cancelation pyramid."

"The new crystal resisted last time." She bit her lip. "And I'm not sure what that would do to a Fiend pyramid."

Sylph seemed almost serene as she smiled, contrasting with the darkness surrounding them, but scaring Thana all the same. She'd looked like that when she'd encased herself in stone. "We'll have to wait and see. All I know is, I'm not leaving you right now."

And Thana was supposed to be thinking about the future, but she focused on Sylph's words instead. The future would have to be fine with not being the center of attention for a while.

Sylph held tightly to her hand the deeper they went. Every once in a while, Gunnar would stop and wait for Thana to scout ahead with her detector. The pyramids she sensed were still on the move, and she tracked the new Fiend pyramid, which drew her senses like a light in the dark.

At one touch near the capstone cavern, the enemy pyramid seemed to flare, and a smattering of dust came from the ceiling as the palace shuddered. With a gasp, Thana turned her attention to the capstone, but it was still dormant, locked, though she could practically feel it straining to be set free.

"Thana?" Gunnar's gaze flicked between her and Sylph, who was breathing heavily but evenly and bore a sheen of sweat upon her forehead.

"Go," she said, and they hurried into the capstone cavern at last.

Everyone sighed at finding it as empty as before, but that just meant they'd have to seek out their enemy.

"Can you cancel the enemy's Fiend pyramid now?" Dina asked.

Sylph looked to Thana. "Should I?"

Thana shook her head. "Let me try." She closed her eyes and concentrated on her cancelation pyramid. Again, the rogue pyramid pulled at her senses. It froze in motion as she touched it, almost as if this was what it had been waiting for.

She hesitated. Pyramids in general weren't sentient, but there was something about this one, a definite anticipation. The capstone felt similar, but she'd always thought that had something to do with the actual creature it controlled. What if it was a peculiarity of Fiend magic instead?

She felt around it, and no other pyramid came to stop her, no dueling cancelation attempt. The way was wide open, even welcoming for her to touch that pyramid with her own.

She drew back, intuition clanging like a bell. The rogues had likely copied what they'd sensed from the capstone, but they couldn't know what it did, and they were curious, and perhaps they expected that canceling it would do something besides the obvious.

She cursed, not used to being in the dark as far as pyramid knowledge was concerned. "I don't want to touch it at all," she said to the expectant faces around her. "I'm not sure what will happen. Even using a cancelation pyramid might set it off."

Gunnar glanced at Sylph as if to get a second opinion, and Thana glared. "I might not have the power of some," she said. "But I possess more knowledge than most." Just not enough at the moment. But more than a *novice*.

He smiled crookedly and dipped his head. "Then we stop them the old-fashioned way. Lady Sylph, another staircase, if you please."

Sylph couldn't pinpoint the exact location of the pyradistés, and Thana didn't want her to try. She was barely speaking now, and sweat rolled down her face. When she made a new staircase, she sighed, and power rolled out from her with such force, the hair stood up on Thana's neck.

No slow rumble accompanied her power now. The cavern groaned, and the rock flowed like water, like it had when Sylph had encased herself.

Thana gripped her hand, terrified of losing her, and was relieved to see her smile weakly. "Can we send her up now?" Thana asked. "Surely we can handle the rest of this."

"I'd rather she stays," Gunnar said as Sylph muttered, "I'm not going anywhere." Good to know she could still talk and that she and Gunnar were getting along.

Thana sighed and gestured forward. The fighters of the Order led the way, and Sylph and Thana followed.

❖

These tunnels had been reinforced like the others the Order had encountered, and they stretched in two directions, but Sylph knew which way to go, lured by the siren call of the Fiend pyramid.

Light shone from that same direction, leading the others, but she could have found her way blind. The desire to reach for the siren tingled through her as if her skin was on fire. She had the remedy to put it out, but she couldn't touch this pyramid, not if even Thana didn't know what it could do.

Nor could she twist the stone around, not with the Fiend's prison somewhere in this direction and with the palace sitting above. She couldn't afford to fracture either of those structures.

Movement came from ahead. A figure rose from a sitting position where the tunnel widened slightly. A light pyramid bloomed in its hand, revealing a dusty face with wide eyes. The mouth opened as if to shout.

A knife appeared in the pyradisté's chest as if by magic, but when Ivar lowered his arm, Sylph realized he'd thrown it. The pyradisté staggered a few steps, staring down in astonishment before pulling the knife out and sliding to the ground. The light winked out.

"Al, you all right?" someone called softly. In the shadows of the tunnel, another figure stirred.

Illis fired an arrow into this one, dropping them. Both deaths took only seconds. Only the pull of the siren pyramid kept Sylph from feeling sick.

Thana made a noise of protest, but Gunnar whispered harshly, "They know about Fiend magic."

She closed her mouth, but defiance still shone in her eyes.

Sounds of digging came from a large, well-lit room ahead, but it quieted all at once, and someone called, "Who is it? We know you're there. We will defend ourselves."

"Your treasonous brethren have been arrested," Gunnar called as the Order halted. "Surrender, and the queen may be lenient."

A hurried conversation echoed from ahead, angry, muffled words ending with, "Enough. What does the pyramid above us do? We've never felt its like, nor the like of the one we made. What powerful secrets is the crown keeping for themselves?"

"Give up, and I'll explain," Gunnar said.

Thana made an angry little growl. Sylph squeezed her hand, something else to hold on to as the siren call beat against her brain.

"This magic could change the face of Farraday, of the world," the voice said, a dreamy quality to the words that Sylph well understood. "And you want to hoard it. But our time has come."

Thana gasped and clutched her cancelation pyramid. Sylph reached for it, and Thana yelled, "No," but Sylph's mind was already there. She had to do something. Canceling the enemy pyramids wouldn't smother her pain, but it was better than nothing.

And as she raced through the enemy pyramids, snuffing them, she came ever closer to the siren pyramid and the delights it promised if she touched it in any way, even to cancel.

A sharp sting rolled up her arm, shocking her. Thana was yelling, shaking her, kissing her, and as Sylph opened her eyes, another sting came from her elbow.

Thana was pinching her?

Affront awakened her. "How dare you?"

Thana's eyes were wide, relieved, and she sputtered a humorless laugh. "Come on." She led the way into a scene from a slaughter. Bodies covered the ground, though the Order was still on their feet. Illis was trying to pull someone out of a hole in the ceiling beside a green-flecked wall that stood out against the gray of this newly made chamber.

The green stone had to be the Fiend's prison. The legs squirmed, and Sylph tried to call a warning that this person held the siren pyramid everyone dreaded, but a pulse went out, and she stiffened.

The Fiend pyramid was active.

The tunnel began to shake, and a low groan echoed from somewhere. No, not just anywhere. It came from the prison, from the thing that slumbered there.

That slumbered no longer.

"No," Thana said. She drew a box from her satchel and took out another pyramid, more Fiend magic, Sylph sensed.

"Gunnar?" Dina asked, as a wave of Fiend magic came from the prince. He stood as still as a statue, and the blue of his irises bled across his eyes as horns sprouted from his head.

Sylph barely had time to be shocked as Thana leaped, grabbed him, and fell into her own Fiend pyramid. She wrapped its power around the prince, seeking to hold something in.

There were too many powers fighting for Sylph's attention. She needed guidance, focus. And by the spirits, she needed to touch the siren-Fiend pyramid, the one made from new crystal, and guidance and focus were as good an excuse as any.

Keeping her grip tight around her stone pyramid, she gave herself to the siren.

The world split in two.

Sylph cried out from the pain of feeling ripped in half. Stone magic was eternal. Fiend magic felt mutable, a power meant for change. Both fought her mind for supremacy, one reaching for the stone, the other toward the greatest source of Fiend magic, the creature inside the prison.

And it reached back.

She gasped to find it intelligent, promising overwhelming power, daring her to imagine her control over stone extended to flesh. She could remake herself and everyone around her however she chose. She could remake the world.

But at what price? Enough of her mind was left to question it, but the answer was surprising. She needn't take the power if she didn't trust it. She could send it back where it belonged, into the captive Fiend. That would end this crisis as definitively as anything else.

Sylph doubted that.

She could sense the presence of the rogue pyradisté as he scratched for the same power, but she was much stronger, and the siren wanted her. And oh, it was tempting. With this power, she could create stone-Fiend hybrids, creatures that could guard against this kind of coup ever happening again. Such creatures already existed, she realized, thinking of those she'd felt in the mountains, chunks of crystal given humanoid form, given life, a perfect union of magics.

But she sensed an undercurrent to the power, the same malevolence she'd sensed in the mountains. The person who had created those creatures, those wild Fiends, hadn't had the good of the world in mind. That was why they carried destruction at their hearts.

No, better to keep away from this power, keep to her stone. She tried to pull further away, taking the enemy pyradisté with her, much as he fought. When she sensed his concentration waver, she opened her eyes to see Illis pull him from the ceiling.

The Fiend pyramid fell.

"No," she cried, knowing that being broken wouldn't stop this magic.

It shattered, its power flowing out. The palace rumbled, and the prince roared, a deep bass growl that shouldn't have come from a human throat.

Inside the prison, the great Fiend twitched.

Thana cried out. Sylph had to keep her safe, had to keep the prison intact, or the Fiend would kill them all when it burst into freedom. She had to fight, to concentrate.

To be closer to the stone.

With a last gasp of air, she gave herself to the magic and sank into the floor.

CHAPTER TWENTY-TWO

Sylph disappeared into the rock as if she'd fallen down a well. Thana cried out but was stuck holding her Fiend pyramid on Gunnar. She had to prevent him from manifesting his full Fiendish Aspect and tearing everyone in the room apart.

But she ached to run to where Sylph had vanished. "Spirits, give her back to me," she whispered.

"What's happening?" Dina yelled as the room continued to shudder, and bits of rock rained from the ceiling.

Nothing good. Thana focused on Gunnar. The sooner she dealt with him, the sooner she could free Sylph. Her predecessor had told her she might have to force the Aspect down in one of the Umbriels if something happened to their Fiend necklaces, but Gunnar's was still intact.

It was probably the only reason he submitted to her at all, pitiful as she was at magic.

"No," she said with a growl. She had practiced with this pyramid, sensing how the energy flowed so she'd know what to look for in case this happened. No matter what circumstances had brought her here, she was going to do her cursed job so she could then dig her love out of the ground.

She closed her eyes. Quashing the Aspect was a contest of wills, and the will of a Fiend could be mighty. She imagined herself trying to pack a crate with a blanket just slightly too big for it or maybe trying to turn a rusty handle. But this was her mind at work, not brute force. She could outthink a cursed Fiend. No, she *would* outthink it.

She focused her will and shoved.

Her limbs trembled as if she'd taxed her muscles, and she grunted again. "Come on," she said with a gasp. To her relief, the Aspect receded a little. "Come on, you bastard."

She pooled the efforts of her pyramid with his necklace and shoved with all her might. Gunnar bellowed, his Aspect resisting her.

"Come...on." She had to get to Sylph. She had to...had to...

With a sigh, Gunnar collapsed. Thana stumbled, gasping for air. At her feet, Gunnar's face was human again, with only two drops of blood where his horns had been.

The tremors in the ground stopped. Thana fought the urge to lean on her knees even as she reveled in her victory. If she could subdue a Fiend, she could rescue Sylph. She staggered forward.

"Is he all right?" Ivar asked as he checked Gunnar's pulse.

"He'll be fine," Thana said, her throat as tight as if she'd been shouting.

Illis dropped from the hole in the ceiling. The man he'd been pulling at lay on the ground. "Looks like they were trying to climb to the capstone," Illis said. "They didn't make it all the way."

"Thank the spirits for that," Thana mumbled as she kneeled next to Dina, right above where Sylph had disappeared. The floor was solid. "Sylph?" She slapped on the stone, but could Sylph even hear her, sense her?

It depended on how deep she'd gone, both into the rock and into her magic.

Thana fought the urge to despair. The room was littered with pickaxes. They could get to her. Digging would be more useful than weeping or beating on the stone and demanding that Sylph be returned. This was a problem that had a solution, and she would find it.

"Watch out," Ivar called.

Thana turned in time to see the pyradisté who'd been pulled from the ceiling lurch upward and gouge Illis's leg.

Dina lunged and stabbed the pyradisté, ending him, and Ivar sprang forward to support his brother.

Thana fought another urge to panic as she stood. "Get him up. Come on."

"It's all right," Illis yelled over her. "I'm okay."

Ivar kneeled at his side. "How deep is it?"

"Not very. Give me a bandage, and I'll be fine." Blood trickled down his leg, mingling with the larger pool of blood from the body on the floor. Dina lifted the body and put it in the corner so Ivar could tend the wound. Illis looked up and caught Thana's eye. "Really."

She mashed her lips together, but she had to believe him and not just because she could continue to focus on Sylph if he was all right. "Okay," she said. "Are the rest of the pyradistés…" She didn't want to say dead, didn't even want to think about the corpses around her, the deaths that should never have happened.

"Yes," Dina said. "What should we do next, Thana?"

Thana nodded to her, grateful for the permission to continue. "Next, right." Everyone looked at her, but she began talking to herself as much as them. "The pyradistés had a Fiend pyramid. They tried to use it, and Sylph stopped them. Then it broke."

Illis scratched the back of his head. "My fault. Sorry."

"You didn't know," Ivar started, but Thana held up a hand.

"What's done is done." She took a deep breath. "Breaking the pyramid released this…burst of energy that tried to bring Gunnar's Aspect out, but his necklace and my pyramid stopped it."

"*You* stopped it, Than," Dina said softly.

Thana gave her a grateful smile. "But the burst also affected Yanchasa." She looked to where Sylph had disappeared. Tears threatened, but she shoved them down. "Yanchasa couldn't have pulled her underground from his prison. That was her power." She looked to Dina again. "Full contact with the stone seemed to help her control her power before."

"When she made it flow like water," Dina said, nodding. "So she went down there to focus?"

"Probably to keep the cavern intact," Thana said, glancing around. "No, she wouldn't need all her will for that." Dread grew in her stomach as she looked at the green-flecked stone of the pyramid that held Yanchasa. "The burst of power…maybe it awakened Yanchasa enough for him to struggle."

Dina put a hand over her mouth, her eyes wide. The brothers cursed.

"If so, she's keeping him inside there," Thana whispered, pointing, and the horror of how close they stood to annihilation gripped her throat. He might be listening to them even now. "Oh spirits, she's pitting her strength against his."

As if to punctuate her words, the ground rumbled again.

"What can we do to help?" Illis asked quietly.

Thana rested her hand on the ground, willing Sylph to hold on. "We put him back to sleep. We perform the Waltz."

The world was stillness. In other places, it raged in fire or furious shudders, but surrounding Sylph, it *would* be quiet.

The monstrous Fiend twitched. The earth trembled.

"No," she whispered. She strengthened his prison, pitting her power against his force, then shifted tiny holes to feed her air, and brought the world to stillness again.

It took all her focus, and it was getting worse, the twitching seemed like the movements a person might make just before waking, and once awake, she didn't know if she could hold him, only that she had to try.

Panic tried to gain a foothold in her mind, but she used all her court training to breathe through it, let it wash over her and leave, a pesky annoyance she didn't have time for. It wouldn't be denied forever. She thought of Thana, who depended on her and waited for her.

No, she couldn't let her mind wander too far. She had to wait for the tiniest shift so she could correct it before it became a quake. Thana would have to remain a specter in her mind until then.

Until when? There was no prison she could make that could match the Fiend's strength. There was no way to put it back to sleep. Her mind was one with the stone, but her body was mortal. How long—

The earth rumbled again, stronger this time, and she sensed massive limbs sliding gently against the prison's walls. Their movement wouldn't be gentle for long.

"No." She focused again and breathed, and the earth settled. She could not begin thinking about the future now. Not because she didn't wish to or because of any pact with Thana. She couldn't afford the loss of focus. She had to remain vigilant, ever present, a statue, waiting.

❖

Thana led the others up Sylph's staircase while they carried Gunnar between them. "This is the second time we've carried his unconscious Highness today," Ivar said.

"And he can stand to lose a few pounds if it keeps happening," Illis said, limping and panting under the strain.

Dina chuckled, and Thana wanted to join in, but she wished they'd save their breath for the task at hand. And any attempt at humor felt wrong at the moment. She was already planning five steps ahead. First, she needed to collect the queen, then they needed two others who—

She pulled up short, crying out as she almost collided with Queen Earnhilt and Calla on the stairs. Everyone sucked in a deep breath before talking at once. The cavern rumbled harder than before, shutting everyone up as they reached for the walls to steady themselves.

Thana took advantage of the moment of silence and summarized what had happened.

When Thana finished, Earnhilt's jaw stood out like iron, and Thana could nearly hear her teeth grinding. She sheathed her blade, stepped near the brothers, and hoisted her son over her shoulders. "Come on," she said, leading the way up.

Everyone glanced at everyone else before following. Thana was just happy it had been Gunnar's Fiend who'd almost escaped and not Earnhilt's.

In the capstone cavern, she laid her son on the floor. "We need two more besides Gunnar and I for the Waltz."

Thana looked to Calla, but she stood placidly. She was probably too far removed from the throne to be born with an Aspect. Umbriel children were born with Fiends because before conception, their Umbriel parent passed it to their other parent during a sexual ritual overseen by a pyradisté using Fiend magic.

Another task Thana had never done and didn't look forward to. Spirits, it looked like she'd have to do it now, though. Fantastic, another task to accomplish before she could go after Sylph.

"The crown prince and his wife are in the Western March," Dina said.

Ivar shook his head. "That's a four-day ride there and back." The cavern rumbled again as if laughing at them.

"And the crown prince's father?" Thana asked.

Earnhilt bit her lip before shaking her head. "I don't know where Gerhart is spending his days now." She turned to Ivar. "Go find Lamont or her cronies, see if they know." He nodded, but she caught his sleeve before he could run off. "If she gives you any shit, tell her that given recent circumstances, I will not hesitate to beat the information out of her."

With a small smile, Ivar was off to do her bidding.

Earnhilt looked to Calla. "And you don't have a Fiend." Calla shook her head, and by her horrified frown, she didn't want one. It was probably too much to hope for that she'd ever be happy about anything.

And that was all the Umbriels Thana knew about. "I don't know if it will work with just two of you," she said before anyone could ask. "We might have to ask for volunteers." She winced as she said it. That meant more people being privy to the court's greatest secret.

Earnhilt frowned. Unless they waited for Gunnar to wake up, she would have to have sex with said volunteer while Thana used a pyramid to pass on the Fiend. Then after the volunteer Waltzed, they'd have to wear an anti-Fiend necklace the rest of their lives and keep their temper in check.

But the most likely candidate, Earnhilt's lover, was lying dead upstairs.

Thana cleared her throat and looked to Calla, but they couldn't ask her to sleep with one of her cousins.

"I'll bear it," Dina said softly.

Earnhilt gave her a gratified smile, and Thana wondered if she knew that Dina had slept with her son as well as her. Depending on who gave Dina a Fiend, everyone would know soon enough. Time was against them, and the need for petty secrets had ended, as far as

Thana was concerned. She'd do what she had to, tell whoever what she had to, in order to get Sylph back.

Earnhilt clapped Dina on the shoulder as if they were about to go into combat together. Thana hoped it wasn't going to be like that, not when she had to be in the room.

Illis limped back when they looked at him. "No, please. I can't." He wiped his lips and looked at Gunnar. "His face, the horns, I..."

Earnhilt lifted a hand. "It's all right, lad. We won't force anyone." She stroked her chin as she thought. "I think I know a few people who might want a way back into my good graces."

Thana did not like using any of the traitorous nobles for this. She didn't know how any of them could be trusted, but Earnhilt seemed certain that once they shared the Fiendish Aspect with the Umbriels, they'd be as desirous to protect the secret and keep the kingdom safe from Yanchasa.

But who to choose? While Thana went to retrieve the two pyramids that would let her pass the Fiend from one person to another, Earnhilt drew up a list of likely nobles while sitting in Gunnar's apartment. She'd said they might as well be comfortable for the ritual, and a corpse was in her room.

Thana hadn't known what to say about that. If Lady Lucia's death affected Earnhilt, she wasn't showing it. Thana suspected she simply preferred to mourn in private and not until the crisis was over. If it had been Sylph who'd died...

She told herself not to let her mind wander there. Sylph was alive, and they were going to save her. Her stupid imagination would just have to accept that.

The palace rumbled every ten minutes or so, prompting them to hurry. Gunnar had awakened when Thana returned to his apartment, and by his frown, he wasn't pleased that he'd be pressured to take part in the ritual of passing the Fiend, but he'd do his duty. From what Thana remembered about the ritual, the magic itself made the act easier. She didn't quite understand how, but she was about to find out.

"What do you think?" Earnhilt asked as she gave Gunnar the list.

He grimaced. "About picking a lover off a list for me or my mother? Equally squicky, thanks."

"Don't be tiresome."

His scowl deepened as he continued to read. "Well, who on here appeals to you, Ma?"

"You're not reading for appeal, boy. It's about trust, loyalty."

"It's a list of *traitors*."

"Not loyalty right now!" she roared. "Going forward."

Thana slammed her hand on a table. "Calm down," she said evenly. "I will not have your Aspects escaping on top of everything else." And to her astonishment, they quieted. She'd never felt more like the monarch's pyradisté.

It couldn't last.

But riding the feeling and keeping her fear for Sylph, for the kingdom, as her motivation, she grabbed the list, and one name stood out, a way to secure the future she was supposed to be sorting for her and Sylph.

"Duke Felix Montague." She was certain he'd agree if it meant he got to keep his lands, his titles, and it would give him a chance to help save his daughter. After what he'd done in the council chamber, she had to believe he cared a little.

And even if he complied solely because he thought it would save his skin, it would tie him forever to the Umbriels, to Thana, too, and from her to Sylph again, to a future for them.

Right now, she'd give anything just for the chance.

She left it to Earnhilt to explain it to the duke while she went into Gunnar's bedroom with him and Dina. Perhaps he'd never have to find out about her and the queen after all. Then all that was left was for them to stare at each other awkwardly, and Thana suspected they were all wishing that the crown prince lived closer or that his father was anywhere to be found.

Dina sighed. "Look, this isn't the first threesome I've been part of."

"It's not a threesome," Thana said as her face burned, and Gunnar mumbled, "Me neither." Thana closed her eyes and blocked out his words.

"I just never thought I'd be having one with you, Than," Gunnar said, and she could tell he was teasing, but she was not in the mood. She glared.

"The secret is, don't think too hard about it. Just lose yourself in the moment," Dina said.

Thana transferred her glare, but she could tell Dina was teasing, too. "Shut up, the pair of you."

Gunnar touched her shoulder. "Sylph will be all right. We'll save her. You can relax a bit."

She shook her head. She did not want to accept his comfort and risk bursting into tears right now. "I'm going behind that screen. You two...situate yourselves. You'll know when the magic starts to happen, or so I'm told." She went behind a changing screen and sat on a stool. She took her pyramids out and tried her best to pretend she'd gone deaf.

As she fell into the pyramids, a warm current ran through her, and a feeling rather like sensuousness flooded her limbs, bringing back memories of Sylph. She let herself linger there as the air warmed. She focused the pyramid energy toward Gunnar and Dina, but she hardly needed to bother. The energy was drawn to them, to their pulses, the same warmth infusing their limbs as coursed through hers.

She became a link in their triangle and had to block out all their talk of threesomes again. She forced herself back to memories of Sylph's smooth skin and breathy exhales. As the power flowed back from Gunnar and Dina into Thana and the pyramids, it sped up before beginning the journey again, picking up speed each time.

Thana's breath came faster, her eyelids fluttering, and the energy changed, becoming darker. It was still powerful, beautiful, intoxicating. Finally, the dark energy came out in a burst, slamming into Gunnar, where it seemed to drag something from him and carry it into Dina. When the pulse passed through her again, the dark energy was gone. It settled back into the pyramids and dimmed.

Thana curled her hands around them and tried not to weep, missing Sylph with an ache that was nearly too much to sit through. She wanted to run from this feeling or to chase it down through the earth and tear at the rock with her bare hands.

The screen moved, and she jolted, realizing that her face was wet. She'd been sobbing and not quietly. Gunnar had at least paused long enough to put his trousers on before he sought her out. He wrapped her in his arms, and Dina pressed into her from the other side.

She wept against them for a moment, happy to lose herself in worry, if only for a breath. Then she realized that Dina hadn't taken the same care to put some clothes on, and that both she and Gunnar were a bit sweaty from the hurried ritual, and she had to break away.

"Thanks, thank you," she said, wiping her eyes. "Get dressed." She hurried to the door. The palace shuddered as she went, and she hoped that using more Fiend magic hadn't made their problem worse.

The tremors didn't stop as she gained the sitting room, and she didn't know if they had time to give a Fiend to Duke Felix even if he agreed. But could they pacify Yanchasa with only three? When a lamp tumbled off a table, she knew they had to try.

Duke Felix waited in the outer sitting room. His finery was rumpled, and he had a bruise on one cheek. The guards hadn't been gentle with him.

Good.

Especially since he had a haughty look on, lifting an eyebrow as if shocked that Thana could look him in the eye. She fought the urge to make an obscene gesture and looked to Earnhilt.

"He's agreed," she said, staring at the walls as if she could hold them still on her own.

"We don't have time," Thana said. "We need to go now."

"With only three?" Gunnar asked as he followed with Dina, both of them clothed.

Thana nodded. "But bring him along." She pointed to Duke Felix. "We might be able to find a use for him."

He didn't do anything so common as sputter or sneer. He went along quietly between Ivar and Illis, and Earnhilt seemed a bit relieved as she followed. Thana couldn't blame her. They might have to give him a Fiend in the end, but at this moment, no one had to have sex with him, and that was a blessing to be cherished.

The palace kept rumbling as they ventured below. To his credit, Duke Felix didn't balk at the sight of the capstone, hadn't balked at all, but Thana questioned if he'd remain silent about everything if he didn't carry a Fiend. She supposed it was enough that he was already in disgrace and that if he went around badmouthing the Umbriels as part Fiend, he'd be in even worse trouble.

And would anyone believe him when the pyradistés who'd held the proof were all dead?

That had burned her at the time, but now, when she had to scramble to fix their mistakes?

No, she couldn't help feeling like death in secret was never warranted.

She really didn't belong in the Order of Vestra. But that was a future to be contemplated later.

In the capstone cavern, Duke Felix peered curiously when Thana fitted the manacles around the legs of Earnhilt, Gunnar, and Dina. Again, to his credit, he pointed to the fourth pair. "And those would have been for me?"

"If we'd had time," Earnhilt said.

He nodded sternly. "But you still think I might be needed?"

Thana had to shrug. If this didn't work, she didn't know how they'd pause to give him a Fiend. As soon as the Waltz began, Earnhilt's Aspect would emerge along with the other two, and if Duke Felix tried making love to her then, she'd rip him to pieces.

Not that he'd even have to get close for that.

A sheen of sweat broke out on his forehead, but he still stepped up and shackled himself. "Just in case."

Thana's admiration went up a smidge from nonexistent. Earnhilt looked at him with respect. Maybe that would keep some of him intact if they had to use him, though the spirits only knew how that would work.

"Don't touch the capstone until I say," Thana said to him.

He nodded. She collected the necklaces of Earnhilt and Gunnar, drew her Fiend pyramid, took the deepest breath ever, and got to work.

"No, no, no," Sylph chanted. Pain arced up and down her spine, and her muscles quivered as if she'd run for miles while carrying a ton of steel on her back. Pebbles rained around her as she shuddered, nearly vibrating from the strain of holding the great Fiend's prison intact.

He was moving, too. She felt his massive limbs rasping inside his prison, could imagine his eyes fluttering and again saw the prince's eyes as they bled all blue and shone with murderous cunning. She'd opened so many airholes that her little pocket within the stone filled with the scent of blood from those dead above.

That seemed fitting.

As the great Fiend once more flexed against his prison, she kept up her chant, painting her mouth and throat in another coat of dust. But she held him, though some of his rumbles had broken through. She hoped Thana felt the urgency, that she could do some—

A spark from above sought to pull her attention away. She tried to ignore it and focus on her task, but the Fiend quieted as if he had also been distracted. Someone was using the capstone, the malevolent heart, a metaphor that became more apt when she knew its function. It had to be Thana, but more than just her. Sylph sensed the same energy that emanated from the Fiend pyramids. But this magic held another note, too, not so much a herald of destruction but of distraction, like a lullaby used on an agitated child.

And it was working. The great Fiend's shudders calmed. Sylph let out a sigh and relaxed a fraction. She focused her magic and sought to bring herself into the light, but before she could move, the great Fiend flexed his power, focusing on her in an instant, reaching for her pyramid from a distance as she'd seen no other pyradisté do but her.

Making them kindred?

No, that was another distraction, maybe from the Fiend, maybe herself, difficult to tell anymore. The sluggish power of the Fiend groped for her pyramid, drawn to her the more she used it, but she couldn't let it go. He would be out of the prison in a moment.

She fell in deeper. She was stone, ancient, unbending, no matter how time battered her. The essence of the Fiend was change, so she would be eternal. Even if all life upon the sphere should die, she would remain.

Her body ceased to matter as she sagged in her stone pocket and gave all her will to the earth.

❖

Something was wrong, and Thana scrambled to find out what. It had been going well. Yanchasa had been quieting, the rumbling around them dying. Then she'd felt a burst of power, not against the capstone, but directed somewhere else, somewhere close. And there were only two other pyradistés in the vicinity.

She opened her eyes and looked to Calla, who was glaring from off to the side. But for once, she wasn't directing her ire at Thana. Holding a detection pyramid, she stared at the ground.

"What is it?" Thana said, fighting to keep her focus on the task at hand. Earnhilt, Gunnar, and Dina had their hands on three sides of the capstone. Their eyes had all bled to solid colors, and while Gunnar's horns sprouted from his forehead, Earnhilt's came from her temples and curved back along the sides of her head. She also sported four crow's wings that had shredded the back of her tunic when they'd burst forth. Dina had two wings and no horns, but a spike jutted from her chin. All three snarled, revealing monstrously sharp teeth.

Duke Felix leaned away from them as far as his shackles would allow, his expression horrified. But he didn't beg to be set free.

"It's that cursed stone pyramid," Calla said. "Your girlfriend and the Fiend are fighting for it."

Thana's stomach shrank as she imagined massive claws reaching for Sylph, but Calla had to mean grappling in a metaphysical sense, power to power, but how was that better? Fiends were said to be made of magic. Surely, they would know how to use it better than any pyradisté, no matter how mindless they might otherwise be.

But Thana also remembered how Sylph had merged with the rock in the cavern, their own stone lady, and how terrifying the idea had been that she might not come back.

"Right." She fell deeper into the capstone through the Fiend pyramid that shielded her from Yanchasa's influence. She called to him, masking herself behind the Fiendish Aspects of the royals. It was all right. They were all Fiends here, and Yanchasa could go back to sleep among his kin.

But she caught a blip of power from Sylph's stone pyramid, and lulling Yanchasa felt like trying to put a child to bed while someone nearby was blowing a whistle. The Fiend wouldn't turn its attention to her while Sylph was using the stone pyramid, but if Calla was right and Sylph stopped using it, Yanchasa could grab hold and tear the whole palace down.

Maybe the world.

"No, look over here, you great bastard," Thana said, pulling harder at the Aspects of those around her, making them growl. Maybe if she created the sense that they were imperiled, that would spark some sort of feeling, and Yanchasa would focus on them again. Though whether to comfort or kill, she didn't know. But once that happened, she could switch back to putting him to sleep.

A flicker of attention came her way, then he turned for the stone pyramid again.

"Spirits curse it!" Thana staggered back from the pyramid, wiping at the sweat on her face. The Umbriels and Dina shifted and snorted, but they couldn't take action while held by the manacles.

"I need four of them," Thana said quietly.

Duke Felix swallowed and grimaced as if the action was as painful as it looked. "I'm ready."

But she didn't know how to give him a Fiend right now, not without the physical joining, and how could they do that? Any of the others would be more likely to eat him than mate with him.

Just as Yanchasa might kill them all, kill Sylph at any moment.

"There has to be a way," Thana muttered. She'd brought Duke Felix for a reason, a plan that wasn't impossible, something lurking in her subconscious that the rest of her hadn't yet realized.

"What are you doing?" Calla asked.

"Thinking." She ran through her knowledge, but nothing came. "Spirits curse it." She'd always known this would happen, that it would come down to her, and she wouldn't be up to the task. "Why did he even pick me? I'm not strong enough to—"

"Hey," Calla shouted as she gripped a fistful of Thana's shirt. "Get a fucking grip, or I'll take over and steal your job and your girlfriend. That what you want?"

Thana blinked, knocked off kilter by the strong swear and the threats. A laugh bubbled up in her, but she fought it down and nodded. "You know, that's the most I've ever liked you."

"Ditto. Now do something."

"Right." No one knew as much about pyramid magic as she did, after all. She needed four people with Fiendish Aspects, and no one could give one to Felix right now, so he'd have to get one from somewhere else. Think, she told herself. Remember every book. Remember—

She gasped. Where had the Umbriels gotten their Aspects all those years ago when they'd first defeated Yanchasa? From the Fiend himself.

She looked at her hand. What was her Fiend pyramid but a siphon? Designed to channel Fiend magic at Yanchasa and placate him, but why couldn't it work in the other direction, too? And what better way to stop Yanchasa than by siphoning some of his energy, weakening him, then using that same essence to pacify him?

"Put your hands on the capstone," she said to Duke Felix as she stepped forward again.

He licked his lips and hesitated before complying until Calla turned her glare on him and stepped behind him as if she might shove. As soon as he touched the capstone, Thana fell into her pyramid again. She could sense the energy that connected Dina and the Umbriels to Yanchasa, but Duke Felix was like a void in the magic, a sandbank in a river. How to change him?

Something Sylph had said came back to her. The essence of Fiend magic *was* change. And it changed humans into monsters, so perhaps all she had to do was let the magic wash over him, almost consume him.

The flow was hard to turn, and she grunted under the weight of it. Yanchasa didn't seem willing to let go of any more power, but he was still distracted. When Thana called to that power rather than sending it away, it moved sluggishly toward her.

She steered it as she might a skiff on unruly waters, swearing with the effort and gripping her pyramid until cramps went through her hand. As the Fiend power filtered up through the capstone, she wrestled it away from the Umbriels, Dina, and herself, and shoved it toward Duke Felix.

He screamed, an agonized sound that harmonized with the crunch of bone and shredding cloth. Thana squeezed her eyes shut harder and tried to block out the sounds, hoping he'd either pass out or enter the same fugue state as the others, who wouldn't remember their transformations. But they'd either been born with Fiends or had received a weakened version, already carried by generations of humans. Duke Felix was getting his from the source.

Now she had Yanchasa's attention.

Thana gasped as the trickle of power flowing into Duke Felix became a flood. He howled, and Thana cried out as well, terror filling her at the idea that Yanchasa might be seeking a new way out since they weren't going to let his body free. She opened her eyes to find a monstrosity standing next to her, horns and wings and spikes and barely any human left at all.

She had to stop it, and her first thought was to kill him, much as that appalled her. Such a creature could not escape this cavern, but she didn't have any weapons.

An anti-Fiend pyramid like the one she'd used on Gunnar's Aspect? But she'd need more than that. The magic had to get inside him. Instinct moved her, and she rammed her pyramid into his chest, turning the siphon back the other way. He screeched, an inhuman sound that filled her mouth with the taste of blood. Agony filled her head, and the sounds of the world faded to a dull roar, but the flow of power reversed.

Thana sobbed through her pain and clenched her teeth. When the duke retained only a little Fiendish essence, she pulled the pyramid from his chest and focused on the capstone. The four Fiendish essences seemed to be working in harmony as they were meant to during the Waltz.

The rumbling of the palace eased, but Yanchasa had gotten a taste of freedom, and he wasn't going lightly. She felt his will fighting to get past the four Fiendish essences, to get to her. She could almost hear him, could feel his rage. She shut her eyes tightly and fought the instinct to drop her pyramid and flee from the room, out of the palace, across the kingdom, as far as she could get from this exemplar of evil.

She held her breath and stood firm. She would keep going. For Sylph.

A whisper in dual voices slid around inside her skull: "She's dead."

"No!" She let anger overtake her, adding to it all her worries about her worthiness, the kingdom, her friends, and Sylph. If this monster thought her sorrow would be greater than her desire for vengeance, it could think again.

With a cry of rage, Thana used the Fiendish Aspects like a battering ram, pummeling Yanchasa under their weight. His control faltered, awareness slipping. Thana didn't let up her assault until she felt him go slack, and even then, she kept blanketing him under the weight of his kindred until they howled.

At last, she dropped her pyramid and ran for the stone stairs.

Sylph came back to herself slowly. She barely recognized her own body. She still sagged in her own stone prison, not sure where she ended and the rock began. The softness, that was her, and the stone scraped against her. It hurt.

It would be so easy to lose herself in the stone magic, to leave her fragile flesh behind. Why would she want it when she could be hard, immovable, indestructible?

Alone.

That idea could piss off, as Thana would say.

Stone couldn't have a nice bath, then cuddle with a lover and sleep for two whole weeks. That sounded wonderful. All she had to do was bring herself into the light. She reached for her power.

Nothing happened.

A twinge of worry went through her. The smooth side of her pyramid still rested in her palm. The stone called to her as it had since this adventure began, but it would not obey. Maybe it could grow tired, too?

Impossible, surely.

Still, when she commanded it…nothing.

Worry turned to panic, fluttering in her like a bird against its cage. She tried to cry out, but only a dry wheeze hissed through the darkness. Every breath hurt her throat and chest, sealing her with dust, turning her to stone from the inside out.

No, this couldn't be how she died. She tried again to call for Thana, to say she was sorry for leaving her like this, to tell her that this feeling had to be love because it filled her and resonated and terrified her more than anything, and her one regret was that she hadn't felt it for longer. But no one had ever told her about it, and she hadn't known she could have it, and that was all so unfair, and—

A ringing sound vibrated through the stone, and she heard the rise and fall of some other noise. Water? Was she hallucinating? Perhaps already dead? No, she could not fathom being dead and still so uncomfortable. That would be most unfair.

Wait. It was voices, not water.

Sylph tried to cry out again, and her head buzzed with the sound, but she didn't know if it reached very far. The voices and the ringing paused before picking up again, louder and faster.

"Sylph?" Thana's voice, muffled by the rock.

"Here." Not more than a whisper, but maybe Thana would hear.

Another voice joined Thana's. They were digging, her pyramid telling her of strikes against the rock. She had to help, desperate to get out now that the normally comforting rock felt more like a trap. She gripped her pyramid. Maybe she could manage something.

Sluggishly, the power flowed from her again, bolstered by her need to see Thana's face.

Someone cried out above as the stone loosened, becoming gravel. Hands replaced tools as the earth shifted, and fingers flitted along Sylph's hair, tilting her face toward light and air. She breathed deep, wanting to call Thana's name, but her voice wouldn't work.

"I've got her head," Thana said. Sylph tried to open her eyes, but they stung with grit.

"I can see that," Calla said, sounding as irritated as ever. "Do you mind helping with the rest of her?"

Thana mumbled something, and they pulled on Sylph's jacket, grunting as they freed her from the ground. She tried to help but could barely move, her muscles quivering and burning at the very thought.

Thana's lips pressed to her forehead. "Sylph, can you hear me?"

"Less kissing, more pulling," Calla said.

"Oh, shut up."

"You shut up."

Sylph wanted to tell them both to keep talking forever as long as it meant she was alive. She managed to chuckle, and they paused in their bickering a moment before starting again, not stopping until they'd laid her on the ground.

"I'm going to check on the others at the capstone," Calla said as she breathed hard. "I hope for your sake they've regained consciousness because I am not helping you carry her on my own."

"Piss off, then," Thana said. There was a smidge of affection in her voice, though Sylph couldn't detect any in Calla's as she grumbled and left.

Sylph groaned as Thana lifted her and laid her head on Thana's lap. With a grateful shudder, she managed to flop her arm up so Thana could hold her hand.

"You'll be all right," Thana said with tears in her voice.

Sylph tried to reassure her, but her voice still wouldn't obey.

"You'll have to speak up," Thana said as she lifted Sylph's hand and kissed it. "My ears are still blown from…well, time enough for stories later. Everyone is alive. That's the main thing."

Yes. And all everything else needed was time. "I love you," she mouthed. Time or not, she'd learned that it couldn't be said often enough.

"I love you, too," Thana said. "I may not have worked out all the details, but I promise, our future will be better than this."

CHAPTER TWENTY-THREE

It was three weeks before Thana had everything figured out. The knowledge of noble pyradistés had spread quickly, but the details about the failed coup were kept quiet. The lesser players had happily traded information in order to spare their lives.

The ringleaders turned out to be Headmaster Cyrus, who had tired of living under the thumb of those with higher stations; and Lady Lucia's sister Anastasia, who no longer wished to live in pyradisté purgatory and wanted a taste of her sister's life at court.

But she couldn't insert herself into the palace without causing a stir. Her family had been telling everyone she'd died young. And she couldn't trade places with her sister without the queen noticing, not to mention the nobles who paid attention to their brethren as closely as Sylph.

The two had joined forces, biding their time, not wanting their coup to be put down as quickly as the last one, when the nobles and royals had cut off access to the crystal north of Allusia. When Cyrus's scouts—who had already been seeking a new source of crystal out of sight of the monarchy—found the remains of a crystal-filled glacier near the northern mountains, Anastasia and Cyrus had decided to put their plans into action and take power.

They'd found willing parties in some of the nobility, those still grumbling that they ought to have won the Troubles. They'd also thought that a noble pyradisté like Anastasia would end up on their side rather than on the side of the pyradistés, who would naturally obey the nobles' council. But Anastasia had chosen the side of the pyradistés, and whether her sister had helped her willingly or had been hypnotized into doing so was a point of contention.

Anastasia claimed that Lucia had aided the rebels of her own accord, but Earnhilt didn't want to believe it. She'd stormed around her apartment that night, claiming that Anastasia's words were simply a desperate woman wanting to avoid yet another charge of hypnotism.

"Why else would they have killed her?" Earnhilt said as she drained an entire cup of wine in two swallows. They'd had Lady Lucia's funeral that afternoon, and Earnhilt had been drinking ever since. Luckily, she'd kept to her apartment all evening, but Thana had to check on her now and again before returning to her apartment where Sylph was waiting.

Thana swallowed her smile and shrugged to Earnhilt's question, not wanting to argue with someone not only deep in her cups but grieving. "Anastasia claims to be innocent of that murder. She says it was a noble who did it, but I suspect it was a pyradisté who didn't want to risk having *any* non-pyradistés in charge or even in a position to sway Anastasia."

Earnhilt stared into her glass. "Any idea which one?"

Thana shook her head. "As pyradistés, their minds are unreadable."

"I know." She spoke softly, swaying a little.

"Why not go to bed, Majesty?"

"So you can get back to your lady's loving arms?" Her tone was wistful, her gaze resting on nothing. Thana didn't want to answer, not when it was true, and Earnhilt's love was in the ground. How much they'd been in love—if they'd ever been—didn't seem to matter now. "Go on," Earnhilt said. "I'm going to brood a while longer, but I'll be all right."

Thana gave her a very awkward pat on the arm, but it garnered a smile. As she was leaving, Earnhilt called her name and said, "I'm glad you made it out alive."

Thana nodded. "You, too, Majesty." As she walked out the door, she was thankful for that, too. The only injury she carried was deafness in her left ear from a Fiendish scream.

It could have been so much worse.

According to the captives, once the pyradistés had begun to plan, they hadn't agreed on how to proceed. Some had wanted to eliminate Thana as soon as possible, seeing her as a traitor to their cause for ever working with the Umbriels and knowing she was the best source of knowledge the crown had about what a pyradisté could do.

She didn't know whether to be upset or grimly gratified by that.

Her visit with Sylph to the academy had been marked, and they'd been followed to the manor house. But the pyradistés who'd escaped hadn't understood Sylph's abilities any better than they understood the pyradistés who'd also been unfortunately affected by the new crystal, most of whom had blown themselves to bits.

Thana had spent a great deal of time these past weeks hunting down any bits of new crystal that remained in Marienne and the surrounding countryside. Most of the accidents she'd traced had been because shipments of the crystal had passed *under* manors or towns where pyradistés had been.

It was a sad business and more charges to be laid at the traitors' feet.

Thana went through her office without stopping, heading for her bedroom. And Sylph. She opened the door softly. A single candle burned on the vanity table, the flickering light highlighting the gold in Sylph's hair where it spread across the pillow. Her eyes were shut, and Thana began to undress as quietly as she could, her mind still processing the traitors' other plans.

Some thought to flood Marienne with new crystal before acting and had focused on tunneling. But they'd gotten distracted by the capstone's promise of power. Luckily, any who'd gotten close enough to try to touch the capstone were dead, and the secret of the great Fiend remained known only to a few.

To make sure no one attempted to scale the Fiendish prison again, Gunnar had left a message on the walls where the pyradistés had died below the palace: "Do not seek the Fiend, or you shall die as these." He'd signed it with a stylized O and V, hoping that a message that came from a clandestine—though sometimes storybook—operation would keep people in line.

Thana doubted such a message would be needed, not when Sylph had filled in her stone staircase and a great deal of tunnel out in the countryside, leaving no way for anyone to get under the capstone cavern again.

Still other members of the cabal had wanted to capture the Umbriels before anything else, thinking that holding them prisoner would force any straggling nobles into line. They thought standing the Umbriels up like puppets would convince the populace that everything was all right. And they might have succeeded, but they'd been unprepared for a power like Sylph's.

So had Thana.

She slipped between the cool sheets, wondering if she could snuggle close without waking Sylph, but Sylph opened her eyes, smiled, and drew her in.

Thana awoke early the next morning and lay still, listening to Sylph sleep. The night before came back in a rush, and she smiled, happy her fatigue had fled the moment Sylph had kissed her with unrestrained passion.

They'd spent a lot of time in Thana's bedroom, with Sylph preferring to hide where few could find her. Gunnar had stopped by once to talk about the rumors in court, most of them about why some nobles had vanished, but many were about that newly discovered creature: the noble pyradisté. A popular rumor tied the stories together, saying that a boatload of nobles had recently discovered they *were* pyradistés and had retired from court in shame.

That story was easier to cope with than the real one: the traitorous nobles had been forced to renounce their titles, which were then handed to their heirs, providing said heirs were not also part of the scheming. Some ex-nobles had been banned from court or exiled from Farraday. And Earnhilt hadn't pronounced sentence on all of them yet.

Like Sylph's father, whose assistance saved him from the noose. He'd recovered from the Waltz with only a few dark memories, a Fiendish Aspect repressed by an anti-Fiend necklace, and a scar on his cheek. And the scar wasn't even from this transformation but from being punched by a guard for resisting arrest before the Waltz. Thana thought it only fitting that he should be marked in some way.

She slipped out of bed, wanting to let Sylph sleep. Since their adventure had ended, she'd been, well, desperate to show her appreciation of Thana's charms. She'd said she was done with putting off showing how she felt.

Thana wasn't going to argue, though she was getting tired of how the Order acted whenever she showed her face, like Illis's chuckles and Ivar's winks, Gunnar's leers, and Dina's proud grins. Even Earnhilt had given her a smirk or two.

Thana donned her robe, lit the candle on the vanity, and sat to comb her hair into a neat ponytail. She grinned at the number of toiletries Sylph had scattered around. Earnhilt had offered them a maidservant, but Sylph had ardently refused, fearing spies. For Sylph's comfort, Thana had agreed that they could see to their own things, though she'd forgotten just how many things Sylph had.

As Thana checked her reflection in her bronze hand-mirror, Sylph yawned from the bed and said, "Is it morning already?"

"I suppose so. Though we've spent so much time in here, I've lost track."

There was a smile in Sylph's voice as she asked, "Was that a recrimination?"

"Absolutely not." Thana sat on the edge of her bed, marveling that this perfect woman should be here. Her tanned skin seemed to shine against the dark sheets, and as she sat up, Thana had to remind herself not to stare.

Sylph chuckled, and Thana knew she'd been found out. Sylph didn't miss much, even if some expressions of emotion were still a mystery to her.

But she was well acquainted with lust by now.

Sylph took her hand and kissed her fingers. "I'm glad to know I can still entice you."

"It's only been a few weeks. I won't go off you for at least a few months."

"How sweet," Sylph said wryly.

"It's not for nothing that I have a reputation as a lothario." She stroked Sylph's cheek as they both laughed at the obvious lie. Thana sighed. "You're the first person to spend the night in here apart from me."

"I'm honored, and I wouldn't say I've been *apart* from you very much."

Thana laughed. "Very nice. Worthy of Dina."

Mention of someone else made Sylph sigh, and Thana regretted it, though they both had to leave this room soon. "My father's fate is to be decided today," Sylph said as if reading Thana's mind. Or maybe it had just come back to her, too.

"Earnhilt saved him for last so you could think on it and render your opinion."

"That seems less like a boon and more like a punishment."

Thana would have argued, but she didn't. Sylph already knew that she'd like to see Duke Felix rotting in prison. "And have you formed an opinion?"

With a groan, Sylph scooted forward and buried her head in Thana's shoulder. Thana held her, telling herself not to get lost in the feel of her warm skin but to think only of giving comfort. She couldn't afford to distract them both, and evidence had shown that Sylph would definitely let herself be distracted given the chance.

"Will you be angry if I say I haven't decided?" Sylph asked.

"No, you can leave it entirely to the queen."

"And what is she likely to do?"

Thana sighed, and Sylph pulled back to look her in the eye. At least she wasn't weeping, but she'd said before that she'd cried out her feelings for her father long ago. Thana fumbled for Sylph's robe and draped it around her before she stood to pace, thinking better when she was in motion, especially when trying to have a care with what she said.

"The nobles involved in the coup have all been forced to abdicate their positions to their heirs, and many have had to surrender all titles and honors, and a few have been exiled from Farraday. Anastasia and Headmaster Cyrus will hang."

Sylph remained silent. She knew all this, but she seemed happy to let Thana think aloud, no doubt used to it by now.

"Your father would be joining them or spending his life in prison if he hadn't helped us with Yanchasa. At the very least, you will be the new duchess, but I doubt your family will lose any land like some did." She pointed at Sylph. "But that's because of your help, not his."

Sylph smiled. "Thank you."

Thana resumed pacing again now that she'd reminded Sylph that she'd done more for the kingdom than her father had. "So the question is really, do you want your father forbidden to leave court and stuck here with no titles save being Duchess Sylph's father? Or do you want him banned from court and stuck at your home up north? Earnhilt doesn't want to exile him, not with a Fiend, but if you ask her, she might." When Sylph didn't respond, Thana kept thinking aloud. "If he's here, the queen could keep an eye on him while you're not at court, and since he no doubt still wants his family to increase its holdings, he'll keep his ears open and report to you about other nobles' schemes."

"True."

"And he'd come in handy if we have to do another emergency Waltz, since the crown prince and his wife don't live here." Thana rubbed her chin. "If he's banned from court, he can run your holdings when you're absent, or you can send him touring other noble houses and making nice."

"Not his strongest quality," Sylph said with a snort.

"Maybe he can make a good marriage."

Sylph laughed delightedly. "Oh, that might be fun to watch after all he's said to me on the topic."

"And the third option, pack his bags and exile him. See if any faithful retainers will accompany him."

"I doubt it."

"And you'll never have to see him again unless you wish to. If you're feeling guilty, you could buy him a house in Allusia."

"What did the Allusians ever do to me?"

Thana barked a laugh. "Allusian servants are famous for speaking their minds. Your father might get quite an education."

Sylph chuckled again, her gaze far away. "You know, it never occurred to me that I would or could someday be without him. He was...like the air I breathed, and I panicked at the thought of not being part of his sphere."

"I remember," Thana said softly, though it did seem like another era.

"And now I keep seeing him hit that man who was going to stab me and imagine him taking on a Fiend, and I can't help but wonder, does he actually care for me?"

"You can ask," Thana said. Sylph shut her eyes as if the very idea pained her. "I can ask for you."

She kissed Thana's cheek. "I don't want to give him the opportunity to sneer at you."

"Let him sneer. His scorn is all he's got left, and he knows it. I'd like to see if he's willing to smile on the peasant who can influence his daughter. If he's even capable of that."

"Don't get your hopes up." The words were joking, but neither of them laughed because this was about the longing of a child for parental affection, even after everything he'd put her through. And if he did care, could he put his pride away long enough to show it? Would his desperate situation help or hinder that?

Thana licked her lips. "There is a way to see past all the scheming and stiff-necked horseshit to his true heart." She hesitated at the question on Sylph's face, hoping she wouldn't be forced to say it, but for all she had learned, Sylph was still a novice when it came to magic.

"A mind pyramid," Thana whispered. She called herself a fool and switched to a normal voice. "Normally, using one on him without his permission would get us in trouble, doubly so because of his position, but Earnhilt will look the other way in this case, I'm sure of it. Then you can see for yourself what he thinks and feels."

Sylph's eyes went wide. "Oh." She stared at nothing for several moments. Thana took the opportunity to dress, not wanting to interrupt her thinking. This had to be her decision, and Thana honestly did not know which path she would choose if their situations were reversed.

By the stricken look on Sylph's face as she also dressed, she hadn't made up her mind. Reading someone's mind against their will was not only illegal, it was considered immoral by most as the ultimate invasion of privacy. The idea made Thana's skin crawl, but this was for Sylph.

"I can do it if you don't want to," Thana said quietly. "I'll tell you whatever I see."

Sylph took her hands and kissed her forehead. "I won't let you sacrifice your principles for love, though I'm happy I'll never have to wonder how *you* feel about me."

Thana's heart warmed, and she led the way into her office. She peeked out the door to see servants bustling up and down the hall. Everyone was no doubt awake, and Earnhilt would send for Sylph before too much longer.

"I need to see him," Sylph said. "I've been putting it off, but..."

Thana nodded. Without prompting, she grabbed a mind pyramid and stuck it in her pocket before leading the way out. When Sylph gave her a questioning look, Thana said, "Oh, I'm coming with you. I can stay by your side, or you can speak to him alone, but I'll be right outside for whatever you need." Lending Sylph her mind pyramid or delivering a swift kick to Felix's backside, it didn't matter to her. Most likely, hers would be a shoulder to cry on, and that was okay, too, even if Sylph's tears would make her want to kick Felix even harder.

Sylph stood outside the guest room that served as her father's cell. Thana waited beside her, but she felt as alone as she had before this whole adventure started. It was fitting. No amount of kindness, love, or support would help now. Afterward, perhaps, but in order to deal with the problem of her father, her heart needed to dwell in the past.

"I'll take the mind pyramid," she said, noting Thana's lack of expression as she handed it over. It was difficult for her not to emote, and Sylph kissed her cheek to show the effort was appreciated. She put the mind pyramid in the opposite pocket from her stone pyramid, not certain if she'd use either, but they both provided comfort.

She knocked since they were still civilized people, but Thana caught her arm as her father called to come in. "Remember, I'm just a few steps away."

Sylph smiled. Yes, the future was always just a few steps from the past.

Her father stood as she entered, and his shoulders seemed to relax a fraction at the sight of her before he clasped his hands behind his back, and all emotion disappeared as if behind a wall. "Sylph." He bowed slightly, a little shallower than a duchess deserved, but it could be considered acceptable since he was her father. She wondered how many times he'd practiced it.

His outfit was perfectly pressed, dark blue trousers and coat with slashes in the sleeves showing glimpses of white that shone like light through bars. And it was close enough to black to be seen as mourning, though no doubt more for his position than for anyone who'd died. His golden hair was immaculately combed. A single red line on his right cheek was the only mark on his freshly shaven face.

Sylph tilted her head, desperately trying not to go to a place of anxiety or fear. She considered touching her pyramid for comfort, but he would have a thousand recriminations for such a sign of nerves. She forced herself to still until she seemed to hear Thana's voice saying, "Who cares? You have all the power here."

True enough. She put her hand in her pocket, and his gaze flicked to the movement, but she wasn't going to let him start anything. "Da," she said before he could comment.

He blinked. He'd always hated that familiar term, and to throw him further off guard, she sat without returning his bow or being invited, even though she was a guest.

He *tsked*, a disapproving noise he hadn't aimed at her since she was a girl.

It nearly made her grin. "Oh, where are my manners?" she asked, holding out a hand. "Have a seat."

He obeyed without remarking that she shouldn't issue such invitations when it wasn't her room. Well, it wasn't really his, either, might not be his palace or even his kingdom if she said so. He had to at least suspect that. She supposed she ought to be glad he didn't grovel. She might have thought him an imposter.

"What do you want of me?" she asked.

He sat up a little straighter. "Is it not supposed to be me asking that question upon receiving a visitor?"

Finally, a response. She smiled, and he seemed even more confused. How long had it been since she'd smiled at him, really smiled? "You've lost your title," she said. "You already know that, but the fate of your person remains to be determined, and soon, the queen will ask my opinion." She crossed her legs and leaned back. Her hands still wanted to shake, but she could pretend that wasn't the case.

He mimicked her posture, never one to be thrown and stay down. "And what will you say? Or are you asking me to plead for an option?"

In a way, she was happy he didn't know her well. It made this easier, even if it caused a hollow feeling inside her. "Why did you save my life, and why did you volunteer to bear a Fiend?"

His hand moved slightly toward his chest where his new anti-Fiend pyramid hid beneath his clothes, but he turned the motion into plucking imaginary lint from his coat.

The hollow in Sylph's chest began to burn. "Be honest with me. You know what I am now. You know what I can do. Do not force me to do it."

He looked a little horrified to hear her talk of magic openly, if obliquely, and her stomach began to churn both under his disapproval and because she was a little horrified to casually threaten powers that had terrified her not long ago.

"You...you would..." He licked his lips and looked away, and she bet his mouth was dry as sand.

"Would you like me to send for refreshment?"

"So you can threaten to poison me, too?" He took a deep breath, and it was gratifying to see him so rattled. He truly didn't know her *at all*.

Her eyes stung, but they stayed dry. "I don't want you to die, Father," she said softly, not able to meet his eyes. "And I don't wish to cause you pain. I only wish to know the truth."

"And that will help you decide my fate?" He sounded incredulous, but there was something else, a hint of disappointment that she would let emotion sway her in this. Even when he could use it against her, he did not want sentiment to rule her heart.

She closed her eyes and breathed deep. At least he'd stayed true to his principles. "No," she lied, opening her eyes. "It will not change my mind. I would simply like to know what was in your thoughts. If you were going to use your actions after the coup was thwarted as lessons, what would the conclusion be?"

He looked away, frowning. She gripped the mind pyramid, so tempted, and no doubt it would come easily to her, as all magic did. Then she could see those wheels turning, know the truth behind all the cursed facades. Did he even possess emotions, or had all her girlish hopes been in vain?

"In the council chamber," he said slowly, "I saw the man with the knife coming for you, and I acted. I cannot answer for my thoughts as I had none. I felt the sting of betrayal from Anastasia. I had been surprised to see you, but at the moment with the knife..." He shrugged. "As you said, I never wished for you to be hurt, either."

Not physically, no.

"As for the *Fiend*," he whispered the word. "I saw an opportunity. Naturally, I hoped you would be saved as well—"

"Why?" She sat forward, feeling as if her throat was being squeezed. She wasn't willing to sit through a lecture on the importance of opportunity. "You have other heirs, the cousins you never hesitate to speak of. What's so special about me?"

He frowned, staring as if she was a madwoman. "As my child, you are my first choice."

She managed to keep her voice steady as she asked, "Do you love me, Father?"

He leaned back as if she'd slapped him. "What?"

"You want me to inherit, but is that it? Did you want me to remain unhurt, to be rescued, because you also love me? Worry for me? Find it hard to consider life without me?" And it was the greatest strain on her court mask, but she kept her lips from trembling, kept any tears inside, and fought the urge to sob.

He continued to stare, but because the answer was no or because he didn't know how to say yes? She clutched the pyramid until the capstone pricked her palm.

"Sylph." He made that same motion toward his necklace but paused, holding his hand over his chest, fingers tapping his palm a few times. His brows were pinched in distress. "I can see you're upset, but I...well. I suppose I must..." He cleared his throat. "I cannot see what you want from me." And his face was as open and real as she'd ever seen it.

Her fingers slipped off the pyramid. He honestly didn't know how to answer. More than that, he didn't know how to love.

She'd been the same before Thana, but no one had ever taught him differently, not even her mother. Or maybe she'd been right before, and he'd never been capable of such feelings. Not wanting to see her hurt was as close as he could come.

Some of her childhood dreams died in that moment—she could almost hear them shattering like glass—but it was better they be buried than continue to limp along without hope.

"I'm sorry I upset you, Father." She stood and bowed, and he nearly leaped to return the gesture. He glanced at her pocket, and she gave what she hoped was a reassuring smile. She would not use the pyramid. If she looked for his emotions and saw confirmation of his emptiness, she would not be able to stop a sob.

She managed to leave on steady legs, managed to grab Thana's hand and ignore all questions until they were behind closed doors, and she could weep one last time for a little girl's love gone wanting.

Later that day, in the royal sitting room, Queen Earnhilt asked Sylph's opinion on her father. She didn't hesitate before saying, "Put him where he will do the least damage and the most good." She cleared her throat and sighed. "Though I admit, Majesty, I have no idea where that could be."

But Queen Earnhilt had faced off against him enough in the council chamber that she knew him as well as Sylph, sad as that was.

No, she was done thinking on that for now.

She took Thana's hand, tired of giving a shit what people might think, as Thana would say.

Queen Earnhilt nodded. "Fair enough. I'll keep him here at court. He can help with the nobles, both as gossip magnet and example, and we'll have an extra in case the Waltz comes up unexpectedly."

Sylph caught Thana's look. Since the queen had brought up magic, there was the opportunity for another topic they'd already discussed.

"Speaking of, Majesty," Thana said, "it's my great pleasure to tell you that Calla will now be the royal pyradisté."

Queen Earnhilt frowned and seemed about to object, but Prince Gunnar cleared his throat from where he stood behind the queen's chair. "Sounds like a fine idea now that she doesn't have to hide any longer." He winked at Sylph and Thana, and Sylph was very glad they'd pulled him into the scheme.

When they'd asked Calla, she'd only said, "About time," and Sylph had to drag Thana away from the room before she'd yelled the place down.

Queen Earnhilt drummed her fingers on the arm of her chair and looked between them. "Conspiracy, eh? Haven't we had enough of those by now?"

"I'll make sure she's got all the knowledge she needs," Thana said.

Queen Earnhilt smirked. "And I suppose you two will ride off north together?"

"Yes," Sylph said, as they'd agreed, but they hadn't discussed this next part, and she hoped it went well. "And we'll be engaged to be married, if you accept, Thana."

Thana's jaw dropped, and she glanced at the queen and prince, but Sylph bet they were just as shocked. Only one other person was in on this secret, and Dina had been sworn to silence.

Sylph took a breath to calm her pounding heart. Dina had assured her that Thana would say yes, but now that she was here…

"I wondered what to call you, you see." She took Thana's other hand. "People will ask who you are, and I could say you're my teacher because you've taught me so much, but that title isn't enough. I can't call you my raven, as they wouldn't understand all the affection there." With a chuckle, she closed Thana's mouth with one finger. "And I can't say that you're my lover, even if it's true, because you would blush every time." And charmingly, she did so right on cue. "So I thought it might do well to say that you're my betrothed, conveying how important you are while leaving it to you when we should marry, if indeed you ever want to." She kissed Thana's hand, noting how her own fingers trembled but from good feelings this time. "I swear now, before the queen and prince, that I shall do whatever you require to keep us side by side."

Tears flowed down Thana's cheeks, and she launched herself into Sylph's arms. Sylph laughed as their hug soon expanded to include the prince and the strong arms of the queen.

"Brilliant," Prince Gunnar said, wiping his eyes when they broke apart.

"I agree," Queen Earnhilt said, a little misty-eyed herself. "Say that lot again, and I might marry you."

Sylph gave a gracious bow. "Dina helped with the words, but the sentiment was all mine."

"And she kept this a secret?" Thana asked, voice rising.

"I certainly did," Dina said from the door to the bedroom. Ivar and Illis followed her out with several bottles of wine, and everyone cheered like in a story.

Thana eyed the members of the Order with suspicion. "I had that secret passageway blocked off."

Queen Earnhilt laughed as she accepted a glass. "They told me they wanted to hide and jump out on you for some mystery celebration. I thought it might be because our current troubles seem at an end."

"That, too," Prince Gunnar said. "And for our new royal pyradisté, who is where, by the way?"

"Didn't want to come," Dina said. "Gonna be loads of fun, that one." Thana gave her a playful shove, but Dina just chuckled. "I will remember the beauty of your joy forever, Than."

Thana blushed again and rolled her eyes, but she wore a smile the entire time.

"To Farraday," Queen Earnhilt said, lifting her glass. "And to Lady Lucia and the others no longer with us."

They drank, their mirth suspended for a moment until Prince Gunnar said, "To Dina, for taking a Fiend."

"And for charitably sleeping with you," Ivar added.

Illis sputtered as he drank, but everyone else cheered. Prince Gunnar narrowed his eyes before he winked, making both brothers turn a little red.

Dina lifted her glass to Sylph and Thana. "To this happy couple, if I can count Thana's leaping into Sylph's arms as a yes to being engaged?"

"Yes, you hooligan," Thana said. She grabbed Sylph's arm, and the look she leveled upward melted Sylph's heart. "Yes."

They kissed among more cheers and drank again.

❖

Later that night, in Thana's bed, they lay in a tangle of sheets, both breathing hard, and Sylph felt a contentment she'd never known before.

"I'm going to write a book about you," Thana said.

Sylph tried to reason why but could consider nothing but bliss. "About this?" she asked, gesturing to the wad of sheets, evidence of their lovemaking.

Thana barked a laugh. "While I'm sure that would sell well, no. About your unique power."

"Is that wise? You've often spoken about its capability for destruction."

Thana was quiet for a moment. "But even if others figure out how to make these pyramids of stone, they might not be as powerful as you." She looked up from Sylph's shoulder with a frown. "Then again, maybe you're right. If someone else is meant to have this power, they'll come to it on their own. I just hate the idea of knowledge being lost." She snuggled in tighter. "Maybe I'll write it, then hide it."

"It won't be the only secret around our house. The prince wants my advice on setting up a spy ring."

Thana shuddered. "The less I know about that, the better."

Sylph kissed her temple. "My raven is always honest and honorable."

Thana kissed her back, eyes sparkling in the light of a single candle on the bedside table. "Do you have any idea how much I love you? Would you like to be my betrothed?"

Sylph bit her lip to keep from laughing and widened her eyes. "How sudden and unexpected."

"Just say yes."

"I don't know. That proposal…lacked grandeur." She squealed when Thana tickled her. "I do not respond to marriage proposals under duress!"

Thana continued her assault, adding in kisses and repeating the question until Sylph couldn't breathe for laughing and cried, "I yield. Yes!" Amid giggles, she added, "You horrid little bully."

"But I got what I wanted," Thana said, arching an eyebrow. "Proving that tickling and kissing are undeniable motivators."

"I'll remember that for the next council meeting."

Thana laughed. "I love you, Duchess."

"And I, you, Duchess-to-be." When Thana's jaw dropped, Sylph said, "Oh yes. You will be what you once hated." It seemed Thana hadn't really considered that, and Sylph felt a flutter of fear until Thana shrugged and snuggled close again.

"I'll work hard to serve as an example to other nobles that one can possess a title *and* avoid being an ass."

"Such an insurmountable task will surely keep you from boredom."

"Life will never be boring with you." She kissed Sylph's shoulder. "Shouldn't we try to sleep? Tomorrow is another future to look forward to, and we'll want to be well rested."

Sylph couldn't help a smile. "Or we could start a future worth looking forward to right now, and to the spirits with being well rested." She caressed Thana's side, driving home her meaning, and returned Thana's smile and kiss.

They blew out the candle together and lost themselves in the blissful present.

About the Author

Barbara Ann Wright writes fantasy and science fiction novels and short stories when not ranting on her blog. *The Pyramid Waltz* was one of Tor.com's Reviewer's Choice books of 2012, was a *Foreword Review* BOTYA Finalist, a Goldie finalist, and made Book Riot's 100 Must-Read Sci-Fi Fantasy Novels by Female Authors. It also won the 2013 Rainbow Award for Best Lesbian Fantasy. She's won five other Rainbow Awards and has been a Lambda Award finalist.

Books Available from Bold Strokes Books

Bet Against Me by Fiona Riley. In the high stakes luxury real estate market, everything has a price, and as rival Realtors Trina Lee and Kendall Yates find out, that means their hearts and souls, too. (978-1-63555-729-9)

Broken Reign by Sam Ledel. Together on an epic journey in search of a mysterious cure, a princess and a village outcast must overcome life-threatening challenges and their own prejudice if they want to survive. (978-1-63555-739-8)

Just One Taste by CJ Birch. For Lauren, it only took one taste to start trusting in love again. (978-1-63555-772-5)

Lady of Stone by Barbara Ann Wright. Sparks fly as a magical emergency forces a noble embarrassed by her ability to submit to a low-born teacher who resents everything about her. (978-1-63555-607-0)

Last Resort by Angie Williams. Katie and Rhys are about to find out what happens when you meet the girl of your dreams but you aren't looking for a happily ever after. (978-1-63555-774-9)

Longing for You by Jenny Frame. When Debrek housekeeper Katie Brekman is attacked amid a burgeoning vampire-witch war, Alexis Villiers must go against everything her clan believes in to save her. (978-1-63555-658-2)

Money Creek by Anne Laughlin. Clare Lehane is a troubled lawyer from Chicago who tries to make her way in a rural town full of secrets and deceptions. (978-1-63555-795-4)

Passion's Sweet Surrender by Ronica Black. Cam and Blake are unable to deny their passion for each other, but surrendering to love is a whole different matter. (978-1-63555-703-9)

The Holiday Detour by Jane Kolven. It will take everything going wrong to make Dana and Charlie see how right they are for each other. (978-1-63555-720-6)

Too Hot to Ride by Andrews & Austin. World famous cutting horse champion and industry legend Jane Barrow is knockdown sexy in the way she moves, talks, and rides, and Rae Starr is determined not to get involved with this womanizing gambler. (978-1-63555-776-3)

A Love that Leads to Home by Ronica Black. For Carla Sims and Janice Carpenter, home isn't about location, it's where your heart is. (978-1-63555-675-9)

Blades of Bluegrass by D. Jackson Leigh. A US Army occupational therapist must rehab a bitter veteran who is a ticking political time bomb the military is desperate to disarm. (978-1-63555-637-7)

Guarding Hearts by Jaycie Morrison. As treachery and temptation threaten the women of the Women's Army Corps, who will risk it all for love? (978-1-63555-806-7)

Hopeless Romantic by Georgia Beers. Can a jaded wedding planner and an optimistic divorce attorney possibly find a future together? (978-1-63555-650-6)

Hopes and Dreams by PJ Trebelhorn. Movie theater manager Riley Warren is forced to face her high school crush and tormentor, wealthy socialite Victoria Thayer, at their twentieth reunion. (978-1-63555-670-4)

In the Cards by Kimberly Cooper Griffin. Daria and Phaedra are about to discover that love finds a way, especially when powers outside their control are at play. (978-1-63555-717-6)

Moon Fever by Ileandra Young. SPEAR agent Danika Karson must clear her werewolf friend of multiple false charges while teaching her vampire girlfriend to resist the blood mania brought on by a full moon. (978-1-63555-603-2)

Quake City by St John Karp. Can Andre find his best friend Amy before the night devolves into a nightmare of broken hearts, malevolent drag queens, and spontaneous human combustion? Or has it always happened this way, every night, at Aunty Bob's Quake City Club? (978-1-63555-723-7)

Serenity by Jesse J. Thoma. For Kit Marsden, there are many things in life she cannot change. Serenity is in the acceptance. (978-1-63555-713-8)

Sylver and Gold by Michelle Larkin. Working feverishly to find a killer before he strikes again, Boston Homicide Detective Reid Sylver and rookie cop London Gold are blindsided by their chemistry and developing attraction. (978-1-63555-611-7)

Trade Secrets by Kathleen Knowles. In Silicon Valley, love and business are a volatile mix for clinical lab scientist Tony Leung and venture capitalist Sheila Graham. (978-1-63555-642-1)

Death Overdue by David S. Pederson. Did Heath turn to murder in an alcohol induced haze to solve the problem of his blackmailer, or was it someone else who brought about a death overdue? (978-1-63555-711-4)

Entangled by Melissa Brayden. Becca Crawford is the perfect person to head up the Jade Hotel, if only the captivating owner of the local vineyard would get on board with her plan and stop badmouthing the hotel to everyone in town. (978-1-63555-709-1)

First Do No Harm by Emily Smith. Pierce and Cassidy are about to discover that when it comes to love, sometimes you have to risk it all to have it all. (978-1-63555-699-5)

Kiss Me Every Day by Dena Blake. For Wynn Evans, wishing for a do-over with Carly Jamison was a long shot, actually getting one was a game changer. (978-1-63555-551-6)

Olivia by Genevieve McCluer. In this lesbian Shakespeare adaptation with vampires, Olivia is a centuries old vampire who must fight a strange figure from her past if she wants a chance at happiness. (978-1-63555-701-5)

One Woman's Treasure by Jean Copeland. Daphne's search for discarded antiques and treasures leads to an embarrassing misunderstanding, and ultimately, the opportunity for the romance of a lifetime with Nina. (978-1-63555-652-0)

Silver Ravens by Jane Fletcher. Lori has lost her girlfriend, her home, and her job. Things don't improve when she's kidnapped and taken to fairyland. (978-1-63555-631-5)

Still Not Over You by Jenny Frame, Carsen Taite, Ali Vali. Old flames die hard in these tales of a second chance at love with the ex you're still not over. Stories by award winning authors Jenny Frame, Carsen Taite, and Ali Vali. (978-1-63555-516-5)

Storm Lines by Jessica L. Webb. Devon is a psychologist who likes rules. Marley is a cop who doesn't. They don't always agree, but both fight to protect a girl immersed in a street drug ring. (978-1-63555-626-1)

The Politics of Love by Jen Jensen. Is it possible to love across the political divide in a hostile world? Conservative Shelley Whitmore and liberal Rand Thomas are about to find out. (978-1-63555-693-3)

All the Paths to You by Morgan Lee Miller. High school sweethearts Quinn Hughes and Kennedy Reed reconnect five years after they break up and realize that their chemistry is all but over. (978-1-63555-662-9)

Arrested Pleasures by Nanisi Barrett D'Arnuck. When charged with a crime she didn't commit, Katherine Lowe faces the question: Which is harder, going to prison or falling in love? (978-1-63555-684-1)

Bonded Love by Renee Roman. Carpenter Blaze Carter suffers an injury that shatters her dreams, and ER nurse Trinity Greene hopes to show her that sometimes love is worth fighting for. (978-1-63555-530-1)

Convergence by Jane C. Esther. With life as they know it on the line, can Aerin McLeary and Olivia Ando's love survive an otherworldly threat to humankind? (978-1-63555-488-5)

Coyote Blues by Karen F. Williams. Riley Dawson, psychotherapist and shape-shifter, has her world turned upside down when Fiona Bell, her one true love, returns. (978-1-63555-558-5)

Drawn by Carsen Taite. Will the clues lead Detective Claire Hanlon to the killer terrorizing Dallas, or will she merely lose her heart to person of interest, urban artist Riley Flynn? (978-1-63555-644-5)

Every Summer Day by Lee Patton. Meant to celebrate every summer day, Luke's journal instead chronicles a love affair as fast-moving and possibly as fatal as his brother's brain tumor. (978-1-63555-706-0)

Lucky by Kris Bryant. Was Serena Evans's luck really about winning the lottery, or is she about to get even luckier in love? (978-1-63555-510-3)

The Last Days of Autumn by Donna K. Ford. Autumn and Caroline question the fairness of life, the cruelty of loss, and what it means to love as they navigate the complicated minefield of relationships, grief, and life-altering illness. (978-1-63555-672-8)

Three Alarm Response by Erin Dutton. In the midst of tragedy, can these first responders find love and healing? Three stories of courage, bravery, and passion. (978-1-63555-592-9)

Veterinary Partner by Nancy Wheelton. Callie and Lauren are determined to keep their hearts safe but find that taking a chance on love is the safest option of all. (978-1-63555-666-7)

Everyday People by Louis Barr. When film star Diana Danning hires private eye Clint Steele to find her son, Clint turns to his former West Point barracks mate, and ex-buddy with benefits, Mars Hauser to lend his cyber espionage and digital black ops skills to the case. (978-1-63555-698-8)

Forging a Desire Line by Mary P. Burns. When Charley's ex-wife, Tricia, is diagnosed with inoperable cancer, the private duty nurse Tricia hires turns out to be the handsome and aloof Joanna, who ignites something inside Charley she isn't ready to face. (978-1-63555-665-0)

Love on the Night Shift by Radclyffe. Between ruling the night shift in the ER at the Rivers and raising her teenage daughter, Blaise Richilieu has all the drama she needs in her life, until a dashing young attending appears on the scene and relentlessly pursues her. (978-1-63555-668-1)

Olivia's Awakening by Ronica Black. When the daring and dangerously gorgeous Eve Monroe is hired to get Olivia Savage into shape, a fierce passion ignites, causing both to question everything they've ever known about love. (978-1-63555-613-1)

The Duchess and the Dreamer by Jenny Frame. Clementine Fitzroy has lost her faith and love of life. Can dreamer Evan Fox make her believe in life and dream again? (978-1-63555-601-8)

The Road Home by Erin Zak. Hollywood actress Gwendolyn Carter is about to discover that losing someone you love sometimes means gaining someone to fall for. (978-1-63555-633-9)

Waiting for You by Elle Spencer. When passionate past-life lovers meet again in the present day, one remembers it vividly and the other isn't so sure. (978-1-63555-635-3)

While My Heart Beats by Erin McKenzie. Can a love born amidst the horrors of the Great War survive? (978-1-63555-589-9)